MARINER'S
COMPASS

THE BEELER LARGE PRINT MYSTERY SERIES

Edited by Audrey A. Lesko

Also available in Large Print by Earlene Fowler

Dove in the Window
Fool's Puzzle
Goose in the Pond
Irish Chain
Kansas Troubles

MARINER'S COMPASS

A Benni Harper Mystery

Earlene Fowler

B

BEELER LARGE PRINT
Hampton Falls, New Hampshire, 2001

Library of Congress Cataloging-in-Publication Data

Fowler, Earlene.
Mariner's compass : A Benni Harper mystery / Earlene
Fowler.
p.   cm.—(The Beeler Large Print mystery series)
ISBN 1-57490-401-9 (lg. print : alk. paper)
1. Harper, Benni (Fictitious character)—Fiction. 2. Women
museum curators—Fiction. 3. Quiltmakers—Fiction. 4.
California—Fiction. 5. Large type books. I. Title. II. Series.

PS3558.O929 M37 2001
813'.54—dc21   2001043196

Copyright © 1999 by Earlene Fowler

Published in Large Print by arrangement with
The Berkley Publishing Group,
a division of Penguin, Putnam, Inc.

BEELER LARGE PRINT
is published by
Thomas T. Beeler, Publisher
Post Office Box 659
Hampton Falls, New Hampshire 03844

Typeset in 16 point Times New Roman type.
Printed on acid-free paper, sewn and bound by
Sheridan Books in Chelsea, Michigan.

For
Karen Gray
Christine "Nini" Nybak Hill
Jo-Ann Mapson

whose love, encouragement, and friendship
supported and sustained me through
the writing of this book.
Thank you cannot cover it all.

ACKNOWLEDGMENTS

MOST ESPECIALLY FOR THIS ONE, THANK YOU, LORD GOD JEHOVAH.

With much thanks to:

Ben Nixon, Division Chief, Phoenix Fire Department (with a special award for being such a smart and handsome cousin), and his beautiful wife, Linda, for her support and for putting up with him; Art Nuñez, Captain, Phoenix Fire Department—for being so open and honest to a stranger about your work experiences; Jim Gardiner, Chief of Police, San Luis Obispo; Sergeant Pete Bayer, Chief Deputy Coroner, San Luis Obispo; Dennis Schloss, Deputy District Attorney, San Luis Obispo; Clare Bazley, Tina Davis, and Elaine Gardiner for good friendship and support; Joe and Leslie Patronik, Morro Bay, for all their enthusiastic help; Sue Morrison—for your friendship and pronto Spanish translation; Judith Palais and Deborah Schneider—for a job always well done; my husband, Allen, because just like rhythm and blues, we were meant to be together.

AUTHOR'S NOTE

ALTHOUGH SAN CELINA COUNTY IS A FICTIONAL county, there is an actual town of Morro Bay on the Central Coast of California. Though I have borrowed from the town liberally, I have also changed streets, places of business, and other points of interest. Morro Rock does exist and is exactly as I described. All characters and incidents in this novel are purely from my imagination, and any resemblance to a person or persons residing in Morro Bay is strictly coincidental. I thank the good people of Morro Bay for allowing me to borrow their town for my creative purposes.

MARINER'S COMPASS

MARINER'S COMPASS IS AN OLD ENGLISH PATTERN that can be traced back as far as the 1700s. The design, taken from the wind roses found on ships' compasses and sea charts, was a favorite of nineteenth-century quilt makers living on the Eastern Seaboard. With its bold mixture of curves and narrow, radiating points, always in multiples of eight, it requires many hours of patient piecing and is often attempted only by advanced quilters. Other names include Sunburst, Rising Sun, and Chips & Whetstones. It is to be noted that a compass is not only meant to point the way to our destination, but its function is also to show us the way home.

PROLOGUE

WHEN I LOOK BACK NOW, THESE LONG YEARS LATER, when age has taught me that the word family is much more complex than I ever imagined, what happened to me all seems so magnified, dramatic in that way things can only be when you're young and your blood flows hot and fast, and tears seem to coat the world, blurring it like dime-store eyeglasses. You're certain that if life doesn't work out exactly how you planned, all nice and neat with tucked-in corners, then you will most certainly die, or worse, keep living with the disappointment stuck in your throat like a peach pit, all rough and jagged and bitter as dirt.

I am here to tell you the pivotal moments in our lives often do not come with any sort of fanfare. Rarely are there snapping flags or warning trumpets or foghorns informing us of changes. They usually come, to quote a wiser source, like thieves in the night—a postcard from the lab: "Please contact your physician"—an intersection at the wrong moment, an egg colliding with a sperm in a miniature cosmic explosion, a quarter in a slot machine, the turn of a steering wheel, a trigger pulled, a lover saying no, a child walking away, a voice over the phone—"I'm sorry to inform you . . ." In an instant, your life is forever altered and you think the rest of your days will become an agonizing before-and-after until you realize from the measured, thoughtful perch of old age that life is simply a series of befores and afters, a long line of them, and each one can either harden your heart to sunbaked leather or turn it pliable and welcoming, into an organ of infinite capabilities, a dwelling place for compassion, a vehicle for grace.

I have had my moments. My mother died when I was six, which I don't much remember. My first husband, the love of my youth, died when I was thirty-four, which I still recall at certain moments with a clarity that can shatter my heart like frozen glass. Since then I have lost many people I've loved. But they remain solid and real in my heart, and I believe with a conviction as fixed as the hills I watch every morning from my front porch that I will see them all again one day, and it will be a glorious time of rejoicing.

When I study the weathered and still handsome face of the man I have loved now for forty years, this second and unexpected gift from God, I am thankful that we do not know the future. I have come to understand that if we could, it would alter life's rhythm in such a way that the song would never be the same; it would never have the same magic, the same joy. And, oh, the joy this man has brought me. I could not tell of it in a multitude of Sundays.

This story is only one of my afters. I thought at the time my heart would break. I know now that human hearts don't break, they either stretch or turn to stone. I've learned it is not the afters themselves but how we handle them that shapes us, that decides our happiness. I discovered that we all hold the key to joy in our own free will. My journey to that discovery wasn't easy, but every heart-rending step was worth the pain.

1

"I HAVE NO IDEA WHO HE IS," I SAID. "ARE YOU SURE it's me?"

"Honey, unless there's another Albenia Louise Harper living in San Celina, California, I'm sure it's you," Amanda Landry said in her pecan-pie-for-breakfast Alabama drawl. Besides being my good friend and an extraordinary quilter, she was also the volunteer legal counsel for the Josiah Sinclair Folk Art Museum and artists' co-op where I was curator. "You are, without a doubt, an heiress."

"What do I inherit?" In the background, I heard aother phone ring. She must have been calling from her office above the new Ross store downtown. "Do you want me to hold?"

"No, ma'am. I know who it is and I'm a-tryin' to hide from him."

I laughed and asked, "Who is it this time?" Amanda's love life was the only place in her life where her sharp intelligence and good sense completely and utterly failed her. Her wisest move so far was she had never married any of her unique and varied suitors. Yet.

"This plumb crazy public defender I went on one lousy date with, and now he thinks he's in love. Lordy, he showed up wearin' white socks with coral Hushpuppies. Coral! It looked like a couple of lobsters died on his feet. What was I thinking?"

"You weren't. That's the whole problem with you and men. But we'll dissect your love life later. Are you sure this is for real?"

"As real as your cattle brand, babydoll."

1

"Who is this Jacob Chandler? I've never heard of him."

"Look, I was just notified by the deputy coroner early this morning myself. Too early. He interrupted an extremely pleasant interlude with Mel Gibson. At any rate, this poor old Mr. Chandler had a heart attack last night, that's all I know. Why don't you meet me at Liddie's around noon and we'll do this all official-like? Since you're the heiress, you can buy me lunch."

"Is there money involved?" Thoughts of the new one-ton truck I'd been eyeing at the Chevy dealership danced in my head. I'd given away my old Harper ranch truck to my brother-in-law last November and had been driving Gabe's restored 1950 Chevy pickup for the last five months. Being curator of the folk art museum as well as still working occasionally at my dad's ranch, I needed a vehicle I could use without worrying about scratching the paint. Not to mention one with a decent radio. Gabe and I had talked about buying another truck, and he was ready to write the check, but I'd wanted to buy it myself since he already carried more of the financial burden in our new marriage than felt comfortable to me. A sudden stream of guilt and shame washed over me. Someone had died, perhaps someone I knew, and the only thing on my mind was what I was going to get.

"There's a bank account," Amanda continued, "but I have no idea how much is in it. I drew up the will a few years ago and don't really remember how much this guy is worth. Don't get rid of that handsome hunk of Latino chauvinism yet. See you at noon."

When Gabe came in from his morning jog, he found me staring at the kitchen floor.

"What's wrong?" he asked, cocking his head and

2

zeroing in with that pervasive gaze many cops pick up during their careers.

I looked up at him and smiled. "How was your run?"

He glanced at the cow-shaped kitchen clock. "Took a half hour longer than usual because Mrs. Potter down the street wanted to talk about whether or not we're going to have Mardi Gras next year and what was I going to do about the naked woman she saw at the last one."

"Naked woman? I don't remember any naked woman."

"I think she saw someone wearing one of those thong bathing suits as part of her costume and was duly shocked."

"Those things are gross, but are they actually against the law?"

He grinned. "Not in any place I want to live."

I rolled my eyes. "I'm assuming you didn't tell Mrs. Potter that."

"No, I told her I'd look into it and get back to her, though I don't even know yet myself if we're going to have Mardi Gras next year. All depends on whether the city council agrees to pay the overtime for my officers and reserves. I can't possibly squeeze the cost out of our budget, but they want both the city and the crowds downtown protected." He shrugged and dried his sweating brown face on a kitchen towel.

I gave his left biceps an encouraging squeeze. "It's only May first so you have almost a whole year to figure something out. And you will. You always do."

"Mrs. Potter's not so sure."

"But I bet you just smiled real pretty at her, and she was like putty in your hands."

He winked at me and didn't answer. My blue-eyed,

3

part-Hispanic husband was a handsome man and was not above utilizing his physical attributes when it suited his purpose. But he was also a top-notch police chief and cared deeply about the people of San Celina. This kind of thing regularly happened to him when he was jogging, some citizen flagging him down, determined to relay some complaint or suggestion they felt he needed to know *right now*. He handled the interruptions with gracious aplomb, jogging in place and patiently listening to their often long-winded diatribes, promising to look into it and always keeping that promise. I was proud of my husband of fifteen months and the way he'd managed, after twenty years of working the roughest precincts in L.A., to adapt to the diverse society of our Central California coastal town with its cornucopia of city-fleeing retirees, rambunctious college students, traditional ranchers and farmers, oil workers, education professionals, and ethnic subcultures.

"Enough about me," he said. "I repeat, what's wrong?"

I opened the refrigerator and poured him a glass of grape juice. "What makes you think anything's wrong?"

He looked at me over his glass, his blue-gray eyes amused. My inability to hide my feelings had been a sore spot between us since we first met. Well, a sore spot for me. He found no end of amusement in it. I stuck my tongue out at him.

"Very subtle, *chica*," he said. "So, what's up?"

I considered making him suffer by not telling him, except I was dying to tell *someone*. "I'm an heiress."

"Who died?" He finished the juice in three gulps and set the empty glass in the sink.

"Someone named Jacob Chandler of Morro Bay."

"Who's he?"

4

"I have no idea. I'm meeting Amanda for lunch at Liddie's, and she's going to read me the will."

He gave a disbelieving grunt. "Are you sure this isn't a joke? You know Amanda." He and Amanda had a somewhat love-hate relationship because his sometimes cute, sometimes irritating male chauvinism alternately amused and annoyed her vehemently feminist sensibilities. They traded cop and attorney jokes like baseball cards—each trying to outdo the other. Deep down, they had a profound respect for one another, but they would rather have eaten worm soup than admit it out loud.

"I don't think so," I said, sitting down on a pine kitchen chair.

"So what did he leave you?"

"Apparently everything he owns."

"Which is?"

"That's what I'll find out at lunch."

He frowned. "I don't like the sound of this."

"Sergeant Friday," I said, using the often appropriate nickname I gave him the first time we met, "it's *Saturday*. Take off the cop hat and quit worrying. He probably just left me his snowdome collection, or something equally strange, to display at the folk art museum."

"You're probably right," he said, pulling me out of my chair and against him. He smelled of clean, salty sweat and spicy deodorant. "So, Ms. Rockefeller, how about a little Mexican rhumba with the help tonight?"

"Sure, you know a young, sexy pool boy who knows how to dance?"

He untied my terry cloth robe and slipped his hands under my cotton tank top. "I was thinking some oak-grilled salmon and a midnight ride on the ranch. It's a

5

full moon. They say it's good luck to make love under a full moon."

"Who says that?" I asked, giving a little shiver when his thumb probed the place on my spine he knew was my weak spot.

"You know, *they* do."

"Buy me Maine lobster, and I might consider it." I squirmed out of his arms and headed for the bedroom.

He followed me, hitting me on the back of the head with his damp, balled-up T-shirt. "Woman, you get more expensive every day."

I picked it up and threw it back. "And who knows, after this afternoon, *you* might not be able to afford me anymore."

I pulled on a clean pair of Wranglers and a white T-shirt while he took a shower. I was sitting at my antique vanity braiding my hair when he came out of our small bathroom and rummaged through our packed closet.

He pulled on new dark blue Levi's and a red polo shirt, toweling his shaggy black hair. "I'll be back from Santa Maria by four. Think about that ride. I was up with your dad on Kenyon Flat last Sunday. The grass is as thick as a mattress." He gave me his sexiest smile.

Laughing, I wrapped a rubber band around the end of my braid. "Geeze, Friday, your *subtle* technique is so hard to resist."

Amanda was already waiting at our favorite restaurant, Liddie's Cafe, the only old-fashioned 24-hour cafe left in town. She waved at me from one of the red vinyl window booths. Seconds after I slid across from her, Nadine, Liddie's head waitress, walked up.

"Looky what the cat drug in," Nadine said. Her brown sparrow eyes glared at us from behind thick pink plastic

6

glasses. She treated everyone from the mayor to the lowliest Cal Poly freshman with the same irritable disrespect. You put up with it or learned that your favorite pie was *always* out.

"How's my boy?" she asked me. She adored Gabe and made no bones about showing it.

"He's going to Santa Maria today. Police business, I think."

"You tell him I have some fresh local raspberries I'm saving for his lunch Monday. Don't you forget, now."

"Nadine, I swear he's gonna leave me for you any day now."

"And he'd be better off by a long shot, tootsie." She licked her pencil and barked, "So, what'll it be, chickadees? I ain't got all day."

"Cheeseburger, Coke, and onion rings," I said.

"Heart attack special, got it," she replied, then looked at Amanda. "And you, Miss Fancy Pants Lawyer Lady?"

"Nadine, I swear I'd like to take you home with me," Amanda said. "You bring to mind my dear memaw back in Alabama, the Lord rest her cantankerous ole soul."

Nadine smacked Amanda on the head with her order pad, which was just the reaction Amanda was angling for. "Someone should wash that smart-alecky mouth of yours out with an old bar of Lava soap."

Amanda winked at me. "I've had some fellow attorneys say that very thing." Her wide mouth turned up in a glorious, toothpaste-selling grin that never failed to melt even the most cynical prosecuting attorney—providing that attorney was male. "Chef's salad and an ice tea. With lots of ranch dressing. On the salad, not in the tea. Ma'am."

"I'll ma'am you," Nadine muttered, her back already to us.

7

"I love her," Amanda said, running her fingers through her thick, sherry-colored hair. "Think she'd consider coming to work for me?"

"You do like living on the edge," I said, sipping my water. "Forget Nadine. Who the heck is this Jacob Chandler, and what have I inherited?"

She pulled a sheaf of legal-sized papers out of her leather briefcase. "I'll tell you all I know, which isn't much." She laid the papers down in front of me and said, "Mr. Jacob Chandler of Morro Bay, California, died of an apparent heart attack last night, and you are his sole heir."

I thumbed through the papers which were full of legalese, then looked up at her. "Give me the *Reader's Digest* version."

"In a nutshell, you inherit his house in Morro Bay, all his possessions, and whatever is contained in his bank account at the Paso Robles Branch of the San Celina Savings and Loan."

"A house? And all his possessions? Who was he?"

"All I know about him is he came into my office when I first opened my practice and asked me to draw up his will. I didn't even know you then, so your name didn't mean squat to me. Frankly, I'd forgotten all about it until I was notified of his death by the deputy coroner. He apparently has no next of kin and is to be buried in a plot he bought some time ago at the Paso Robles cemetery. The mortuary address where they took his body is in there. Everything's been picked out and paid for. You just need to set a date for burial. I'm the executor, and they're waiting for instructions from me. And I'm waiting for instructions from you."

"This is so weird," I said, pushing the papers aside

8

when Nadine brought our lunches. "I swear I don't know him."

Amanda searched the plates of food. "Where's my dressing?"

"You don't need it, missy," Nadine answered. "That blue suit of yours was looking a tad snug in the hips the last time you was in here." She swung around and stomped away.

Amanda sighed and dug into her salad. "I sure do miss my memaw."

"So, what do I do?"

She forked a slice of turkey breast. "You go check out your new house and then call a realtor."

"But I have no idea who this man is!" The thought of a stranger leaving me something as valuable as a house, not to mention all his worldly possessions, was intriguing, but also a little unsettling. I picked up the will again, trying to glean some answers from its neat black and white lines, but for all they told me, they could have been the phone book.

"Here's the house keys." Amanda pushed a set of keys across the table to me. They were attached to a small, hand-carved cowboy boot. I ran my finger over the intricately carved boot—tiny stars, roses, and horseshoes covered the shaft. Someone—Mr. Chandler?—was a very talented wood-carver. I peered closer at the key ring and looked up at Amanda in surprise.

"My name is carved on this!" *Albenia* was cleverly hidden in fancy script among the elaborate decorations.

"Looks like Mr. Chandler knew *you*," she said, grabbing one of my onion rings. "By the way, there's one little stipulation to the will."

"I knew there had to be a catch."

"To inherit his estate, you must reside in the house for

two consecutive weeks starting the day the will is read to you."

"What?"

"Alone. No overnight guests."

"What?"

She laughed. "You said that already."

"You have to be kidding."

"No, ma'am, it's part of the will. If you don't comply, the estate goes to the Federal Government to help lower the national debt."

"What?" I squeaked.

"And before you ask, yes, it's all legal and above-board. There's nothing you can do except follow the will's instructions or let the money go to our wonderfully screwed-up government." She stole another onion ring and dipped it in the ketchup spreading across my plate.

I groaned. "Gabe is going to have a fit when he hears this. He was suspicious about it from the start."

"This truly is the weirdest inheritance I've come across in my entire legal career. Are you sure you don't know who this guy is?"

"Haven't a clue." I slipped the key ring in my purse and picked up my hamburger. "But you can be darn sure about one thing. I'm gonna find out."

2

AFTER SPLITTING A PEACH COBBLER AND LISTENING TO Amanda complain at length about her lobster-footed defense attorney, I drove downtown to Blind Harry's Bookstore and Coffeehouse owned by my best friend, Elvia Aragon. The window display was full of pastel figurines, books of poetry, and frilly cards extolling the virtues of motherhood, hoping to entice window-shoppers into remembering their mothers next Sunday with a gift from Blind Harry's. It was unusually warm for the first day in May on the Central Coast. Cal Poly students crowded the streets dressed in tank tops and skimpy shorts, trying for an early start on tans they'd regret twenty years later. Finals were still a week or two away, and the mood was as festive as a Fourth of July block party.

"Where's *la Patrona?*" I asked the young girl behind the front counter in Blind Harry's. "Upstairs or down?"

Elvia's elegant, soundproofed, French country-style office was upstairs, but my friend, having grown up in a household of seven children, was often found in the downstairs coffeehouse peacefully attending to her paperwork amidst the noise and confusion of her beloved customers.

"She and Emory are eating lunch in her office," the clerk said, fingering the blue streak in her long black hair.

"He said they didn't want to be disturbed."

"Great, thanks," I said, heading up the stairs.

"Wait," she called after me. "He really said they—"

"Oh, he doesn't mean *me.*"

Elvia and I had been best friends since second grade when we were fortuitously seated next to each other for the entire year, starting a relationship that to this day was the closest either of us had to a sister. The oldest child in a family of six brothers, she was tough, stubborn, beautiful, smart, bossy, loyal, and demanding. And I would do anything for her. She was also nosy as an old hen-turkey and would throttle me if she heard about my inheritance from anyone else. Worse, she'd make me pay up my charge account at her store.

11

I burst into her office, hoping to catch Elvia and my cousin Emory in flagrante delicto. Their heads were together all right, intently studying something on her computer screen. Two half-eaten Caesar salads sat on the corner of her executive desk.

"Sorry to break up such a romantic moment," I said, grinning.

Elvia glared at me. It annoyed her to no end that I was right, and she actually did enjoy dating my cousin. "What do you want?"

Emory came around the desk to hug me. "Sweetcakes, I've been meaning to call you."

"Sure, sure," I said, kissing his smooth cheek, then sitting down in one of her rose-colored visitor chairs.

"You always do this whenever you get a new girlfriend—ignore your favorite cousin."

Elvia glared at me again. She hated being referred to as his girlfriend, but I figured the more I said it, the more it would seem inevitable to her. My goal was for them to get married. As was Emory's. The only fly in the ointment was one stubbornly single Latina woman.

"What's cookin'?" he asked, sitting down next to me. He was dressed in his everyday work wear of expensive wool slacks, tailor-made dress shirt, and Hugo Boss sports coat. He'd landed a job at the *San Celina Tribune* in November after moving here lock, stock, and Razorback loyalties from his home state of Arkansas in the belief that close proximity rather than absence makes a woman's heart grow fonder. In that short time he had managed to talk the newspaper into giving him his own column and one of the best offices in the building. The fact that he had an independent income thanks to his father's successful smoked chicken business gave him the sort of easy going

12

confidence that always seemed to procure good employment.

"You'll never guess in a billion years," I said.

"Lord have mercy on us all, your application has finally been accepted at the sheriff's academy."

I mimed slapping him upside the head. My reputation for stumbling into dangerous situations, some of which included dead bodies, was a source of gleeful entertainment for Emory, who kept threatening to send my resume and clippings to the San Celina Sheriff's Department so I could start getting paid for my criminal investigations.

"No, I've inherited the house and all the worldly possessions of a total stranger, and I wanted you two to be the first to know." I left out the will's weird stipulation until I could break it gently to Gabe.

The word inheritance caused Elvia to turn from her computer screen. "Any cash involved? I know a great investment . . ." Her Chanel-red lips treated me to her most winning smile.

Elvia had been slowly buying Blind Harry's from its absentee owner, a Scottish man who lived in Reno. She'd been bugging me to invest in the store with my spring cattle money, which I'd resisted because I needed to buy that new truck. Emory, of course, would have gladly bought any or all of Blind Harry's stock, but she wouldn't even consider his offer.

I held up my hand. "Whoa there, Nellie. I haven't even seen the house yet. It's in Morro Bay, and I'm going out there in just a few minutes. I just wanted to tell you both the real story before it hopped a ride on the San Celina gossip train."

"As soon as you find out how much, we'll talk," Elvia said confidently, turning back to her screen.

13

"Now get out of here, both of you. I've got work to do."

"Yes, ma'am," I said.

"But we haven't finished our lunch," Emory protested.

I grabbed his hand and pulled him out of the office, shutting the door behind us. "When are you going to learn that the way to Elvia's heart is to ignore her, not sit at her feet like a pathetic little Chihuahua?"

"Don't tell *me* how to woo a woman," he said, following me down the stairs. "We've had exactly seven and a half dates. I'm wearing her down. I can feel it. We'll be married by the end of the year."

"Right. You haven't even kissed, and already you're naming the babies."

He grinned and ran a palm across the side of his thick blond hair.

I pinched his forearm. "Quit looking so smug. When?"

"Last night," he whispered. "But she said if I ever told anyone, especially you, she'd boil me in Tabasco sauce and feed me to that spoiled cat of hers, so you'd better keep your big mouth shut."

I held up my hand. "Cattlewoman's honor."

He walked me to my truck three blocks away and lingered for a moment while I buckled my seat belt.

"So, what's the story behind this inheritance?" he asked casually.

"Get that nosy journalistic sparkle out of your eye. I've been in the news enough in the last year. There's no story."

"I disagree. I'm sensing a real human interest saga here, little cousin. Let me come with you." The gleam in his green eyes grew deeper.

14

"No," I said, starting the truck. "I want to see it myself first. If, and that's a big *if*, there's anything remotely interesting about him, I'll consider . . . hear me now, cousin . . . *consider* talking to you about it for the paper." He was going to kill me when he eventually heard the stipulation of the will. It was exactly the type of story he'd love to write—and I'd let him . . . maybe. But before I decided anything, I wanted to see the house, get some sort of handle on this man's identity and motives.

"You women," he said, heaving an exaggerated sigh. "You'll be the death of me."

"Pipe down. You're beginning to sound like Aunt Garnet. Gabe and I are going out to the ranch this evening. Anything you need to tell Dove?"

"No, I'll be calling her myself tonight about that column she wants written on the city's plans to sell the historical museum. It's going to run in tomorrow's paper."

"I think what the city's doing is crappy."

The historical museum, located in the old brick and stone Carnegie library, was the pride and joy of my gramma Dove and her cronies in the San Celina County Historical Society. Acquiring the lease five years ago had been the result of constant haranguing and calling in of every marker these influential seniors had from their countless years of community service. But recently the city council, led by our new mayor, had been making rumblings about how the museum wasn't a moneymaker and how much they needed the space for something that could generate tax revenue for our growing city. It was rumored that the old library might be sold to a hotel chain that planned on turning it into a theme restaurant.

15

I blew a soft raspberry at the county buildings. "Your article better wake up people into seeing what's happening to our town."

"That's the whole plan. It's going to be a tough fight against 'Boxstore Billy,' though. He's determined to, as he says, 'usher San Celina into a bright and prosperous new millennium.' "

Our newly elected mayor, William Davenport, was a dark horse candidate who no one had expected to win at the special election held in December because our old mayor resigned due to health reasons. Mayor Davenport proved to be slightly less "Committed to Retaining San Celina's Old-fashioned Values" than he professed in his enthusiastic campaigning.

"What he's doing is taking everything unique about this town and making us look just like every other town in the United States," I said.

"You know I'll muckrake as best my little Southern heart can." He slapped the side of the truck. "Now, canter off to claim your inheritance, my calamitous little cowgirl, and remember, I get the scoop."

"There is no story," I repeated to his disbelieving face.

After he left, I opened the envelope containing the will and glanced down at the address: 993 Pelican Street. I had no idea where that was in Morro Bay, so I felt under the seat and found a street map for San Celina County. Pelican was one of the small streets overlooking the Embarcadero. The Embarcadero, with its incredible view of Morro Rock, paralleled the bay and was the first place tourists headed when they hit town. The shell boutiques, fish-and-chips restaurants, art galleries, saltwater taffy parlors, and nautical knickknack shops drew visitors like kids to cotton candy.

Morro Bay wasn't a big town—tiny, in fact, compared to San Celina. The population was just over 9,500—one quarter the size of San Celina. It was known mostly for its great fish restaurants, perfect summer weather, and mysterious Morro Rock jutting out of the cool green ocean, the last of a chain of volcanic peaks that marched through San Celina County down to the sea. The greatest number of tourists arrived sometime around June, and Morro Bay's surfing, sportfishing, bird-watching, and camping businesses thrived until the visitors disappeared as quickly as they came after Labor Day. It was a town that held special memories for me and Gabe. Since it was only twelve miles from San Celina, we did much of our dating there, wandering through the funky antique stores and art galleries, gradually getting to know each other away from curious eyes in San Celina. We'd usually end up at one of the seafood restaurants perched over the bay or at the house of Aaron Davidson, Gabe's first partner and best friend. Rachel, Aaron's wife, would serve us sun tea and homemade oatmeal cookies while Aaron and Gabe would reminisce about their old LAPD days. Rachel and Aaron lived there for eleven years, but after Aaron's death last September from liver cancer, Rachel sold their house and moved back east to live with her daughter. Gabe and I hadn't been back to Morro Bay since.

The twenty-minute drive to Morro Bay on State Highway 1 gave me time to contemplate this new twist in my life. Who was Jacob Chandler? Why would he leave me all his possessions? Had I met him somewhere and not remembered? Perhaps helped him with his packages, opened a door for him, said hello, performed some small kindness that compelled him to name me as his heir? You heard about things like this in tabloid newspapers or in movies, but never in real life. Nobody left an entire estate to a perfect stranger just because she picked up some spilled apples.

The road to Morro Bay bisected mile after mile of brilliant green hills. I felt a rancher's joy at seeing the feed look so lush and healthy this year. We'd had consistent rains this winter, and it was about as perfect a spring as I'd seen in ten years. Heifers and their calves stood knee deep in emerald grass that rippled and danced like thick green waves. Ahead of me, out of the perpetual fog that often lingered in Morro Bay until past noon, the smoke-stacks of the PG & E power plant appeared, pointing its three aggressive fingers to the sky. Morro Rock, named by the Portuguese explorer Juan Cabrillo, loomed next to it, still shrouded in white, misty clouds.

I drove down Morro Bay Boulevard, the town's main north/south street, going past shops and cafes that commingled in my memories with both Jack, my late husband and childhood sweetheart, and Gabe, my intense and very present second husband. I passed the old Bayside Theater still holding on in its faded glory with two evening showings and a Saturday matinee. Small-town America, rapidly being lost in San Celina, still survived in Morro Bay. Across from the theater was a quilt shop I'd visited often—The Fabric Patch. It was run by a bubbly, enthusiastic woman named Tina Davis who loved quilts, kids, quilters, Morro Bay, and her husband Tom, not necessarily in that order. Since San Celina didn't have a quilt store, during the last two years as curator of the folk art museum, I'd called upon her regularly for quilting information and supplies. She was one of the few people I knew in Morro Bay, so I'd definitely have to talk to her about Mr. Chandler.

I glanced back down at the map. Pelican paralleled

Morro Bay Boulevard, so I turned right on Maddox Street until I came to Pelican Street. I turned south, cruising slowly, looking for 993. The houses in this part of Morro Bay seemed like dollhouses. Though most were of a similar, California bungalow design, each uniquely reflected the owner's personality. The houses were painted in myriad blues, grays, whites, pinks, and faded yellows. The yards were embellished with salmon-shaped wind socks, elaborate rock gardens filled with ceramic ducks and gnomes, hanging baskets filled with lush asparagus ferns, and sprinkled everywhere the wild yellow monkey flowers that sprouted out of every nook and cranny each spring.

Pelican Street ended at an ice-plant-covered bluff overlooking the Embarcadero. I parked in front of 993 Pelican Street and studied the house from the safety of the truck's cab.

The house, *my house,* sat on the corner of Pelican and Grove streets. The front of the house faced Pelican, and the detached garage faced Grove, a street-alley consisting only of garages. It was a one-story house painted pale yellow with white trim. A fence of neatly trimmed thick green bushes surrounded the yard. At the entrance to the front sidewalk someone had patiently trained the bushes into a seven-foot arch and attached a white picket gate to two wooden posts. Red and pink impatiens surrounded a tugboat-shaped mailbox. I climbed out of the truck and opened the mailbox. Inside there was an electric bill and a bunch of advertisement papers.

Still not ready to go inside, I looked out at the Embarcadero and Morro Rock, which would be the view from the house's back deck. Hidden in the ice plant was a small staircase leading to the parking lot of a surf shop named Pinkie's Boards and Bikinis. In the distance, the sailboat masts rocked in the brisk May winds. Catty-corner from the house was a small motel decorated with blue and gray gingerbread edging and balconies off each room. The sign in front—in shiny black calligraphy—stated, "The Pelican Inn—Your Second Home by the Sea."

I took a deep breath and walked up to the gate feeling apprehensive, intrigued, and, I'll admit, a little excited.

That's when I found out what else I'd inherited besides the house.

3

THE DOG AND I STUDIED EACH OTHER FOR A LONG thirty seconds. He was a handsome Lab mix, the color of creamy milk chocolate. I guessed by the shape of his head and long snout, not to mention one upright, tent-shaped ear, that some German shepherd flowed through his blood. His eyes, the color of dark sage honey, made me wonder if there wasn't also a sly old coyote grandparent. He broke the face-off and walked slowly toward me. The muscles in my arms and legs tensed. Growing up around animals, I knew how unpredictable they could be, but before I could hold out my hand for him to sniff, he sat down next to me and with great familiarity leaned his seventy some-odd pounds against my left leg, heaving a deep sigh as if to say, "What took you so long?"

I scratched behind his floppy Labrador ear and said, "So, did you come with the house or are you just visiting?"

His tail thumped against the concrete walkway. I stooped down and felt along his collar. A large wet

20

tongue kissed my cheek. "Well, you certainly have a friendly streak," I said, finding his ID tag. "Scout," I read out loud. His thick tail whump, whumped again.

"Good solid name," I said, stroking his velvet head, reveling in the touch and smell of canine. Though we had three ranch dogs who followed Daddy or whoever was driving a ranch truck everywhere, I hadn't had a personal pet since five months before Jack died. We'd had Poacher, our Border collie, put to sleep because of a brain tumor. It broke our hearts not only because we loved him, but because, along with our brass bed, he'd been with us since the first year of our marriage. I missed the companionship of a dog—their honest emotions and joyful acceptance of you no matter what your mood.

"Look at me, Scout, acting like you've come with the house. You're probably one of the neighbors' dog. Did Mr. Chandler sneak you treats? Is that why you're hanging around?" I ran my hand down his healthy, padded rib cage. His shiny coat and bright eyes indicated he wasn't a stray; he obviously belonged to somebody. I glanced around. The neighborhood was quiet in the thinning fog; no one to ask without knocking on doors. Finding out who owned Scout would be my second task after inspecting Mr. Chandler's house.

I stood up and dug in the bottom of my purse for the boot-shaped key ring. "So, want to join me while I check out my inheritance?"

A small sound grumbled from the back of his throat.

"I'll take that as a yes."

The expensive oak front door had a two-foot oval stained glass window. The pattern was an old sailing ship, the full sails made of a milky white glass, the sun behind it an improbable red-pink.

The key slid smoothly into the lock, and I turned the knob, my stomach lurching slightly. I touched Scout's head, thankful for his comforting presence. The door opened directly into a small living room. The house smelled of smoky vanilla, like that from a pipe. To my left a doorway led to the kitchen. Directly in front of me, a short hall ended at three closed doors which, after a quick inspection, turned out to be two bedrooms and a bathroom. Back in the living room, I walked over to the sliding glass window running the length of the west wall. The curtains opened to reveal the freshly painted wooden deck I had seen from my truck and a million-dollar view of the Embarcadero and Morro Rock. Two redwood lawn chairs with bright kelly green cushions and a matching table sat waiting for occupants. I gazed for a moment out at the busy harbor scene below and the ocean beyond. The sunsets from this perch were probably magnificent.

I turned back and really looked at the living room—clearer now in the light. There was no doubt that Mr. Chandler was a man who loved both wood and the sea. Everything in the living room celebrated the beauty of wood from the built-in teak bookcases to the oak mantle carved with small anchors and dolphins setting off the stone fireplace to the dozens of hand-carved duck decoys.

I walked around the room, studying the furniture and wood carvings, trying to get a handle on this man's identity. The detailed workmanship of his carvings was unbelievable. A walnut dolphin, looking as if it sprang from a burl of wood, danced on its tail; a mare with a colt lying at her feet made from some kind of light, very grainy wood; walking sticks carved with the heads of dogs, cats, horses, and gargoyles; a tiny wren perched on a hunk of rough wood, looking as if it would take flight any minute; a cormorant in smooth wood whose wings lifted as a hinged lid to reveal five small wooden fish inside. I counted fifteen duck decoys—some so realistic I expected them to shake their feathers and quack when I touched them. On the walls were framed prints of old sailing ships and one hand-carved bas-relief plaque in pale, almost grainless wood—"Raise the stone and thou shalt find me; cleave the wood and there I am."

I read it out loud, saying each word slowly. It seemed religious, but didn't sound like anything I'd ever read or heard.

The sofa was a plain navy cotton with an Irish Chain lap quilt hung over one arm; the chair opposite it a wine-colored recliner. A refinished trunk, the wood trim perfectly restored and flawless, served as a coffee table. On the table was a pipe stand cradling two very used pipes and a carved horse's head on a pedestal. I picked it up and ran my thumb over the horse's muscled neck. There was something vaguely familiar about it. Mr. Chandler had been true to the wood, a light hard wood I couldn't name, following the grain, letting the wood tell him where to carve. I turned it over and read the named carved on the base—Harley.

I sat it back down on the trunk, my hand shaking. Harley had been my first horse. A chestnut-colored, part quarter horse, part standard breed with a single white star on his forehead, he'd died of old age when I was twenty-two. I picked up the pale oak carving. He'd even gotten the scar on Harley's neck right—a scar from a protruding nail in the old corral behind the barn.

How did he know what my first horse looked like? A tiny ripple of apprehension scuttled crablike down my spine.

Scout nudged my hand, and I absently scratched behind his Lab ear, which I'd discerned was a favorite spot. "Who is this guy, Scout? You want to give me a clue?"

All I got was another Morse-code tail thump.

Since I'd been curator of the folk art museum I'd become a lay expert on a variety of different arts and crafts. Whenever a new artist was accepted into the artists' co-op or whenever we installed a new exhibit, I read everything I could find at the library and Elvia's bookstore about that particular subject. We'd had a wood carving exhibit cosponsored by the San Celina County Wood-carvers Guild last winter. Their museum and headquarters was north of here near the town of San Simeon. It was one place I could begin my inquiries about Jacob Chandler.

A perfunctory inspection of the remainder of the house took only a few minutes. It was tidy in the way that lifelong bachelor quarters are, though the conclusion that Jacob Chandler had never been married was purely speculative on my part. Here I was already making judgments before possessing all the facts, something I was trying to avoid. His queen-size bed, a simple, walnut four-poster, was covered appropriately with a Mariner's Compass quilt made with navy, slate blue, and gold fabric. The pattern, looking just like its namesake, had sixteen points radiating from a gold center. The workmanship was expert. An Ocean Waves lap quilt in blues, teals, and greens was folded neatly over the bed's footboard. The room held only one nightstand and a chest of drawers, both in the same dark wood as the bed. The three hand-made quilts I'd found told me that someone in Mr. Chandler's life was a quilter.

"Or he is," I said to Scout. "There I go again, making

assumptions." Next to his bed was a fancy L.L. Bean dog bed in a hunter green plaid. "So, is this your bed? If it is, it looks like you're used to the best, my friend." Scout's tail wagged politely.

Predictably the bookcase in his bedroom held many wood carving manuals and books on old sailing ships and an Audubon book on North American birds. But there were also some well-thumbed poetry collections—Frost, St. Vincent Millay, Yeats, and Kipling. He also seemed fond of puzzle and game books—chess strategy, Mensa quiz books, cryptograms, logic puzzles, a Scrabble dictionary.

A game player. Something told me that wasn't a good sign.

"One thing for sure, Scout, I have plenty of time to go through everything if I'm going to be staying here the next two weeks, so right now I think I'll take a quick tour of the yard and then see where you really belong, though I'm half tempted to offer ten bucks for you." I encircled his muzzle in my hand and gave it a little shake.

He wiggled away, barked joyfully at the game, then licked my hand.

"Okay, fifty bucks. But that's as high as I'm going. Then I have to go home and let Gabe know what's going on."

Scout followed me back through the simple white and yellow kitchen where there was a door leading to the backyard. Next to the door was a ceramic dog dish with *Scout* painted on the side, confirming, along with the bed, where he belonged.

I checked out the garage first. Inside the clean and neat structure was a light blue Honda Accord that looked a couple of years old. The glove compartment held only his registration, a blue packet of AAA maps, and a couple of flares. I popped the trunk open from a lever inside the car and found only the spare tire, a jack, and an old blanket. The unlocked garage cabinets were stocked with plant food, insecticides, and some used gardening tools. Mr. Chandler obviously did his own gardening.

And, I thought, standing in the backyard and observing his work, he really loved it. The yard was crazy with flowers and plants, only half of which I could name. Impatiens mixed with rosebushes and rows of freshly planted tulips. A row of purple iris ran along a side fence so covered with ivy that only small windows of splintery gray wood showed. Blue and green tiles etched with boats, pelicans, and starfish led to a gray, lava-stone birdbath in the corner of the yard, its base surrounded by new red tulips. In the brightening sunlight something silver glinted in the loose black dirt surrounding the birdbath. I bent down to pick up what turned out to be a half-buried quarter.

"Hey, neighbor!" a loud, bass voice bellowed out.

Startled, I jerked up, scraping my forehead against the rough edge of the birdbath. "What the . . . ?" I touched my stinging forehead, then inspected my fingers stained with blood.

An older Hispanic man peered at me over the ivy-covered fence. He muttered some Spanish words, then, "Oh, kid, I'm sorry. Just a minute." His head disappeared, and I stood there dumbly, my hand reaching instinctively down to Scout's head. In less than a minute I saw a piece of the fence move, and the man came through a hidden gate, a small first aid kit tucked under his arm. He had strong, heavy features with silver-streaked black hair that touched his shoulders in a shaggy, casual haircut. His skin glowed the same reddish-mahogany as my stepson Sam's after a day of surfing. He wore faded jeans, an orange and white Hawaiian shirt, and a split leather cowboy hat—a sort of Pancho-Villa-meets-the-Beach-Boys look. His age appeared to be early sixties.

"I didn't know a gate was there!" I exclaimed.

The slight pouches under the man's black eyes smoothed out when he smiled. "Story goes that the original owners of these two houses were a married couple who couldn't live together but still liked to visit a couple of evenings a week."

I laughed. "Sounds like the perfect setup to me."

"Now, you don't mean that," he said.

"You might be surprised."

"Believe me, kid, at my age you very rarely are. Hey, *amigo*," he said, reaching down and scratching under Scout's chin. "Had a craving for enchiladas today, not tri-tip steak. Guess you're stuck with the canned stuff tonight."

Scout's wagging tail beat furiously against my leg. "You two know each other, I see."

"Me and *el perro loco* here are old friends. Since I've only lived here three months I'm still enamored with the local custom of barbecuing tri-tip over oakwood, so he gets a lot of my scraps."

"You're not from around here?" There went my burgeoning hope of picking his brain for information about Mr. Chandler.

"Leased this house three months ago. I'm originally from Phoenix. I'm trying to decide where to spend my retirement years. I have one daughter in San Francisco, one in Hollywood, and one in Santa Monica." He rubbed the back of his fingers on his brown cheek. "Not one city I consider habitable, so I thought somewhere in between might be good. Besides, this

27

ocean air is good for the complexion." He grinned at me.

"Something I'm sure your wife especially appreciates," I said.

His dark eyes flickered. "Wish that were so. She died five years ago. That's also why I moved. It was about time to let the old place go. Start a new life."

"Oh, I'm sorry," I said.

"Thank you. He held up the first aid kit in his hand. "Since that scrape on your head is my fault, how about letting me take a look at it?" He grinned at me again.

"Don't worry, you can trust me. I'm a fireman."

I laughed. "That would be great, except I'm not on fire."

He shook his head and pointed to a blue wooden bench under a pepper tree. "You sound like one of my daughters. You modern young women, always the smart remark for everything. Why, in my day—"

"Okay, okay," I said, holding up my hands in mock surrender. "I'll let you bandage my wounds as long as I don't have to endure an 'In my day, women were seen and not heard' lecture."

He raised his thick black eyebrows. "You do know my daughters, don't you?"

"No, but I have a father."

I sat down on the bench. Scout flopped down, resting his head on the tops of my feet.

"Lift your bangs," the fireman said, sitting down beside me. He inspected the scrape closely, then tore open an alcohol swab and started cleaning around it. "Trust me," he said. "I was a paramedic about twenty years ago." I jerked back when the alcohol hit my raw skin.

"It's going to sting a little," he said.

"You're a day late and a dollar short there, buddy," I commented.

"Cut an old fart some slack. I'm not as quick on the draw as I once was." He winked at me. "So, what was all the ruckus about this morning?" he asked as he tore pieces of tape with his teeth to fit the gauze pad covered with antibiotic cream.

"Mr. Chandler passed away last night."

He carefully taped the bandage to my forehead. "The guy who lived here? I'm sorry to hear that." Only inches away, he looked sympathetically into my eyes. "Was he a relative?"

"No," I answered, feeling funny about accepting sympathy for a sorrow I didn't feel.

When I didn't elaborate, he didn't press. He ran a finger lightly over the taped edges, flattening them into place. "All done." He snapped the first aid kit closed and held out his hand. "Richard Manuel Jose Trujillo. Formerly of Phoenix, Arizona. Call me Rich."

I took his hand and said, "Benni Harper. San Celina, California."

"So, Benni Harper of San Celina, what brings you to Morro Bay?"

I hesitated, then blurted out, "How well did you know Jacob Chandler?"

His face grew curious. "Jake? Not well. We talked over the fence a few times. You know, weather and whatnot. He recommended a few restaurants and the fishing boat I go out on sometimes." He shrugged. "We were just neighbors. We didn't run in the same circles here in town. Actually, I haven't really gotten to know many people yet. Me and the fire chief are old buddies from way back, but other than that I'm still a relative newcomer here myself."

I hesitated again. Did I want to tell this person, this stranger, about the weird circumstances of my inheritance? A silent voice warned me to keep that information to myself. On the other hand, how would I convince people to talk to me if they didn't even know who I was or why I was here? I felt irrationally guilty, as if *I'd* done something wrong, when in reality I was an innocent bystander drawn into the life of a man I'd never met. Another feeling of uneasiness seized me when I realized that a good chance that relatives or friends of Jacob Chandler might expect his will to read quite differently.

"Hey, kid, are you all right?" he asked.

"Yes, fine." I stood up abruptly. Scout jumped up and crowded next to my leg.

Rich stood up, and I looked at him for a long moment. His dark eyes seemed kind, and I had to start *somewhere.*

"To be honest," I said, reaching down and stroking Scout's head for comfort, "I didn't even know Mr. Chandler. I just found out today that he died and left me everything he owns, which apparently includes Scout here."

"That's the strangest thing I ever heard."

Should I tell him the stipulation of the will? No, the silent voice cautioned again. Gabe's instinctive cop suspiciousness had obviously rubbed off on me. Mr. Trujillo would find out soon enough, since I was destined to be his neighbor for the next two weeks. One thing was for sure, I wanted Gabe to check the place out before I uncurled my bedroll and settled in.

"Did you . . ." I didn't know quite how to say it. "What kind of impression did you get of him?"

He pulled at one of his short sideburns, considering my question. "I'd say he was about my age—early sixties. Liked to garden and fish, like a lot of us who retire here. Showed me some of his wood carving. The guy was really talented. Oh, and he was a diabetic."

"He was?" I hadn't seen any indication of it, but then I hadn't looked through the kitchen cupboards yet.

"Yeah, he told me when he found out I was once a paramedic. I'm borderline myself, but I can still control it by diet. Oh, one other thing. He and the lady across the street were in and out of each other's places a lot." He pointed to a blue and white clapboard house next door to the Pelican Inn.

That must be the woman who found him. There was one of those potential disappointed persons who worried me. How close were she and Mr. Chandler? "Well, thanks. I guess I'll be seeing you around."

"I'll look forward to it. Sorry I couldn't be of more help."

"That's okay. Well, Scooby-doo," I said to my new dog, "we've got exactly one hour to figure out how to break it to my husband that we have a new family member."

Rich bent down and scratched Scout's throat. "Hope he likes dogs."

"He does." At least, I hoped he did, because I'd already decided one thing. There was no way I was giving up this one.

Rich said, "Well, show him this. It's a sure bet." He straightened up and said, "Scout, friend."

Scout immediately sat down and lifted a paw.

"That's great!" I said. "Does he know any other commands?"

"I think all the regular ones—sit, stay, come, down. Jake told me he trained him right from a puppy. Said he didn't like unruly dogs—especially big ones."

"That has to work in Scout's favor, right?"

"I'd say it probably does." He grinned at me. "If not, you have a bit of sweet-talking to do tonight. Somehow, I get the feeling that between you and Scout there, that husband of yours doesn't stand a chance."

Rich waved good-bye and disappeared back through the gate into his yard. I locked up the house and opened the passenger side of the truck. Scout jumped in as if we'd done this a million times.

"Okay, my furry friend, you're going to meet the real alpha dog in this outfit. Best be on your most adorable behavior, 'cause *el Perro Patron's* got *mucho grande* power in this county."

With the nonchalant confidence so reminiscent of his unmet competition, he licked his lips and yawned.

I was sitting cross-legged on the sofa mentally rehearsing my explanation when Gabe burst through the front door at a little past four-thirty.

"Sorry, I'm late. I got hung up on . . ." He was stopped dead in his tracks by Scout's raised hackles and low growl.

"Scout, no," I said quickly, surprised at his instant protectiveness.

The dog continued to growl.

Gabe scowled and took a step forward.

Scout's rumble deepened.

I jumped up and grabbed Scout's collar. "Scout, stop."

The look on my husband's face became darker. Then I remembered what Rich had told me.

"Scout, friend."

The dog immediately sat down and lifted a paw.

Gabe frowned at the dog. Scout continued to offer his paw.

"Better shake it, or who knows what he'll do," I said.

Gabe cautiously walked over and shook it. Scout immediately licked his hand, and Gabe's face softened. "You posturing *pendejo.*"

Scout was home free.

Gabe sat down next to me on the sofa, scratching behind Scout's ears, and asked, "Okay, I'll bite. Who's he and what's he doing in our house?"

"His name is Scout. He's . . . well he's mine now."

"He's what you inherited from this guy?"

"Not only Scout, but a house in Morro Bay. Not to mention all its contents. It was so weird, Gabe. The minute I walked up, Scout greeted me like he'd known I was coming, and he hasn't left my side since. And you should see what's inside the house. It's—"

His face hardened, and he snapped, "You went inside this house without letting me check it out first? Are you out of your mind?"

"It's in a perfectly nice neighborhood overlooking the Embarcadero. I even met one of my neighbors. He—"

"Benni, I swear, someday I'm going to lock you in our house and wear the key around my neck. I had no idea a house was involved. There could be a bomb there, or it could be a meth lab, or—"

I interrupted him with a laugh. "For cryin' out loud, Gabe, a bomb?"

He jumped up and started pacing, his face turning burnt sienna as he moved right into lecturing without taking a breath. "Not to mention it could have been a setup. Someone could have been just waiting for you to walk through that door. You really don't have any idea how stupid it was to go to that house alone, do you?"

I folded my arms across my chest. "Don't call me stupid."

He stopped in front of me, his face pained. "Sweetheart, I wasn't calling you stupid. What you did was . . ."

I narrowed my eyes at him.

He inhaled deeply. "Injudicious."

"Now there's a five-dollar way of saying stupid."

"Okay, imprudent."

"That hole you're digging is getting deeper by the minute, Chief Ortiz." This was not going like I'd planned. In fact, it was much worse than I'd expected. He was going to have a stroke when he heard the will's stipulation.

I gnawed the inside of my cheek, contemplating how to phrase it.

His fingers tugged irritably at one side of his thick mustache. "Okay, tell me the rest. Don't make me guess what that guilty look on your face means."

"I resent that! I don't have a guilty look."

He sat down on the sofa and started tickling me. "Spill it, Señora Ortiz."

"Stop it, stop it!" I tried to wiggle away. Scout started barking when Gabe pushed me down and lay on top of me, his hands still tickling my sides.

"Scout, save me!" I cried, laughing so hard tears flowed from my eyes. My new watchdog just stood there and continued barking, his tail wagging triple time. "He's going to bite you," I said, gasping.

"He knows we're just playing," Gabe said, stopping long enough to kiss me long and hard. "Are you going to confess now, or am I going to have to continue torturing you?"

I scrubbed my lips across his mustache. "Forget the tickling, but this isn't so bad."

"The torture is I won't kiss you again until you confess."

I pushed him off me. "Chief Ortiz, you'd better watch that uppity attitude of yours. You aren't *that* irresistible."

Gabe sat back on the sofa and ran his fingers through his messy hair, no longer laughing. "Seriously, what's the rest of the story?"

I told him the requirements of the will in one long run-on sentence. His face turned from cynical to incredulous to immovable stone.

"Absolutely not. I won't allow it," he said in his police chief voice.

"You won't *allow* it? Excuse me, but the last time I checked *Roget's Thesaurus,* wife and slave were not synonyms."

"It's crazy. Let the government have the whole thing."

"No way!" I protested, standing up and heading toward the bedroom to pack, Gabe and Scout fighting for position to follow me. I opened the closet door and pulled down a canvas duffel bag. "I'm going to follow the will's instructions right down to the last comma so I can inherit that house. It has to be worth at least two hundred thousand dollars. Maybe more."

"If it's paid off."

"I'm sure it is, or Amanda would have told me." I started throwing jeans, underwear, and T-shirts into my bag. Remembering the funeral I was going to have to plan and attend, I added a plain cotton navy dress and a pair of pumps. Then I tossed in a couple of flannel shirts, since it was always ten to fifteen degrees colder in Morro Bay than San Celina. "Come with me to the house and look through it. Like I said, it's in a perfectly nice neighborhood. Good locks on the doors. I even met one of my neighbors. He's a fireman."

35

Gabe leaned against the doorjamb, his arms crossed. "Oh, wonderful. I feel so much better about your safety now."

I laughed at his superior expression and grabbed my flannel-lined Levi's jacket. "C'mon, I thought there was some kind of brotherhood between cops and firemen."

"I have the utmost respect for firemen. They manage to get full-time pay and benefits for a part-time job. You have to admire anyone who can pull off a scam like that. Not to mention they're usually darn good contractors. But then, they have all that spare time to work on it."

I laughed and zipped up my bag. "I'm going to tell Barry you said that." Barry Dolenz was San Celina's fire chief and an occasional racquetball partner of Gabe's.

"I've told him that a million times. He doesn't argue because he knows I'm right."

Before I could answer we heard an Arkansas drawl call out, "Knock, knock" from the front screen door.

"In the bedroom," I called back.

Scout stood up when Emory entered the room, but no threatening sound came from his throat.

My cousin stopped short when he saw the dog. "How do you do?" he said politely, crouching and holding out his hand. Scout walked over and sniffed it cautiously, then allowed his head to be stroked.

"Why didn't he growl at him?" Gabe asked.

"Maybe it has to do with how fast you were moving toward me," I said.

"Off to claim your inheritance?" my cousin asked me, glancing down at my bulging bag, then smiling at Gabe. "Guess you'll be singing the empty bed blues for a few weeks, Chief. Join the club."

I gave Emory a warning look that only made him grin wider.

Gabe, arms still crossed, grunted irritably.

"He wants me to let the government have it all," I said.

"Cousin Gabe, I declare, is what she says true?"

Gabe faced my cousin, his hands outstretched. "There's something not right about this whole thing, Emory." He jerked a thumb at me. "Would you talk some sense into her?"

Gabe knew that if he won Emory over, that would be a big boost to his side. Emory and I had been close since childhood, our friendship deepening when he stayed with my family the summer his mother died. I was twelve, on the verge of adolescence and hating it with all my stubborn tomboy heart. He was eleven, a skinny, bespectacled egghead terrified of all animals except fictional ones. I taught him to ride, gather cattle, look for kittens in the barn, wrestle with dogs, and fend off the bullies who liked to steal his glasses. He read me *The Red Pony* and *Huckleberry Finn,* explaining what they really meant, taught me all twelve verses of a salty sea chantey he learned at Sugartree Baptist church camp the summer before, didn't laugh at my blossoming figure, and showed me how to be quiet and listen to my own thoughts. Hiking in the woods all summer, we'd talked of our mothers—mine had died when I was six—what we remembered about them, how much we missed them. Things we didn't tell the grown-ups. He knew me like no other person in the world, and Gabe respected that.

"Gabe," Emory said, "you might not believe this, but I'm here to tell you that my sweet little cousin takes everything you say and feel into deep and loving consideration, but she also has a contrary streak the width of the treacherous Mississippi River itself. So if I were you, I'd not waste my breath and just pray the

37

Good Lord protects her." He checked his watch, then straightened the cuffs of his cream-colored dress shirt. "It's coming on five o'clock, and I have a date with the woman of my dreams. Wish me luck. And don't forget, I get first dibs on this story about your mysterious inheritance. I'll drop by to see you in the next couple of days. What's the address?"

"It's 993 Pelican. Good luck with Elvia," I said, not promising anything.

Gabe shook his head. "Emory, I don't know why you waste your time on such a headstrong and stubborn woman."

Amusement flashed in Emory's green eyes. "Mighty fine vitreous house you're residing in there, Chief Ortiz. Want to borrow my Windex?"

"Get out of here," Gabe said good-naturedly, "before I arrest you for being a smart-ass."

After Emory left, Gabe tried every argument he knew to get me to reconsider. I patiently gave a counterpoint to each of them.

"Geeze, Gabe, you really don't want this house and money to go to the government, do you? Maybe we could buy a house. I could buy a truck!"

"I make more than enough money to buy us a house and you a truck."

"I don't want your money."

"*Our* money."

"Easy for you to say—your name is on the paycheck. At any rate, I think getting a house for a mere two weeks' stay is darn good wages. I'll only be twelve miles away, and as you can see, under pretty good protective custody." I gestured at Scout, who watched our argument, his head on his paws, his brow wrinkled with worry.

Gabe finally threw up his hands in defeat. "I'm not going to talk you out of this, am I?"

"No, but I'll miss you like crazy." I went over and circled his waist with my arms, burrowing my face in his solid chest. The scent of him through his polo shirt, a musky-gingery scent that never failed to both arouse and comfort me, made me rethink my decision for a moment. A lonely bed in a strange house for two long weeks wasn't something to look forward to.

Weakening, he nuzzled the top of my head. "Let me make a few phone calls. Then we'll take a look at this place."

The sun was setting by the time we arrived in separate cars at my new house. Morro Rock had turned an orange-gray, and there was only a slight haze in the air, scented briny from the ocean. Three vehicles were parked in front of the house—one was a truck painted with the logo *John's 24-hour Locksmith.*

"These locks are perfectly all right," I exclaimed, climbing out of the truck. My frugal rancher's heart hated to see money wasted.

"Let me have your keys," Gabe said. His stubborn bottom lip told me the energy it would take to argue him out of it would be wasted.

He spoke to the man sitting in the locksmith truck for a few minutes, then handed him the keys. By the time he walked over to the other two cars, a man had climbed out of each vehicle. Both men held a dog on a short leash—one a yellow Lab, the other some kind of hound.

Next to me, Scout stood up, his body tense and ready, his quivering tail sticking straight out, ready to defend his home turf.

"Scout, sit," I said, touching his head. Reluctantly he obeyed, but his German shepherd ear stood up straight and stiff as a sail in full wind. His front legs trembled with the desire to challenge these intruders. "Stay," I told him, ignoring his pleading expression. "And don't give me that look. One snarling alpha dog is about all I can take right now." I walked over to where Gabe was talking with the men.

"Everything," he was saying. "Even the yard. Especially the garage."

"What's going on?" I demanded.

One of the men, a thin, straw-haired guy in ostrich cowboy boots, raised his sandy eyebrows and looked embarrassed. The other, an older man in a tweed jacket and New York Mets baseball cap, just laughed.

Gabe nodded at them, and they walked away, both avoiding my question. "Since you're insisting on staying here, I'm just doing the best I can to protect you. I'm having the place searched by bomb and drug dogs."

My mouth opened in astonishment. "You truly take the word paranoid to unparalleled heights."

My words didn't ruffle him. "After they're gone, I'm going through the house myself. Then you can stay, though *for the record,* I'm still very, very unhappy about it."

I didn't answer, still annoyed at what seemed to me an overreaction.

He brought his large hand up to my cheek. "You know you can't change who I am. I'm suspicious by nature, and I'd do anything to keep you from being hurt. Doesn't that count for something?" He dropped his hand down to my neck and massaged it lightly.

"I suppose," I said, melting slightly under his touch. I did know how hard this was for him, this loss of control, and I was really trying to make an effort to understand the fears he carried inside him concerning the people he cared about, frozen solid there because of the things he'd seen in Vietnam, during his time as a street cop, and working undercover narcotics in East L.A. But I couldn't allow him to make my life into the safe, easy prison he wanted it to be.

When the locks were changed and the house and garage given a clean bill of health by the bomb and drug dogs, we fed Scout and walked down the steps in the ice plant to the Embarcadero. We ate dinner at a fish restaurant and then strolled along the water's edge. The streets were fairly empty even though it was a Saturday night because an unusually strong cold wind had come up. We silently watched the masts of the sailboats sway, the rigging clanging against each other, each of us lost in separate thoughts and fears.

It was past ten when he finished searching the house to his satisfaction. Gabe found insulin, needles and a compact blood-testing kit in the nightstand, confirming what Rich had told me about Mr. Chandler's diabetes. During his search, which included, in spite of my teasing, looking behind every light switch and plug plate for bugs, he also found both savings and checking account books. The savings account balance was a little over nineteen thousand dollars. The checking account held eleven hundred and twenty-seven dollars and fifteen cents. I stuck them in my purse with the intention of asking Amanda if I had access to this money yet.

Mr. Chandler's wallet was in his nightstand. Now I had a face to go with his name. Jacob Chandler smiled slightly in his driver's license picture, which revealed the basic information: he was sixty-four years old, five feet seven inches, one hundred forty pounds, and wore corrective lenses. His hair was gray, eyes brown, and he was clean shaven. There was only one other picture in his wallet. It was a photograph of me standing in front

41

of Blind Harry's, the front window decorated for Mardi Gras. My hair was just past my shoulders, which meant it had probably been taken this last February.

"Creep," Gabe said, one fist slowly clenching. "He was stalking you."

A ribbon of fear ran through me at the word "stalk." I almost told Gabe about the carving of my childhood horse, then stopped. He was nervous enough. I pushed the fear back down. The man was dead; there was no way he could hurt me now.

"I'm staying," I said, touching his jaw gently.

His eyes turned a familiar smoky blue. "Put the dog in the kitchen and come into the living room," he said, his voice raw and husky.

When I commanded "stay," Scout obeyed, looking up at me with sad eyes as if being parted from me was a cruelty beyond bearing. "Scooby-doo, you *are* a heartbreaker," I said, stroking his smooth head.

In the living room, Gabe had built a fire in the natural stone fireplace. We sat on the sofa and started kissing, eventually making love on the smooth cotton sofa. It seemed to be an unspoken agreement that we wouldn't use the bedroom of this mysterious man. There was a skittish intensity to our lovemaking, as if we were teenagers making clandestine love with sleeping parents in the other room. Our feverish passion surprised us both.

I touched my fingertips to the teeth marks on his shoulder. "Oh, I'm sorry."

"I don't want to leave," he murmured softly under his breath and trailed a calloused fingertip down between my breasts, its roughness lightly scratching my skin.

"I wish you didn't have to."

At the front door he tugged off his black leather jacket and wrapped it around my shoulders. "When I was a

42

teenager and I liked a girl I always left my jacket at her house. That way I knew no matter what happened, we had to see each other one more time."

"Unless she mailed the jacket back to you," I said, laughing, hugging the buttery-soft jacket close to me. "Or sent it by a friend. Or—"

"Leave it to you to ruin a romantic moment. Be careful. And once more, for the record, remember I hate this."

"Duly noted and date-stamped," I said, taking his face in my hands and kissing him again.

"I'll come by early tomorrow," he said. "Want to have breakfast?"

"Absolutely."

"*Buenas noches, mi corazón*. Dream sweet. Don't forget me."

"As if I could, Friday."

I shut the door quietly behind him and I was alone.

Behind me canine nails click-clicked across the kitchen floor, and then Scout leaned against my left leg, heaving one of his big sighs.

Well, not totally alone.

4

BACK IN THE LIVING ROOM THE FIRE HAD BURNED down to glowing embers. I was too agitated to attempt sleep, and though it was superstitious and childish, I wanted to find out just *exactly* where Mr. Chandler had died before I slept in the bed. Gabe had searched the house his way, looking for things that could possibly hurt me, but now it was my turn. Somewhere in all these books and papers must be some information about his

43

identity. The coffee table trunk looked promising.

Just as they do most people, trunks have always fascinated me. They seemed like something from a bygone era—people my age didn't own trunks as much as our parents and grandparents had. Gabe had quickly glanced through it, but now I could spend as much time as I wanted inspecting the contents.

The smoky-vanilla smell that I was already starting to associate with this mysterious man floated up from inside the trunk. The removable top tray contained a faded maroon autograph book, a bone-handle pocketknife engraved with the initials G. M., a flat translucent white stone that I assumed was some kind of sharpening stone, and a stained and tattered old book— *Treasure Island*. Inside the flyleaf was an inscription in an obviously feminine handwriting—"To G. Because you've always loved the hunt more than the treasure. Love, G." I flipped through the book looking for other inscriptions, but that was it. What did it have to do with this Jacob Chandler? Was it a clue because it was inside the chest and not on the crowded bookshelves, or just a book he'd picked up in a used bookstore because he liked it or it held some personal meaning?

I opened the maroon autograph book. There were entries sprinkled throughout its coarse, brownish paper pages.

Some were dated June 1957. Were they someone's high school memories? There was nothing to indicate even the part of the country they were from.

Mary McKinney
Shirlee Barsky
Gwen Swanson
Doris Kent
Phil Blue

Margaret Sicker
Avis
Goldie Hassel
Dorsey
Caroline Canthon

The friendship verses were those typical of the era: "In your chain of friendship count me as a link"; "When the golden sun is setting and your heart from care is free/While of absent friends you're thinking, will you kindly think of me?"; "True friends are like diamonds, precious and rare/False friends are like autumn leaves, found everywhere"; "When you are dirty and in the tub/Remember me with every scrub."

On the back cover was the only clue to the owner of the book.

"Weezie," it read, "I know you will have many a friend and many a lover/So to give them all room, I'll write on the cover. Best friends till powder puffs. Love, Gwen."

Weezie? Obviously a nickname and the owner of the autograph book. Again the questions were how were they connected to Jacob Chandler, and why was this important enough for him to keep in this trunk? Was Gwen one of the G's in the *Treasure Island* book?

I set the book aside and peered inside the trunk. A rolled canvas cloth revealed his wood carving tools. There were twenty-eight of them in two staggered rows so the tools cleared each other. Under the tools was a green leather scrapbook. As I flipped through the pages, my first thought was that there was no way I was going to show Gabe this, at least until he got used to me staying here. Each page featured an article about me— the time the *Tribune* took a picture of me demonstrating a cutting horse for schoolkids during the Agriculture Day sponsored by the Cattlewomen's Association; the article about Jack's fatal car accident on Highway 1; the times I made the newspaper because of the murders I stumbled across at the museum, at Oakview Retirement Home's Senior Prom, and at Laguna Lake; the picture of me and Gabe announcing our marriage. The articles went all the way back to February 1, 1978, and included the newspaper's wedding picture of me and Jack. My eyes burning with fatigue and my blood churning with anxiety, I put the scrapbook back in the trunk. How long had this man lived here, and how long had he been watching me?

I looked down at Scout and said, "Looks like we have some work cut out for us. It's a good thing I finished that Mother's Day showing." During the month of May we were having a special exhibit of arts and crafts made by or for San Celina mothers. "But that's for tomorrow, or rather, later today. Right now, I'd better get some sleep." His eyebrows seesawed, listening to my words.

I contemplated taking a shower, but held off, not just because of my strange surroundings, but because I didn't want to wash away the musky scent of my husband, the mingled smell of us. I grabbed a pillow and the quilt from the foot of the bed and settled down on the sofa, hugging Gabe's leather jacket to my chest. Scout hopped on the sofa and curled up at the other end. I tucked my feet into his warm body and watched darkness for at least an hour before drifting off to sleep.

I woke to the stereo racket of Scout's bark and a loud pounding on the front door. The unfamiliar sounds startled and disoriented me for a moment. The mantle clock showed seven-thirty. I stumbled to the door and tried to discern through the stained-glass design who was out there. Though the door was a beautiful piece of artistry, it made for lousy security. Next to me, Scout's spirited barking didn't let up.

"Hey, Benni!" Sam, my eighteen-year-old stepson, yelled. "Are you being eaten by wolves in there?"

I grabbed Scout's collar and told him "friend" while opening the door. "How'd you know where I was?" I asked, gesturing for him to come inside. He was dressed in baggy shorts and a torn, gray Cal Poly Cougars sweatshirt. He clutched a bulging white paper sack.

He let Scout sniff his hand then gave him a vigorous ear scratch, receiving a welcoming tail wag. I fixed my eyes on the paper bag, which was emanating a toasty, nutty scent.

"Bless you and the Chevelle you rode in on," I said, grabbing it from him. Inside were two cups of hot coffee and two warm maple bars—a wicked addiction Sam and I shared as often as possible out of sight of his health-conscious father. "What are you doing here so early? Were you out surfing?"

"Elvia told me the whole story yesterday." He flopped down on the sofa and took the coffee I handed him. "No offense, *madrastra*," he said, using the affectionate Spanish word for stepmother, "but you look like crap."

I looked down at my rumpled clothes and ran a hand through my wild, curly hair. "Don't tell anyone, but I was too creeped out last night to sleep in the bedroom so I slept with Scout on the sofa." Between the coffee and the maple bar, within five minutes I was on the way to feeling human again.

"This is so cool," Sam said, twisting his head to inspect the whole room. "You have all the luck. Getting a house left to you. And a dog, too. Did this guy have any money? Hey, do you need someone to house-sit for

47

you until you sell it? I'm cheap. Or maybe you should just keep it and let me live here. It'd be a good investment, and I'd be a great tenant. Only one wild party a month, I swear." He grinned at me with the smile that had already captured way more than its share of hearts at Cal Poly, where he'd been attending classes since January.

He was living with Dove and Daddy out at the ranch and had been since last September. As I knew would eventually happen, he was chomping at the bit to escape Dove's watchful eye. I was sympathetic, but not enough to turn my house over to a bunch of college students.

I couldn't bear to wipe away the hopeful look on his face. "I don't even know what I'm going to be doing five minutes from now, Sam, but when the time comes, I'll keep your proposal in mind." I finished up my maple bar and took another few gulps of coffee. "Look, your dad's going to be coming by soon, and we're going to breakfast. You're more than welcome to join us, but right now I need to take a shower."

"Sounds cool," he said, nodding. "You know me, I never turn down a free meal. Actually I already talked to Dad, and he said to tell you he's probably going to be late, maybe noon or so. I'll hang around until then."

I instantly grew suspicious. "Why's he going to be late?"

He shrugged and tried to look innocent. Unfortunately for him, he was about as proficient at hiding his feelings as me.

"How was the surfing this morning?" I asked, testing him.

"It was okay."

I grabbed his arm and brought it up to my nose.

"Hey, what are you doing?" He jerked his arm back.

"You didn't go surfing this morning."

"Did too."

"Your hair's not wet, and you don't smell salty. Your father told you to come over and baby-sit me, didn't he?"

He looked as guilty as a two-year-old with a lapful of unrolled toilet paper. "Man, I'll never make it as a spy, will I? Don't tell Dad, okay? He really trusted me to pull this off."

"Where is your dad?" I asked.

The intense struggle of conflicting loyalties on his face was both painful and amusing to watch.

"Stepson, who are you most afraid of here?"

His dark brown eyes widened. "No contest. Dad by a mile."

I scowled at him. That wasn't the answer I wanted. "Okay, let me rephrase the question. Who slips you money when you're broke and hungry? Who ran interference when you decided to get your *other* ear pierced? Who talked your father into buying that Chevelle for you? And who—"

He held up his hands. "I give up. He's home sleeping."

"Sleeping? Why . . . ?" Then it dawned on me. "I'm going to smack him silly. He staked out this house last night, didn't he?"

He sipped at his Styrofoam cup of coffee and didn't answer, but his eyes revealed the truth.

"Never mind, I'll take care of your father. So, since your assignment is morning watch, we might as well catch up. How's school?"

He spent the next hour complaining about his classes, teachers, and the finals he had coming up. "I'm meeting my mom in Santa Barbara for Mother's Day. I every

49

made reservations at a fancy restaurant."

"She'll be very impressed," I said. "And thanks for reminding me. I have to get something for Dove and order some flowers for my mom's grave."

His young face grew curious. "You go there much?"

I shrugged. "Usually just on Mother's Day. Sometimes I take flowers on her birthday."

"Your husband's buried there, too, isn't he?"

I laughed and tossed a throw pillow at him. "No, but he might be after I get through with him for pulling that ridiculous stakeout stunt."

Sam caught the pillow and held it in front *of* him, his face serious. "You know what I mean."

"Yes, I do," I said softly. "And, yes, Jack's there, too."

He was silent for a moment, then said, "Dad said your mom died when you were six. That's really little."

"Yes, it was."

"Was it hard having your mom die when you were so little?"

I studied the tops of my hands, hands that were already ten years older than my mother's when she died. "When you're that young, you mostly just tuck it inside you and don't think about it except in little pieces."

"That's so sad," Sam said.

I felt my chest tighten, remembering Dove telling me in the ranch house kitchen that while I was at school that day, Mama had gone to heaven and that I would see her again, but not for a very long time. I was eating an oatmeal cookie with raisins, and I recall picking out the raisins and laying them on my plate, carefully arranging them in a circle as Dove talked. I looked at Sam's solemn face. "Actually I don't remember that much."

I stood up and stretched. "Think I'd better shower

before your dad gets here. I haven't checked the television, but I'm sure it works fine." I tossed him the remote.

In the sparkling clean bathroom I threw away Chandler's used soap and half-empty tube of Pepsodent toothpaste. In the cupboard I found two new bars of Zest soap and a new tube of Colgate baking soda gel toothpaste—both both my favorite brands. Was it a coincidence? Or had this man actually followed me around in the store and watched what brands of soap and toothpaste I bought? That was beyond creepy. By the time I'd finished showering, dried my hair, dressed in jeans and a red long-sleeve shirt, I heard Gabe's voice in the living room. It was only a little past ten o'clock, so he must have had trouble sleeping.

He and Sam were laughing at something—music to my ears since it didn't happen often. Sam was at the age where he annoyed his father more than pleased him— and vice versa.

Much to Sam's relief, I didn't confront Gabe until after we'd all eaten breakfast, gone back to the house, and Sam left to help my dad clear cattle roads. Then I lit into my husband, pacing in front of him on the sofa.

"I will not have you sitting outside this house for two weeks. Not only are you too old to do that, you are way over the line. I swear I'll call the cops if you're out there tonight, and, buddy-boy, I'll be watching."

He listened calmly to my ranting, then said, "I could sit out there until the moon turns to blue cheese, and the Morro Bay police wouldn't do a thing."

I stopped pacing and glared at him. Oh, yes, how could I forget? The *brotherhood*. There were times I really, really hated being married to a cop.

He grabbed my hand and pulled me down next to him

51

on the sofa. "Sweetheart, I'm just concerned for your safety."

I sat there stiffly. "Why can't you understand that this makes me feel like a child? No more discussion. You're going to stop it."

He looked at me silently for a moment, then said, "Okay. I won't stake out this house again."

I was instantly suspicious. He was giving in much too easily. "What about your officers?"

"You know I'd never use the city's money for my private problems. I'll continue to worry, but I'll back off and let you handle this."

My face must have screamed my disbelief.

"Benni, who's not trusting who now?"

"All right," I said reluctantly.

"But I do have one confession to make."

"What's that?"

"Last night I called a friend of mine who's a private investigator down in Santa Barbara and told him to run a check on Jacob Chandler. I hope that doesn't crowd your boundaries too much."

"A private investigator? Can't you just run some kind of record on him at the station? As a matter of fact, I was going to ask you to do that."

"No, contrary to popular belief, cops can't just run criminal records on anyone they please without a reason."

"Not even you? Who would know?"

"Maybe no one. Maybe the Department of Justice when they audit our records. At any rate, there are privacy laws, and it's a felony. I could lose my job over it."

"So you hired a private eye?" I laughed, the idea striking me as funny. "On television, it's always the other way around, a private eye trying to get information from a cop by slipping him fifty bucks."

"I don't know many cops who are willing to risk their jobs for fifty bucks. Anyway, I've known this guy since my L.A. days. He was a good cop and a whiz on the computer, which is mostly what private investigation is these days."

"So, what did he find out?" I asked eagerly.

He pulled a slip of paper from his back pocket, glancing at it as he gave me the facts. "Not much. Chandler seems like a normal, if somewhat bland character. He was born in Houston, Texas, in 1930. That would make him sixty-four as of February. He served in Korea in the Army in 1950 and was given an honorable discharge in 1954. Shortly thereafter, he went to work for a trucking company that same year. Then in 1957 he got a job as a salesman for a restaurant supply company. His area was the Southeast. Never married and had no record of any children. He has one sister, a Rowena Ludlam, last know address Lubbock, Texas. He retired from his sales job when he was 54—that was 1984— came to Morro Bay, bought this house with cash from a private trust, and opened up a checking and savings account at San Celina Savings and Loan—Paso Robles branch. He has no credit cards and no credit history except for owning this house."

"Why wouldn't he leave everything to his sister?"

"Good question, except he wouldn't be the first person estranged from family. I have her address and phone number here, so that could be a place for you to start. I have no idea if it's any good." He laid the piece of paper on the trunk top, his face troubled. "You know, I get nervous when I have so little information on someone. He looks too clean."

"Too clean? How can a person be too clean?"

"There's just not enough history. He was sixty-four years old. Most people leave a paper trail seven or eight miles long by that age. It's like he deliberately kept his trail skimpy, and that makes me suspicious."

"Everything makes you suspicious. To me it sounds like he's a loner who saved his money and retired to a small coastal town after years of being a traveling salesman. Doesn't sound suspicious to me, just kinda sad."

"A loner who was very obsessed with you. That's not normal, Benni, no matter how you look at it."

I sighed and nodded, laying my hand on Gabe's forearm. "I'm going to do my best to find out who he was if for no other reason than to try to understand why he chose me. I have an eerie feeling there's something more to all this. Something deeper."

"That," Gabe said, "is exactly what worries me."

5

"WE'D BETTER DRIVE OUT TO THE RANCH SO I CAN explain all of this to Dove," I said. "She's probably already heard about it through the grapevine, and frankly I'm surprised she hasn't called."

Sure enough, while helping her peel apples for pies, I received a lecture from Dove for humiliating her by making her hear the news thirdhand from Edna Dunsworth down at the Farm Supply. When Gabe went out to the barn to visit with Daddy, I tried to encourage Scout to follow him, but the dog refused to leave my side.

"Looks like you've made yourself a friend," Dove commented, scooping up my pile of apple skins and dumping them in the white plastic compost bucket.

"If I didn't know better, I'd say he was trained by the big pooch himself," I said wryly. Scout wagged his tail slowly, almost apologetically, as if he understood what I was saying.

"Some dogs are like that. Takes to one person right off, and there's never anyone else in their eyes and they aim to protect them." She flipped her long white braid back, her pale blue eyes mischievous. "Some men, too."

"Yes, he's annoyed as all get out about this whole thing," I answered her nonverbal question. "He'd just as soon let the money go to the government, but there's almost twenty thousand dollars in the bank, and that house has to be worth at least two hundred thousand. How can I throw away money like that?"

"Gabe's got a point. It is right strange."

"Yes, but then again, maybe this guy was just a lonely man who randomly picked me as the object of his—"

"Perverted obsession?" Gabe finished as he walked into the room, followed by my father.

"No," I answered, though I had to admit I couldn't think of a better description. "Are you sure you've never seen this man before?" I asked Dove. His driver's license and the picture of me from his wallet were the only pictures I'd come across so far.

Dove looked at the license and the candid photograph of me again. "No, don't look a bit familiar. What about you, Ben?" Daddy peered over her shoulder, polishing a red apple on his cotton shirt.

"Nope, but I sure don't take to the idea of this old boy carrying a picture of my little girl in his billfold." The webbed wrinkles around his eyes deepened as he took a large bite out of his apple. "Son, you better watch out for her."

"Doing my best, sir," Gabe answered, raising his

eyebrows at me, "but she doesn't make it easy."

"Never did for me, don't reckon you should have it any better," Daddy said, chuckling.

"You two chauvinists just dry up or go back out to the barn," I said, then turned to Dove. "Let's forget about Mr. Chandler for two minutes. Tell me what's going on with the Historical Museum."

Dove straightened her entire five feet and glared at the room. "If those mealymouthed, noodle-brain council members think they're selling our Historical Museum to some hotel chain, they got another think coming."

"What happened at the meeting with the mayor on Friday?"

"That man has more than his share of tongue oil, that's all I have to say. To think that I voted for him. Is there any way I can take my vote back?" She looked over at Gabe, who, because of his police chief status, she considered her political advisor.

"I don't believe so, *abuelita*," he said. "You might be able to start a recall, but that takes getting signatures on a petition, then another election. A lot of work. Especially since the mayor was voted in by a special election."

Her wrinkled face looked sly. "Don't y'all worry. Me and the ladies have a plan, and it's a lot quicker than any recall. They aren't getting away with it, that's a natural fact." She went over to a lump of bread dough lying under a damp tea towel, slapped it down on a wooden breadboard dusted with flour, and started to knead it with her strong fingers. "He's got me so mad I've made more bread than Ben and I could eat in a month of Sundays. Y'all better take some with you."

"Yes, ma'am," I said. "We both will."

Her blue eyes darkened in a searching look. "Ain't

56

good for married folk to sleep apart, honeybun. You see it don't last any longer than need be."

"I won't," I said, not looking at Gabe who was no doubt smirking.

"By the way," Dove said, "Elvia called. She said she was tired of hearing about things secondhand from Sam. Said you'd better call her pronto. I told her to join the club."

"I'll call her right now," I said, ignoring her carping. It took me four tries to find her—her house, the store, her mother's house. I finally tracked her down at Emory's house downtown.

"I've called all over creation looking for you. Maybe I should start checking here first," I teased her when she came to the phone.

"Shut up," she said, "and tell me what's going on."

"I can't do both."

"Benni!"

"Okay, okay." I quickly told her everything I knew so far.

"Well, just be careful," she said. "This sounds very, very weird."

"I'm fine. My number's in the Morro Bay phone book under Jacob Chandler. I'll be easy to track."

"All right. Let me know if I can help, *amiga*."

"You bet, girlfriend."

On the drive back, four loaves of plastic-wrapped molasses-wheat bread sitting in my lap, I stared out the truck's window, thinking about Jacob Chandler and the second night I'd spend in his house. Pelican Street appeared almost before I realized it.

Gabe put the truck in park. "I'll walk you in," he said. "Check things out."

"Oh, sure," I said, hopping out and heading down

the front walk, Scout trailing after me. "Don't kid me with your noble pretensions. You're just hoping for a repeat of last night's episode on the sofa. Well, you can just—"

I stopped when Rich walked up.

"Oh, hi," I said.

"Hi back." He looked curiously at Gabe.

"This is my husband, Gabe Ortiz. Gabe, this is Rich Trujillo, my next door neighbor. I told you about him."

They shook hands and nodded. Gabe's face was stiff and wary.

"So," Rich said, smiling at me, "how's your head?"

I touched my forehead where a scab had already started forming. "Fine."

"Good."

He cleared his throat, the smile never leaving his face.

"Well, you two have a nice evening. Nice meeting you."

Gabe stared at him, not answering.

"Geez Louise, Friday," I said after Rich was out of earshot. "I thought you were going to start growling like Scout."

"Why would he ask about the scrape on your head?"

"I told you I did it on the birdbath. He bandaged it for me."

"You didn't tell me *that*."

I gave an irritated exhalation of breath. "Gabe, for cryin' out loud, you are really getting paranoid."

"How long did he say he's lived here?"

"Three months. He's a retired fireman from Phoenix. I'm sure that'll be a cinch for you to check out."

"No doubt."

Inside the house, I turned and shook a finger in his face. "I think you were rude to Mr. Trujillo."

58

He grabbed my finger and kissed it. "Does he know why you're here?"

I was silent for a moment, not wanting to tell Gabe how much I'd opened up to my new neighbor. "He's a perfectly nice person."

One black eyebrow lifted in skepticism.

"I didn't tell him everything," I said defensively.

"See, that's exactly what worries me about you. You're too trusting with strangers."

"And you think everyone and his grandmother has a hidden criminal agenda. Can you imagine what he thought?"

He shrugged, unconcerned, and gave a wide yawn.

"You are too old to be trying to get along with only three hours sleep, *papacito*," I lightly scolded.

"Am not," he said, yawning again. "Besides, it's only six o'clock."

"Don't argue with me. You need to go home and go to bed."

"I hate leaving you here."

"I know, but you don't have a choice."

Just as he was walking out the door, I remembered something. "Gabe, I know this sounds silly, but is there some way you can find out exactly *where* Mr. Chandler died in this house?"

"Sure, I'll see what I can do." Using his cell phone, he called Morro Bay's police chief, who gave him the number of the officer who took the call. Luckily the officer was home.

"The recliner in the living room," Gabe informed me. "He was sitting there when his neighbor, a Mrs. Tess Briggstone, found him. She has a *key* to his place." I-told-you-so was written all over his face.

I made a face at him. "And?"

59

"She lives across the street. The story is she grew worried when he didn't show up at his usual time at her store on the Embarcadero. She apparently owns one of those knickknack shell shops, and they had coffee and doughnuts together every morning."

"That fits with what Rich told me about them."

Gabe frowned at the mention of my neighbor's name.

I pushed him in the chest. "Quit being such a suspicious old bear. Thanks for finding that out for me. Now I can sleep in the bedroom."

He didn't answer. At the door he kissed me, then started in. "Be careful. Keep the doors and windows locked. Call me tomorrow."

"I will, I will, I will. Now go before all my willpower flies out the window and I lose my inheritance because I can't bear to have you leave."

"Going without me for one night is cruel and unusual punishment, isn't it?" he said solemnly.

"Get outta here before I smack that macho arrogance clean out of you."

I listened to his laughter as he went to his car, lonely for him even before the sound of his Corvette faded away.

I looked down at Scout, patiently waiting at my side.

"Scout, my loyal sidekick, we've got work to do. We'd better get cracking."

The first thing I did was look for a notebook. I found an almost new steno pad in the small desk in the spare room and started listing the things I needed to do. The first was to set a date for his funeral service—the sooner the better. Then I needed to go see this Tess Briggstone, who was obviously a close enough friend to have a key to his place, and ask her for a list of Mr. Chandler's friends. Then I had to . . .

I sat drawing stars and triangles on the steno pad, stumped. Then what? All I had so far were the items in the trunk—the initialed knife, the Robert Louis Stevenson book, the scrapbook, and the little bit of information that Gabe's private investigator had found. Not many clues at all.

I methodically searched the rest of his desk, reading his bills and anything else that might give me a lead. In the back of the last drawer, underneath boxes of old checks, bank statements, and utility statements, I found a five-by-seven manila envelope. Inside was a roll of exposed film and a folded piece of paper. I opened it and read the neat, handwritten message.

Carving is a very special art form and needs a cool-headed approach. Don't hurry the process. Study each cut before you make it so you don't cut what you might later regret. Remember, there are no shortcuts. Take your time. Do your research. Think.

A lesson in wood carving? The twelve-exposure roll of Kodak film felt cold in my hand. It certainly didn't take a Sherlock Holmes to figure out he wanted me to develop this film. I added to my list—one-hour photo developer.

After searching the living room, including fanning through every book on the bookshelves, I checked out the kitchen. The refrigerator contained only a quart of milk, some orange juice in a pitcher, and some leftover Chinese takeout in white unmarked containers. Looking through the cupboards, where I found the normal staples as well as a few cans of soup and vegetables, it occurred to me that eating anything left in this house might not be smart.

I glanced at the plain yellow clock over the kitchen table—nine p.m. Maybe the grocery store out by the highway would still be open. In the last cupboard I checked, another small alarm went off inside me. Sitting on the shelf next to a round blue box of Morton salt and some paper plates was an unopened green can of Van Houten German Cocoa. The kind I'd come to use exclusively since I was eighteen after discovering I liked its dark richness better than the American brands. Our local gourmet food store ordered it special for me.

I carefully placed the can back on the shelf. Fear tumbled like rough little stones in my stomach, but, I told myself firmly, it was just another coincidence.

I discovered the grocery store was open until midnight and stocked up on my comfort foods—Coke, barbecue potato chips, Ben and Jerry's Cherry Garcia ice cream, as well as fruit, oatmeal, milk, bread, cheddar cheese, and coffee. I also bought all new staples—not even trusting this man's flour, sugar . . . or cocoa. On the spur of the moment, thankful that so many grocery stores had become one-stop shopping meccas, I bought a new set of queen sheets. Sleeping in a stranger's bed was bad enough, but I would at least have new sheets touching my body.

Back at the house, after putting the sheets on to wash, I started checking out the bedroom, the last room left. The search went quicker simply because the room was smaller, it only contained a bed, a nightstand, a bookcase, and a chest of drawers.

I opened the closet and discovered in five seconds how Scout knew me the first time we met. It wasn't something Gabe would have noticed because he had searched the house like a cop, for signs of illegal activity or things that would jeopardize my safety. I searched it looking for signs of things connected to me and found the biggest one hanging in plain view. To anyone else, including Gabe, it would look like just another Levi's jacket. But I knew this jacket intimately since I'd owned it for five years before it mysteriously disappeared right after I'd moved to town two years ago. I'd assumed at the time that I accidently left it somewhere, which was not an unreasonable deduction considering how scatterbrained I was those first few months after Jack died.

I touched the frayed hole on the elbow. It had happened while mending a fence only weeks before Jack's accident. The hole was surrounded by a blue ink heart that Jack had drawn one night while we ate dinner at Liddie's.

Somehow this man had found—or taken—my jacket and used it to familiarize Scout with my scent. Of all the things he'd done, this upset me the most. I tossed the jacket on the bed and continued searching the closet.

Mr. Chandler seemed fond of khaki pants and flannel shirts from Mervyn's and owned three pairs of Vans slip-on deck shoes. The boxes on top of the closet revealed only old issues of *Wood-carvers* magazine and more old bills. I stood back and surveyed the room, feeling like I'd missed something. On the nightstand stood a simple wood-based lamp and a cordless phone. The *phone*.

I went back into the living room and checked the message light on the combination phone/answering machine. It read two. Like ours at home, it had a replay button.

"You have two old messages," the machine said.

"Jake," a grainy-sounding, older woman's voice said,

"how about Chinese tonight? Call me at the store."

Friday. April 30th. 11:08 A.M.

That explained the Chinese take-out boxes.

"Hey, buddy," the second message said. It was a male voice—age indistinguishable. "A chess game on Sunday? Whatta ya say? Got a whole smoked salmon says I got a move that'll beat you in a half hour."

Friday. April 30th. 2:27 P.M.

That was it. No great information there except that he liked Chinese food and played chess with someone. Gabe had probably already listened to the two messages and discounted them.

I stared at the phone a minute then recalled something I'd seen on television. It was hokey but heck, it worked sometimes. I hit the redial and waited. The phone rang four times, and then an answering machine came on.

"Cafe Palais," a smooth, male Southern voice said. "We're at home now makin' our beaten biscuits and burgoo for y'all, but we'll be open bright and early at six A.M. as always. Leave a message if you've a mind to. Thanks for calling."

Beaten biscuits and burgoo. Someone was from Kentucky, if I remembered my regional Southern cooking correctly. A French-sounding restaurant that served Southern food? I'd have to check that out even if it didn't have a thing to do with Mr. Chandler. I added another item to tomorrow's growing list.

The phone rang, and I didn't need to be any sort of detective at all to know who was on the other line. After scolding him for still being up, I told him about the roll of film and the note and my long-lost jacket.

"Manipulative pervert," Gabe said in a disgusted voice.

"A little nuts, maybe, but I don't think he's a pervert."

64.

He grumbled unintelligibly over the phone.

"Go to bed. Things will look better in the morning."

Scout settled in his bed next to mine. My pure fatigue and his comforting presence helped me fall asleep almost immediately.

The next morning, fog shrouded everything in a deep, pillowy silence. A distant foghorn sent a muffled heartbeat through the dense air. I flipped on the heater and every light in the cold, smoke-scented house, trying to give the place a cozier feel, but it still felt like exactly what it was, a stranger's house. I made some coffee, fed Scout from the supply of canned dog food I found under the sink, then at nine o'clock called Amanda's office.

"So, how's it going?" she asked.

"Things are getting weirder by the minute." I told her about the scrapbook, the unexposed film, and the note Mr. Chandler left me.

"A wood carving lesson?" Amanda said. "This guy sounds like a real kookabird. How's Chief Macho Man taking it?"

"About like you'd expect." I told her about the bomb and drug dogs, the changing of the locks, his staking out the place, what his detective friend had uncovered via his computer databases. "That's why I'm not going to tell him about the scrapbook just yet. He swore he'd back off and let me handle this."

"Bless his heart, he is thorough. So, did you just call to chitchat, or is there something I can do for you?"

"I need the mortuary's number so I can arrange his funeral. A simple graveside service tomorrow is what I'm thinking. My goal today is to find out who his friends were and break the news to them as gracefully as possible."

"In a town that size, it shouldn't be too hard to locate them. Then what?"

"Take the film to be developed and check out Cafe Palais."

"Looks like you're cookin', babydoll. Let me know if there's anything I can do to help."

"Count on it."

I dressed in black Wranglers, boots, a red-and-black plaid flannel shirt, and Gabe's black leather jacket. After sticking the film in my purse, I checked the address of Cafe Palais in Morro Bay's thin telephone directory. It was down on the Embarcadero, so I wouldn't even have to drive. Then, unable to put it off any longer, I called the mortuary and discovered that all the arrangements had been made by Mr. Chandler, down to the coffin's flower spray. All I had to do was give them the date. Tomorrow was fine.

With Scout at my heels, I picked my way down the staircase in the verbena-speckled ice plant, ending up at the back of Pinkie's parking lot, my pant legs and boot tips wet from the dew. Though I wasn't sure where on the Embarcadero the restaurant was located, I took a chance and turned right.

The damp, chilly air caused me to shove my hands deep into the pockets of Gabe's leather jacket as I passed stores that hawked every beach souvenir you've ever bought and thrown away three months later—seashell wind chimes, china music boxes shaped like whales and mermaids, fool's gold paperweights, framed prints of sad-eyed baby seals, hand-painted refrigerator magnets saying "Fish and Play in Morro Bay!" On this early Monday morning, minus the tourists, the Embarcadero looked more like its original self—a working place for fishermen and the businesses that support them. All of the fish restaurants were closed, so I guessed the only people eating down here would be

66

locals. I passed Bay City Donuts and noted the gray formica tables were crowded with people, most in their sixties or seventies. Definitely a place I would have to visit. The owners probably knew more about what was really going on in this town than the police chief.

The direction I chose was correct. Cafe Palais was located in an unattached building directly in line with Morro Rock, separated only by the calm, gray waters of the bay. At this time of morning, Morro Rock looked almost mythical as pewter-colored fog weaved around its crown. The cafe was painted a clean, Navajo white with royal blue trim and matching scalloped awnings. The crowded parking lot out front told me that this was also a popular spot for locals.

"Stay," I told Scout. He dropped down in front of the window planters filled with yellow marigolds.

Inside the cafe, I gazed over the full tables and booths, looking for an empty spot. The decor was French country with an emphasis on coffeepots and geese. Pots of every shape and size decorated the walls covered with a blue, white, and yellow-flowered wallpaper. Geese were equally represented in framed prints, brightly painted china knickknacks, and copper molds. Interspersed between the prints and copper molds were beautiful little handmade quilts—sizes ranging from the breadth of my palm to the size of a rectangular cake pan.

"Honey, there's a spot opening up over by the window," one of the waitresses said, sailing by with three plates balanced on one arm and a coffeepot in her other hand. "I just gave 'em their check." Sure enough, two wind-dried old men wearing identical navy and gold Greek fishermen's caps stood up, tossing crumpled bills next to their empty plates.

I weaved through the noisy crowd and sat down on one of the padded ladder-back chairs. In a few seconds, a busboy cleared the table, and another waitress handed me a blue plastic menu. She held up the coffeepot in question, pouring when I nodded yes. She looked to be in her late twenties with walnut shell brown hair cut in a shaggy style that made the most of its thick texture though it slightly overwhelmed her pinched, oval face. She wore a denim skirt and a blue-and-white-gingham blouse. A goose-shaped name tag on her left shoulder said "Neely." Dark brown eyes flicked over me quickly before she started her litany of featured dishes.

"Morning specials are a mushroom and smoked bacon frittata with fresh avocados on the side or stuffed French toast with an orange/cream cheese filling. Both come with Martin's home-style red potatoes with onion, coffee or tea, and fresh fruit of the day. Also, Eve's power drink this morning is banana/apple zest with wheat germ," she said in a low-pitched, malty voice that didn't seem to fit her sharp features.

"I'll take the French toast special," I said, handing the menu back. After she walked away, I sat there for a moment trying to figure out the best way to bring up Jacob Chandler. If she knew him she might not even know he'd died, and I sure didn't want to be the one to break it to her in such a public place.

I worried the problem for the fifteen minutes it took for me to get my breakfast. Since I hadn't thought to bring something to read, I spent the time studying the other customers, wondering if any of them knew Jacob Chandler. Unless the grapevine had done its usual small-town trick, the weekly newspaper, I'd noticed outside, came out on Thursdays so there was no way his death would be public knowledge until then.

When Neely came back with my breakfast, I casually asked, "Have you lived here long?"

She refilled my coffee cup, her face neutral. "About six years."

"Here in Morro Bay?"

She nodded, her face wary. "I'm originally from Modesto and came here to attend Cal Poly, but couldn't afford to finish. I liked it here so I stayed."

"Have you worked here a long time?"

"Four years last September. Why?"

Oh, geeze, there was no offhand way to ask, so I just said it. "Do you know a man named Jacob Chandler?"

Her left eyebrow jerked slightly, but her ivory skin didn't color. "I'll get Eve or Martin."

She maneuvered deftly as a cat through the chattering ocean of people. Between bites of my French toast, I watched her through the food-service opening, talking to a dark-haired man. Her hands made feathery gestures in the air between them. He glanced over at me, and, catching his eye, I turned with embarrassment back to my food. In a few minutes, a tall, slender blond woman with friendly brown eyes and neat, pixie-cut hair came to my table.

"Neely said you were asking about Jacob Chandler."

I nodded and set down my fork. "Can you sit down for a minute?"

"Certainly," she said. "Please, continue eating your breakfast. Martin takes great pride in having his food eaten when it's at its best." She glanced over at the dark-haired man in the kitchen and gave him a small wave. "By the way, I'm Eve Palais, and that man under the chef's hat is my husband, Martin. We own this place."

"Nice to meet you," I said, reaching out a hand. "Benni Harper."

She shook it and said, "Same here. Now, Neely said you were asking about Jake."

"Yes, Jacob Chandler. The man who owns the house on 993 Pelican Street. Were you friends?" I stumbled slightly on the word "owns," not knowing exactly how I was going to tell her he'd died. I picked up a slice of potato and stuck it in my mouth. Martin was a marvelous cook, no doubt about it. He put just the right amount of onions and garlic in the potatoes.

"I guess we were as close to friends as Jake allowed. He ate here three, maybe four times a week. He and Martin sometimes went fishing. And they both belonged to the Wood-carvers' Guild, though Jake stopped attending the meetings these last few months. He was having some heart problems, he told us." Her face drew tight, her peach-tinted mouth turned slightly downward. "I hate to be the one to tell you this, but Jake died on Friday. Was there any special reason you were looking for him?"

At that moment I would have given anything to flee this uncomfortable situation and not come back. "I . . . I know. I'm his heir." I looked down at my half-eaten French toast, twirling my fork in the cream cheese filling.

"Oh, you're the one," Eve said in a low voice.

The way she said it told me I'd already become a subject of speculation among some people in town.

I looked back up, directly into her eyes. "Yes, I suppose I am. I've set up a graveside service for him tomorrow in Paso Robles, but I have no idea how to contact any of his friends. He didn't have an address book, and I found your name by punching the redial on his telephone."

She nodded and said, "Clever." She must not watch

too much television otherwise she wouldn't have been quite so impressed. "Actually, I don't know all of his friends, though he spoke to a lot of people when he ate here. But I do know who can help you."

"Who?"

"Tess Briggstone."

The woman Rich saw coming in and out of Mr. Chandler's house frequently. The lady who found him in his recliner. And, I guessed, the woman on the answering machine.

Eve glanced around the room which, now that it was nearing ten o'clock, had started emptying out. "Sometimes she eats breakfast here with one of her sons, but I haven't seen her this morning." She looked back at me. "She and Jake were pretty tight. As a matter of fact, she lives across the street from him, next to the Pelican Inn."

I nodded, not wanting to give away anything I knew.

"She owns a gift shop down on the south end of the Embarcadero. Both her sons work the fishing boats sometimes. A couple of times a week they work in the store. And she subs for me once in a while in the summer. She also makes these little quilts to sell." She pointed to one of the small, hand-quilted miniature quilts I'd noticed when I walked in. It was a tiny Pinwheel quilt with rust, gold, and black fabric. The stitching was expert and the piecing perfect on first inspection. That explained Mr. Chandler's quilts.

"Beautiful," I murmured. "She sounds like a busy lady."

Eve looked over at the register, checking for anyone wanting to pay their bill. "Like most of the working people here on the Central Coast, one job isn't enough to support you unless you're working for the college or

71

one of the oil companies. Most people have to juggle a couple of plates to keep the meals coming in." She laughed, touching her chest with slender fingers sporting a wedding ring set with a large, tear-shaped diamond. "Listen to me, even my metaphors include food. Martin warned me that would happen. This restaurant is our dream. My husband's from Kentucky, and I'm from New York. We met at a singles resort seven years ago, fell in love, quit our stockbroker jobs, and invested every penny we own in this place. We've never regretted it." She gave me a curious look. "Pardon my boldness, but are you a relative of Jake's? As far as we knew, he didn't have any family."

I shifted uncomfortably in my chair, trying to think of the best way to tell this bizarre story. "Actually, I have no idea who he is."

"Are you saying he left everything he owned to a perfect stranger? Why in the world would he do that?"

"That's what I'm trying to figure out, but right now it's my responsibility to get his funeral planned. It'll be one o'clock tomorrow at the Paso Robles Cemetery. Apparently he'd already bought a plot there."

"I'll post the information on the bulletin board up front right now," she said, standing up. "Are you going to be in town long?"

"A couple of weeks," I said. I didn't tell her about the conditions of the will. Let everyone just think I was staying there to take care of the odds and ends of clearing up the estate.

"If there's anything you need, give us a call here. Jake was a nice man. We'll miss him." She started to walk away, then turned back, her face concerned. "His dog . . ."

"It's okay. Scout and I took to one another right off. I'm going to keep him."

Her face turned soft. "He loved that dog. Scout waited for him outside this restaurant every time he ate here."

I smiled at her. "He's out there now."

She nodded approvingly. "You know, if anyone knows anything about Jake, it would be Tess. It might be good for you to talk to her."

"I was thinking that myself." I stood up and put a ten down on the table, figuring that more than covered my meal and the tip. "Tell your husband it was great."

"We serve breakfast, lunch, and dinner. We open at six A.M. and close at nine P.M. Believe me, you haven't eaten anything until you've tried one of Martin's Kentucky Brown sandwiches."

"Sounds intriguing. What is it?"

"Now, you're just going to have to come back and find out, aren't you?" she replied, still smiling. "Martin and I probably won't be able to make the service since I'm sure Neely will want to go. She and Tess are very close."

Outside, Scout stood up when I walked out the door. I gave him an absentminded pat and started walking south on the Embarcadero. A few blocks into my walk I realized I hadn't asked Eve the name of Tess Briggstone's gift shop. I didn't turn back. If I couldn't find it, I'd ask at one of the other local businesses. I passed the giant chessboard, the oversized anchor memorial honoring the Fishermen Lost at Sea, Joe and Leslie's Seaside Books, a place I knew I'd eventually end up visiting. If it was anything like Elvia's store, the people who worked there would know a lot about what went on in this town. My problem was solved when I passed the bookstore and next to a store called the Bay City Shirt Shack was a small building with grass-green awnings and the name Briggstone's Fine Gifts across the top. I stopped in front of the shirt store for a moment and studied the window display of tropical-colored Flojos, surfboards, novelty T-shirts, and bumper stickers. One said—"Morro Bay Native—Tourist, Go Home."

Sounded good to me right then.

I read all the bumper stickers until I couldn't delay entering the gift store one more minute. At the open door I turned to Scout and said, "Stay."

"No, that's all right, honey," a raspy, older female voice called out. "Scout's an old friend of mine. He's allowed in here."

I stepped across the threshold. The woman speaking to me stood behind a glass case of silver jewelry. She walked around the case and held out her hand. Her long acrylic nails were painted a bright tangerine; small sparkly rings decorated almost every finger. "You're my new neighbor," the woman said. "I'm Tess Briggstone. Welcome to Morro Bay."

She was about four inches taller than me with a narrow tanned face that had seen a lot of weather—both physically and emotionally. She wore stretchy blue jeans and a large shirt covered with orange and red orchids. Hair dyed the color of a Kansas sunset was piled on top of her head in a neat bun bisected by a thin black pencil.

"Thank you," I said. Her handshake was firm and no-nonsense. "I'm Benni Harper."

Scout walked over and nudged her leg, and she scratched underneath his chin. "Hey, old boy, how're you holding up? Got a treat for you." She walked behind the counter and tossed a rawhide chew stick at Scout, who trotted over to the corner of the store and settled down to work on it.

The woman looked back at me, her blue-shadowed eyes blank. "So . . ."

Before she could continue, the door opened, and two young men in their twenties walked in. They were dressed in old flannel shirts, grime-encrusted jeans, and stained orange gimme caps advertising Union Oil. Both were strawberry blonds with reddish-brown skin that was already looking as coarse as beef jerky from the daily exposure to sun and wind. They were stocky with broad chests and the puffy features of heavy drinkers. One of them, the handsomer of the two, wore rubber boots. He was slightly broader in the chest and had a spoiled, mean expression around the mouth. The other man's expression seemed more genial.

"Duane," Tess complained, "I told you I didn't want you wearing those smelly old boots in here."

"Sorry, Ma." He walked behind the counter and picked up her purse. "We need twenty bucks for breakfast."

She gestured at the two men. "These are my boys, Cole and Duane." Duane, pocketing the money he took from his mother's purse, grunted without looking at me. Cole raised his thick blond eyebrows and gave me a slow once-over.

Tess folded her skinny arms over the colorful orchids spread across her chest. "So, you're the young lady Jake left his things to. How do you know him? Far as I knew, he never had any family. Leastwise, none he spoke of."

I felt my face turn warm, feelings of guilt irrationally sweeping over me. Then I straightened my spine. I hadn't done anything wrong so I pushed those feelings aside. "To be truthful, Ms. Briggstone, I never knew Mr. Chandler and I have no idea why he left me his estate."

A disgusted snort came from Duane. "Told you he

was a jackass, Ma. He was just leading you on. What're we going to do now? Huh?"

Tess turned around and said calmly, "Duane, you shut your mouth and go on and get your breakfast."

He swore under his breath and pushed the front door open so hard the glass rattled. Cole came over and laid a hand on his mother's shoulder. "Ma, he's just letting off steam."

"He's got to learn some control."

"Whatever," he answered with a shrug. "I'd better catch up with him."

After he left, Tess turned back to me, her face rigid with embarrassment. "I'm sorry, Miss Harper."

"It's okay." When she didn't answer, I figured the ball was now in my court. I cleared my throat. "The reason I'm here is because Eve Palais said that you and Mr. Chandler were good friends and that you'd know who would probably want to come to his service tomorrow."

She nodded. "Yes, I would. Where and when?"

"Paso Robles Cemetery at one o'clock. It'll be a graveside service. Is there . . . would you or anyone like to. . ." I paused, willing myself to talk calmly. "What I'd like to know is if you'd like to say anything, or perhaps his other friends . . ."

"That's all right," she said, her face unemotional. "I'm sure whatever you plan will be fine. We'll be there."

"Okay . . . thanks." I turned to leave, then stopped and faced her again, deciding it was probably better just to state my intentions. "I'll be staying in his house for the next two weeks, and one of the things I'll be doing is trying to figure out why he made me his heir. If you have any idea, if he ever said anything that might shed some light on it, could you tell me?"

Her weathered face remained neutral. "I'll think about it, but offhand I have to tell you he never mentioned you once in all the years I knew him."

I left the store quickly and stood on the street, my heart beating fast as a bird's. Obviously Jacob Chandler and Tess Briggstone had meant something to each other, so why didn't he leave his estate to her? Why had he dragged me into his life like this? This guy was really starting to piss me off. A few blocks from Tess's store, I sat down on a bench and watched white egrets float across the bay, their impossibly long legs stretched out like tree limbs, as I tried to figure out what I should do. After an hour or so, the sun started peeking out from behind the gray clouds and Gabe's heavy leather jacket started getting warm, so I decided to drop it by the house before tackling the other things on my list.

On the way back to the house, I passed by a one-hour photo shop so I dropped off the roll of film. Their technician was out at lunch, but I was told the film would be ready by two.

"No problem," I said, glancing at my watch. After dropping off Gabe's jacket, maybe I'd head back down to the Embarcadero and talk to some of the other shop owners about Mr. Chandler.

I walked down Grove Street toward Pelican. Grove was actually an alleylike street consisting only of garages. The fronts of the accompanying houses on the west side faced the ocean, those on the east side Gull Street. Rich was in front of his garage in cutoff jeans and a green and blue Hawaiian shirt, washing his white, crewcab pickup. True to Gabe's assertion, it was equipped with a contractor's toolbox. A faded bumper sticker read, "I Got Hot at the Phoenix Fire Department Chili Cook-off."

"*Buenos dias*, kid," he said.

"Hi," I replied, slowing down.

He turned off the hose and wiped his hands on his tattered shorts. "You can tell me to take a flying leap if I'm out of line here, but can I ask you why your husband staked out your house last night?"

I didn't answer, certain my face revealed what I thought of his question.

"I know, I know." He held up his damp hands in apology. "I have to confess to you that firemen are the nosiest people in the world. I'll tell you a trade secret. Half of us are hooked on soap operas. It just seemed mysterious to me, you inheriting this stranger's house and your husband not staying with you. Especially curious since he's a cop, and cops aren't known for being the most trusting people on earth."

"How did you know he was a cop?" I asked, surprised.

He laughed. "I bet he flipped when he heard your neighbor was a fireman, didn't he? Made the comment about it being the best part-time job in the world. Said we're all pretty good contractors to boot."

I couldn't help laughing with him. "Are you psychic, too?"

He picked up the garden hose and started rolling it. "No, but I've been a fireman for thirty-nine years and I've known lots of cops. Most of 'em I've liked, but I've never met one that wasn't always looking over his shoulder or was sure everyone he met was up to something. You know that old cop saying, don't you?"

"Which one?"

"There are cops and there are assholes. If you're not a cop, you're an asshole."

I shook my head in amazement. He did know cops.

"I'll bet you a fish dinner he's already in the process of having me checked out through the Phoenix PD. Don't worry, my buddies there will vouch for the fact that I'm an upright if slightly immature individual. Hope he doesn't call my daughters. They might not be so generous in their recommendations. So, what's on your agenda today?"

"Right now, getting rid of this jacket and then who knows?"

He tossed the bucket of rags into the garage and said, "Hey, you up for some leftovers? I made tomatillo and green chile enchiladas last night, and since I'm used to cooking for a bunch of hungry firefighters, I made way too much. It tastes better the second day, I swear. Especially with lots of sour cream and guacamole."

I hesitated, Gabe's suspicions ringing through my head.

"You can have it to go if you prefer," he said, amused by my reluctance. "But honestly, you don't want to miss this. I won the best main dish award ten years in a row at my station. I was taught by an expert—my late wife, Maria."

My instincts told me this guy was all right, so I said, "I'll be over as soon as I get rid of this jacket."

He wasn't lying about his cooking. The enchiladas were the best I'd ever eaten and I wasn't even hungry when I sat down. "You could open your own restaurant," I said.

"I've been told that before. The problem is, I only like to cook what appeals to me at the moment so I couldn't have a set menu. People would have to take their chances."

"Believe me, they wouldn't regret it. So, tell me about your daughters."

"Twenty-seven, twenty-nine, and thirty-two. A teacher, an attorney, and a social worker. Smart as whips and so beautiful I threatened every young buck in the Phoenix Fire Department with a slow, torturous death if they even looked cross-eyed at them."

"So you've cautioned your daughters not to date firemen."

"You bet. I'm nothing else if not a good and caring father."

Maybe it was the easiness with which he talked about his daughters or the softness that came over his face when he said his wife's name, or maybe it was just how the intimate act of eating often puts people in a more familiar frame of mind, but before I realized it, I'd told him everything—the strange conditions of the will, the scrapbook I'd found, the film, and the wood carving message.

"This gets stranger every time I talk to you," he said, resting his elbows on the kitchen table, his dark eyes interested. "It would make a great plot on *One Life to Live* though. What does your husband think?"

"He doesn't like it, naturally," I said much too quickly, irritated at myself for telling him about the scrap-book before Gabe. And for spilling my guts so easily to a virtual stranger, albeit a charming one, just like Gabe said I would.

"So what are you going to do?"

"Try to figure out why he left his estate to me. It doesn't make sense, because I've found out he had relationships with other people. Close ones. As a matter of fact, I met the woman you told me about."

"The redhead I saw going in and out of his house."

"Tess Briggstone is her name. She owns a gift shop down on the Embarcadero. She has two sons."

80

His dark face was thoughtful. "I've seen them around. To be honest, they look like a couple of losers to me."

"Why do you say that?"

"Just the fact that two men that age shouldn't still be living with their mother. They sit around on weekends drinking beer and playing music loud enough to broil steaks. They screech up and down the alley at three in the morning in trucks that need mufflers more than I need new knees."

I nodded, taking in the information, though I wasn't sure if it would be of any use to me.

"Maybe I'm just an old fuddy-duddy, as I'm often accused of by my daughters, but a couple of men pushing thirty ought to be living on their own, raising their own families." He stood up and started clearing the table. "Sometimes I sound so much like my own father, it scares me. *Pollo ruidoso*, my daughters call me. Noisy chicken."

I carried my plate over to the sink and started running the hot water.

"Leave those," Rich said. "I'll do them later."

"Okay. Thanks for lunch. Your awards were absolutely deserved. Well, I'd better go pick up my film. See you later."

"You bet."

My film was ready, and I eagerly sat on the brick planter out front, flipping through the twelve photos. They were typical tourist shots of Morro Rock, the bay, and the marina down by the PG & E plant. Only one was different.

It was the James Dean monument at the intersection of Highways 41 and 46 near the town of Cholame—a name from the Salinan or Yokut Indians meaning either "the enchanted valley" or "beautiful one" depending on which county historian you believed. I'd been to the spot many times with my friends as a teenager, attracted by what we thought was the romantic way James Dean had died. Now, the thought of his young body mangled in a fiery automobile accident only made me sick at heart for the ridiculous and never changing stupidity of youth.

I gazed closer at the photo. There was a card propped next to the Tree of Heaven that canopied the monument. Printed on it was the number 226. What in the heck was that supposed to mean?

"Very funny, Mr. Chandler," I said, stuffing the photos back in the envelope. What next? Go out to the monument? What if it was a wild goose chase? The thought of driving out there for nothing irritated me.

"Let's go see Emory," I said to Scout. "No one has a more devious mind than him, so maybe he can make heads or tails out of this. Besides, we'd better drop by and see the chief and let him know we made it through one more night."

"Sweetcakes, this is gettin' more peculiar by the minute," Emory said, settling comfortably in his leather office chair. You'd think by the look of his office he'd been there five years instead of five months. Anyone else who had breezed into town and snatched a prime reporting job the way he had would be hated by everyone from the janitor to the city desk editor. But I'd learned never to underestimate the power of a genteel, Tupelo-honey-tongued, upper-class Southern gentleman. The women mooned about his office like lovesick poodles, and even the men found Emory amusing with his self-effacing humor and his never empty mini-refrigerator filled with imported beers, soda, and handmade, chocolate-covered bourbon candies Fed-Exed from Louisville.

"You're telling me," I agreed, helping myself to his crystal candy dish of Godiva chocolates. "What's this?" I held up a dark chocolate candy heart. He knew all of Godiva's selections by sight. Behind him hung an expensively framed calligraphy of his favorite saying—"American by birth, Southern by the Grace of God."

"Hazelnut praline center in a dark chocolate shell. Have you told the chief about this scrapbook yet?"

"No, and I wasn't going to because I knew he'd just worry, but now I feel obligated."

"Why's that?"

Settling down in one of his visitor chairs, I told him about spilling my guts to Rich and feeling somewhat guilty about it.

"As well you should," Emory said. "You don't know this man from Adam's house cat. His noble profession notwithstanding, you'd best keep any further confessions and discoveries to those you know and love."

"You mean you." I popped the candy into my mouth, letting the rich sweetness dissolve in my mouth. Hazelnut praline, just like he said.

"When are you going to let me start writing the article?" he asked.

"When my two weeks are up."

"What?" He grabbed the candy dish as I was reaching for another.

"Hey!"

"You shall not enjoy a smidgen more of my bounty until I get something in return."

I sat back in my chair and propped my boots on his desk. "Emory, I'm here to invite you to the funeral service tomorrow, and I'm going to tell you what's happening every step of the way. I just don't want you writing the article until it's all done. No one's going to scoop you because no one else knows about it. Besides, do you really think I'd talk to another reporter?"

"There are other people involved," he said, his voice petulant. "They could tell someone."

"Quit pouting, Emory. It's so wussy. If we wait until it's over and I find out why Mr. Chandler left all his worldly goods to me, you'll be able to write it with more authority. It's always easier to write a story when you know the ending, don't you think?" I leaned over and took a piece of paper from his desk and started making a paper airplane.

"Sometimes," he conceded. He leaned back in his chair and pointed an aristocratic finger at me. "Keep me informed every step of the way. Promise me."

I laughed and pointed my airplane at him. "You are beginning to sound a mite like a certain police chief I know, dear cousin." I stood up and sailed the airplane across the desk, hitting him in the chest. "Gotta go, Joe, it's three o'clock. I want to stop by and French-kiss my husband so he won't forget me, then get back to Morro Bay before the quilt shop closes." I picked up a nut-covered Godiva chocolate and held it up.

"Pecan caramel truffle. Going to do some quilting during your lonely nights?"

I bit into the candy and inspected the contents. Right again. Dang, he was good. "No, I know the lady who owns the store, and she's lived in Morro Bay quite a while. I'm going to see if she knows anything about Jacob Chandler. And by the way, the reason I actually stopped by was to ask you to do some checking for me."

"I thought Gabe had an investigator working on the case."

"He gave me the lowdown on Mr. Chandler, what there is of it, and I'm going to try to call Jacob Chandler's sister today, but I want to see if your sources can dig up anything else. And I want you to check on the other people on this list—see what you can come up with." I handed him a piece of paper listing Tess, Cole, and Duane Briggstone of Morro Bay and Richard Trujillo of Phoenix. "There may be more after the funeral because I'm going to try to get names. Do you think having a guest book at the graveside services is too obvious?"

"A bit, sweetcakes. But I'll come, nose around a bit, and get names."

I went around the desk and gave him a quick hug. "I was hoping you'd say that. Besides, I need you there for moral support. I don't know who else besides this Tess woman feels like they have a claim to his estate, and I need someone to help me absorb all the bad vibes."

"I'll be happy to be your bodyguard, provided I'm allowed to ask questions."

"Emory, that's exactly what I'm counting on."

Gabe's corvette, the same pale blue as the afternoon sky, was in its parking space at the police station, so I pulled into the visitor's parking lot. In the reception area, Rod, the desk clerk and an avid animal lover, buzzed me in and, as I expected, commenced to making a big fuss over Scout.

"The chief said you'd inherited a dog. He's adorable!" Rod exclaimed, crouching down to stroke Scout's head.

"Yeah, he's a charmer, all right. Gabe's in, right?"

"Yes, ma'am," Rod said.

"C'mon, Scout," I said and walked through the maze

of desks and hallways, greeting people and stopping every so often so someone could pet Scout. Walking down the hallway toward Gabe's office, I said, "You know, Scooby-doo, I'm getting jealous here. Try and reel in that charm a little."

He looked up at me with patient eyes, as if to say, this is my burden, live with it. I left him with the dispatchers, telling them I'd be back in a few minutes.

Gabe's secretary, Maggie, wasn't at her desk, but his door was open, so I breezed right in. He was sitting at his desk looking very authoritarian in his gray Brooks Brothers suit and khaki-and-gray-print tie.

"Hey," I said. "I waited all night for my dancing pool boy, and he never showed up. What gives?"

He looked up and smiled. "Hmmm, I'm sure I gave him the right address. That was 663 Seagull, right?"

"It's 993 Pelican, and you know it. Oh, well, guess I'm stuck with the old fart again." I went around the desk and gave him a quick kiss. "I kinda like them already trained anyway. How's your day going?"

"Same old stuff. How was your second night? I tried to call this morning, but you weren't there."

Leaning against the edge of his desk, I gave him a quick rundown on what Eve had told me and showed him the photograph taken at the James Dean memorial. He sat back in his chair and studied the photo.

"I suppose you feel compelled to go out there," he said.

"It's the next logical step, wouldn't you agree?"

An unintelligible but definitely deprecating sound rumbled from his throat.

Then I told him about meeting Tess and her sons, about setting up the funeral for tomorrow.

"I'm glad Emory's going to be there," he said. "Otherwise, I'd come with you."

"Bad idea. A lot of people know who you are, and you know how people clam right up when the police are around. That's exactly what I *don't* want them to do. The secret of who he is and why he singled me out might be located in the memories of his friends."

He kicked the toe of my boot with one of his black dress shoes. "You are a real pain in the posterior, Ms. Harper. Anybody ever tell you that?"

"Only a certain unnamed law enforcement official who has no confidence in my ability to take care of myself, but whom I'll keep anyway 'cause he's pretty good in the sack for an old guy."

"I trust you. It's just the rest of the world I don't trust."

Finally I reluctantly and with not a little guilt told him about the scrapbook. The longer I explained, the more his jaw tightened.

"I know, I know," I said, heading off his words. "It is creepy beyond imagination. But don't forget, Gabe, he's dead. He can't hurt me now."

"By the way," he said, ignoring my comment, "I checked out your fireman this morning."

I made a face at him but was glad he hadn't made too big an issue over the scrapbook. "He's not *my* fireman. What did you find out?"

"He's what he says he is and, according to my sources, a nice guy. He retired an assistant chief, was very respected by his colleagues, and was even quite active in community affairs before his wife died."

"I told you he was okay. My instincts about people are impeccable," I said in a teasing voice.

He ignored my joking. "At any rate, he is still a stranger. All I'm asking is that you don't go off half-cocked the way you normally do."

I stood up, irritated now. "I think I'll leave before I say something I'll regret. And for the record, that last remark was a ten on the jerk scale."

His phone picked that inopportune time to ring. "We'll talk about it later," he said, reaching for it.

"No, we won't, because there isn't anything to talk about."

The phone rang again. "I'm not happy about this situation."

"You've made that perfectly clear."

The phone shrilled a third time. He inhaled a deep breath, held up a hand at me to wait, and answered it. "Gabe Ortiz," he said into the phone. I started to walk out.

"Let me call you right back," he quickly told his caller. "Benni, I'm just trying to—"

I interrupted what was certain to be another lecture. "What choice do I have? To fulfill the conditions of the will, I have to stay there. There's nothing I can do about that. I don't understand why we're going through all this again. You've checked out the house. You've checked out Mr. Trujillo. Everything's fine, right?"

"On the surface."

"Apart from tearing the house down and injecting my poor, innocent neighbor with truth serum, I'd say you've done all you can do to protect me, so any responsibility you have is covered, okay? Just let it go."

His face was troubled. "I wish it were that easy."

"Gabe, for once just let me do something without fighting you the whole distance."

"I'll try. That's the best I can offer you."

"Good enough. Are you free for dinner tonight?"

"Unfortunately, no. I have a dinner date with Sam and some tickets to go see a jazz guitarist in Ojai. We planned it weeks ago, but I can cancel . . ."

"Not on your life. You and Sam need to spend as much time together as you can. Call me when you get in."

"Might be after one A.M."

"Forget that then. Call me tomorrow. Or I'll call you."

He came around the desk and pulled me into a hug. "I'll miss you. Now get out of here before I'm tempted to lock you up."

"I'm gone," I said, relieved that he seemed to be taking the situation with a bit more resignation and almost a little humor.

I finally located Scout in the detectives' department, where he was being thoroughly spoiled, and headed outside. I sat in my truck planning my next move. Since I obviously had tonight free, I could nose around Morro Bay more, but first I had to make an obligatory stop at the folk art museum.

It was quiet at the museum today. Even our neighbors, the Coastal Valley Farm Supply and San Celina Feed and Grain Co-op, seemed unusually subdued. Usually the sound of noisy ranch trucks and customers picking up supplies filtered over to us here at the museum. Only a few cars were in our newly graveled parking lot, and the hacienda looked almost like what it must have a hundred and fifty years ago when the Sinclair ancestors lived there. I could almost picture a corseted lady standing on the second floor balcony under its red-tiled roof staring out to the green velvet hills, waiting for her husband to return from town or checking on the cattle.

D-Daddy Boudreaux, my very capable and loyal assistant, was bent over, whitewashing a section of the front wall where some vandals had knocked a chunk out of the adobe. He whistled a cheerful Cajun tune that had probably been passed down in his family for 200 years. At seventy-two years old, he'd been the most hardworking and reliable assistant I'd had so far.

"Looks great, D-Daddy," I said, inspecting his work. "But everything always has since you've been here."

He straightened up and beamed at me. His thick white hair caught the afternoon sunlight and glistened. He was still a handsome man, a fact that had not gone unnoticed by the senior ladies in our museum docent program. He looked at Scout standing calmly at my side. "Who's the hound dog?"

"This is Scout. Scout, friend." He sat down and lifted a paw, his red tongue hanging sideways from his mouth.

D-Daddy gave a delighted laugh and shook it. "What a fine dog. Where'd he come from?"

"My inheritance. I suppose you heard about it."

He nodded. "Gossip flows round here like Mississippi floodwater."

"I thought so. I'll leave my current address and phone number in your mailbox. I'll only be there two weeks, and I'll be checking my messages at home, too. Since we're basically all set for the exhibit, I'll be in and out."

He leaned against one of the long porch's rough wood posts. "This man, he sound crazy to me."

I laughed. "You're not alone in those thoughts, but he's dead so he can't really hurt me, can he?"

D-Daddy shook his head doubtfully. "Even the dead have their ways of hurtin' folks."

"On that cheerful note, I'll let you get back to your work. I'm going to make one last run-through on the exhibit."

"Let me know if anything needs fixing, you."

"Sure will."

I walked through the double Spanish doors into the

museum. A volunteer was rearranging handmade handkerchief dolls on one of the shelves of the gift shop. I waved at her and continued into the main hall.

The name we'd voted on for the exhibit was "From a Mother's Heart." We'd opened the entries to the public with the only criteria being that the item had to be handmade by or for the entrant's mother or mother-in-heart. The response from the one article we'd run in the local free paper had been overwhelming, and eventually we were forced to turn people away. Recording and cataloging the entries had been a nightmare, and I'd spent a lot of days working until midnight getting the exhibit ready in time for Mother's Day weekend. It had been hard, tiring work, but definitely worth it. This was by far the most heart-wrenching and provocative exhibit we'd presented. The stories that accompanied many of the pieces caused more than one set of eyes to tear up. And that was just among the co-op members and volunteers. No matter what type of relationship you had with your mother, it was a powerful one, maybe the most powerful of your life.

As I wandered through the exhibit, I marveled at the talents of these women, these mothers, and the love that emanated from their handwork. There were many baby quilts, of course. I'd hung those in a group in one corner of the hall. And a great many baby sweaters and booties, also a special grouping. But the scope of what women create while raising their families amazed me. There were handmade rivercane, pine-needle and corn-shuck baskets; birdhouses made from "found" items; rag rugs, which I'd discovered in my research were often referred to as salvage craft because of how scraps of fabric were ingeniously transformed into something useful; a couple of handmade brooms made of sedge grass and buckeye saplings. One braided handle broom made of palmetto fronds had been passed down through four generations of Houma Indian daughters and mothers. Upstairs I'd organized the displays of dolls and textile crafts other than quilts—samplers, tatting, embroidery, needlepoint, and lace-making.

This was where my contribution to the exhibit hung—an embroidered sampler made by my mother when she was eighteen and pregnant with me. To anyone else it looked just like another printed cross-stitch sampler, the kind that was popular back in the fifties and sixties. In the center was the requisite baby in a cradle. In each corner was a different picture—a stork, a baby rattle, a bottle, and a pair of tiny shoes. My date and time of birth were stitched across the bottom. A fancy multicolored alphabet made up the border. Nothing special in terms of artistry, but very special to me because it was the only thing I owned made by my mother.

My first memory of the piece was when I was twelve years old and my father, without a word, hung it in my bedroom. I never asked him where it had been for six years, why he hadn't shown it to me before. Daddy never talked much about my mother. What little I knew of her came from Dove, her mother-in-law. Dove said my mother had been an only child, like me, and pretty much kept to herself. Her parents had died in an automobile accident when she was sixteen, and she was taken in by her distant cousin, Ervalean, Emory's mother, in Little Rock. Ervalean was only three years older, but mature enough to encourage my mother to finish high school. Mama was seventeen when she graduated and went to work as a waitress. She met my dad when he came to the city to pick up tractor parts and ate breakfast in the cafe where she worked. They married three months later, when she was still a month shy of her eighteenth birthday.

None of this was written on her biography under the sampler. Instead, I told about how she much liked to sing and that she loved green beans, pink roses, Judy Garland movies, pecan pie, and the singer, Kitty Wells.

At least, that's what Dove told me.

I straightened the sampler and stared for a moment at the black-and-white crinkle-edged picture I'd hung next to it. It must have been taken someplace in Arkansas, since I appeared to be about two years old. She perched me on her hip, standing in front of an old country store with a Standard Oil gasoline pump. Her hair was very light and teased into a bouffant that fit the year written on the back—1960. She was smiling, squinting into the bright sunlight. I was staring at whoever was taking the picture, my round baby face on the edge of tears.

She was so young. I'd long passed the age at which she died—twenty-five—and it often struck me how strange it was to think of myself as experiencing ages, physical changes, and even feelings that my mother never did. I still remembered myself at twenty-five, strong and healthy and, in my youthful mind, invincible.

But not really. Because somewhere deep inside I knew, I'd known since I was six, that life hung on a fragile thread. *How scared she must have been.* How full of despair knowing that her child would grow up unprotected by her. A few times I'd asked both Dove and Daddy if there was something, anything she told them to tell me. Daddy's blue eyes would turn cloud-gray, and he'd turn back to whatever he was working on, saying, "She loved you, Benni. You were her life."

Dove told me all she knew, which wasn't much.

93

"Alice was not one for chitchat," she'd say. "Kept to herself. She always seemed kind of . . . I don't know . . . sad. Even when she was smiling. But she lost her own folks so early. She had lots to be sad about, I reckon."

With a finger I touched her face in the picture. "Mama," I whispered, testing the feel of the word on my lips. After all these years, it felt strange, like a foreign word for which there was no translation into a language I knew.

"Benni?" D-Daddy's voice from the entrance hall jerked me out of my thoughts.

"Coming," I called back.

He handed me a stack of envelopes. "Mail's here."

I flipped through it quickly, then said, "There's nothing of any importance. Can you just put it on my desk? I'm going over to the Historical Museum and see what's cooking with their latest project."

"That new mayor man," D-Daddy said, shaking his head. "He'll be the ruin of this town, yes, sir."

"You're not the only one who thinks so," I agreed.

The Historical Museum was usually closed on Monday, but I followed my instincts and was rewarded for doing so. Through the windows of the front door I could see Dove and three of her fellow historical society members sitting around a small foldout table. I tapped on the glass and was let in by June Rae Gates, my former seventh grade math teacher.

"Benni, it's so good to see you," she said. "We were just talking about you not five minutes ago."

"All positive, I hope," I said.

"Maybe," she answered gaily. "Maybe not."

"So, what's going on, ladies?" I asked, sitting down on a folding chair.

"We're planning our assault on Mr. Boxstore Billy,"

94

said June Rae. "We're bringing out the big guns and going to—"

"Be careful what you say around her, June Rae," Dove said. "Don't forget, she's with the establishment now. She's married to the fuzz." Dove smiled at me innocently. "How's things in Morro Bay?"

I laughed out loud. "The fuzz? The establishment? Too much *Mod Squad* being watched, girls. What's going on here? Has the Gray Panthers been recruiting you all?"

Dove's eyes lit up. "We called the AARP, but I clean forgot all about them! Make a note, June Rae. So, how's the search going?"

"I'll tell you, but you all have to promise to keep it quiet. Emory wants to do a story on it, and he's afraid someone's going to scoop him."

"Loose lips sink ships," June Rae said. "You can trust us."

I told them about Gabe having the house searched by bomb and drug dogs, my new neighbor, the scrapbook, the wood carving instruction clue, the James Dean memorial picture, and the funeral services the next day.

"Look for the murderer in the funeral guests," Goldie Kleinfelder said. She once owned a stationery store and still did calligraphy on the side.

I laughed. "Goldie, no one's been murdered. Mr. Chandler died of a heart attack. I'm only looking for clues as to why he chose me as his heir."

"Are you sure it was a heart attack?" Edna McClun asked. She'd been an extra on two *Diagnosis Murder* episodes when she visited her sister in Los Angeles recently and now considered herself an expert on murder.

"I'm positive, ladies," I said. "He had a heart

condition. He had diabetes. The coroner would have done an autopsy if there had been any doubt. It was just his time to go."

"Or maybe someone decided it was his time to go," Edna insisted, not willing to give up so quickly.

"You all watch too much television," Dove carped, slamming the flat of her hand down on the table. "We've got more important things to think about. Any particular reason why you're here, honeybun?"

"Nope, just checking to see how things are going. Looks like you've got everything under control. Anybody bake this morning?" I looked hopefully at the empty paper plates in front of them. That was actually my underlying motive for dropping by. All these women were Mid-State Fair blue ribbon winners, and they never had a meeting without someone bringing goodies.

"In the back room," Dove said. "Then get out of here. I have a hard enough time keeping these old ladies on the subject without you coming by and stirring things up."

They were all protesting and laughing as I walked behind the counter at the front of the museum and into the back room where they kept their coats, purses, and various office and personal supplies. Sure enough, it was Edna's turn, and she'd made lemon bars and chocolate-cinnamon muffins. I grabbed two of each and stuck them in a plastic sandwich bag I found in a drawer.

"So," I said, walking back into the main room, "what do you have planned for Mayor Billy anyway?"

"Don't you worry about that," Dove said, pushing me between the shoulder blades out the door. "You'll find out soon enough."

She closed it with a determined click of the lock.

Only half joking, I prayed as I walked down the steps. Please, Lord, soften the judge's heart and let her sentence be suspended.

6

I SPENT THE REST OF THE DAY LOOKING THROUGH the house one more time, hoping I'd missed something. The mail came, bringing only a catalog for wood carving supplies. Back in the kitchen, I laid out all my evidence or clues, or whatever they were, on the round table.

The *Treasure Island* book with the inscription to G. from G.

The knife with the initials G.M.

The autograph book.

The flat white stone.

The picture of the James Dean monument with the mysterious number.

I stuck the picture in my purse. Tomorrow, after the funeral, I would drive out on Highway 46 to the monument.

I picked up the book and flipped through the pages again, hoping for something I'd missed before—an underlined word or sentence, or perhaps a piece of paper stuck between the pages.

Nothing.

I read through the autograph book again and decided to write down the names of the people in my notebook. Maybe somewhere in my search I'd run across them, and there were too many to remember offhand.

That left one last thing to do. Something I'd been putting off because I had no idea what to say. Gabe had neatly listed all the information his private investigator buddy had found on a piece of San Celina PD stationery. Just the sight of his neat, dark handwriting made me miss him.

I picked up the phone and dialed the phone number listed for Jacob Chandler's sister in Lubbock. It was five-thirty P.M. here, so that meant it was seven-thirty there. The phone rang six times, and I almost hung up when an elderly lady answered.

"Hello, hello? Can I help you?" her crackly voice asked.

"Mrs. Ludlam? Mrs. Rowena Ludlam?"

"Yes, who's calling? I don't want any time-shares, young woman."

"I'm not selling anything, Mrs. Ludlam. I . . ." My mouth turned dry. How do you tell a perfect stranger that her brother has died?

Just tell 'em, honeybun, Dove would say. We old folks are tougher than you youngsters give us credit for.

"Mrs. Ludlam, my name is Benni Harper, and you don't know me."

"Young woman, what are you selling?"

"Ma'am, I'm not selling anything. I've . . . I'm afraid I've got some sad news for you. About your brother, Jacob."

"Jake!" she exclaimed. "You've seen my brother Jake? Where is he? Is he all right? Where's he been? Oh, my stars, Mother's last words were about wanting to see her Jakie one more time. I'll never forgive him for that. Where's he at? Why's he wanting to contact us now?"

I let her words peter out before continuing. "Mrs. Ludlam, I'm sorry to tell you that your brother passed away of a heart attack."

"Jake's dead?" Her voice corkscrewed into a squeak. "We always thought he was dead, but we never really knew and always wondered, but I always thought of him as dead, but Mother always hoped and hoped, and now he is dead. Isn't that the oddest thing?"

I didn't know quite how to answer that. "Yes, ma'am," I finally said.

"What did you say your name was? Where are you calling from?"

"I'm Benni Harper and I'm calling from San Celina, California. Well, actually I'm calling from Morro Bay, which is twelve miles from San Celina, but I live in San Celina and—"

She interrupted my rambling. "How do you know my brother? Are you with Social Services? Was he homeless? How did you know to call me? Did he ask you to call me before he . . ." A second of silence, then, "Oh, Lord, we haven't heard from him for over thirty-five years. Young woman, are you sure it's my brother?"

"Well, his papers say he's Jacob Chandler and—"

"What papers?"

"His driver's license and his house and—"

"He had a house? You mean he wasn't homeless?"

"No, ma'am. Can I ask you something? When was the last time you saw your brother?"

A short silence, then, "My stars, I'm trying to think now. Must've been about 1956, no, 1957. That's it. It was 1957 because that was the year Mother won the blue ribbon for her knitted afghan at the state fair. Took her eight months and then she upped and gave it to Janeen Rylie down at the church for a prayer pal gift. She probably let her cat sleep on it. He went down selling to New Orleans and never came back."

"Selling?" That fit what Gabe's private investigator friend had found out.

"My brother was a traveling salesman. Sold cleaning products to restaurants. Found his car sitting outside a town called Lake Charles. Never did find him, though. We figured he just ran off. Left a fiancée and a whole apartment full of new furniture. We heard she married someone else. A man named Bowman. They moved to Des Moines."

"You never heard from your brother again?"

"No, we didn't, and I'm still mad about it. I don't know why he up and took off, but he didn't need to go and do that to Mother. They had their moments, but there's not a thing worse in the world than dying not knowing what happened to one of your children."

Thinking about how easy it was for Gabe's friend to find her, I asked, "Mrs. Ludlam, why didn't you hire someone to find him?"

"With what money, young woman?" she snapped. "We was poorer than church mice all our lives. And why, pray tell? Besides, he made it clear he didn't want us to find him."

"How? I thought you hadn't heard from him."

A disgusted *humph* came over the line. "Land sakes, I'm so used to telling that story to save Mother's feelings it's almost the truth to me now. But since he and Mother are dead now, I suppose there's no harm in telling you. He did contact me once. Sent a postcard about a month after they found his car. Said, 'Weenie, don't look for me. Going to Alaska. Jake.' Came from Phoenix, Arizona. Had some cactus on it."

"You sure it was from your brother? You recognized his handwriting?"

"And, pray tell, who else would call me Weenie?

100

He'd tortured me with that nickname from the time I can remember."

"You called his job?"

"He upped and quit, they said. They said they sent his last paycheck to general delivery in Phoenix and never heard from him again."

"You never told your mother about his postcard?"

"I thought it'd be kinder to let Mother think he'd gotten in some accident than for her to know he'd just run off. To be honest, she'd always spoiled him, so I'm not surprised." Her voice turned sly. "Why are you calling anyway? Is there some kind of inheritance or something?"

"I'm still looking into it," I hedged. "Can you answer another question?"

"Depends." Her voice was suspicious now.

"I just wondered if you could give me a quick description of your brother." I picked up his driver's license.

" 'Bout five feet eight or nine, brown hair, brown eyes. Just your average Joe."

It all matched though his hair was gray on his license.

"Young woman, is there some kind of inheritance?"

That made me feel guiltier than I already did. Not only did Mr. Chandler abandon his friends here in Morro Bay, but he'd done even worse to his blood family. "I'll get back to you about that as soon as I can. Things are very unsettled right now." I hoped she wouldn't ask me again if I was with Social Services. I wouldn't outright lie, but if she just didn't ask . . .

Her breathing grew ragged over the phone. "Is there going to be a service?"

"Yes, tomorrow."

Her voice softened, and for the first time sadness

crept into its bitter edge. "Could you take a picture of him? I'd like to see him one more time."

"I could photocopy his driver's license picture. It's the only picture I've found of him so far."

"That would be nice, but I mean how he looks now. Laid to rest."

I swallowed hard. "I'll see what I can do. I am sorry, Mrs. Ludlam."

"You know, I did love my brother at one time. I surely did." She hung up the phone with a quiet click.

I called the mortuary where they held Mr. Chandler's body and, after a bit of verbal stumbling around, asked if anyone could take a picture of the body for me. I found the thought of it grotesque, but if this small thing made Mrs. Ludlam feel better, I would do my best to accommodate her.

"Certainly," the man over the phone said. "It's requested more often than you realize. We have a Polaroid camera here. I'll send the photograph with our representative tomorrow."

"Thank you," I said, relieved I wouldn't have to take the picture myself.

At seven o'clock, my stomach told me that Rich's enchiladas had been consumed much too long ago. I fed Scout, then we walked down the steps to the Embarcadero, following a fiftyish man and his wife carrying a couple of camera cases and a tripod.

"Hope we're not holding you up," the man called out four steps below me as he carefully picked his way down. He wore a gray sweatshirt that said across the back—"Dwight Yoakum World Tour—Bakersfield to Bangkok—Country All the Way." The woman, a fluffy-haired, bleached blonde with thick eye makeup, turned her head and smiled at me.

102

"He'd throw himself on the ground to save that camera," she said. "If I fell, I'd just have to fend for myself."

"Your hair would break the fall," he called up cheerfully. She blew him a loud raspberry.

"No problem," I said. "I'm in no hurry."

"We're going to try to sell some pictures to travel magazines," she said when we all reached the surf shop parking lot. "Maybe recoup some of the money he's spent on photography equipment."

He grinned at me, his face pink with embarrassment. "Now, Susan, this young lady doesn't want to hear about my hobby."

She rolled her eyes at me. "Hobby? Try obsession."

"Beats chasing women, love," the man said.

I smiled at her. "He's got a point there."

"Know any good restaurants?" the woman asked. "We just got here."

"Cafe Palais." I pointed across the street. "I had a great breakfast there this morning. I'm going to try their dinner now."

"Cafe Palais. I like the name," the woman said. "We'll try that."

The cafe was crowded again, suggesting that we'd chosen wisely since on a Monday night off-season they were probably locals. Eve was so busy that she only stopped by my table for a moment and said a quick hello and reminded me to try Martin's famous sandwich.

The Kentucky Brown sandwich turned out to be as wonderful as Eve had promised. It was an open-faced sandwich consisting of crustless toast with a layer of turkey breast covered with a rich homemade Mornay sauce topped with sliced tomatoes, crispy bacon strips, grated cheese, and bread crumbs.

"This is wonderful!" I said to Eve when she refilled my coffee cup.

She smiled. "Martin's specialty. He worked during his college years in the kitchen at the Brown Hotel in Louisville where the hot brown was invented. I tell him it was only his sandwich that convinced me to give up Manhattan."

I laughed. "Doesn't do well to let them get too big a head."

"That's what I say."

She turned to walk away, and I blurted out, "Eve, can I ask you something?"

She looked at me curiously. "Sure, what?"

"It's about Mr. Chandler." I set my fork down and looked straight into her intelligent eyes. There was something about this woman that I sensed was honest and street-smart. If there was anything about this man that was off-kilter, surely she'd have sensed it in the years she'd served him meals.

"What about him?" she prompted.

"Did he strike you as being . . . weird in any way? I mean, like, did he ever get, you know, strange with you?" I bit my lip, embarrassed about what I was asking.

"You mean did he ever harass any of my waitresses or me?" She shook her head no. "He was a real nice man. Tipped good but not extravagantly. Was polite but not too forward. I'll give him this—he never left his table in a mess, and we appreciated that. He'd talk about the weather or his wood carving or sometimes someplace he'd seen when he was a traveling salesman. He'd seen a lot of the country. We had a long talk about Coney Island one time and about New York hot dogs. I don't think he was a sex pervert, if that's what you're asking,

104

but honestly, do we ever know anyone? I mean, this thing he's done, making you his heir, that took us all by surprise. We honestly thought . . ." She stopped, realizing she'd gone too far.

"That he'd leave it to Tess," I finished.

She ducked her head and didn't answer.

"It's okay. I've figured out that they had a special relationship. Believe me, this is as confusing to me as it is to all of you."

"It's just that she really needs . . ." She stopped again, her face pink. "I shouldn't be talking about this."

"She needs what?" I asked.

Eve tightened her lips and shook her head. "Tess's money problems are her business, but she's a nice person, and I feel bad for her. Duane's legal problems ate up what savings she had—"

"Legal problems?"

"Look, I've said enough already. I know Tess won't hold it against you, but it wouldn't be fair if you didn't know she did get help from Jake."

"And now that's cut off," I said softly.

"I think she should have kicked both those boys out a long time ago, but that's just me. Enjoy your sandwich."

The sandwich was delicious, but halfway through I stopped eating, feeling slightly sick to my stomach either from the richness of the sauce or the complex, troubling situation I'd been drawn into.

Outside the restaurant I untied Scout's leash from the bench and just started walking, hoping the excercise would help me sort out what I'd learned about Mr. Chandler. He'd apparently abandoned his family in the middle fifties, showed up here in Morro Bay in the early eighties. What had he been doing the rest of that time? And, more importantly, why had he ended up here obsessed with me?

A heavy mist filled the air with a chilly wetness, but that didn't deter me, and I walked past the giant chessboard, a place I needed to come back and hang around when it was occupied and eavesdrop a little, past the Coast Guard buildings, and followed the road leading to Morro Rock. It took me about forty-five minutes to reach the parking lot at the rock's base. Standing next to the huge black rock, peering into the gauzy fog surrounding it, I tried to quiet the noise in my head. Watching the screeching gulls and the elegant black cormorants fly low over the water, feeling the crash of the waves against the breakwater, tasting salt every time I licked my lips cleared my head only a little as it skittered from possibility to possibility about this mysterious man. In the falling dusk, the ocean looked almost metallic, like tarnished silver. I sat on the edge of a rock, running my hand over and over Scout's damp head, wondering if Gabe and Sam were having fun— and wished I was with them, sitting in a cozy club somewhere, being warmed by a good blues guitar.

Then I sneezed twice. "I'm going to get pneumonia if I don't get something warm to drink," I told Scout.

"Let's head back." Though the walk had done me good, I still was no closer to understanding this situation.

I stopped at Greta's Koffee Haus on the Embarcadero. A canvas awning provided Scout with shelter, though the damp weather didn't seem to be making him near as uncomfortable as me. Those Labrador genes, no doubt. The combined smells of marzipan, cinnamon, butter, and hot coffee teased my senses the minute I walked into the tiny, six-table bakery/coffeehouse and convinced me that dessert was the logical answer to my dilemma.

I'd settled down with a slice of chocolate-chip coffee cake and a small café au lait when Rich walked in. He bought a cup of coffee and, with a questioning look, gestured at the empty chair across from me.

"Be my guest," I said, sipping at my coffee.

The bell over the door jangled, and the photographer and his long-suffering wife walked in, minus their plethora of camera bags. They smiled and waved at me, then started perusing the glass bakery case.

"I saw Scout sitting under the awning outside," Rich said.

I nodded. Though Rich was a nice guy and I certainly felt sympathy for him, I really wanted to just concentrate on my own problems. Which, apparently, was obvious.

"Hey, it looks like I'm bothering you," he said softly. "Sorry, I'll . . ." He started to stand up.

That made me feel like a heartless jerk. "No, please sit back down. I'm just a little distracted." I stirred my coffee idly and asked, "What do you have planned for tomorrow?"

He shrugged. "Since I've retired, I just take each day as it happens. Maybe I'll go fishing. Maybe I'll watch *Oprah*."

We sat in silence, listening to the photographer and his wife commence with the eternal marital debate of the wisdom of caffeine consumed this late in the day. Rich and I smiled in mutual recognition. The wife won, and they ordered decaf.

When I finished my coffee cake and stood up, he followed suit. "Want some company on the walk back?" he asked.

"Sure." I said. Outside Scout stood up to greet me, his tail wagging furiously. On the way back, we casually

107

complained about the difficulties of adjusting to a seaside town—how our towels never seemed to dry out, how the damp air made my hair as curly as corkscrews, how the ferns in our yards looked like something out of a Michael Crichton movie.

When we reached my front gate, he asked, "Anything new on the investigation?"

"A little," I said, figuring it wouldn't hurt to tell him some of what I'd discovered since Gabe's background check had cleared him. "Keep this between you and me?"

"Absolutely."

On my front porch, where I'd forgotten to leave a light on, I dug through my purse for my boot-shaped key ring. While digging, I told him about my conversation with Rowena Ludlam and her request for the picture of her brother in his coffin.

"He sounds like a real coward to me," Rich said stiffly. "What kind of man just walks away from his family?"

I didn't answer. Naturally I agreed with him, to a degree, but if I'd learned one thing in the last few years, it was don't judge things until you've seen the whole picture. People and situations aren't always what they seem. Maybe some families deserved to be walked away from.

I inserted the key, then turned the knob to open the door.

A strangled scream caught in my throat, and I jerked my hand back.

With the instincts of a father, he grabbed my upper arm and pushed me behind him. "What is it?" I showed him my palm. It was covered with blood.

7

HE KICKED THE DOOR OPEN DOOR WIDER WITH HIS foot, reached inside, and flipped on the porch light. I held my hand away from me, a gamut of emotions and questions racing through my mind—whose blood is this, what are we going to find inside, how could I stay here now?

"Let me look," Rich said, grabbing my wrist. He touched the red dripping off my palm and brought his finger to his nose. "It's paint."

"What!" I pulled my hand back and stared closer at it. It was only then that the sharp, metallic smell of fresh paint reached my nose.

Rich inspected the doorknob, his face shadowed in the yellow porch light. "Someone's playing a joke on you."

"Some joke." I peered hesitantly into the dark house. What else was waiting for me inside?

"Let me go in and look around," Rich said.

"That's okay, I can do it."

"Kid, now's not the time to be cocky. We'll both do it," he said, walking ahead of me.

After a thorough search by both of us and Scout, we concluded that the prankster hadn't been inside.

"I have some turpentine in my garage," Rich said. "I'll clean off your doorknob for you." He looked down at my stained hand. "And you."

"Thanks. Maybe we should report this to the police."

He kept his face blank. "Up to you."

My mind quickly calculated how long it would take for someone at the Morro Bay Police Department to contact Gabe, who would be out here quicker than I could get the door locked, nagging me again to give this thing up.

"It's probably just some kids or something," I said.

He didn't comment.

After he'd cleaned off the knob and my hand and after multiple assurances that I'd be fine, Rich went home. I sat on the sofa playing with Scout's ears, wondering what this little incident meant. If the person was trying to unnerve me, it had worked. But who and why? To scare me out of the house so I'd lose it? But what good would that do since it would just go to the government?

The person playing the prank probably didn't know that.

I double-checked all the doors and windows, then took the quickest shower on record. It took me over an hour to fall asleep, even with the light on and the comfort of Scout sleeping next to my bed.

Since the funeral wasn't until one o'clock, I decided I had plenty of time the next morning to visit my friend Tina, who owned The Fabric Patch downtown, and find out if she knew anything about Mr. Chandler. I was pulling on my boots when Gabe called.

"Hey, good-lookin'," I said. "How was the blues?"

"Great. Sam and I had a good time. We didn't fight once."

"Such big boys. I'm so proud of both of you." He laughed. "Who's being condescending now?"

"It'll still take me years to catch up with you."

"What did you do yesterday?"

"Not much. Went and checked on the Mother's Day exhibit. Then I visited Dove at the Historical Museum. Word of warning, they're plotting something dastardly. Had dinner at Cafe Palais again then walked down to

Morro Rock. Stopped off at Greta's Koffee Haus and had dessert. Talked to my neighbor a little. Cleaned the red paint off my doorknob. Took a shower and went to bed."

"Back up there. What red paint?"

"It's nothing. Someone smeared some red paint on the front doorknob. Messy, but Rich had some turpentine and cleaned it up in no time."

He was quiet a moment.

"It's just a prank," I said.

He remained silent.

"Gabe . . ."

"I'm making a real effort to keep my promise not to get upset, but I don't like the sound of that."

"And I appreciate your effort."

I could almost hear his struggle over the phone. Then he asked, "Tell me your schedule. Knowing what you're doing will make me feel better."

"I have no problem with that. The funeral is today. One o'clock at the Paso Robles Cemetery. Before that, I'm going to my friend Tina's quilt store downtown and see if she knows anything about Mr. Chandler. How about dinner?"

"Sure, but why don't you come into town? I have to attend a city council meeting at seven o'clock. They're voting on the Historical Museum issue, and I want be there to soothe frazzled nerves. Angelo's at five-thirty?"

"See you then. Maybe I should come to the council meeting, too."

"That might not be a bad idea. It may take both of us to hold Dove back."

I ate breakfast at Bay City Donuts and didn't hear any gossip about Jacob Chandler, though I was thoroughly entertained by a story about three widow ladies in a casserole competition for a new widower in town. I walked through the quilt store's door at five minutes after ten.

Entering Tina's shop was like walking into a fabulous amusement park made especially for quilters. Just the smell and colors of the fabric inspired me as I threaded my way through the crowded aisles. She and her husband Tom had retired here after his career as an Air Force pilot. For twenty years she'd followed him, uncomplaining, all over the world, and now, she said, it was her turn. With their kids off in college, she was living her dream, which he cheerfully and wholeheartedly supported. Mostly, Tom told me once, his sharp pilot's eyes teasing, because all her fabric purchases were now a tax write-off. When he wasn't working on his Cessna Skyhawk, used for flying fishermen to remote lakes in the Sierra Nevadas, he was moving bolts of fabric, checking in inventory, or repairing something in the store.

Tina's shop reflected so much of her upbeat, bubbly personality that you couldn't help but want to linger awhile, pour yourself a cup of almond-flavored coffee, and peruse the dozens of quilt and craft magazines in the small area in back she called the Community Corner. Next to the overstuffed chairs, a corkboard wall held pictures of finished and nearly finished quilts; baby and wedding announcements, and accompanying pictures of the quilts made for them; letters from quilters who'd visited her shop or had once lived here; requests of all kinds from those needing scraps of certain fabrics to finish a quilt to questions about quilting stores in other areas. It was a place where everyone in the San Celina County quilting world checked while on a "fabric run."

"Is Tina here?" I asked the white-haired lady behind the counter.

"She's in the quilting room." She pointed to the back of the store.

Tina's dark head was bent over a lap-sized red, blue, and off-white muslin quilt.

"Is that fabric a reproduction or the real thing?" I asked.

Her head flew up, and her eyes, as dark as her curly hair, sparkled. "Benni! Gosh, it's been ages since you've been here. How're things at the folk art museum?"

"Fine, though I'm taking a little break for personal reasons. That's why I'm here." I picked up the edge of the quilt and held it out so I could see it better. "Fifty-four-forty or Fight? That's definitely a pattern meant for a revolution."

"Dove commissioned it three weeks ago, and I've been working furiously on it. The Historical Museum must be doing a display on the Oregon Territory. That's what my quilt book said this has to do with—the fight over the Oregon Territory between the United States and Great Britain. She says she needs it by tonight."

I laughed and sat on a folding chair next to her. "I suspect it's about territorial rights, but Oregon's definitely not involved here." I filled her in on the battle between the mayor and the ladies of the historical society.

"So, I'm part of a radical movement," she said, clipping a thread and laughing. "I like that. Wait'll I tell Tom. So what brings you here? Though I suspect I know."

"You heard, then." I wasn't surprised. Not much happened in this town that didn't eventually make it to

Tina's ears, though, being naturally kindhearted, she was always discreet as a cat if it was something bad.

"I heard you inherited a house over on Pelican and that you don't know the man who left it to you." She threaded her needle, then looked up at me, her eyes curious. "That's about it. Nothing too scandalous."

"That is why I'm here. What do you know about Jacob Chandler? I mean, if you know him at all."

She knotted her thread, then stuck the needle into the pincushion bracelet on her wrist. "I knew him, but not really that well."

"How?"

"Actually, Tom knew him better. I think I told you the last time we talked that I finally got Tom to do something besides work on that airplane."

"Right, but I can't remember what you said he was doing."

"Wood carving. He's just started, but he really likes it. He knew Jake from the wood carving meetings. He's here this morning rearranging some of the heavier stuff in the back room. Do you want to speak to him?"

"Sure, if his boss will let him take a break."

Laughing, she stood up, laying the quilt on the large craft table next to her. "I hear she's a cruel taskmaster, but I think she'll let him stop working for five minutes or so."

I spread out the quilt on the craft table and ran my fingers over the fine stitching while Tina went for Tom. The pattern of triangles and squares that when finished made up an eight-pointed star pattern was beautiful and striking in the bright blue and red conversation print fabric, set against the off-white muslin.

A nervous feeling started itching at my stomach lining. I had a strong suspicion this quilt wasn't going to

114

be raffled. "Dove," I said under my breath, "what in the world do you have planned?"

Tom came in, drying his hands with a paper towel. He was still as neat and trim as a twenty-one-year-old; I had no trouble picturing him playing an extra in the movie *Top Gun*. "Hey, Benni, when are you going to let that hardworking husband of yours take some time off and fly with me to Lake Tahoe?"

"You two alone in Tahoe?" Tina said. "In your dreams, sweet pea."

"I'd be glad to get rid of him for a weekend," I shot back. "Then me and Tina can go on a road trip and hit all the fabric stores in California."

He groaned dramatically, tossed his paper towel across the room, and made a basket. He bent his elbow and clenched a fist in victory, grinning at us with his Tom Cruise smile. "Not a chance. You two would spend more than if we played the five-dollar poker machines for three days without sleeping."

"And don't you forget it," Tina said.

Tom asked, "What's this about you and Jake Chandler?"

"I want to pick your brain about him. Tell me everything you know."

He cracked his knuckles, his clean-shaven face thoughtful. "I didn't know him real well. Had breakfast with him and some other guys a few times before a wood-carvers' meeting. Some of us would commute together to the meetings up in San Simeon. He seemed like a nice enough guy. Told me he served in the Navy in Korea. Then I think he was a salesman or something. Mostly we talked about sports, the projects we were working on, politics."

"The Navy? He definitely said the Navy?" That didn't

115

fit. Gabe's investigator friend had said Jacob Chandler had served in the Army.

"Yeah, I teased him a lot about it. He said that's why he wanted to live in Morro Bay. He loved anything to do with ships and the ocean."

"What else did he tell you about his past?"

He shook his head. "Not much. But then again, men aren't like women. I've seen Tina in the course of a half hour tell our whole life story up to and including what we had for breakfast that morning to a waitress serving us lunch in a roadside cafe."

"I do not!" She giggled and hit his arm with the rolled fat quarter of fabric.

"Careful now with the merchandise, honey," he said with mock seriousness. "That's our future you're beating me with. But you know men aren't as interested in all the nitty-gritty personal details as you women."

"Isn't there anything that sticks out in your mind?" I asked.

"You really should talk to Beau Franklin," he said. "He probably knew him about as good as anyone here in town except for Tess Briggstone."

"I've spoken with her, but to be truthful, it was a little awkward."

Tom looked confused.

"They were together," Tina explained to him. "It was probably a shock that he died . . ."

Tom's face showed his comprehension. "And that he left all he owned to a perfect stranger and not his lover."

Her face noncommittal, Tina looked down at the quilt spread across the table and picked at a loose thread. "She's had some tough times this last year and she cared about him. This can't be easy for her."

Remembering the quilts on Mr. Chandler's bed, I was

willing to bet that Tess was a customer of hers. I didn't want to make Tina betray her loyalties, even if she might be a rich fountain of helpful information.

He looked back at me and said philosophically, "The drama of small-town relationships, huh? Well, like I said, Beau Franklin knew him best. They played regularly at that giant chessboard down on the Embarcadero."

"Where can I find this Beau Franklin?"

Tina said, "I heard the funeral's today."

I nodded. "One o'clock."

"They were friends, so I'm sure he'll be there. If not, he's in the phone book. His wife, Anita, comes in here a lot. She's a cross-stitch fanatic, but she likes to get ideas from the quilt books."

"I'll look for him there. Is there anything else you can think of?"

They shook their heads. "He seemed like just another senior citizen who had retired in Morro Bay," Tina said. "Thanks, anyway. And, Tom, I'll pass on your invitation to Gabe."

I started out when Tom's voice stopped me. "Benni, there is something that did strike me—well, all the guys—as odd."

I turned around. "What?"

"He wouldn't enter his wood carvings in any competition or even sell them. And, believe me, he was the most talented carver I've ever seen."

I considered his statement. "Maybe he just wanted to keep them for himself."

He shrugged. "Could be. The rest of us talked about it a lot, though not around him, of course. I mean, he was downright paranoid. He wouldn't even let any of them be displayed at the museum. After a while he stopped going to the meetings, and we assumed he'd stopped carving. I don't know if it means anything, but it was strange."

"Thanks, I'll file it away in the computer." I pointed at my head.

Back at the house, there was a message on the answering machine from Emory.

"Might want to change that voice on the answering machine," he said. "It's rather weird leaving messages to a dead man. Now, don't get riled, sweetcakes, but I'm gonna be a tad late to the buryin'. But don't you fear, I'll be there in time to interrogate the guests."

I glared at the machine. Great, now I'd have to brave the lion's den alone.

I quickly ironed my navy dress, slipped on leather pumps, then grabbed a Hershey bar for lunch. "Stay," I told Scout when I walked out the door. He flopped down on the front porch with a sigh. "I know you hate not coming, but someone has to hold down the fort."

I climbed into the truck and started the ignition.

"Hey, neighbor!" Rich called out. I turned off the truck and rolled down my window.

He was dressed in neat blue chinos, a blue-and-green-plaid-shirt and a blue knit tie. "Are you heading out for the funeral?" he asked.

"Yep."

"Want some company? I'm going that way, too."

I gave him a grateful look. "Rich, that would be wonderful. My cousin was supposed to meet me there, but he's going to be late. I really dreaded walking in there alone."

As we pulled out on Pelican, we passed the Pelican Inn where the photographer's wife was sitting at the patio table in front painting her nails. She waved at us as we drove by.

118

On the drive to Paso Robles, I unwrapped the Hershey bar and offered Rich half.

He shook his head, his broad face disapproving. "That better not be your lunch, young lady."

In spite of my churning stomach, his comment managed to get a smile out of me. "Did Gabe pay you to say that?"

"I have three daughters. Nagging comes natural."

Paso Robles Cemetery overlooked the town with treeless mountains rising up in the distance, mountains bisected by a treacherous two-lane highway that eventually led to the vast Central Valley. We drove slowly through the wrought iron gates and up the narrow road, braking once when a flock of partridges darted in front of us. At the top of the cemetery, near the mission-style grounds buildings where both American and black and white MIA flags lay quiet against the metal pole, it was obvious where Mr. Chandler's service was being held. People were gathered under a crooked Valley oak tree a small distance away. We parked next to the Memorial Rose Garden.

There were about twenty people at the funeral, most around Mr. Chandler's age—early to late sixties. The slamming of the truck doors caused people to glance toward us. Curious and judging looks froze their faces as Rich and I walked across the dry, papery grass—not that I was surprised. I certainly didn't expect to be the most popular girl at the funeral. Blue jays and blackbirds fluttered in the trees above us. Purple and white lupine bloomed in wild patches, and traffic from the highway sizzled through the tall sound break bushes, sounding like the ocean.

About thirty feet from the gathering, I stopped, not certain what to do. The only folding chairs open were

119

in the front row next to Tess and her sons. When the minister saw me and Rich, he pointed at the empty chairs.

Rich cupped my elbow with his hand and whispered in my ear, "Walk in like you own the place. Don't look left or right. Remember, you haven't done anything wrong."

"I feel like throwing up," I whispered back.

"Sorry, not allowed. Chin up, kid, and just put one foot in front of the other."

I could feel the eyes of Jake Chandler's friends studying me as we claimed the seats in the front row, my face warm with embarrassment at this charade. On one side of Tess sat Neely, the waitress from Cafe Palais. Tess's older son Cole sat on the other. Tess's face was a hard, emotionless mask. She dipped it in a single nod of acknowledgment when we passed in front of her. Neely scowled slightly and, knuckles taut, clutched the white vinyl purse in her lap. I still hadn't figured out the relationship between those two, but with the look on Neely's face, it was obvious she thought I didn't belong here. Certainly something I wouldn't dispute. I sat down next to Duane, whose smirk was entirely inappropriate. Rich took the chair on the other side of me, giving me an encouraging wink.

The coffin was covered with a large spray of peach roses. There were a few other multicolored standing sprays. The funeral was short and bland with the predictable reading of the Lord's Prayer and the Twenty-third Psalm. While the minister said his words, I stared straight ahead at the coffin, feeling guilty that my emotions were not moved except for the vague sympathy any normal human feels at the death of another. A stifled sob from Tess made me feel even worse. I truly had no business being here. At the moment, the only emotion I felt begin to roil inside me was anger at this man who would play such cavalier games with people's emotions.

After the last prayer, I waited a few seconds, then stood up to leave. What I wanted to do was bolt across the smooth lawn like a nervous mare, but I'd been raised to have manners, and awkward or not, I felt the need to say something to Tess, who without a doubt loved this man.

"I'm so sorry for your loss," I said to her.

"Thank you," she answered, her eyes boring into mine with an intense emotion that could have been either sorrow or anger. Neely took her arm and, without a word to me, led her away. Cole looked at me a long silent moment, then followed his mother.

Duane waited until his mother and brother were some distance away before he said in a mimicking tone, "I'm so *sorry*." Before I could answer, he swung around and caught up with them.

"Smart-ass punk," Rich said. "What's his problem?"

I shrugged, weary of the whole thing. "Who knows? I'm sure they've all had a field day speculating about my relationship with Mr. Chandler."

"So, ready to let me buy you lunch? That Hershey bar is probably about ready to wear off, I'll bet."

I didn't answer, gazing out over the crowd until I found who I was looking for. Sure enough, Emory had finally showed up and had his notebook out talking to a group of mourners. I looked away, not wanting people to guess we knew each other until he could pry some information out of them.

A dark-suited man came up and informed me he was with the funeral parlor. "Ms. Harper, my sympathies for your loss. These are for you." He handed me two envelopes. "One contains the cards from the flower arrangements. The other is your request on the phone yesterday."

The photograph. "Thank you," I said, sticking them in my purse. "If there's any outstanding expenses, please send them to the Morro Bay address."

"It's all been taken care of," the man said. "Mr. Chandler saw to that himself. If anything, there may be a refund."

"Okay, thanks. Can I ask you something?" I kept my voice low so the people lingering close by couldn't overhear.

"Certainly, Ms. Harper. I'm here to assist in any way I can."

"Do you know how long ago Mr. Chandler arranged all this?"

"I certainly do. I took care of him myself. Almost a year now. June, I think it was. He was a very pleasant fellow. Knew exactly what he wanted. Even picked the Bible verses he wanted the minister to read. Said he didn't want his loved ones having to worry about a thing."

"Thank you," I said.

" 'Scuse me," a gruff voice said behind me.

I turned and faced a short, square-shouldered man with plastic eyeglasses and thick, wavy gray hair. He appeared the same age as most of the mourners, early sixties, and wore a dark brown leisure suit that looked uncomfortably snug on his bulky frame.

"Beau Franklin," he said, holding out a hand as square and blunt as a block of wood. He gestured to the lady standing next to him. She was so thin it looked painful for her to even move. She cradled her large black purse as if it were a baby. "My wife, Anita."

Beau Franklin—where did that name ring a bell? Tom Davis's voice echoed through my head. The man he suggested knew Jacob Chandler better than anyone. Just the man I wanted to talk to.

"I'm sorry for your loss," he said. His wife nodded silently.

"Thank you," I said, feeling again like a fake. "But, as I'm sure you've heard, I really didn't know Mr. Chandler. I should be offering condolences to you."

He nodded thanks briskly, clasping his hands in front of him in the way ministers do when they are trying to appear calm and collected. "We'd been friends since he moved to Morro Bay."

An awkward silence passed. "Mr. Franklin," I said, "I'd like to talk to you, but I don't think this is an appropriate time. May I call you?"

"I'll come by the house tomorrow," he said. "You up by ten?"

I nodded.

"Ten it is, then. I'd be glad to talk to you about Jake now that you brought it up. He and I have some unfinished business." The folds in his deeply tanned face sagged. Solid brown eyes, the color of ditch water, darted from me, to Rich, and back to me. "Tomorrow, then."

Rich and I watched him pick his way down the hill, his wife holding on to his arm like it was a life raft.

"Wonder what his agenda is," Rich said.

"Who knows?" I answered, staring after the couple. "But how much do you want to bet his unfinished business involves money?"

"Ms. Harper, Ms. Harper, can I talk with you a minute? Please, just a minute." I felt a finger tap my shoulder. "Emory Littleton, *San Celina Tribune*."

123

Rich looked at me with the nonverbal question—*should I get rid of this guy?* Even without Scout here, it appeared that I had a watchdog.

Catching Rich's look, Emory's smile never faltered. "I just need to ask Ms. Harper a few questions."

Rich ignored him and asked, "Benni, do you want to talk to the press?"

"Not really," I said, trying not to laugh so Mr. Chandler's friends wouldn't have that much more to gossip about. "But I think this one is okay."

"You think?" Emory said in a low voice. "You're breaking my heart, sweetcakes."

Trying to keep a straight face while Emory led me away from the crowd, I gestured at Rich to follow. When we were out of earshot, Emory said, "Do you realize the dander you've aroused in this happy little group? I truly fear I'll have to throw myself in front of you when they start the stoning."

"And mess up your new Armani jacket? We should all live to see the day."

He fingered the lapels of his tweedy sport coat. "It is rather dashing, isn't it? A lot of chickens gave up their lives for this jacket. But I'm sure you'll agree it's worth every penny of my daddy's hard-earned money."

I turned to Rich and said, "Hard as this is to believe, this crazy man is my cousin, though there are times when I've contemplated whether I actually want to claim him. Emory, this is my neighbor, Richard Trujillo."

"How do you do," Emory said, sticking out his hand.

Rich's jaw relaxed slightly. His fatherly protectiveness was sweet, but if it continued, I was going to have to diplomatically lead him back to his own corral. One overly protective Latino man in my life was more than enough.

Emory's expression turned serious. "Now, I'm going to pretend I'm taking notes here and I'll fill you in on what dirt I've tilled in this garden of dastardly deceitfulness."

"You actually got some information? You've only been here ten minutes!"

He brushed a lock of curly hair out of my eyes. "I'm a journalist. Gossip and innuendo is my bread and butter, my little sweet tart." He flashed a wicked smile. "You *do* realize that's exactly what all these fine folks are thinking you are?"

I swatted at his hand. "Stop it. You're supposed to look like you don't know me. What did you find out?"

"Found it all out from one talkative little widow who was dying to tell someone what she heard. There's always one in every group, the one who watches everyone else, getting her thrills out of reporting others' peccadillos. Apparently your Ms. Tess Briggstone wasn't the only one expecting a little something extra when Jacob Chandler passed away."

"Who else?"

"That rather stout man and his sad-looking wife you were talking to."

"His name's Beau Franklin. He told me right up front that he and Mr. Chandler had some unfinished business. He's coming by my house tomorrow at ten to talk about it."

"That fits with what my chattering little source told me. Your Mr. Chandler had apparently gone into some sort of speculative business with Mr. Franklin, and Mr. Franklin's investment has yet to be returned."

"For what?" I asked.

"She didn't know. Just knew they had a deal going that was supposed to bring in some quick money, which

125

apparently Mr. Franklin is desperate for, though she doesn't know why. She overheard Chandler and Franklin at one of the senior potlucks a few weeks ago when she was washing dishes in the kitchen. Beau was getting mighty agitated at Jake. Asked him when was he going to get the stuff so Beau could recoup his money."

"Get the stuff? Wonder what he meant by that."

"I don't know, but I don't like the sound of it. Could be anything these days from drugs to black market CDs. Makes me a tad nervous about you stayin' in that house, that's a fact."

I waved my hand impatiently. "Believe me, Gabe's had that house practically dipped in alcohol. Whatever stuff he's talking about isn't inside that house."

"Nevertheless," Emory said doubtfully, leaving it at that.

"Ponder on it, cousin, and get back to me if anything bubbles up out of that diabolical brain of yours."

"I'll poke around. By the way, what's Dove got cooking over there at the Historical Museum, anyway?"

"I have no idea. Gabe seems to think something is going to happen at the city council meeting tonight, so you might want to be there."

"With bells on." Emory checked his flat, gold watch. "Gotta go. I'm interviewing the mayor at three."

"Traitor," I teased.

"No, ma'am, just doing a little spyin' for our side." He flipped a little wave at Rich. "Nice meetin' you, Mr. Trujillo. You'd best be on full alert hanging around my cousin here. She attracts trouble like a lightnin' rod on a Kansas silo."

"Get lost, fashion boy," I said.

"Your cousin, huh?" Rich commented, watching Emory climb into his shiny black Cadillac Seville. "I do see the family resemblance."

"We don't look that much alike," I said.

"I didn't mean your looks."

At the truck he asked, "You ready for lunch now? I sure am."

I turned the ignition. "I'm not really hungry. I think I'll go out to the James Dean Memorial and try to figure out what that number 226 means, but I can drop you off first."

"I could go with you," he offered.

"Thanks, but you've wasted enough of your day. I'm sure you have better things to do."

He closed the passenger door and turned to me, his forehead wrinkling. "Like what? Frankly, if I spend another day fishing or just wandering around Morro Bay I'm going to go crazy. I'm enjoying this." He smiled sheepishly at me. "I mean, not Jake dying, but . . ."

I smiled back. I knew exactly what he meant. How to fill your days and weeks when you'd spent most of your life as a couple and now weren't anymore. "Well, I certainly don't mind the company, but first I have a quick errand in Paso Robles. Then we're off to Cholame."

At a local stationery store that advertised Federal Express, I paid the overnight price to send the Polaroid picture of Mr. Chandler to his sister in Lubbock, hoping it would give her some sort of closure to the pain of his desertion.

Heading out of Paso Robles on Highway 46, I gave Rich the tourist guide information about Cholame and the James Dean Memorial.

"Like Dove would say, Cholame is a 'poke and clean' town. Poke your head out of the window and you're clean through it."

Rich laughed. "So what is there?"

127

"A pretty decent cafe and the James Dean Memorial. It's right before Highways 41 and 46 split off. One road goes to Fresno, the other Bakersfield."

"We can have lunch at the cafe, then."

I gazed out over the rolling green meadows, remembering how Jack and I and our friends used to come out here even before the memorial was built in 1977. We'd sprawl across the hoods of our trucks, throw rocks across the road, drink warm Cokes, and spit sunflower seeds at each other. Something wild in us drew us to that spot, the place where James Dean's own explosive youth was ended so quickly, so irretrievably.

I came here a few times after Jack's death, sitting in our truck and staring at the steel and concrete monument, trying to discover some answers about why he was taken from me so young. I never came to any great conclusions and eventually relegated this place, like so many others, to a back room in my mind labeled, "Jack." Now, here it was again, placed before me for some other inexplicable reason.

We pulled into the parking lot of the Hi-Way Cafe. Without speaking, we stepped out of the truck and walked over to the memorial. At this time of day, during the middle of the week, we were the only visitors. Behind us, in the fields full of wild alfalfa, young bull calves playfully butted heads. Yellow-eyed blackbirds flitted through the thin leaves of the Tree of Heaven that grew in the middle of the monument. The sun beat down warm on our shoulders, glinting off the monument's steel posts. During the hot summer months, this place was unbearable except after sunset. I knew ranchers who loved the desolate, sometimes forbidding Carrizo Plains of San Celina County where the San Andreas Fault meandered through the dry, cracked

128

landscape, but it took a certain toughness to appreciate and tolerate this land's isolated beauty.

Rich read out loud, "His name was James Byron Dean. He was an actor. He died just before sundown on 9/30/55 when his Porsche collided with another car at a fork in the road not 900 yards east of this tree, long known as the Tree of Heaven. He was twenty-four years old."

He didn't look up but continued staring at the plaque. "I remember when this happened. He was a year younger than me. I'd been a firefighter for a little over a year. Around the same time, a buddy of mine . . ." He looked at me, his face heavy with grief, but it wasn't for James Dean. "We were booters in the academy. He died in a house fire. Roof collapsed on him. Left a wife and five-year-old son. The thing was, I couldn't believe someone my age could die. It's still hard to believe."

"I know what you mean. My mom died when she was twenty-five."

"That's really rough on a kid. How old were you?"

"Six."

He shook his head sympathetically. "My friend's son grew up to be a pharmacist. A real nice kid. He was a big help when my wife needed so much medication that I couldn't keep it all straight." We both stared at the monument for a long, silent moment.

"Let's have lunch," I suggested, wanting to get off the subject of parents, spouses, and friends dying too young. "We can inspect the monument in detail afterwards and see if anything relates to the number 226."

"Good idea."

The cafe smelled of that wonderful flavor combination that could seduce just about any red-

129

blooded American citizen no matter what their race, creed, or color—fresh baked pie and the intoxicating scent of grilling hamburgers. We took a seat in one of the green Naugahyde booths and ordered the hamburger, fries, and cherry pie special from our young, frizzy-headed waitress.

"I'm going to look around," I told Rich. He nodded and went over to the old fifties jukebox to peruse the music selections.

"No rap," I called over my shoulder.

"Don't worry, kid. I'm more a Frank Sinatra kinda guy."

Since we were the only customers, I wandered freely about the small room, inspecting the framed black-and-white photographs of James Dean over every booth showing him dressed in everything from Western clothes to a tuxedo to a plaid shirt and nerd glasses holding a white kitten. Different clothes altered his look entirely. They were costumes really—props—the ones he chose, or were chosen for him, determined how we saw him, how we judged him. Who was he really? That was a question that could be asked of any of us: How much of what we show the world truly reveals who we are?

Something about this Mr. Chandler bothered me. It was as if he was trying to reveal himself to me, but it was all so planned, so manipulated, that it seemed like all he was revealing was that he was an insensitive, controlling man who didn't even remember his lover in his will.

At this point, I was pretty certain I wouldn't have liked Jacob Chandler very much.

I looked through the James Dean T-shirts, hats, postcards, and key chains, not seeing anything that gave me a hint as to what the number 226 meant. I'd glanced quickly over the memorial when I was outside, though I knew most of it almost by heart and there was no 226 there, either. Was it some kind of latitude/longitude reference? Was there someplace 226 miles from this spot I should go? Was there something in James Dean's life where that number was significant? If there was, it had to be here somewhere. If nothing else, it appeared that Mr. Chandler was methodical and logical—that number was there for a reason.

I went back to our table when the food arrived and ate my hamburger and fries absentmindedly. Rich, taking my cue, didn't press me for conversation. We listened to his selections: "Fly Me to the Moon," "A Hundred Pounds of Clay," "Peggy Sue," "Something to Talk About."

"Bonnie Raitt?" I asked, putting more catsup on my fries. "Kinda wild. I'd never have guessed that about you, Rich."

His chin jutted out slightly in defiance. "I have my cooler moments." Then he softened his stance with a sheepish smile. "Besides, I've always had a weakness for redheads with attitude."

We were halfway through our pie when the music ran out.

"My turn," I said, scooting out of the booth. Leaning over the jukebox, I perused the selections—a combination of big band, fifties tunes, and country/western classics. "Oh, for cryin' out loud," I exclaimed.

The teenage waitress, coming by with a pot of coffee to refill Rich's cup, asked, "What's wrong?"

I turned to her. "Do these records get changed often?"

A look of disdain crowded her face. "Not often enough for me. Isn't it gross? My mom owns this place. I'm working on her getting some singers from this decade, and she's considering it. She said she'd consider giving up anyone except Carole King. She refuses to get rid of old Carole." She rolled her kohl-blackened eyes. "She's the *queen* in my mom's eyes."

"Rich, get over here and look at this."

He stood next to me and looked at where I was pointing.

Number 226. Carole King. "I Feel the Earth Move."

Rich's brown face clouded with confusion. "I don't get it."

"That's because you're not from around here. But he knew I would."

"So, what does it mean?"

"Our next stop is Parkfield."

"Where and what is Parkfield?"

"You think this is the boonies, wait'll you see Parkfield."

"I still don't get it."

"Earthquake capital of the world," our young waitress filled in. "The people who live out there are crazy. When the big one hits, they are moose meat."

Rich turned to me and grinned. "Sounds like fun. Let's go."

8

"You weren't kidding," Rich said as we bumped along the gravel road toward Parkfield. It was open range, and I had to stop more than once for a lazy heifer or bull wandering across the road to where the alfalfa was undoubtedly greener. Above us, turkey vultures swooped low in the sweet-tasting air, so close we could almost count their wing feathers.

I laughed. "I guarantee that Parkfield isn't a tourist trap on the level of Morro Bay and I doubt that it ever will be. In the summer, it can get up to 110 degrees out here. The people who live and ranch out here are tougher than me by a long shot. Tough as baked-in-the-sun bull hide."

He looked out the window, a small smile tugging at the corner of his mouth. "Somehow, I think you might give them a run for their money, Benni Harper."

"You're just being flattering 'cause I know the way back."

"Could be," he said with a chuckle.

In a half hour we pulled into the tiny town of Parkfield—population 34—with more earthquake-predicting gizmos than could be found even at Cal Tech. We parked in front of the Parkfield Inn, where, painted across a rusty old water tank, an advertisement welcomed visitors to the "Earthquake Capital of the World—Sleep Here When It Happens." The inn was a pleasant, rustic building next to an old guntower-like structure colored a faded yellow with Shell Products still visible in weathered red. Across the street was a log cabin cafe and farther down a gift shop in a real caboose and freight car called appropriately the Parkfield Caboose.

We climbed out of the truck and looked around. A golden retriever trotted by, not giving us a second glance. The absence of human voices was so apparent, the chirping of the birds and hum of the insects so loud, it caused both of us to stand quietly for a moment, enjoying the peace.

"Not much here," Rich finally said in a lower than normal voice. "Shouldn't take us too long to question all thirty-four people."

I hitched my purse over my shoulder. "Guess the cafe would be the logical place to start. How about something to drink?"

"Sounds great."

After buying two Cokes from the woman behind the counter, Rich walked around the cafe, reading the framed newspaper articles about the town while I chatted casually with the waitress, finally getting up enough nerve to show her Jacob Chandler's driver's license and ask her if she knew him.

"He doesn't look familiar," she said, wiping down the counter with slow circles. "Why are you looking for him?"

"It's a long story," I said. "He's not a criminal or anything. Actually, he passed away last week. I'm just kind of trying to figure out who he was."

She nodded in understanding. "Lots of people seeking their roots these days. Sorry I can't help. You might try Risa or Marc over at the caboose. They might've known him."

I didn't correct her when she assumed I was looking for a long lost father or relative. "Thanks, I'll do that."

Out on the porch, Rich and I finished our drinks and walked the short block over to the gift shop. As we did, I told him about the two other times I'd been out to Parkfield. "They have an old-fashioned ranch rodeo every year. I rode barrels in it once. Jack—he was my first husband—he rode bareback broncs and roped."

"You were married before?" Rich asked. On our walk over, I told him about Jack, how we'd known each other since high school, were married at nineteen, and how I found myself widowed at thirty-four.

"I kind of figured you and your husband hadn't been married long," he said when we reached the caboose.

134

"Why is that?" I asked.

"Rhythm," he said.

"What?"

"You haven't worked one out yet. I was married forty-one years. You say you were married fifteen so you know what I mean." His dark eyes were kind and a little sad. "Rhythm," he repeated.

I did know what he meant. And he was right. Gabe and I hadn't established one yet. My face must have showed my dismay.

"Don't worry, kid," he said, patting my shoulder. "You two are still young. Now at my age . . ." He gazed out over the soft green fields behind the caboose.

We climbed the metal steps of the caboose and walked single file down the narrow passageway. At the end of the caboose sat a man in Western clothes, including a pale gray cowboy hat that was stained in the right places for a working cowboy. He was filling out some kind of order form.

"Afternoon, folks," he said, nodding.

We nodded back.

"There's more out in the freight car in back," he said in a pleasant, wind-graveled voice. "Ropes used by Blaine Santos himself—PRCA Champion. He sponsors the rodeo out here, you know."

"Thanks," Rich said. "We'll check it out."

The man went back to his work, and we poked around through the Western memorabilia, magazines, bandannas, and knickknacks. I picked up a mug shaped like a barrel with a curvy cowgirl-shaped handle. Her mouth opened to a red, surprised "Oh."

"How much is this?" I asked the cowboy/store owner.

He studied it for a moment, then said, "Six bucks, okay?"

135

"Sure." As I handed him the money, I said, "By the way, the lady over at the cafe said you might know this man." I showed him Mr. Chandler's driver's license.

He put down his pen and looked at the license, then back up at me. "Benni Harper?"

I nodded.

"I have something for you. Come on back." He stood up, squeezed past us, and climbed down the train steps. We followed him back to the freight car.

"Wait here," he said. "I'll bring it to you." He climbed up into the freight train and called back to me, "Sure you don't want a Blaine Santos rope to add to that mug?"

"No, but thanks anyway."

In a few seconds he came back down and handed me a square, cardboard, teapot-sized box. "How is old Jake anyway?" he asked.

I hesitated for a moment. "I'm sorry, Mr . . . ?"

"Just Marc."

"I'm sorry, Marc, but he passed away last Friday. He had a heart attack."

He dropped his head and stared at his worn boots. His eyes were shiny when he looked back at me. "Hope he didn't suffer. He used to come out here three, four times a year. We'd have lunch and talk about bumming around the country. We've both seen some road, that's for sure. He was a good man."

"His funeral was earlier today. I'm sorry—I would have told you, but he didn't leave an address book or any list of his friends."

He brushed my apology away with a sweep of his hand. "I'm not one for funerals. You his daughter? He never mentioned he had any family."

"No," I said, not wanting to explain my odd

136

inheritance to yet another stranger. "Just a friend." I hugged the box to my chest. "Do you mind telling me when he gave you this?"

"Not at all. 'Bout six months back. We had lunch like usual, then right before he left, he gave me this box. Said you'd be coming for it. Didn't know when, but me and Risa have been here quite a while and probably will be here till the big one drops the caboose in a crevice, so I've just held on to it until you came." He grinned at me. "Didn't even peek either, though I'm dying to know what's in there."

After that comment, I couldn't bear to just walk away, so I opened the sealed box and dug through the tissue paper, pulling out a breathtaking glazed pot in deep blue and greens with an unusual red undertone.

"Beautiful," Rich said.

"I'll say," Marc said.

Inside the pot was a folded piece of paper. I left it there. I wanted to read it alone. I turned the pot over and looked at the potter's elaborate calligraphy initials on the bottom—A.N. Though I knew many ceramic artists in San Celina County, the style and initials didn't strike a familiar chord.

"Well, thanks," I said, holding out my hand.

"No problem," Marc said, shaking it. "Sorry to hear about Jake. Risa will be, too. They really hit it off, both being from the South and all."

"Texas?" I asked.

He shook his head. "Risa's from Tennessee. I don't know where Jake was from, but he sure wasn't a Texan. We once had a big ole friendly argument about what true barbecue is. He said if it ain't pork, it ain't barbecue. And that ain't no Texan, I'll tell you that, 'cause I lived in Texas for ten years and I can spot one a

137

mile away." He hesitated for a moment, then said, "I don't know who you are to him, but I feel like I have to tell someone this. When Risa was real sick and the gift shop wasn't doing so well, he paid for her medicine. Went down to the pharmacy in Paso Robles and just put three hundred bucks on retainer there for us. We didn't even know it until we went to go pay. This was a man I had just met like I did you two, by him coming into the gift shop. I've never had anyone do something so kind before. I'll never forget that." He touched his hat in farewell and walked back toward the caboose.

On the ride back, I glanced every so often at the package sitting between me and Rich, anxious to read the paper inside the pot. What did it say? Did the pot itself have any meaning?

I dropped Rich off at his house and, after giving some well-deserved attention and dinner to Scout, sat down on the sofa and opened the folded paper. In his precise, block printing was another carving lesson.

To begin the piece, start with the design. Your perspective is yours alone. Patterns, ideas, and inspirations are everywhere, sometimes in the most obvious places. See things with a child's unspoiled vision. Don't take anything on face value. Study your subject completely, then try to visualize your carving. Use all five senses to experience the object you want to carve. The more you learn about your subject, the more truthful your work. Remember, there are no rules, and in the end there are no shortcuts. Take your time. Don't let your goal keep you from relishing the journey.

I read it two more times, knowing he was trying to tell

138

me more than just how to make a good carving. But if there was any hidden clue in this ambiguous message, it was flying right over my head. With the note stuck in my purse to show Gabe over dinner, I headed out to the truck. Scout followed me and sat expectantly next to the passenger door.

"Scout, go back," I said, pointing to the yard. He sat and stared at me, his face longing. "Back," I repeated. He whined deep in his throat.

"I'm sorry, fella, I know I left you alone all day, but tomorrow will be better, I promise." I stooped down and slipped an arm around his shoulders, giving his chest a vigorous scratching. "I'll be home soon. Guard the house." He walked dejectedly over to the front porch and flopped down, his eyes accusing. The guilt worked enough to make me feel terrible, but not terrible enough to change my mind.

During dinner, I told Gabe everything that had happened at the funeral and later at the James Dean Memorial and Parkfield. He read the note, studied the small pot, running his thumbs over the glossy lip, his face thoughtful but calm.

"What next?" he asked.

"Find the seller or possibly the maker of this pot. Maybe that's who he wants me to talk to. I'm getting the drift of this game now. It's sort of like a scavenger hunt. I'm going to drop it off at Barnum's Craft Gallery, over in the old Springfield Dairy building. The manager has been involved with local potters for years, so maybe he'll be able to identify this person with the initials A.N. I'm assuming that's who Mr. Chandler wants me to see."

He smiled and ate a bite of ravioli. "Good solid detective work."

I smiled back, pointing a soft bread stick at him. "Did it hurt you to say that, Chief Ortiz?"

"Only a little."

After dinner he drove me to Barnum's, where, fortunately for me, Geoffrey Renault, the manager I'd mentioned, was working that night.

"Set it behind the counter," he said after I explained my problem. "It doesn't ring a bell right off, but I'll take a closer look at it after things slow down a bit." He ran twig-thin fingers through his red shoulder-length hair.

I glanced around the room crowded with customers. "Thanks, Geoffrey. I'll come by after the city council meeting. You're open until nine-thirty, right?"

"Righto, sweetie. You tell Dove and the rest of the ladies to kick some council butt. I'm rooting for them." He gave Gabe a mischievous smile. "Quite the radical family you've married into, Chief Ortiz."

"Tell me about it," Gabe said.

When we arrived, the council chambers were almost full. I spotted Dove in the front row with at least fifty senior citizens. She caught my eye and waved at me and Gabe, then held a raised fist over her head.

We took seats in the second to last row. "I am not optimistic about the next two hours," I said.

"I'm sure they'll come to a mutual agreement," Gabe said, patting my knee.

He was wrong.

During the next two hours, person after person stood up and testified in favor of keeping the museum where it was. But there were also almost as many saying that the city needed the money and the Historical Museum was nothing but a useless drain on the city's budget. Some man called it a play area for bored, rich old ladies with no lives. Edna and Big John Rutledge had to physically hold Dove back on that one.

After hearing all the testimony, the council voted. The count was three to three. The deciding vote was Mayor Davenport's.

With a serious, pseudo-concerned expression on his tanning-parlor brown face, he voted to sell the museum.

A roar went up from Dove's group in the front row. From somewhere a tomato flew across the room and landed with a juicy smack on the table in front of the mayor.

While he stood up sputtering, trying to gain control, Gabe swiftly moved into the crowd, followed by five or six patrol officers who seemed to appear from nowhere. In minutes, the agitated seniors had been gently herded outside.

I caught up with Dove on the courthouse lawn. "Are you all right? Did you throw that tomato?"

Dove shook her head in disgust at an elderly man in a French beret arguing with a patrol officer, trying to convince her to handcuff him. Gabe stood behind the officer, trying to suppress a grin. "I warned Elmo no vegetables, but he got overly excited. Said it was one of them flashbacks from the sixties. He was a teacher up there at Berkeley. You know how they loved tossin' good food at folks back then. Crazy old coot. I think he just took too much heart medicine."

"I'm sorry you lost," I said, putting an arm around her shoulder. "What are you going to do now?"

She smiled. A smile that made me very, very nervous. "Don't you worry about us. We've been through worse, this group. We have a backup plan. We're all meeting at the museum in ten minutes."

"Do you want me and Gabe to come?"

She patted my hand. "No, you go spend some time with your husband. This business about you living apart isn't good."

"We're doing fine. Let me know if there's anything I can do."

"Count on it, honeybun."

After the crowd was dispersed and Mayor Davenport managed to sneak out the back door of the council chambers without having to face his irate former supporters, Gabe and I walked back to my truck parked five blocks up a dark side street.

"What happens now?" I asked when we reached my truck.

"The historical society will probably have to put all the displays in storage somewhere until they can find another facility."

"It's not fair."

"No," he said, pulling me to him, "it's not. It's politics and it stinks, but the city council and the mayor were elected by the people of this town to make this kind of decision. Dove and her friends fought hard, but in this case, they lost and they're going to have to accept it."

I laid my head against his chest. "I really want to do something to help them, but for the life of me I can't think of what."

He took my face in his hands. They were warm and sure and made me want to stand on this dark street forever just to feel his thumbs stroke my cheeks. "*Querida,* as bad as I feel for their plight, right now all I want to do is kiss you and imagine what I would do to you if you were coming home with me."

I had to admit his plan had definite appeal. "Maybe I'll drop by the house for a few minutes before going

142

back to Morro Bay. What did you have in mind?"

He tangled his fingers in my hair and pulled my head back, kissing me hard. The salty-sweet taste of his tongue and the solid feel of his hips pressing me against the truck's passenger door was familiar, but it took my breath away nevertheless.

Then I remembered Geoffrey and the pot. Abruptly I pulled back from him. "What time is it?"

With a slightly annoyed look on his face, he checked his watch. "Nine-thirty-five."

"Shoot, I have to try and catch Geoffrey. I need to find out who this potter is."

"Couldn't you do it tomorrow?"

"I suppose," I said, feeling chagrin at interrupting the romantic moment. "But it would bug me all night. Look, I could come by afterwards."

"Forget it," he said, his voice cool. "I have to get up early anyway. Give me a call when you get back to Morro Bay."

He walked around the front of the truck and opened the driver's door. "You'd better get moving or you'll miss your friend."

"I'm sorry," I said, standing on tiptoe and kissing his jaw. "I'll make it up to you."

"Drive carefully," he said, his expression neutral. That bothered me even more than anger.

"You, too," I said to his back as he walked away. Guilt ate at me, not to mention the desire he'd stirred that would now simmer all night, but the lure of finding out one more clue about this mystery man was irresistible. More irresistible, apparently, than making love to my husband. For the first time I really began to wonder whether I would have been better off letting the government have the inheritance. Let Tess and her sons and Beau be angry with

Uncle Sam instead of me and not create yet another tiny fissure in my delicate cliff of a marriage.

I caught Geoffrey walking out to his Volkswagen Beetle, carrying the box holding my pot.

"I wondered what happened to you," he said, holding out the box. "I left a message at your house. I'm sorry, but this pot was not created by anyone I've seen or represented, but I've only been here on the Central Coast for ten years, so take that into consideration. It's exquisite, though. If you find out who did it and they're interested in showing in a gallery, send them down."

"Thanks," I said, cradling the box against my chest. "I'll do that, when all this is over. But you know pottery in this area better than anyone so you were my biggest hope. Any suggestions about where I should go next?"

"Thanks for the flattery, but there are lots of people who are more knowledgeable than I am. Have you tried the people in Harmony?"

Harmony was a little town north of Morro Bay. Infinitesimal was probably a better description. With a population of about thirty-five, give or take a cat or two, the town consisted mostly of artists and craftspeople who sold their wares in the old Harmony Valley Creamery buildings.

"That's a great idea. I'll do it tomorrow."

He looked at me sympathetically. "Heard about what happened at the council meeting. Please give my condolences to Dove."

"I will, but don't count them out yet. If I know my gramma, there's an ace or two she hasn't played yet."

"Good for her," Geoffrey said. "Tell her to let me know if she needs bodies to walk a picket line. Me and some of my friends could dust off our radical chants and modify them for the occasion."

I laughed at the eager look on his middle-aged face. "I'll pass it on. You may be getting a call."

"Power to the People," he said cheerfully. "Just have her make sure to stock up on bottled mineral water and low-fat bagels. We're too old to be protesting on empty stomachs and we definitely don't want to dehydrate."

"You wild and radical guy, you. Thanks again."

Back in Morro Bay, I called Gabe immediately, an apology and detailed plan of future physical appeasement ready. The only reply I got was from the answering machine.

"I'm back and okay. See you tomorrow," I said, slightly irritated. Where was he? Why demand I call the minute I arrived safely when he wasn't even there to take the message? Or maybe he was there. I pictured him sitting there listening to my voice, and that really pissed me off. *Fine, play your stupid games,* I said silently to the phone.

Then I called Elvia and updated her on the developments and whined as one only can to a very old girlfriend about how annoying men are.

"And you're bugging me to make it permanent with Emory," she said.

"Yes, then we can suffer together."

"I'm telling you, *gringa blanca,* if you keep them at a distance, they treat you like a queen. Show them any weakness, and they'll have you scrubbing floors and slapping out tortillas in no time flat."

I sighed. "Gabe mops the floors in our house." The thought of his kiss and what I knew came after was making me really regret my decision to choose following another clue rather than go home with him.

"Go to bed," Elvia said. "Watch *Jay Leno.* He's the safest man I know. Gabe'll get over it and be moaning

145

mamacita at you again before you know it." She paused for a moment. "And, Benni, be careful. You're the only best friend I've got. *Buenos noches.*" She hung up with a sharp click.

"Back at ya, *mi amiga*," I said softly to the dial tone.

The next morning I walked uptown with Scout and had breakfast at a small cafe called the Egg Place. When I finished, it was only nine o'clock. I wasn't sure what time the pottery studios in Harmony opened so I decided to walk back down to the bookstore on the Embarcadero. I hadn't yet bought a card for Dove for Mother's Day, so this seemed a good time to work that into my schedule.

Stopping by the house for a bathroom pit stop, I found a message blinking on the answering machine. Rowena Ludlam's voice crackled on the tape.

"I don't know what kind of joke you're playing, young woman, but it's not a bit funny. This ain't my brother Jacob. He ain't a stinkin' lizard."

She hung up the phone with a loud click.

He wasn't her brother? He wasn't a lizard? What in the heck did she mean by that? I quickly dialed her number. She answered on the sixth ring.

"Mrs. Ludlam? This is Benni Harper, the person who—"

"I know who you are. What's the idea of sending me a picture of this strange man? What kind of scam are you trying to pull? I don't have a penny but my Social Security, so don't think you can get anything out of me."

"Mrs. Ludlam, I assure you this is not a scam. That's the man who died, who owned this house. Are you sure it's not your brother? I mean, you haven't seen him for over thirty-five years. People do change."

146

"They don't grow fingers, do they?" she snapped.

"Huh?"

"This man has all his fingers. Jacob lost his right forefinger in a bicycle accident when he was four. Like I said, he ain't a lizard."

"I'm sorry. I . . . I don't know what to tell you."

"You can tell me what happened to my brother and why this man has his name."

"I'll look into it and call you. I promise." I hung up before she could answer, my heart like a clenched fist in my chest.

Who was buried in that coffin? And where was the real Jacob Chandler? What did all this have to do with me?

I left the house and started walking, hoping the brisk, morning air would clear up some of the confusion this latest revelation had caused. I walked the length of the Embarcadero twice, Scout following me, tail and ears up, his whole body reveling with the pure joy dogs take in this simple activity. When I passed the bookstore—Joe and Leslie's Seaside Books—for the second time, I remembered the card I had intended to buy before Rowena Ludlam's phone call.

The store sat at the end of the Embarcadero in one of the newer gray wood buildings. Next door, from the tiny Morro Bay Aquarium, the sound of barking sea lions and honking seals echoed through the clammy morning air.

It was ten o'clock when I reached the front door just as the clerk was unlocking it.

"Good morning," she said, her genial voice welcoming. "If there was a prize for being first, you'd win it today." She held the door open for me.

"Thanks," I said, walking in. "Do you carry greeting cards?"

147

"Best selection in town. Over by the romance novels, back wall."

I slowly perused the cards, feeling as I did every year at this time, a thick, sad feeling that lodged somewhere between my heart and my stomach. To be honest, I didn't think a lot about my mother. When your mother dies so early and you have someone who is as warm and loving a substitute as Dove has been, you don't feel as set adrift as you might had you been left literally alone. I'd always had someone there to feel my forehead when I had a fever, argue with about cleavage in prom dresses, and cajole about later curfews. Dove knew children, knew how to raise them, and she loved me as fiercely as if she'd born me herself. I had no doubts about that. The hole left inside me when my mother died had almost been filled by Dove's love and intense protectiveness. Almost.

This time every year, when I had to choose a card to express my sentiments to the woman who for all intents and purposes was my mother, it always hit me like a swift, unexpected blow that she wasn't really; she was my father's mother. Every year I bypassed the cards printed especially for mothers and studied the cards made for grandmothers. It never failed to occur to me that I'd never bought a Mother's Day card in my life and never would.

I grabbed a four-dollar Hallmark covered with violets, Dove's favorite flower, and walked quickly away from the card section. I wandered through the store, picking up a few paperback novels that looked interesting to help kill the long evenings I still had left in Morro Bay. At the counter I asked the friendly, peppery-haired lady, "So, are you Leslie?"

The woman smiled. "Oh, no, my name is Eleanor.

148

Eleanor Newhard. Leslie and Joe haven't owned this store for about a year now. They sold out to me and bought a sailboat. Last I heard, they were in Fiji somewhere."

"Sounds like a dream come true."

"Not to me," she said, shaking her head as she rang up my purchases. "I'm living my dream now, just wallowing around in books. Of course, that's how I've spent my whole life. I was a librarian in Long Beach before I bought this store with every penny of my retirement fund. If it doesn't work out, guess I'll have to hire out as a fish cleaner on my little brother's boat."

"Your brother's a fisherman?"

"Has been his whole life. So was our father. Ray owns a party boat now. He hasn't done commercial fishing in years. Too old and too many regulations, he says."

"Have you been in Morro Bay long?"

"Two years. I volunteered at the Morro Bay Library for a while, then I started working down here for Joe and Leslie. When this place came up for sale, I said, 'What the hay, I'll give it a whirl.' Now I have all the books in the world and no time to read them." She smiled at me and handed me a shiny red bag. "But I love it. Everyone in town comes in here or the library eventually. There's not much that goes on around these parts that I don't know about." She smiled at me. "Ms. Harper, new heiress."

I smiled back, thinking, *Benni, you've hit a solid gold source here.* "Then I don't have to tell you that I knew practically nothing about Mr. Chandler. Can you fill me in?"

"Now, Jake Chandler, there was a strange character. Nice a man as you'd want to meet, but just a tad different."

"As in?"

She studied me with sharp, knowing eyes that I was willing to bet could see through book bags hiding torn pages from library encyclopedias to guilty hands that had written silly graffiti on the library's bathroom walls. Not a woman you could lie to. "He just wasn't all he seemed."

"What do you mean?"

"When you've worked with the public as long as I have you get to know people. You watch them and you just get to know when someone is hiding something, and that man was."

"Anything specific that made you think that?" Though I held a certain respect for feelings of intuition, what I wanted were hard facts.

She thought for a moment, her face serious. "There was this one time last summer. I had this nice young clerk working with me for the summer. Polite young man from North Carolina whose grandmother was a longtime customer. Jake was over in the craft section. I remember I'd sent him over there because I'd gotten in a new book on wood carving. I called out 'Garrett' just as loud and clear as a foghorn, and darned if Jake didn't turn around and say, 'What?' the same time as my clerk. The minute he did, his face turned beet-red and he flew out of here like the proverbial bat. I thought he was just embarrassed because he was losing his hearing or something, but I'd never noticed him having any more problems before that or after. Now, I don't need a sledgehammer over the head to tell me that there was something fishy going on. Why would he answer so quickly to a name completely different from his?"

That answered one thing—who the "G" was in the old copy of *Treasure Island*. Garrett. I had a first name now.

Eleanor looked at me curiously, waiting for a reply.

"Maybe it was an old nickname," I said lamely.

"Perhaps," she said, shaking her head. "But you should have seen his face when he realized what he'd done. He looked. . ." She thought for a moment. "Scared. That's what I say . . . flat-out scared."

I thanked her and left with my bag. Okay, so now I had a first name. Garrett. It wasn't much, but it was something. On the walk back to the house, I went over the possibilities in my mind.

Maybe this Garrett person and the real Jacob Chandler changed identities. Like the prince and the pauper. Two people who for some reason wanted to leave their lives, start whole new ones without the hassle of inventing a new identity. Maybe there was a Garrett somebody living up in Alaska, happy and content with his children and grandchildren, carving walrus tusk or something. It happened.

Well, on soap operas anyway.

That only left one other possibility. That the real Jacob Chandler was dead. That he'd been dead for thirty-five years. That this Garrett somebody had stolen his identity and made a new life for himself.

Which meant the fake Jacob Chandler was possibly a murderer.

Suddenly all I wanted to do was run home and leave this whole mess. I made the decision to call Gabe as soon as I got to the house and tell him that I was abandoning this quest and would let the government have everything. If Jacob Chandler had gained everything he owned because he murdered an innocent man thirty-five years ago, I didn't want one penny of his money.

The phone was ringing when I walked through the

door. I caught it before the answering machine picked up.

"Hello!"

"Benni?" My cousin's voice sounded strange. "Thank goodness I got to you before anyone else.'"

Emory, what's wrong?"

"Sweetcakes, hold on to your hat. We've got ourselves a little hostage problem downtown here, and apparently the only person they'll speak to is you."

9

"WHAT?" I SPUTTERED. "WHO?"

"Take a breath, cousin. In a pecan shell, Dove and six of her friends have barricaded themselves in the Historical Museum and refuse to leave until the city agrees to give the museum back. They've called all the radio and television stations and, bless their radical little hearts, have stirred up quite a little tempest."

"What?" I yelled into the receiver.

"Yaow! he exclaimed. "Thank you kindly—I needed the wax cleaned out of that ear. Anyway, the only people they'll let in are you and me. But me *only* if I'm accompanied by you. Am I making sense here?"

"Does Gabe know?" I asked.

"I'm on my cellular, and he's standing right here. You can talk to him yourself."

"Benni?" Gabe's rich, baritone voice was not happy.

"What's going on?"

"All we know is that a phone call came in about a half hour ago that something was happening at the Historical Museum. A patrol car rolled on it and discovered Dove and her friends. She told the patrol officer through the

152

door that they're staying until the city agrees to sign a long-term lease. You'd better get down here."

"I'm on my way."

I drove the twelve miles from Morro Bay in record time. The streets in front of the Historical Museum were already cordoned off with yellow police line tape, so I had to park three blocks away. I clipped a leash on Scout and headed to the museum. The front lawn was crowded with tourists, about ten or so picketers, the news van from KKSC—our local television station— and a few uniformed officers. I walked over to where Gabe was standing beside Emory. His eyes blazed a bright blue; his jaw was as stiff as metal pipe. I looked up at the second floor of the Historical Museum. Outside of an upper museum window, flapping gently in the late morning breeze, hung the Fifty-four forty or Fight quilt Tina had been working on yesterday.

"Hi, guys," I said, touching my husband's arm tentatively. His face relaxed slightly. He reached down and gave Scout a quick chest rub.

"I'm glad you're here," Gabe said. "Go talk some sense into her."

I glanced at Emory, whose blond eyebrows raised slightly. *Not a chance,* they proclaimed, and I silently agreed. Gabe obviously didn't know Dove as well as he thought.

"I'll try," I said, handing the leash to Gabe. "Let's go, Emory."

We walked up the steps to the Historical Museum, and I could hear the voice of the reporter from the television station say, "Start rolling." Our ascent was recorded for replay on the four o'clock news.

We knocked on the wood-and-glass door, and a face peeked around the window shade that covered the upper

153

half. Edna McClun called, "Halt, who goes there?"

"Oh, for cryin' out loud, Edna, let them in," Dove's voice snapped.

The door opened a crack, and Emory and I squeezed in. Edna slammed the door behind us and bolted it. We followed her past the reception counter into the center of the museum, normally used for lectures and demonstrations.

I gazed around the room in amazement. There were cots, bags of groceries, and gallons and gallons of bottled water. I turned to my grandmother. "Dove, what in the heck is going on?"

"We're staying until the mayor changes his vote," June Rae Gates said.

I looked at Emory in dismay, but he didn't see my glance. He already had his notebook out and was taking notes.

"Make sure you spell my name right," Edna said. "It's M-c capital C-l-u-n."

"Yes, ma'am," he said, writing feverishly.

"Dove, you can't stay here," I said. "It's . . . it's . . ." For the life of me I couldn't think of one other thing to say.

"Honeybun," she said, "we have to get them to listen, and this seemed the best way. We've called CNN and the television stations in L.A. and San Francisco. The Gray Panthers and some other groups are going to take turns picketing. We're just trying to make a point. All we want is our museum to stay the way it is."

"How many of you are here?" Emory asked.

Dove turned away from me and said, "Seven. Eight if you want to count Elmo Ritter's cat. Fool man can't go anywhere without it."

"Seven," Emory murmured, his face thoughtful. Then it brightened. "The San Celina Seven!"

Dove smiled widely. "I like that, Emory." She turned to the others who had gathered around us. "See, I told you he was a clever boy."

I groaned. "Dove, the similarities between you and the Chicago Seven are tenuous at best."

"Sounds good, though," Elmo said, holding his hissing Siamese. He was the man yesterday with the French beret trying to get arrested. "We needed a hook. All good stories have a hook."

Emory grinned. "Elmo, you are my kind of man."

I chewed my bottom lip, trying to hold back the screaming fit I truly wanted to throw. "What," I said patiently to Dove, "do you want me and Emory to do?"

"Emory's already doing it," she said. "He's going to be our media source. You are going to be our hostage negotiator."

"Don't tell me you've got a hostage?" I felt my stomach drop. I hadn't seen the mayor out there . . . they wouldn't . . . no, they wouldn't . . . kidnapping was . . . "Please tell me everyone is here voluntarily."

"Of course we are," June Rae said. "She meant we're holding the building hostage until that ole backstabbing Boxstore Billy sees fit to change his vote." She turned to the tiny, white-haired lady standing next to her who looked vaguely familiar. "Sorry, Melva."

"It's all right, June Rae," the woman said, her diamond-studded hands flashing in dismissal of the remark. "I sure didn't raise him like that. That sneaky side comes from his father's genes. They were rum runners back in the Prohibition, you know."

"Oh, geeze," I said, "please don't tell me you're Mayor Davenport's mom."

She gave a dainty sniff. "I'm merely a concerned senior citizen who is fighting for a cause she believes in."

155

Emory gazed upward and crowed. "Oh, Lord, thank you. I'm going to win a Pulitzer."

I smacked Emory's arm with the back of my hand. "You're going to win a knuckle sandwich if you don't start helping me talk them out of this."

"Emory," Dove said, "you get all their names down, and Edna will fill you in on our demands. I need to talk to Benni alone." She grabbed my upper arm and hustled me to the storeroom behind the reception counter, closing the heavy oak door behind us.

"Dove," I started, "Are you out of your mind? It's against—"

"Now, hush, child. We aren't hurting a soul and we wouldn't do this if we weren't ready for it. We have plenty of water, food, good bathroom facilities, and everyone's heart medicine. And I didn't let anyone in on this who couldn't handle it healthwise. You know I'm not a foolish woman."

I leaned against the counter. "I know. It's just that I feel like I'm caught in the middle. You know how this looks for Gabe."

Her face grew pensive. "Honeybun, that's the only thing I regret. You know I'd never in a million years hurt Gabe, but it can't be helped. We can't just lay down and let those money-hungry politicians take away everything we've worked so hard for. We might be old, but we still have beliefs and feelings. Try and understand that."

I went over and put my arms around her. Her bones underneath my fingers felt so fragile and vulnerable. "I do, Gramma. I'm just worried."

She hugged me quickly, then pushed me away. "Now, there's something else I wanted to tell you. I'm probably not going to be home on Mother's Day since

Melva says that son of hers has a stubborn streak as long as a boa constrictor, so I wanted to tell you something."

"What's that?"

She gave me a long, searching look. "Your mama . . ." She paused, hesitating, then started again. "Your mama left you something that she wanted me to give you at a certain time of your life, and, well, I've been thinking, I'm getting along in years, and things aren't going the way she probably thought they would, and I'm sure not wanting you to find it after I pass on and wonder why I didn't give it to you before—"

"What is it, Dove?" I asked, breaking into her explanation.

She inhaled deeply, her pale blue eyes shiny. "Your mama has a baby blanket that was given to her by her girlfriends back in Sugartree, and she wanted me to give it to you when you had your first child, but . . ." Dove's voice trailed off, and she looked down at the ground.

"But it looks like that's not going to be happening," I finished for her. "It's okay, Dove. It's something I've been dealing with."

She looked back up. "There's still plenty of time for you and Gabe. Don't think there isn't."

I grabbed her pale, calloused hand whose touch was the only one I remember as a child. What had my mother's hands felt like? Why can't I remember? Were they work-roughened like Dove's or soft and smooth? Did she have long, beautiful nails or did she clip them off once a week like I always had? How had she touched me when she checked for a fever—with her palm or with the back of her hand? "I know, Dove."

"I just think there's times you have to rethink the promises you make people. If something happens to me,

I don't want you to thinking I was keeping something of your mama's from you."

I covered her hand with both of mine. "Nothing's going to happen to you," I said fiercely. "But thanks for telling me. Where is it?"

"It's in the top of my closest wrapped in a sheet," she said. "Talk to your daddy when you drop by and tell him I'm all right. I told him last night what we were going to do today, and he's not happy by a mile. See if you can soothe his nerves a little."

"I'll try. Now, you take care of yourself. Promise me you'll abandon this if any of you start feeling sick."

She smiled at me. "Don't you worry about us. We made it through the Depression."

When we came down the museum steps, Emory and I were bombarded by questions from reporters, bystanders, television people. Gabe pushed through the crowd, slipped his arm around me, and nodded at Emory to follow him. He walked us across the street, where the police had set up an Incident Command Post.

"Fill me in," Gabe said curtly.

"Where's Scout?" I asked, glancing around. He pointed to a tree a few feet away where Scout was tied. Three giggly teenage girls were giving him enough attention to last the rest of the week.

With Emory throwing in his two cents' worth every so often, I told Gabe what the senior citizens wanted. Just as I finished, the mayor, William Davenport himself, pushed into our small circle.

"Gabe, this is unacceptable," he said. "I demand you arrest those rabble-rousers. I don't care what their ages or who they are. That is city property they are holding hostage."

Gabe stared down at Mayor Davenport's thick head of

silver hair. "Bill, I'm finding out the details now."

The mayor turned to me and said, "This is the work of your gramma, young woman, and I'm warning you I'll see her in jail, I will. Don't think I won't." He poked my shoulder once with his forefinger.

Gabe grabbed the mayor's hand, his voice low and uncompromising. "Do that again, Bill, and I'll break it."

The mayor looked up at Gabe, surprised. His tanned face blushed dark red. "Your job is to uphold the law in this city."

"When and if there are arrests to be made in this situation, I'll order them. Right now, I think the prudent thing to do is wait and see what they have planned."

"I'll tell you what they have planned," he sputtered. "Making me look like a fool."

"Not a difficult task," I muttered. Gabe shot me an impatient look that said, *Your smart mouth is not appreciated right now.*

Next to me, a chuckle erupted from Emory.

"And what's so funny, young man?" the mayor snapped at Emory.

"Are you certain you want all the people involved booked and arrested?" my cousin asked. "That would give them criminal records, you know. All these sweet, nonviolent senior citizens."

"Yeah," I said. "Do you realize. . ." I stopped when Emory's face begged me to let him break the news. I held out my hand in acquiescence.

"I don't care," Mayor Davenport said. "Age doesn't give them the right to break the law." He turned back to Gabe. "I demand you take steps to remove them from the property."

Gabe said, his voice just barely tinged with sarcasm, "What do you propose I do, call in the SWAT team?

Throw in canisters of tear gas? What do you think that would do for your image?"

The mayor contemplated his reasoning for a moment. "All right, let's try to talk them out of there. But I don't want this turning into a media circus."

I gazed out over the milling crowd and thought, *Too late, buster.*

Gabe turned to Emory and said, "Do you have the names of the people inside?"

Emory's face almost split from his smile. "Yes, sir." He read off the names. "Dove Ramsey, Edna McClun, June Rae Gates, Elmo Ritter, Goldie Kleinfelder, Maria Ramirez, and Melva Davenport."

A strangled cry came from the mayor's throat. "What?"

Emory looked up and opened his eyes slightly with mock innocent curiosity. "Any relation to you, Mayor Davenport?"

A shocked expression spread over Gabe's face. Behind him, a couple of patrol officers burst into laughter, quieting only when Gabe gave them a stern look.

"This can't be," the mayor said. "My mother would never agree to something like this. It's kidnapping, plain and simple. They went down to her condo in Santa Maria and kidnapped her."

Gabe's face turned sober at the word. Kidnapping was a serious charge, and things were moving in an ominous direction.

"She's in there voluntarily," I said quickly. "I talked to her myself."

Mayor Davenport turned to me, his thin nostrils flaring. "It simply can't be."

I glared back at him. "I guess you don't know your

160

mother as well as you thought. She fooled you just like you fooled the people who voted . . ."

Before I could finish, Gabe's big hand closed around my elbow and firmly steered me a short distance away. "Benni, you're just adding fuel to the fire."

I jerked away from him. "I don't care. He's a creep."

"Nevertheless, right now we need less angry words, not more. Is it true that Mrs. Davenport is in there of her own free will?"

"Absolutely. She's pretty mad at her son and plans to stay the duration." I gave him a small smile. "She said his bad genes came from his father's side."

His thick mustache twitched slightly. "Let's not get into genetics here. Why don't you take Scout and leave for a while?"

"But Dove . . ."

He reached down and trailed a finger down my jaw, tapping it gently on my chin. "Don't worry about Dove and her friends. I'm going to have officers staked out twenty-four hours a day until this is resolved."

"I suppose," I said, my voice doubtful.

He stroked my cheek with the back of his hand. "Don't worry, *niña*, I'll make sure our *abuelita* is safe."

I nodded silently.

His eyes grew sharp and searching. "Is there something else?"

I touched his hand briefly. Now was definitely not the time to tell him about Mr. Chandler's stolen identity, about my plans to abandon this crazy inheritance. I'd just be there when he got home tonight and explain everything then. "No, I'm just worried." I kissed his palm. "I'll talk to you later."

I retrieved Scout from his teenage admirers and told Emory I'd be in touch. Then I drove out to the ranch to see my dad and find my mother's quilt. After a friendly but thorough sniff-off with the three ranch dogs, Scout flopped down on the porch.

Inside, Daddy was sitting at the breakfast counter eating a tomato and mayonnaise sandwich.

"How's Dove?" he asked.

"Fine."

He nodded at the pot of coffee on the counter. "Want some?"

"No, thanks," I said, sitting down next to him. I traced a finger over the tiny squares of the blue gingham tablecloth. "There's quite a hullabaloo going on downtown."

He nodded and kept eating. "Figured there would be."

"You okay with this?"

He grunted like an old bull. "Does it matter?"

I laughed lightly. "Guess not. She's gonna do what she's gonna do."

"That's a natural fact."

"You got enough food?"

"She left a bunch of casseroles. Reckon she's been planning this awhile."

"No doubt. Well, I'll keep you posted."

"Figured you would."

"I'm getting something out of her room." I paused for a moment. "She's giving me the baby quilt Mama's friends made."

A shadow passed across my father's face then was gone. "Well," he said, nodding. "Well, now."

I stood up. "Don't worry. Gabe's going to have officers posted twenty-four hours a day."

"I trust the boy. Always have."

"So have I."

"So, then." He ate the last of his sandwich and

162

drained his coffee cup. "Got some fence down over in the west pasture. I'll be over there most the afternoon."

I nodded, picked up his empty dishes, and set them in the sink.

Entering Dove's room without her there seemed almost sacrilegious to me. It smelled slightly of the Jean Nate talcum powder she often used and strongly from cedar—she was crazy for cedar chips, believing they kept away everything from moths to mice to head colds to gout. Her old cherry wood Shaker-style furniture—head-and footboard, chest of drawers, one nightstand—were more familiar to me than any piece of furniture I'd ever owned. I sat on her double bed for a moment, studying for the thousandth time the pink and mint-green Arkansas Snowflake quilt. I was eight years old when she and her friends quilted it—in one day—while I lay underneath the quilt rack reading *Black Beauty*. I could close my eyes and still remember the murmuring sound of their voices; the thick, warm summer air; the restless shuffling of their feet; the sight of the fabric pushing toward me as their needles rocked through the layers of cloth. I remember the taste of the lemon cake one of the women brought, how it tasted just like the lemonade Dove had made, and how tickled they got when someone made a joke I've long forgotten about men and puckered lips.

I stood up and opened her closet doors. Using a footstool, I looked over the neatly hung flowered blouses and jeans to the top of the closet. Back in the corner, under a teetering bunch of shoe boxes wrapped in a faded blue sheet, lay the quilt. Holding back the shoe boxes with one hand, I pulled it out.

I spread the small signature quilt across her bed. It was a Sawtooth Star pattern with sixteen eight-inch squares. The fabrics were primarily pinks and pale blues with a muslin backing, which told me they had probably started the quilt before I was born, since back in the fifties parents didn't have the medical means to find out the baby's sex ahead of time. Embroidered names, vines, flowers, and messages decorated ten of the blocks. "When this you see, remember me—Ida Pendleton." "Welcome, Little One—Rose Mae Lovelis." "Love to the Little One—Glessie Wilcox." "Bless you and the little baby—June Willows." "Happiness Always—Caroline Maplegrove." "Love from your sister-in-heart—Gwen Swanson." "Friendship is a Sheltering Tree—Agnes Bickles." "Hands to Work, Hearts to God—Elizabeth Clark." "Train up a child in the way he should go—Proverbs 22:6—Carlene Kelligrew." "As the twig is bent, so grows the child—Congratulations—Juby Renault."

The border was a Wild Goose Chase pattern of running triangles. The quilting wasn't elaborate, but precise and neat. I turned the quilt over to look for a quilt label and was in luck. Back before quilting started its renaissance in the late sixties, it was still considered a craft for bored housewives or old ladies sewing for missionary causes. Not many women back then thought to record the date or the maker of the quilt. These ladies did, though, and the white cotton label said in beautiful, curlicue script: *Presented to Alice Louise Banks by her loving friends in honor of the birth of her first child— Young Women's Sunday School Class—Little Rock First Baptist Church—March 1, 1958.* Twenty-two days before I was born.

I reread each name, studying their signatures and messages, imagining what these women talked about as they stitched the quilt, who they were to my mother, what their problems were, where they were now.

164

The quilt looked almost brand-new. Did she ever lay it over me or did she keep it wrapped up, a memory of the friends who so carefully put in every one of these tiny stitches? I read over the names again, a vague déjà vu feeling coming over me. Then it occurred to me. The autograph book in Mr. Chandler's trunk. This was the second time in less than a week I'd read the long-ago sentiments of a group of people. I glanced over the names on the quilt again, and suddenly one jumped out at me.

Gwen Swanson.

I jumped up and ran into the living room where I'd left my purse, emptying it on the floor, pawing through it until I found the pocket-size notebook where I'd recorded the names of the people in the autograph book.

Gwen Swanson.

I sat down on the floor, my heart racing like it was going for a trophy.

A coincidence? I wanted to think so. But I knew it wasn't. Somebody named Gwen Swanson had signed an autograph book in the possession of this stranger. Gwen Swanson was also a friend of my mother's.

There it was.

The thinly threaded link between Mr. Chandler—or whoever he was—and me.

My mother.

I clutched the notebook against my chest, frozen, not knowing what to think, where to go from here.

My mother and . . .

And who?

Any plans I had of abandoning the search for Mr. Chandler's real identity were over now. I didn't have a choice but to see this thing through all the way to the end, whatever that might be.

165

10

IT WAS PAST THREE O'CLOCK WHEN I RETURNED TO Morro Bay. I called Gabe's office, and Maggie, his secretary, informed me he'd gone back to the museum after a morning full of meetings about the incident.

"That grandma of yours is a real kick in the pants," she said, her voice going into a high-pitched, delightful laugh.

"I'm sure this will look a lot funnier to me in retrospect," I said with a sigh.

"You'll be able to dine out on this story for years," she assured me. "Like I said, the Grand Poobah's been here and gone already."

After telling her I'd track him down eventually, I spread the baby blanket over the sofa to look at it again. I pulled out the autograph book and turned to the page Gwen Swanson had signed. There was no doubt about it—the signatures were the same.

What now?

I sat for a moment on the sofa staring at the quilt, then pulled it up to my face and inhaled. What did I expect to smell? I had no conscious memories of my mother's scent, just a vague one of her voice. My recollections of my mother were as hazy as the perpetual morning fog surrounding Morro Rock. I was barely six when she died of breast cancer, and my image of her was intermingled with that of my first grade teacher, Miss Rodale. My teacher had been a skinny, ginger-haired woman who smelled of spearmint and had long, beige teeth that she covered with a pink-nailed hand whenever she laughed too hard. She was gone when I returned to second grade the next year, and I assumed with the

166

skewed logic of a seven-year-old that she died like my mother had in late June when the wild mustard and monkey flowers were blooming a cheerful yellow on the hills around our ranch. For years I took it for granted that any adult who moved out of my own personal sphere had died, until I grew old enough to understand that there were places outside of San Celina where people continued to live their lives.

I remember very little about my mother's funeral; what I do recall is tinged with a child's dramatic memory—my father on a rearing horse, cursing and angry, bringing it under control with a crop and racing down the long driveway at the ranch; the sharp, sickening scent of carnations; the cold, sweet taste of chocolate icebox pie that someone fed me, the meringue dissolving like sugared air on my tongue. I remember waking up in Dove's bed, the very one I sat on this afternoon. It was dark, and she was lying next to me, still wearing her silky Sunday dress. I lay there for the longest time stroking the sleeve and listening to her breathe.

Daddy and I didn't discuss my mother much as I was growing up. Though he was as Southern as the rest of the Ramsey clan, I'd heard it said by my aunts that when he moved to the Central Coast from Arkansas, he'd taken on a Western taciturnity that seemed to suit his personality better. Most of what I knew about my mother was gleaned from Dove.

I was born in Arkansas, and we came to California when I was barely three, using the small insurance settlement from her parents' fatal car accident to put a down payment on the Ramsey Ranch. Dove had encouraged them to leave even though she'd miss her oldest son, because she knew he needed to start his own

167

life. He'd carried the burden of being a man since he was fourteen and his own daddy died, leaving Dove with five kids to raise. Later, when Mama was dying, Dove sold her farm, packed up her last child living at home, my uncle Arnie, and came west to help.

I left the quilt spread out on the bed and took Scout out to the backyard. While contemplating this latest discovery, I sat on the bench under the pepper tree and tossed a tennis ball to him. Should I tell Gabe about this new information? The situation in San Celina worried me, and though I knew Gabe wouldn't let Dove be hurt or arrested, I also knew how hard this was for him, the narrow fence he was being forced to walk. Though I desperately wanted to share with him the connection between Mr. Chandler and my mother, I also didn't want to add to his stress. I'd give him a day to get used to the situation with Dove and tell him about this tomorrow. Until then, I'd just keep digging.

The question was where? I tossed the ball against the fence, and Scout bounded after it. Just watching his joy at the game relaxed me and put me in a less agitated state of mind.

The gate in the fence opened, and Rich stepped through. Scout ran over to him with the ball. Rich grabbed it from his mouth and tossed it straight up in the air. Scout jumped like a puppy, causing me to laugh out loud.

"You should do that more often," he said, coming over and sitting down next to me.

"I would if there was more to laugh about."

"So, what's new on the investigation?"

I hesitated, tempted to tell him about the discovery of my mother's connection with Mr. Chandler. But my loyalty toward Gabe stopped me. If I wasn't going to tell my husband, I shouldn't tell anyone.

"My friend, the potter, suggested I try Harmony. It's a little town up the coast where a lot of artists live and work. He said maybe someone there would recognize the pot. And there's still the Wood-carvers' Guild. Maybe somebody there . . ." Before I could finish, Scout stood up, tail wagging, and Beau Franklin walked around the corner.

"I came by at ten o'clock, and you weren't here," he said, his eyes boring down on me.

My hand flew to my cheek. "Oh, Mr. Franklin, I'm so sorry. I completely forgot about our appointment. I . . . there was a family emergency in the city and, oh, I'm really sorry."

He scowled at me. "My time is valuable."

"Please sit down, and we'll talk now. Would you like something to drink?"

He shook his head and stood there, his arms folded across his broad chest.

"You need me to stay?" Rich asked in a low voice.

"No, I'll be fine," I said. "Thanks, anyway."

Rich gave Beau an unsubtle, warning look, then left through the side gate. "Come over when you're through," he called over his shoulder. "I've made tamales."

"I'll be there." I turned back to Mr. Franklin. "I have a couple of questions about Mr. Chandler, if you don't mind."

"Before your questions, I have something to tell you. Jake Chandler owed me ten thousand dollars, and I want it back."

I was speechless for a moment. "Ten thousand dollars?" Then I became suspicious. "For what?"

"None of your concern for what," he said, his arms still folded. "I want a cashier's check and I want it today."

169

I looked at him for a long moment, then said, "Just a minute. I'll be right back." Inside the house I dialed Amanda. Fortunately she was in her office. I explained quickly what Mr. Franklin was demanding.

"Not unless he's got some kind of proof," Amanda said. "A notarized note or something. Don't let him bamboozle you, cowgirl. Without proof, he can't get a dime from Jacob Chandler's estate."

Back outside, I informed Mr. Franklin of my attorney's demand for proof.

"My word is my proof," he snapped. "I gave him ten thousand dollars in cash to invest for me, and I want that money back."

I folded my arms across my chest. "Sorry. Until I have proof I'm not paying anything. You could just be trying to scam me."

He jumped up from the bench. "Young woman, you're going to regret this."

"I'm sorry," I said. "Until you have proof . . ."

His cheeks flushed a splotchy red. Scout sensed his anger and immediately came to my side and sat down, his German shepherd ear alert. I slipped my hand under his collar and felt him tremble with anticipation. "I think you'd better leave," I said.

He jabbed a finger at the air in front of me. "I'll get my money one way or another." He turned and walked away.

When he'd turned the corner, I sank to my knees and buried my face in Scout's neck. A hand touching my hair startled me, and I jerked my head up.

"Are you all right, *mija*?" Rich asked. He held a tire iron in his other hand.

I stood up and gave a shaky laugh. "I'm fine. He's just not happy with what my attorney said to tell him about the money he says he's owed."

I glanced at the tire iron and gave him an accusing look. "You were listening the whole time."

He grinned sheepishly. "So sue me."

"For heaven's sake, what were you going to do, start a rumble?"

"Hey, don't think I can't. I grew up in Quatro Milpas."

"Where?"

"A barrio in south Phoenix. It's a mountain preserve now, but back then you didn't mess with us *vatos*."

I held up my hands and laughed. "Okay, okay, sorry to doubt your warrior capabilities. Amanda, my attorney, says he doesn't have a legal leg to stand on. With no proof that Mr. Chandler owed him money, I have nothing to worry about."

His dark face grew troubled. "Legally, maybe not. But I'm afraid he's not concerned with legalities at the moment."

"Mr. Franklin is just full of hot air. When he calms down, I'll talk with him again and see if he'll give me any information about what it was he and Mr. Chandler were involved with. If it sounds believable, then maybe I'll consider paying it."

"Believable it might be," he said. "It's legal I'm worried about."

"What do you mean?"

"I mean this Chandler guy doesn't sound on the up-and-up, and that makes me think that anything he'd be involved with wouldn't be either."

"Like what?"

"Like anything illegal. Drugs are the first thing that come to mind."

"Mr. Chandler a drug pusher? You're beginning to sound like Gabe."

"Your husband isn't a stupid man, Benni. I'd tell him about this incident as soon as possible."

"I will."

"And watch your back, young lady."

"Believe me, I've gotten real good at that." I patted his shoulder. "Now, where are those tamales you promised me?"

After another wonderful dinner where Rich entertained me with stories from his many years of fire fighting, I went home a little before eight o'clock, exhausted from the emotional highs and lows of the day. I called home and caught Gabe, who assured me that Dove and her fellow conspirators were well guarded and that negotiations were still in progress.

"I'll be up there first thing tomorrow morning to see if a night on Army cots has weakened their resolve," he said.

"She's pretty stubborn when she wants something."

"A family trait."

I didn't comment.

He cleared his throat and said, "Meet me at the Historical Museum at eight A.M. in case I need you to talk to them."

"You got it, Friday." Then I told him about the incident with Beau Franklin.

"Just what I was afraid of. Did he threaten you?"

"Not me personally. He just said he'd get his money one way or another."

Gabe was silent a moment. "I'll do some checking into his background. Be careful."

"I will," I said, glad he didn't make an effort to talk me out of pursuing this. There was no way I could stop now, though I wasn't ready yet to tell him why.

Since it was too late to head out to Harmony, I spent

172

the rest of the evening studying every aspect of my mother's quilt and rereading the autograph book, looking for a clue to Mr. Chandler's identity. I thought about trying to track down these women and seeing if any of them knew of someone named Garrett in my mother's life. That would take more extensive investigating abilities than I had at my disposal, but there was always Gabe's private detective friend. He probably had all sorts of CD-ROMS that could locate the current status and addresses of these women. I redialed my home phone, then hung up before it rang, realizing in a split second that Gabe would want to know why I wanted these women traced, which would naturally lead into the fact that Mr. Chandler was somehow connected to my mother. I would have to figure out a way to find these women myself. Maybe Amanda knew of a private investigator.

By ten o'clock my eyelids were already drooping, so I went to bed. Scout's presence in his bed next to me was all the security I needed to fall asleep in a few minutes.

The clock radio next to my bed said 1:32 A.M. when Scout's barking jerked me out of a sound sleep.

I bolted straight up, my heart pounding. Scout dashed out of the bedroom, barking, then ran back in. I grabbed the pair of sweats lying across the foot of my bed and jammed my legs into them, awkwardly hopping toward the door.

As I reached the front door, a figure appeared in the filmy glass. I hesitated a moment before turning on the porch light.

"Benni!" Rich's voice yelled from behind the door. "Wake up!" I fumbled with the lock and flung the door open. "Your garage is on fire!"

I followed him out to the front yard where a fire truck

had just pulled up, followed by two Morro Bay police cars and the paramedics. The garage was already half engulfed in thick smoke. I grabbed Scout's collar and pulled him close. In the next few minutes, the small alley turned into a teeming mass of firefighters and hoses. In twos and threes, neighbors came to their doors and watched the spectacle. I looked over at the Briggstone house. Tess, Cole, and Duane all stood on their front porch, their faces so shadowed no expressions were visible. Next door to them, the photographer and his wife and a couple I assumed to be the Pelican Inn's managers also watched the fire. Adrenaline careened through my veins as I watched the firefighters spray the garage. When I started to shake in the damp misty air, I felt Rich's arm go around my shoulder.

"It'll be okay," he said, squeezing my shoulder.

"What happened?" I asked. "Did you call the fire department?"

"Your guardian angel was working overtime, *mija*. I had insomnia and got up to get something to read when I smelled smoke. Looked out my side window and saw your garage on fire. I dialed 911 before I came over."

For the next fifteen minutes, we silently watched the firefighters bring the fire under control. When they were finished, the roof and one wall was completely gone, and the car inside badly scorched. The arson investigator arrived shortly after the fire truck and police cars.

"I'll be back," Rich said and walked over to the tall, gray-haired man wearing a dark blue windbreaker. They talked for a few minutes, then came over to where I was standing.

"Ms. Harper, I'm John Sterling. I'll be investigating

this fire. Do you mind answering a few questions?"

I shook my head no and answered all his questions as thoroughly as possible—what time I came home, when was the last time I was in the garage, was there a gas mower or gas can in the garage, were garage doors and windows locked, was the window on the alley side broken the last time I looked, was anyone mad at me?

That last question caused me to glance at Rich. He nodded at me, and I told Sterling briefly about the situation with the house and about the Briggstones. Before he could answer, Gabe's Corvette pulled up. His red emergency light was hooked on his dashboard, so I knew he must have been really worried. He hated using it. He hopped out of the car and came over to where we were standing.

"Are you all right?" he asked, placing both his hands on my shoulders, kneading them gently. Though his face was dark and intense, his familiar touch caused my tight muscles to relax. Scout whined and pushed his body against my leg.

"Yes, Rich saw the fire and called 911. Then he came and woke me."

He turned to the two men and asked, "What's the story?"

"John Sterling, Arson Investigation," the man said, holding out his hand. "You are?"

Gabe shook it quickly. "Sorry, I'm a little tense. Gabe Ortiz, San Celina Police. Ms. Harper is my wife."

Mr. Sterling gave a sympathetic smile. "Well, I don't know much yet because I haven't gotten in there to poke around, but the captain over there said it appears by the burn pattern on the floor that it started in a small trash can on the west wall. Most likely an accelerant of some kind—lighter fluid or gasoline. I'll know more once I can check it out. It'll probably take an hour or two for me to make an assessment."

When my shivering became too much to hide, Gabe, after thanking Rich for his help, convinced me to go inside the house. Once we were alone, he hit the roof, as I expected. "It could have spread in minutes to the house. You could have been killed. I want you home *now*."

"You know that's not possible," I said, my teeth chattering slightly in spite of myself.

"No, I don't know that."

"I'm sorry, Gabe, I just can't quit."

"*Carajo!* Does the money mean that much to you?"

"It's not the money."

He was silent for a long moment, watching me. "All right," he finally said, his voice tired.

It was past three A.M. when the fire department finished mopping up and the arson investigator finished his second set of questions, promising to send me a copy of the report for my insurance claim. While Mr. Sterling questioned me again, Gabe had gone outside to speak to a Morro Bay police officer who had come back to check things out.

"I don't want any special treatment," I told Gabe when he came back into the house. He didn't answer. A few minutes later he reluctantly left, but not before he hugged me and said, "I'll call you *mañana. Te amo.*"

I clung to him for a moment. "I love you, too, Friday."

Standing in the doorway, I watched him hesitate at his car as he looked over at the Briggstone house, which was dark now.

"Gabe, not tonight," I called softly from the doorway. "No one's going to try anything more tonight."

He gave a curt nod and repeated that he'd call me in the morning.

I finally settled back into bed, but sleep eluded me. I lay in bed listening to Scout give wild little moans while stalking dream rabbits, and watched the room change from black to soft gray to pale orange. Finally at six-thirty I gave up and went to fix myself a pot of coffee. Pure caffeine and a lot of it was definitely going to be on my day's menu. Standing at the kitchen window waiting for the coffee to finish, I stared at the garage's blackened walls. Who set the fire? My first thought was the Briggstones, then Beau Franklin. But why? Did they think it would drive me away so that the will was broken? Maybe I should just make it clear to them that even if I failed, they wouldn't get a penny. Maybe then they'd leave me alone. If, of course, it *was* them pulling these pranks.

I'd definitely have to look further into it, but my first stop would be town to see how the San Celina Seven had managed through their first night, then off to Harmony, a play on words that amused me even with only a few hours sleep. Harmony was something in short supply in my life these days.

The photographer and his wife from the motel across the street were walking by when I got into the truck at around seven-thirty. The huge aquamarine ring on her right hand caught the sunlight and flashed.

"Nice day," he commented.

"Guess you're going to take advantage of it," I said.

"As they say, make hay."

His wife rolled her eyes at his remark. She nodded in the direction of my garage. "You all right?"

"Yeah, fine." I didn't elaborate, and she didn't either.

At a quarter to eight I pulled up in front of the

177

Historical Museum. No reporters were around this early, but Gabe was already there at the command post talking to a patrol officer.

"Oh, good, you're here," I said, walking up to them. "Saves me a phone call to check in and tell you I'm fine. What's going on?"

"We called them about a half hour ago," Gabe said. Pale lavender circles tinged the skin under his eyes. He glanced down at his watch. "They'll see you and Emory at four and give another statement then."

"I'll be here." He looked so tired I didn't want to burden him with more problems, but I wanted to tell him what I'd found out from Rowena Ludlam before any more time passed. "Can we talk in private for a moment?"

"Let's walk," he said.

As we walked, I told him about my phone call from Rowena Ludlam and the undeniable fact that because of the missing finger, my Jacob Chandler was not the original Jacob Chandler.

"I'm not surprised," he said. "That's probably the reason he has so little credit history. Trying to keep a low profile. After that fire last night, I'm really worried now."

We stopped in front of the steel bear and Chumash Indian girl fountain next to the mission. The trickling water, normally a soothing sound, didn't ease the turmoil inside me as I watched his troubled face.

"Do you think he was hiding because of something illegal?" I asked.

He stuck his hands deep into his pockets. "I'd say you could count on it. Not many people disappear into deep cover just on a lark." His eyes turned gray and serious. "The question remains what happened to the real Jacob

178

Chandler, and did your Mr. Chandler have anything to do with it?" He looked away. "I want you to drop this whole crazy thing even more now."

"I know." There was nothing more to be said. I wouldn't, and he knew it. But at least we'd come far enough that we wouldn't argue about it. Now would be the perfect time to tell him about Mr. Chandler's connection to my mother, but something in me couldn't yet, not just to save him more stress, but because it was still so confusing and troubling that I had to keep it to myself until I grew used to the idea.

"I'll talk to Hank and see if he can keep an extra close eye on those two lowlifes across the street from you." Hank was Morro Bay's police chief.

"I don't actually know if it was them, though they're my first guess."

"It won't hurt to have someone talk to them."

I nodded without answering, leaving it up to him. Just like me, he had to do the things he felt were right.

"What are you doing today?" he asked.

"I'm going to Harmony to see if anyone there recognizes the maker of the pot I told you about last night."

"And then?"

I shrugged. "Depends on where the pot leads me. I'll be back here by four o'clock, no matter what. I promise."

He put his hand underneath my hair, his fingers lightly massaging my neck. I closed my eyes briefly in pleasure. "You know," he said, "I love Dove as much as if she were my blood grandmother . . ."

I leaned into him, touching my head to his shoulder, and sighed. "I'm trying to talk her out of this, really I am."

He kissed the top of my head. "I know."

I looked up at him. "Let's look at the bright side. How long can Dove really last?"

We stared at each other a moment, then burst into laughter.

"I don't even want to think about it," Gabe said. "I swear, I'd buy the friggin' museum myself and give it to them if it were possible."

"You and me both," I replied.

The coastal drive to the town of Harmony had always been one of the prettiest drives in the county, especially in the spring when the deep green hills contrasted with the ocean's cobalt blue, white-tipped waves. Thousands of tourists each year drove this stretch of State Highway 1 heading to Hearst Castle, Big Sur, and Monterey, some of them stopping at Harmony, intrigued by its improbable but hopeful name.

It was said the town's peaceful name dated from the 1890s when a feud between locals over the location of a road started with shouting and proceeded to shooting. After a death occurred, some wise dairy farmers organized a truce, and in the spirit of peace, the town was named Harmony after the Harmony Valley Creamery of the same name. Now a town of thirty or so people, it was privately owned and operated as an arts and crafts Mecca. It consisted of one street with five or six buildings, the largest one the old white Harmony Valley Creamery Association, which now held a pasta restaurant and various shops that displayed local artists' sculptures, blown glass, and pottery. I parked the truck in front of the paint-peeled dairy building and walked into the courtyard carrying the box containing the pot. Benches made from old wagon wheels and varnished boards crowded the red brick courtyard, stained wine barrels overflowed with wildflowers and asparagus fern, and ancient wood-burning cookstoves sprouted yellow marigolds from their burners. It was quiet and peaceful, so perfectly in tune with the town's name that I wanted to sit on one of the rustic benches and watch the blackbirds flit among the olive trees, smelling the sweet, dusty scents coming from the herb gardens that meandered around the rusty metal sculptures. A Thursday morning in early May was obviously not one of their busier times. But I had no time to linger. My destination was a weathered white barn in the back. "Pottery Works" was painted in black calligraphy letters over the heavy sliding wood door. Inside the airy room, haunting music, the kind that might make you dream of swimming whales, radiated from hidden speakers. No one greeted me when I entered, so I wandered around the room, admiring the pottery and sculptures, recognizing some of the work from members of our co-op, but finding none that resembled the pot in my arms.

"Can I help you find something?" The voice, as soft and full as the music, seemed to float from nowhere.

The sixtyish woman came out from behind a doorframe covered by an Indian-style curtain. Her long gray hair hung in two braids tied with leather strips. She wore an electric-blue fringed suede jacket and black leggings. The fringe slapped against her body as she walked toward me.

"Actually, you can," I said, holding up my box. "I was given this pot as a gift, and I was wondering if you could identify the potter."

"I can certainly try." She gestured over to the counter.

I set the box on the counter and carefully pulled the pot out of the shaved paper packing. Her powdered face lit up in a smile.

181

"Oh," she said with a sigh. "Haven't seen one of those in a long while." She stroked it with her fingertips. Her nails were painted the same bright blue as her jacket. "It's an original Azanna Nybak. One of her early works, if I don't miss my guess."

"Azanna Nybak?"

"Wonderful artist. A fifth-generation San Celinan," she said, her eyes never leaving the pot. "She lives by herself on her family's ranch outside of Cayucos past Eagle Rock Reservoir and doesn't come to town but once a year for the lighting of the Christmas tree. Sends one of her ranch hands in for supplies a couple of times a month." She looked up from the pot and raised her gray eyebrows. "How did you say you got this again? She hasn't made a pot in years—not since her two sons were killed in a boating accident in Mexico. This is worth quite a bit of money. Offhand, I know of half a dozen people who'd pay you top dollar for it."

"It's not for sale. It was a gift. Do you think she'd talk to me?"

She shook her head, doubtful. "She likes to be left alone. Last person who showed up uninvited at her ranch was chased off with a shotgun."

"Oh," I said, biting my lip in disappointment. I was certain that this pot, and this Azanna person, held the clue to the next step. Did it even occur to Jacob Chandler that maybe this woman wouldn't want to be a part of his little game?

The woman ran her fingers through the suede fringe on the front of her jacket, untangling it. "Why do you want to see her?"

I thought for a moment. I was growing tired of repeating this strange story, but unless I told her, I'd end up at a dead end.

182

"How positively intriguing!" she exclaimed after hearing a condensed version of my quest.

"So, do you think there's any way you or someone you know could arrange for me to speak with her? I won't take much of her time."

She held up a finger. "Wait here." She walked through the curtains and was gone for about ten minutes. While waiting, I carefully packed the pot back into the box. A huge smile covered her lined face when she returned.

"Good news, Benni Harper. I called, and she said she'd see you. Get back on Highway One and turn off on Crazy Creek Road. Go past Eagle Rock Reservoir and keep going. It's about ten miles. When you come to an old almond grove, that's the turnoff for her ranch. Follow the dirt road another three miles and you're there."

"Thanks." I picked up the box and headed for my truck.

I was already speeding down Pacific Coast Highway toward Crazy Creek Road when I realized she'd called me by name—and that I'd never given it to her. As I drove I couldn't help but wonder now that I knew of the tenuous yet certain connection of Mr. Chandler to my mother if this Azanna Nybak knew my mother.

Within twenty minutes the reservoir appeared to my left. Eagle Rock Reservoir was a place I used to sneak off to with high school friends at night when we'd told our parents we'd be in town at the movies. We'd park our trucks along the side of the rarely used road and scoot down the small dirt embankment on the heels of our boots to throw rocks into the dark water and spook each other with fake bear sounds. At the old almond grove I turned onto a dirt road and followed it past well-maintained corrals and ancient wooden calf chutes.

I turned a corner, and the house appeared. It was a white, three-story farmhouse with a picket fence covered with blue morning glories and flowering honeysuckle. A small widow's walk jutted out from a third-story window. The yard was as neat as a store-bought pie and at this moment empty, except for a six-foot bronze sculpture of a nude man and woman, limbs intertwined, faces not on each other but heavenward. I parked next to it, scattering the black-speckled chickens and three spectacular peacocks pecking at its base. I climbed out of the truck and read the small plaque on the sculpture—"Love Looking."

The barn, as clean and white as the house, lay to my left; a gazebo with one high-back wicker chair lay to the right of the yard. A finely groomed black cocker spaniel trotted out from behind the house to greet me. He ran his nose up and down my legs, smelling Scout's scent.

"You don't look like a ranch dog," I said, stooping to pet him.

He barked, and at that moment the sound of a shotgun blast tore through the air. I flinched and instinctively ducked. Unperturbed, the spaniel kept wagging his stubby tail.

The sound came from behind the house. I pocketed my keys and cautiously followed the second shot. When I came around the corner I encountered the shooter standing at the edge of the used brick patio. I watched this six-foot-tall woman, wearing a green and gold paisley caftan and spiky hair the color of red wine, as she calmly called "pull" to the young cowboy in leather chaps. He pulled the lever on a homemade skeet shooter, and a clay pigeon shot into the deep blue sky. I watched her fire at five in a row, and though she wore a black rhinestone-studded patch on one eye, she didn't miss one. Without speaking, she nodded at the cowboy. He stood up and walked away from us, his ringing spurs the only sound in the quiet. The woman turned and looked at me with one kohl-ringed aquamarine eye.

"Have a seat, Benni Harper," she said, pointing toward a couple of redwood lawn chairs with cushions made of red crushed velveteen.

I sat down. The cocker spaniel flopped down at my feet with a giant sigh, laying his head on my feet. I reached down and stroked his head.

"Typical man," she said, sitting next to me and nodding at the dog. "Fickle as a . . ." She paused for a moment and laughed, a laugh as deep and velvety as our chairs' cushions. "As a man, by golly. There's nothing else to compare them to."

"Ms. Nybak, I came to see you . . ." I started.

She held up a hand that seemed to belong to a different woman than this brilliant peacock sitting in front of me. Hers were ranchwoman hands—brown and calloused and square-nailed. "I know why you're here. When did he die?"

I told her what I knew of Jacob Chandler's death and about his funeral. "I'm sorry. I would have contacted you, but he didn't leave an address book."

She waved her hand in absolution. "That was Jake. He loved his secrets. And his games."

"So I've discovered."

Her smile was sad. "He was a lonely man. We understood each other."

Impatient, I asked, "Do you have something for me?"

Her arched eyebrows rose at my tone. "You have two weeks, my dear. Relax and enjoy the journey. Would you like some sun tea?" She rang a silver bell on the

185

table next to her. In a minute or so, a different young cowboy in Wranglers, a blue chambray shirt, and a silver and gold platter-shaped buckle came out of the back door carrying a tray with a very old-looking blue and white teapot, two delicate matching teacups, and a plate of poppy seed tea cakes. He set it on a round redwood table in front of us.

"Thank you, dear," Azanna said to him. "Did the salt mix we order arrive at Farm Supply?"

"Yes, ma'am. I'm driving into Paso this afternoon to fetch it."

"Very good. Have a couple of beers at the Rawhide and put them on my tab. You've worked hard this week."

"Thank you, Miss Nybak. Would you like me to pour?"

"No, dear, I can do it. Carry on."

He nodded, then, without a glance at me, he turned and went back inside the house.

A bronze sculpture fine enough for a museum sitting in the yard with the chickens and peacocks, cowboys with the manners of English butlers, a sharpshooting woman with rancher's hands and a queen's demeanor. Alice's Looking Glass had nothing on me.

I waited, realizing it was probably futile to try to rush this whole scenario. I crossed my legs, trying to keep my jittery foot still.

She poured us both tea, offered me a linen napkin and a tea cake, and when we'd both eaten one, she spoke again.

"Don't be too impatient with Jake. I told him this might make you angry, but he insisted that he wanted to do it." She stopped for a moment, her eyes misting. "I didn't know it would happen quite this soon, though. It was a heart attack, you say?"

186

"That's what the coroner thinks. They found him at home. Well, actually a neighbor did."

"Tess Briggstone, I'll venture to say."

"Yes."

She shook her head. "He cared about her, but those sons of hers are bad news, and she won't ever see it. How're they handling you inheriting Jake's estate?"

"Not too well." She and Jake had obviously been good enough friends that he told her all about this ridiculous scavenger hunt he'd concocted.

"How's that handsome police chief husband of yours dealing with this?"

"How do you know so much about me?"

"Jake, of course. He'd been following your life for a long while. But then, I guess you probably have found that out."

"Why?" I asked.

"Can't tell you that, my dear. Old Jake might rise up from the grave and smite me. We were good friends, Jake and I. Very good friends. Without him, I would have never made it through the death of my sons. That's where I met him, you know. In Mexico, when I went down to try to get their bodies." Her one turquoise-colored eye misted over. "I would do anything for him."

"What was he doing in Mexico?" I asked.

"I have no idea. He was very conversant in the language. Spent quite a bit of time there, I assumed. I don't know how he did it, who he paid off or how much, because he wouldn't tell me, but I got my sons' bodies in one day. He wouldn't let me pay him, so I sold him the house you're living in for a good price. He wanted to settle down in this area without any fuss, and I helped him do that."

"You did?"

"The house was built by my maternal grandfather. He was a sea captain and a woodworker, built those teak bookshelves himself. I knew it would suit Jacob, and being fiercely single, I have no one to leave it to. Are you comfortable there?"

"Yes," I said, still shocked.

She smiled at me and sipped her tea. "This ranch came from my father's side, in case you were wondering."

"So, what now?" I asked, setting my half-finished tea on the table.

She pulled an envelope out of a hidden pocket in her paisley caftan and handed it to me. "This is my part of the relay."

I opened the plain white envelope and found another hand-printed note and a black and white matchbook. "Zalba's French Basque Restaurant, Bakersfield, California." I opened it up to find . . . matches.

"This is it?" I asked.

"That's it. And I'll be honest with you, I have no idea what it means. I'm assuming someone at this restaurant has something to give you."

"When did he give you this?"

"About six or seven months ago." She looked down in sadness. "He never told me he was having heart problems."

I fingered the smooth book of matches. "Did you ever know anyone named Alice Ramsey?"

"The name doesn't sound familiar."

"How about Alice Louise Banks?" I asked, trying my mother's maiden name.

She shook her head no.

I looked at her for a long moment, at a loss for something else to ask. The thing that was so frustrating

188

about this situation was my lack of control. I was being forced to float along the current this man had set in motion, like a raft on a treacherous, unpredictable river. I stood up and held out my hand. "Thank you for the tea and cake, Ms. Nybak."

She rose and stood looking down at me, adjusting the black rhinestone eyepatch with her rancher's hand. "I'm sorry I can't make this easier for you, Benni. He was my good friend. Once, something more. This was his last request."

"I understand," I said. Only I didn't. I didn't understand the point of this man's ridiculous, tyrannical game.

When I reached the highway, I pulled over at the first scenic vista, found a comfortable seat on the rocks overlooking the ocean, and read his folded note. It was, as I expected, another lesson in wood carving.

You cannot beat wood into compliance. Wood responds to a gentle touch. You must cajole, not demand. If you honor wood, it will tell you the secrets hidden in its depths. Wood has personality. It can be hard or soft, easy to work with or difficult as an old uncle. There are many paths to good work. Beautiful carvings have resulted from flawed wood, and bad carvings have come from apparently unflawed materials. A wood-carver often must use the woods that are attainable, whether or not they are perfect for his purpose. Utilize flaws like knots, dry rot, fungus infections, holes, lines, unusual roots, and other deformities to create your own unique finished piece.

What did he mean by this? What did he mean by any of it? Why couldn't he just spell things out? I jammed the page and matchbook into my leather backpack and headed toward San Celina. I made it to the historical museum with five minutes to spare.

There were even more TV cameras than there were the day before. One van had *Hard Copy* written on the side. It was pulling away from the curb as I walked up. Thank goodness no one had informed them about my four o'clock meeting with the San Celina Seven.

A group of senior citizens wearing matching gray sweatshirts leaned on picket signs. Printed across each of their backs in bright red lettering was—"Heck, No, We Ain't Old." I wasn't quite clear on how that slogan had anything to do with saving the museum. Next to the protesting seniors were tables covered with cakes, brownies, and cookies. The sign said—"San Celina High School Mustang Pep Squad—Half of proceeds to go to saving the Historicule Museum." The other half, I surmised, should go to spelling lessons.

After a quick check on Dove and her cohorts, taking their orders for crossword puzzle books, a couple of spools of white quilting thread for the quilt they were working on, and two avocados for Elmo Ritter who had a craving, I went back outside and was assaulted by a half dozen reporters. I gave a quick statement. No, they weren't weakening; yes, they were absolutely serious; I had no idea whether the mayor's mother had breast-fed him or not. The last question was from our local advocates of breast-feeding. I guess they figured a man as sour and contrary as Mayor "Boxstore Billy" Davenport must have been raised on chemical formulas.

Gabe was waiting for me at the command post across the street.

"Where's Emory?" I asked.

"They let him in earlier. He told Dove he had to get ready for a date with Elvia. She granted him special dispensation in the name of romance." He gave a half smile. "What did our *abuelita* have to say?"

"That unless Bill concedes to renewing the lease for another twenty years, they aren't budging. Was that really a *Hard Copy* news van I saw driving away?"

"Yes," he said curtly.

"Did they interview you?"

"Yes, but they probably won't use it. I told them we were in negotiations with the seniors, and other than that, no comment. Last I heard, they were hunting down Bill. He's made it a point to stay away from here since he found out his mother was involved."

I couldn't help but giggle. Gabe shot me an irritated look.

"I'm sorry," I said, still laughing behind my hand. "It's just so ironic and so . . . right."

He didn't answer, and I didn't blame him. All he wanted to do was keep peace in the city, and it seemed right now that everyone was fighting him on that. "Are you hungry?" he asked, changing the subject.

"Starved. Let's go to Liddie's. I feel like comfort food."

Over my chicken potpie and his steamed vegetables, I brought him up-to-date on my quest for Jacob Chandler's identity—about my trip to Harmony and meeting Azanna, but still leaving out the connection to my mother.

"My next step," I said, "will be to call the restaurant and see if they have something for me. I might have to drive out there to get it."

"I don't like the thought of you driving 46 alone with all this going on." He tore off a piece of dinner roll and

191

took a bite. "Not to mention it's a death trap of a road at any time."

"I've driven it a hundred times. I'll be fine."

He sipped his iced tea and didn't answer. That meant he didn't approve but wasn't going to argue with me.

I smiled at him. "I have the cellular phone you bought me. I really will be okay."

"When are you going?"

"*If* I go, it'll have to be tomorrow. Saturday's going to be a busy day at the folk art museum with the Mother's Day exhibit, and I should at least make an appearance."

In the parking lot, I gave him a quick kiss good-bye.

"You're always leaving me," he complained, pulling me back against him. I rested my face in his neck, rough with early evening stubble. His arms held me strong and close, and for a brief moment I let myself relax, eventually pulling away with regret.

"I need to get back and feed Scout. I've been leaving him alone too much lately, but I feel better if he's there watching the house. I don't trust those Briggstone guys."

"And you shouldn't. Have they approached you at all?"

"No, I think they're too cowardly for that. Practical jokes like paint on my doorknob are more their style, I think."

"Setting your garage on fire is a little more than a practical joke."

"We don't actually know they're the culprits. Mr. Chandler sure didn't realize what a bed of snakes he'd left behind for me to deal with."

Gabe's face grew sober. "Or he didn't care. Seems to me his game takes precedence over the people he had relationships with or his concern for your safety. I find that very calculating."

"I agree with you mostly, except that on this wild goose chase he's led me, I've also discovered another man. All the people he's left these wood carving instructions and clues with have been people he's helped out in some very rough times. They have nothing but good feelings about him. I think what he's trying to do is tell me about himself. The person I'm discovering is an enigma—sometimes he pisses me off, and then I hear some incredibly nice story about him from one of these people, and my bad opinion of him wavers. To be honest, I don't know which is the real man."

Gabe brought a warm hand up to my cheek. "In my experience, *querida,* anyone who is that manipulative and wants to be in that much control is not a good person."

"This from a man who secretly dreams of being king of the world," I said, laughing as I laced my fingers through his. "I don't have a choice. I have to see this to the end."

"You're wrong. You do have a choice. He's only in control because you're allowing him to be, and I don't understand why."

I released his hands. "Let's not get into that, okay?" If we talked too much longer, I'd be tempted to tell him about Mr. Chandler's tenuous connection to my mother.

"Okay," he said reluctantly. "I'll call you tonight."

On the drive back to Morro Bay I thought about what Gabe had said regarding control. Was wanting to be in control always bad? There were all sorts of situations where control was important. A total lack of control meant chaos. That was crazy. A good leader is in control . . . both of the situation and themselves. Like this thing with Dove. If Gabe wasn't in control, wasn't keeping everyone within their legal boundaries, a lot of people could get hurt. A crowd without control is a mob. Of course, ultimately we don't have control of anything important. Where we come from, who we love, when we die. Well, these days maybe that last one was up for debate. But the fact remained we couldn't control *that* we die. There was no doubt that for the moment, like it or not, Mr. Chandler's morbid game of emotional "catch me if you can" put him in control.

The question still remained, though, even more so now that I knew he was connected somehow to my mother. Why?

11

WHEN I GOT BACK TO MORRO BAY, I IMMEDIATELY called the Basque restaurant in Bakersfield. After speaking to three different people who couldn't make sense of what I was asking with the scant information I offered, they finally told me that I should probably talk to the owner, Gabriel Zalba. He was gone for the day but would be in tomorrow at eleven A.M. As much as I dreaded the long, boring trip, it seemed best if I drove to Bakersfield and talked to him in person.

I spent the rest of the evening watching television and playing with Scout. About nine o'clock, Rich brought over a piece of fresh-baked pineapple upside-down cake, and we talked for an hour or so.

"Sure you don't need any company on the drive?" he asked.

"Thanks, but I'll be fine. This man might tell me more if I'm alone, you know?"

His disappointed face made me feel bad, but my first priority was not to fill a lonely widower's days, but to get this mysterious situation resolved.

194

"He's going to be mad at me, but I'm leaving Scout here," I said. "To watch the house."

He nodded. "That's probably a good idea. I'll keep an eye out also."

Later when Gabe called, I told him I was driving to Bakersfield tomorrow. For a change, he didn't argue and just asked me to call him when I returned. I almost missed his zealous protectiveness. Almost.

The next morning at eight o'clock, as I was getting in my car, I saw the photographer and his wife loading camera equipment into their blue Taurus. I walked across the street and asked, "So, where are you going today?" It was nice to just shoot the breeze with people who weren't involved with this crazy quest business, people who were just vacationing, taking touristy pictures, and were normal. The woman pushed up her tooled silver bracelet and said, "Hearst Castle and maybe that lighthouse up there."

"Piedras Blancas," I said.

"That's the one. Also, we heard that there's a bunch of sea lions somewhere around that area."

"There are, and the poor things are constantly harassed by tourists. I'd use a telephoto lens if you have one. Sea lions can be aggressive when they feel threatened."

"We'll be careful," the man said. "We believe in the credo—'Take only pictures, leave only footprints.' " He paused for a moment to reattach the red tape covering one of their taillights.

"What happened there?" I asked sympathetically.

"A tree jumped in back of him yesterday," the woman said with a chuckle. He gave her an irritated sideways look.

They were in front of me when I drove through the

195

center of town. A lively conversation was taking place, no doubt about her smart remark about the tree.

The three-hour drive on Highway 46 to Bakersfield was not a fun one, especially since I'd traveled it so many times in my life. I took a portable tape player and stuck on a long-playing tape of George Strait—my favorite singer for long, tedious trips. His silky caramel voice would make the miles fly.

The curvy, narrow highway passed thick-leafed avocado orchards, mobile home ranches, and U-pick raspberry farms. During one thirty-mile stretch, Cal Trans workers in their brilliant orange vests caused me to slow down to thirty-five mph every ten minutes or so while they repaired yet another section of this dangerous road. Wind blasts from passing Peterbilts and Kenworths shook Gabe's old truck, and though I loved this vehicle emotionally, I longed for a good, solid Chevy one-ton with a stereo tape deck, air-conditioning, and convenient drink holder.

About ten miles out of the rural suburbs of Atascadero the road started to climb, and the engine was forced to work harder. The land grew more desolate and treeless as I approached Shandon and Cholame. Just past the James Dean Memorial, deserted this early on a Friday morning, a doe froze at the side of the road, and I instinctively touched my foot to the brakes. But I passed her before she moved, and in my rearview mirror I watched her bound across the road and up into the cattle-dotted hills behind the monument. I counted off the familiar travel markings to Bakersfield—the fork in the road outside of Cholame where 41 and 46 split, the sign stating 90 miles to both Bakersfield and Fresno, the Pacific Almond groves where a few white almond blossoms still dotted the green groves, and Blackwell's

Corner, a store and cafe whose single claim to fame was being the last place where James Dean stopped before his rendezvous with fate.

I crossed the 5 freeway, the quickest way through Central California, driven best at midnight, and drove past Wasco State Prison slapped stark and cold in the middle of an alfalfa field. Then came 99, the freeway straight into the heart of Bakersfield—home of Buck Owens; trailer parks; used tractor lots; restaurants with dark, fifties-style cocktail lounges; cozy pastel California bungalows set on old streets canopied with full, leafy trees; and Dewar's Candy and Ice Cream Parlor—where Daddy always took me as a girl when he came here twice a year to visit friends. I pulled over at a Burger King, bought a Coke, and studied my age-softened Bakersfield street map. I was only a few blocks away from Zalba's. Killing time, I took another sip of Coke, dreading my mission. Each time I encountered another of these people Mr. Chandler had steered me to, I wondered if this one would be the one to unlock the mystery of who he was . . . to my mother and to me.

Zalba's French Basque Restaurant was larger than I expected. Set on a street of car dealers and fast-food restaurants, its newly paved, tar-scented parking lot was already filling up, even though it was only 11:15. It was dark and cool inside with framed photographs on the wall of men playing jai alai. It took me ten minutes waiting in line to talk to the hostess.

"I'm here to see Gabriel Zalba," I said.

The young, dark-haired girl whose name tag stated Christina looked at me curiously. "Which one?"

That threw me. "I don't know," I admitted.

Her expression grew even more curious. "What is it about? Are you a vendor? Old Gabriel doesn't do much

197

anymore except watch Young Gabriel work. I bet it's Young Gabriel you want to see."

"I'm not a vendor." I wasn't about to tell my whole story to this young girl. Maybe I'd just speak to both of them. Then it occurred to me. "How old is the older Mr. Zalba?"

She shrugged, her maroon-colored lips drawing downward in a concentrated frown. "I don't know. Old." At her age, which I guessed at sixteen or seventeen, everyone over forty was old.

"Sixties?" I asked. "Seventies?"

"Yeah, like that. His hair's, like, all gray. Young Gabriel is, like, my dad's age. Only some of his hair is gray."

"I think it's Old Gabriel I need to talk to."

She put on her hostess smile. "Okay. Wait here." She started to walk away, then turned back and called to me, "Oh, yeah, who should I say wants him?"

"Benni Harper."

A few minutes later she came back. "Follow me, please," she said and led me through the restaurant and sat me at a booth. "Your waitress will be right with you."

"Wait," I said as she started walking away. "I don't want to eat. I want to see—"

"Mr. Zalba says you have to eat first. He'll see you after you're through. Would you like something to drink?"

"Just water," I said.

She brought me my drink, and in the next hour I was served by a quiet, pretty waitress named Connie. While I studied the pictures of sheepherders and sheep on the dark paneled wall next to me, I ate a traditional Basque meal: vegetables with onions and carrots, thick and

198

tangy sourdough bread with real butter, pink beans with a sauce hotter than any Santa Maria salsa I'd ever eaten, sliced pickled tongue, salad, french fries, green beans, rice with beets, spaghetti, and beef brochettes with onions and bell peppers. Someone knew I didn't like lamb, a Basque specialty. For dessert she brought me chocolate mousse topped with vanilla sauce. The one thing you had to say for the Basques, they didn't believe in people going hungry. I had just taken the last bite of my chocolate mousse when I was joined by a sixtyish man with gray curly hair and black, red-rimmed eyes.

"Miss Harper?" he asked, dipping his head in an acknowledging nod.

"Yes, are you Gabriel Zalba?"

"Yes, I'm pleased to make your acquaintance. May I join you?"

"Certainly."

He slid into the booth across from me and smiled, first at me, then at our waitress when she came to get my empty dessert cup. "Connie, bring me some coffee. please." He looked at me in inquiry. "Miss Harper?"

"No, thanks. I couldn't eat or drink another ounce."

When she walked away, he asked, "So, your meal was satisfactory?"

"It was marvelous." We studied each other for a moment. I sensed that this wasn't a man to be rushed, but as pleasant as this all was, I was not here on a social call. "My husband's name is Gabriel," I said to start some sort of conversation.

"Yes, I know."

"How?"

"Jacob told me."

Okay, now things were moving along. He'd at least admitted knowing him. I pulled the matchbook out of my purse and laid it down on the table in front of him, telling him my story. When I finished, his coffee arrived, and I had to wait while he methodically poured in cream and sugar, tasted it, then added a little more cream.

"So, you do know him," I said, hoping to hurry him along.

"Me and Jacob were friends. A long time. He saved my life."

"He did?"

"Not literally, but without him I would not have this restaurant. I would not have my son's respect or a legacy for my grandchildren. He was a good man. He loaned me money, but more importantly, he told me not to give up, convinced me when I was still just a dishwasher at someone else's restaurant that I could start my own restaurant. He did this . . ." He paused to think. "Thirty-five years ago. Young Gabriel was four, not yet in school. Jacob sold paper goods to the restaurant where I was working. I'd gotten in a fight with the owner's son, a spoiled boy who was cruel and liked to anger me because I had a wife who loved me and a beautiful son. Jacob saw how he needled me, and Jacob made it a point to call me once a week, tell me to not let Joaquin bother me, to watch and learn everything about this business so one day I could open my own restaurant. He told me to save money. He helped me fill out the loan papers for this building and its equipment. On our opening day, I served him our first meal. He was my friend."

Not knowing how to break the news that Jacob Chandler had died, unable to look him in the eye, I compulsively folded and refolded my pink cloth napkin. "I'm so sorry, Mr. Zalba. Your friend . . . Mr. Chandler, he . . ."

He reached across the table and patted my nervous hands, his face tight and controlled. "I know. You wouldn't be here if he were still alive. He told me you'd eventually come. But Jacob knew I would need time before I could speak to you. That is why he bought you dinner."

"He arranged this dinner?"

"Yes."

I sat back in my booth, again irritated and amazed by this elaborate game, but also touched by the story this man told me. There was no doubt Mr. Chandler was an enigma. Like two different people almost. I closed my eyes briefly, then opened them. I was learning the rules. "So, do you have something for me?"

"Right here." He pulled a package out of his tweed jacket and handed it to me. I opened it and found a box containing another wood carving lesson and a stone the length and thickness of a pencil, cut in a triangular shape, made of the same white translucent material as the flat stone in the trunk. I unfolded the piece of paper.

Buy good tools. Keep them simple. You don't need an expensive set of tools to discover the treasures in wood. It is possible to carve your whole career with a few tools. Add to your tools gradually as the need arises. Treat them with respect, and they will not fail you. Keep them sharp. Sharpening is done on an abrasive stone and is followed by polishing on a leather strop. Use the best quality stone you can find. The stone is important. If you nick yourself, bandage the cut because you most likely will nick yourself in the same spot. Always remember your mind and your powers of observation are your most valuable tools. Don't underestimate them.

The stone lay cold and smooth in my hands. "Do you know what this is?" I asked Mr. Zalba.

"It looks like a small sharpening stone."

That's what I figured. I looked back at the note, and the words *The stone is important* seemed to stand out. Did he mean something about this stone and the other one? I stuck it and the note back in the pasteboard box. "Is that it? Did he have anything else for me?"

"Just the box. Please, where is my friend buried?"

"The Paso Robles Cemetery—under a pepper tree in back of the stained-glass memorial. Someone at the office can give you exact directions. The headstone won't be there for a few weeks. We had his service a few days ago. I'm sorry I couldn't tell you, but he didn't leave an address book. If I'd known . . ."

He waved his hand in dismissal. "I will go and say my own good-bye."

"Mr. Zalba, can I ask you a couple of things?"

"Anything."

"Did you know an Alice Louise Banks or an Alice Ramsey?"

He shook his head. "No, I'm sorry."

"Did he ever say anything about where he came from, who his family was?"

Blunt fingers circled his mug. Distress and sorrow were apparent in his face, and I felt horrible about questioning him right now; but I didn't know what else to do. "Jacob never talked about himself. Always asking about the children and my wife, Rosa. I'm sorry, but I knew very little about him. He was alone, I think. Except for you, he never mentioned anyone to me." He slid out of the booth, and I followed him.

Taking my hand in both of his, he looked deep into my eyes. "Miss Harper, I don't know who you were to Jacob, but he cared for you deeply."

"What did he say about me?" I asked, feeling desperate and suddenly afraid.

"Only that his biggest regret was not having the courage to speak to you. This he told me himself. Go with God's blessings, Miss Harper, and think of Jacob with good thoughts."

I didn't answer. I wanted to do as he asked, and maybe someday I could. But right now irritation was the only emotion I was willing to grant Jacob Chandler, no matter how many kind things he did for people.

Outside, in the sunny parking lot, I shivered under my flannel shirt even though it was seventy-five degrees. The sky was a bright, brittle Central Valley blue. I leaned against the front grill of the truck for a moment, watching traffic pass, trying to get my bearings. Across the street, the Denny's coffee shop was even more crowded than Zalba's. Those poor people, I thought, remembering my incredible Basque meal, choosing a fried tuna melt over the wonderful meal I'd just eaten. I glanced over the cars. It was then I noticed it.

A blue Taurus. Or rather the back of a blue Taurus.

Not unusual, by any means. A million of them made every year probably.

It was the broken taillight on the passenger side that caught my eye. A broken taillight taped in the exact same way as a car I'd seen only hours before in Morro Bay.

I pretended to glance past it, feigning interest in the cars speeding down the busy street. Out of the corner of my eye, I could discern the outline of two people sitting in the car. Even from across the street, I could tell one of them had very light hair, fluffy hair.

Light as in bleached blond. A hand rested casually on the open window ledge. A large aquamarine ring caught the bright sunlight and flashed.

Though fear made me want to bolt and run like a new calf, I made myself casually stand up and walk around to the driver's side. Once inside, I gripped the steering wheel, my mind racing. What was that couple doing in Bakersfield when they had distinctly told me they were going to the north coast? No photographer would choose a Denny's parking lot in Bakersfield over pictures of Hearst Castle, Piedras Blancas lighthouse, and lazing sea lions.

Unless, of course, their purpose wasn't to photograph the natural beauty of the Central Coast but to follow me.

Now you're being paranoid, my practical self said to the self that was frantically waving red warning flags.

I drove the truck slowly out of the parking lot and headed toward downtown. There was only one way to find out, and that was to try to lose them. I drove all over Bakersfield, stopping once in a shopping center and went into a grocery store. Inside the cool building, I stood slightly back from the window and watched the Ford Taurus drive past my truck and park three rows over. I wasn't being paranoid—these people were following me.

I wandered around the store for a few minutes, trying to calm my panic and formulate a plan. The drive back to Morro Bay loomed long and desolate in front of me. So I wouldn't come out of the store suspiciously empty-handed, I picked up a six-pack of cold Cokes and a bag of barbecue potato chips. On the way to the check stand, I paused at the kitchen utensil aisle and perused the kitchen knives, finally dismissing the idea that a steak knife would be much protection and wishing that, illegal or not, Jack's old .45 was tucked under the truck's seat. For me, following the law to the letter was one of the harder parts of being a police chief's wife. As the clerk rang me up, I debated calling Gabe.

No, I decided. He'd insist on me waiting here or perhaps driving to the nearest police station until he arrived. By that time, the people would be long gone, and I'd never find out who they were and why they were following me. Better to just act as if I'd not seen them and head back home before dark. They'd made no move to harm me, and if I were to confront them, it would be better to do it on my home turf. I'd drive back, then call Gabe immediately so he wouldn't accuse me of running off half-cocked.

Satisfied with my sensible decision, I started the drive back to Morro Bay. I caught the Taurus in my rearview mirror a few times when we had long, straight stretches of road, but these people were discreet and knew how to follow someone—which made me grow increasingly nervous. I would have preferred their efforts to be less professional. Then another thought occurred to me. Could they have had something to do with the fire?

Relief flowed through my tense body when I reached Morro Bay's city limits. The Taurus was nowhere in sight and hadn't been for the last half hour but then, these people knew where I lived. Scout greeted me with the enthusiasm given a soldier home from battle. I stooped down and rubbed his chocolate-brown head hard, pushing his soft ears back so they lay flat against his head. His eyes closed in pure pleasure.

He followed me inside, where I immediately went to the window facing the bed-and-breakfast where the Taurus couple was staying. They drove up ten minutes later. While I was watching them, the doorbell rang. At the door I called out, "Who is it?" though it was unnecessary since Scout's tail was beating furiously against my leg.

"It's Rich."

I opened the door wider. "Come on in. Guess I didn't have to be so paranoid and make you announce yourself. Scout here's a pretty good indicator of who's safe and who's not."

He reached down and scratched behind Scout's floppy ear. "Not really, kid. Don't forget, he's known those Briggstone boys a long time and probably thinks they're all right. As much as I like to give our canine companions their due, sometimes they aren't any better at judging character than us humans. They react well to positive treatment just like us, without thinking about how that person petting them and giving them treats might just sell other dogs for scientific experimentation."

"Good point. I'll keep that in mind. What's up?"

"I made *arroz con pollo* and was wondering if you were hungry. I'll confess right off that I have an ulterior motive, besides wanting your lovely company. I want to hear what happened at the Basque restaurant in Bakersfield." The expression on his face was eager and hopeful.

I glanced up at the clock. It was a little past four-thirty. Gabe would probably want to have dinner with me, but I couldn't bear to disappoint Rich. Gabe and I could have coffee later. The information I had about the couple following me wasn't horribly urgent. A few more hours wouldn't matter.

"Okay, let me call Gabe and tell him I'm back and that I'll meet him. I'll be over after that."

206

"Did I interrupt dinner plans between you two? Look, the chicken can wait. It tastes just as good heated up the next day."

I squeezed his forearm affectionately. "No, I want to have dinner with you. Gabe and I will have plenty of time to talk. And, boy, do I have a lot to tell you."

After telling Gabe I got back okay and making plans to meet him at Blind Harry's at seven o'clock, I went over to Rich's with Scout and told him the latest link in Jacob Chandler's chain, including my discovery about the fake photographer and his wife.

"You are going to tell your husband right away, aren't you?" he asked, his dark face worried.

"Yes, Papa," I said, teasing, "as soon as I see him. I'm going to let him handle this one with no hassles from me. I don't even have the urge to confront these people myself since I have no idea who they are or what their business is following me."

"I wonder if Jacob had other people he owed money to," Rich mused, spooning more chicken and rice onto my plate.

"I'm going to gain ten pounds living next door to you," I said, taking a large chunk of white meat and tossing it to Scout.

"You need energy to carry on your investigation," he said, pushing the bowl of homemade guacamole toward me. "You're just like my daughters, trying to survive on Wheat Thins, diet Coke, and popcorn."

"That shows how little you know about me, Señor Trujillo. I'll never be accused of being anorectic." Scout whined next to me. "No more for you, Mr. Scout, or we'll be renaming you Mr. Tubby."

"Just to prove to you I'm not as lazy as I look, I've been doing a little investigating of my own. Discovered

207

an interesting fact about why the Briggstone boys are harassing you."

I sat forward eagerly. "You did? What?"

He rested his elbows on the table. "I've become pretty buddy-buddy with Ray Newhard down at the docks. He owns Ray's Sportfishing, and I tease him that I helped pay for his new galley because I've done so much fishing these last few months. I asked him what he knew about the Briggstone boys. After discovering that there was no love lost between him, Duane, and Cole, I told him just enough of your story to get him interested." He gave me a questioning look. "Hope that was all right."

"Knowing this town, he'd probably heard about it anyway."

"You're probably right, though he didn't act like it. Besides just confirming what you and I already know— that Duane and Cole are a couple of losers who work just enough at the docks to buy beer and *Playboy* magazines—he said about a month or so back he overheard them at the Masthead, that bar downtown where fishermen hang out, bragging about being 'all set' when their mom married that old fart she'd been seeing. Apparently they said they might not even have to wait that long, that they knew for a fact he had a lot of money, and it was easy to get to."

"Between his checking and savings account he had about twenty thousand dollars. I wouldn't classify that as a lot of money. As for easy to get to, it is if you have the authority to draw it out, which they don't."

Rich stood up and started clearing the table. "Maybe there's more. Maybe he has it hidden in the house somewhere."

I handed him my plate. "If it was, Gabe or I would have found it. And it couldn't have been in the garage,

208

or Duane or Cole wouldn't have tried to burn it down."

"So maybe it's something worth money, like drugs."

"I think you're really reaching. Jacob Chandler didn't seem the type to deal drugs. And you forget, this house was thoroughly sniffed out by a professional drug dog."

He started rinsing the dishes, his face skeptical. "I'm not sure there is a type, Benni. And those frequent trips to Mexico that lady told you about. What were those about?"

"You said he liked to fish. Maybe he went fishing."

Rich shook his head doubtfully. "We do know he's manipulating you on this crazy scavenger hunt, and I'm afraid there's something at the end of it that might harm you because someone else wants it."

It hadn't occurred to me that there would be anything at the end of this hunt except his identity. "Like Duane and Cole. And maybe that pseudo-photographer and his big-haired wife."

"Could be. That's why you'd better tell all of this to your husband pronto. Let him decide what's the best thing to do."

"I will as soon as we're through here." I took my plate over to the sink and started running hot water.

"Leave those, kid. I want you to get to town and tell your husband about those people now. Maybe I should follow you there, just in case."

"Thanks, Rich, but honestly, I'll be fine. If they didn't do anything on the trip back from Bakersfield, I doubt they'll harm me on the twelve-mile trip to San Celina."

"Okay, but I won't rest easy until I see your truck back here safely."

After saying good-bye, I put Scout in the back of the pickup, not having the heart to make him stay home alone again, and headed for San Celina. Gabe was waiting at our usual back table downstairs in Blind Harry's book-lined coffeehouse. In the background, a flannel-shirted girl played a beautiful Spanish guitar to a packed Friday night crowd.

Gabe came around the table to wrap me in a big hug. He wore a soft wool sweater that smelled distinctly of his scent, and I rested my cheek against his shoulder, feeling my stomach finally calm down. It was time to tell him about Jacob Chandler's connection with my mother. I don't know why I held back even for a day. This man loved me and wanted to help me. It had been a long, hard journey this last year and few months, learning to trust each other, learning to be vulnerable.

There was no area in my life, even Jack's death, that had affected me like losing my mother. It had taken me years to understand that. And yet Gabe and I had never even talked about my mother. With Mother's Day coming this weekend, a day that was always so difficult for me, this seemed like a good time to start.

"Miss me?" he asked.

"More than you know," I said, kissing his jaw, then his mouth. "Ouch, you need a trim on that mustache."

"That's what happens when you leave a husband on his own," he said, pulling out my chair. "He falls to pieces. Want me to get you something?"

"In a minute. Have you talked to Dove?"

"They were fine as of half an hour ago," he said, sitting down across from me, right underneath the John Dos Passos section of Elvia's informal lending library of books. He sipped his black coffee. "I talked to her over the phone myself. She said to tell you that you could come by with her Mother's Day present anytime Sunday and that, if because you've been so busy running all over creation you hadn't bought anything, an

210

extra large pepperoni pizza from Nick's would be the perfect gift."

I laughed. "No problem. She's actually right. I bought a card but hadn't thought of an appropriate gift. Pizza it is. I have some other stuff to take them, too." I gave him a curious look. "You seem much more relaxed about it tonight."

He shook his head in amazement. "I know and I have no idea why, especially since I'm getting no less than ten phone calls a day from Bill asking me what I'm going to do. I finally told him that my job was to keep the peace, protect citizens and property, and that I was doing my job, so maybe he should just see about doing his."

"Good for you. Wonder how his family has been treating him since they found out his mother is one of the San Celina Seven."

"Not kindly, I'm sure. That's probably why I'm getting all the phone calls." He scooted his chair around closer to me and took one of my hands. "Let's forget about them. Tell me what happened in Bakersfield."

So I did. He listened to my story, his eyes never leaving my face. His expression darkened slightly when I told him Jacob Chandler's comment to Mr. Zalba that his biggest regret was not having the courage to speak to me, and Mr. Zalba's belief that Jacob Chandler had cared deeply for me.

"What's wrong?" I asked, pausing in my story.

"If he'd cared at all, he wouldn't be putting you through this painful ordeal."

I squeezed his hand. "It's not that bad, Friday." I finished telling him about the visit with Mr. Zalba and showed him the latest message and the white stone. "It's the same kind of sharpening stone I found in the trunk.

211

At least, I think it is. You know, the line 'The stone is important' seems a little too obvious to ignore."

"What kind of stone is it?"

"I don't know. I need to take it someplace and find out. Maybe a hardware store?"

"Or one of the geology professors at Cal Poly."

"Great! I never thought of that. Of course, there's still the wood carving museum. Man, I need an extra ten hours in a day."

A shadow of a frown passed across his face, stiffening it. "Didn't this guy even consider that you might have more important things to do than fool around with his asinine games?"

I stuck the stone and note back in my purse and took a deep breath. "There's something else I need to tell you, but you have to promise me to stay calm." First I would tell him about the couple following me, then about my mother's connection with Jacob Chandler.

His eyes darkened with worry. "What's that?"

I told him about meeting this couple, their car's broken taillight, spotting them in Bakersfield after my meeting with Mr. Zalba, and my certainty, after my wild ride around Bakersfield, that they were following me.

"Maybe I'm being paranoid, but it's too much of a coincidence if you ask me. Let me tell you, the whole drive back from Bakersfield I was ready to jump out of my skin. Maybe the Briggstones hired them. Maybe Beau Franklin did. According to Rich, who heard it from Ray who owns a sportfishing boat, the Briggstones think that Mr. Chandler has some kind of treasure or something hidden. Rich is thinking drugs, but I said that you'd already had the place checked out by the drug dog. They haven't actually tried to break into the house so they must not think there's anything there, though

212

with Rich next door it wouldn't be easy for them. Maybe they did start that fire and are trying to scare me away 'cause there is something in the house. I don't know. What do you think? Do you think the couple could be involved with the Briggstones or Beau Franklin?"

I paused to take a breath, waiting for him to hit the roof and to rant about me being in too much danger, how could he protect me from this new threat, demand I come home immediately, if not sooner.

Except he didn't.

His face was flushed but not with anger. I'd lived with him long enough to know embarrassment when I saw it.

"What's wrong?" I demanded, leaning toward him.

He sat back in his chair, his ocean-blue eyes cajoling, his smile downright sheepish. "I . . ." He stopped and smiled wider. He shifted in his chair and looked at the backs of his hands. "It's . . ." He stopped again.

For the first time since I'd known him, he was speechless. My eyes widened. Then the realization hit me.

"You didn't . . . No, even *you* wouldn't . . ."

He didn't answer, but the truth was unmistakably there in his eyes.

I slammed my hand down on the table, sloshing coffee. "Dang it, Gabe, this is the most outrageous, annoying thing you have ever done. I was scared to death that whole drive back from Bakersfield. How dare you have me followed! I ought to . . . I don't know what . . . report you to someone. I swear, if we weren't in public, I'd smack you silly. You *promised* that you wouldn't stake me out." I inhaled, ready to keep going when he interrupted.

213

"I kept my promise. I didn't stake you out, and neither did any of my men. Dan and Sandi are old friends of mine from L.A. He and I worked Narcotics together, and now he owns his own investigating firm."

"Small technicality, Friday, and I ain't buyin' it. Did it ever occur to you that I might, I just *might,* catch on? Why didn't you tell me?"

"Because you would have told me not to do it. I couldn't be there to protect you—"

"Spy on me."

"*Protect* you, so I did the most expedient thing—hired a stand-in."

"I'm sorry, but I see that as a lack of complete trust in me and my ability to assess a situation. I've kept you informed about every little second of my comings and goings just like I promised, because trust has always been an issue between us. Apparently I'm the only one who is concerned about changing that."

He scowled and sat forward, resting his elbows on the table. "If I had told you I wanted to have Dan keep an eye on you, you would have refused."

"You're darn right."

"Sometimes when you love someone, you have to go against her desires and do what is right for her."

I pointed a finger at him. "Listen up, Chief. I'm not your child. I'm not incompetent or stupid or foolish—"

"I never said you were any of those things."

"No, but your actions do."

"Look, what did you expect me to do? I'm going crazy here. My wife is staying alone in a place where there are people who want to harm her. She's driving all over creation, *unprotected,* following some nutty treasure hunt set up by a dead man who, as far as I can tell, was a sick control freak, while her grandmother

214

holds hostage the town's historical museum, causing me no end of headaches in trying to rearrange my officers to keep her and her friends protected. Not to mention I have the whole city council, the mayor, and the local press on my ass asking what I'm going to do about her. What am I going to do? What a laugh. What can I do?"

"Leave my gramma out of this."

"Believe me, sweetheart, I'd love to. Unfortunately, protecting this city is my job and one I'm determined to do no matter how much I'm undermined by the women in your family."

I stared at him flatly. "Let's not go any further with this because we're only going to say more things we regret. Just call off your watchdogs and let me deal with this situation without interference from you."

"No problem. Forgive me if I showed too much concern for your safety. I won't make that mistake again."

"Why is everything so black and white with you? Why can't you understand there's a difference between control and concern?"

"Why can't *you* understand that your way of showing love is not the all perfect, only way to show it?"

I stood up and slammed my chair into the table. "I don't want to talk about this anymore. Especially here."

"So when do you suggest we talk about it?" he asked, remaining seated.

"How about . . . oh, *next year.*" I walked out of the room without looking back. I knew I was acting childish. Just like he was. It never failed to amaze me how quickly adults resort to playground tactics when fighting. I guess everything we needed to know we did learn in kindergarten.

I contemplated dropping by the Historical Museum to

215

see how Dove and her group were faring, but she'd know the minute she saw me that something was going on between me and Gabe, and at this point I wasn't up to her third degree.

On my drive back to Morro Bay, I thought about what Dove was to me, a convoluted mix of mother and grandmother. A real grandmother, one where that was the only relationship, would have probably been completely on my side. At least, that's the way Elvia's grandmother always was. And my other friends' grandmothers, too. I'd spent my whole life observing the relationships between my friends and their mothers and grandmothers, fascinated and envious of the fact that most of them had both and that the relationships were so different. Dove had never been able to be a doting, indulgent grandmother to me, as she was to the rest of her grandkids, because she'd become my surrogate mother from the time I was six.

My thoughts wandered to what my mother would have advised. Would she have told me to give in to Gabe, placate him, tell him what he did was okay because his intentions were good? Or would she have told me to stick to my guns and make him see my way? Or maybe she wouldn't have given any advice. Maybe she would have said that we'd have to work this out between us, that I was a smart girl, that she'd raised me to make up my own mind, fight my own battles, that no matter what happened she'd love me, she'd always be there. The lie all mothers told their children. One their children believed because the possibility of it not being true was too much to bear.

Except sometimes you had to bear it.

I'd never know what my mother would have told me to do about Gabe. I didn't have a clue as to what type of person she was, what type of person she would have ended up being by the time she was fifty-three. In my mind she would always be twenty-five. I had no sense of her voice anymore, the smell of her, the way she walked, the way she cleaned a house. Did she vacuum or dust first? For some reason, I desperately wanted to know that one small detail.

The house was dark when I parked in front. The skeletal shell of the garage roof looked spooky in the shadows. The pungent, dusky smell of burnt wood still permeated the air. Thankful that Scout was with me, I walked up to the front door, my stomach feeling like a chunk of ice. The doorknob was cold in my hand as I fumbled with the lock. Underneath my foot, plastic crunched. I flipped the porch light on and bent down to pick up the cassette. I'd cracked the case, but the cassette inside was intact.

I quickly closed the door behind me, went through the house switching on every light, and turned the wall furnace on high to eliminate the damp chill. Standing in front of the heater, I contemplated the unmarked cassette, wondering if it was another clue from Jacob Chandler. But who had left it here? He had so many people involved in this stupid game that it could have been anyone. I stuck the cassette into his stereo and after fiddling around with the unfamiliar knobs and switches, music started to play.

It was an old eighties pop song. One you still heard too often in elevators, in dentists' offices, and on oldies stations. The music had always intrigued me, but the words left me feeling a little sick, a little scared.

I stood there, feeling my heart beat faster as I listened to Sting and the Police sing the line ". . . I'll be watching you."

217

12

THE NEXT DAY I MOPED AROUND THE HOUSE UNTIL past noon, wanting to call Gabe but refusing to give in. Finally I decided to call Emory at the newspaper and see what he'd come up with in his investigations.

"Sweetcakes, are you doin' okay? Rumor on the street has it you and the Man had words last night."

"Geeze, Emory, do you have the tables at Blind Harry's bugged?"

"No, but thanks for the idea. Seriously, is everything okay?"

"Gabe and I just had a small disagreement about the words control and concern and how they are not synonyms in any way, shape, or form."

"Hmm, sounds serious enough for me to steer clear of. What can I do for you?"

"I was wondering if you'd found out anything on Duane and Cole Briggstone."

"Sure did. You were on my list to hunt down today anyway so you've saved me some time." I heard him shuffle some papers. "Okay, here we are. Duane is a low-life, but then, we already knew that."

"Details, Emory, details."

"He was busted five times in the last two years. Twice for drunk driving. Once for possession of illegal narcotics—speed. And twice for petty burglary. His mama bailed him out every time, by the way, but he did spend a little time in the county jail. Got all that from a cute little receptionist who works for a bail bondsman who's a friend of a friend."

"You know, if Elvia finds out you're flirting with other women, she'll drop you like the proverbial hot tamale."

His laugh rumbled over the phone. "Never fear, cousin dear, I only did what was absolutely necessary to obtain needed information for Elvia's very best friend in the whole world, so how could she be upset with me?"

"You're incorrigible, but I still love you. What else?"

"Nothing on the older brother, Cole. He appears to be the good son or at least the smart one who never gets caught. Here's another interesting fact, Mama Briggstone's store is in Chapter Eleven."

"Really? That explains why her sons are so upset about me being named Mr. Chandler's heir. Their gravy train will be shut off. How bad off is she?"

"It was hard getting details since I haven't cultivated any contacts yet in Morro Bay, but I did find out who owns the building where her store is located and tracked down the property management company in charge of it. Tess Briggstone is three months behind in her store rent."

"What about their house?" I walked over to the window, Scout following me, and peered through the blinds at their house. It was closed up tight, and no one appeared to be home.

"It's a rental, too. The owner is an attorney in Santa Monica. His office says he's out of the country until Memorial Day, and I couldn't even pry out of his secretary who the management company was so I have no idea if they are also behind on that rent. I could keep digging if you want."

"No, that's okay. It really doesn't matter. All your information just confirms what we already knew, that these people are desperate for money. The question is how desperate."

"That fire tells me they're pretty desperate," Emory said, his voice worried. "I'm chancing your wrath here,

219

but are you sure that house and Chandler's measly savings account is worth risking life and/or limb?"

"Don't be so dramatic, Emory. You're beginning to sound like Gabe. I have to see this thing through to the end."

"Why?"

I paused a minute, thankful we had the distance and physical anonymity of the phone between us. One look at my face, and he'd instantly know there was something I wasn't telling him. It had been that way since we were children—this ability to read each other. "I just have to, Emory. You know I hate quitting anything."

He was silent for a moment. "What aren't you telling me?"

"Now you're *really* beginning to sound like Gabe." But I didn't answer his question.

His exaggerated sigh was audible over the phone. "Fine, have it your way. You'll tell me when you're ready."

"Thanks for getting me the information. You're definitely in the running for being my favorite cousin."

"Ha, I won that award years ago. I'm in the cousin Hall of Fame."

I laughed. "What are your plans for tomorrow?" I knew, just like me, Mother's Day was hard for him. It was our tradition to call each other and talk for hours, but this was the first Mother's Day he lived near enough to visit. We'd have to figure out a new custom.

"I'm invited to the Aragon house for their traditional fete."

"What a treat for you. That's the only day of the year the Aragon men cook. Don't be surprised if you're handed an apron."

220

"I'll do whatever it takes to fit in. What are your plans?"

"Same as always. I'll meet Daddy at Mama's grave and put flowers on it, then we'll probably eat at Liddie's. Oh, and I'm bringing pizzas to the San Celina Seven. That was Dove's Mother's Day dinner request."

"Their little escapade has made the Associated Press, you know. That means any paper in the country could pick it up."

"No, I didn't know. Think they'll hear about it back in Sugartree? Aunt Garnet will burst a blood vessel. Worse, she might feel compelled to fly out here and set Dove on the straight and narrow."

He chuckled. "Heaven help us all. I'll see you later."

"If not today, then definitely tomorrow. I always bring flowers to Elvia's mom for Mother's Day. Besides, I have to get a picture of you in an apron for future generations to ridicule."

"Just make sure you get my good side."

Talking to Emory raised my spirits considerably, so I took a shower and planned my day. As I dressed, I studied Gwen Swanson's embroidered signature on the baby quilt I'd left draped over the footboard. Maybe Daddy would know who she was. The only way to find out was to drive out to the ranch and ask him.

Before I left I called a florist and ordered flowers for Señora Aragon and for my mother's grave. Yellow roses for Elvia's mom, pink roses for Mama. The same as every year. I assumed my dad initially started the custom of pink roses for my mother, and I just took over the ordering when I was sixteen. Were pink roses my mother's favorite flower? Did they have some personal significance to my dad? I'd never asked because we never talked when we took the flowers to the cemetery.

Our yearly visit consisted of the same ritual—my father taking off his hat, standing silently for a few minutes staring at her headstone, then walking away, leaving me to arrange the flowers in the sunken vase and brush the grass off her stone. We always ate at Liddie's afterwards. We never talked about her.

Outside, the private investigator and his wife were loading up their Taurus. I walked across the street to them.

"Sorry I blew the gig for you," I said.

The woman smiled at me and shrugged. "Happens," she said.

Gabe's friend hefted a leather suitcase into the trunk and slammed it shut. He turned to me and said, "Gabe's a good man. He was just trying to look out for you."

"Yeah, well, it's more complicated than that."

He tossed his camera bag into the backseat. "Good luck. Maybe we'll meet again under more agreeable circumstances."

"Maybe."

"Just one piece of advice." He jerked a thumb over at the Briggstones' house. "Watch your back with those two jokers. They're not very smart, but they're mean."

"Don't worry, I intend to."

THE RANCH FELT EMPTY AND SAD WITHOUT DOVE'S visible and often audible presence. The clothesline was bare, and no crackly voice singing, "Bringing in the Sheaves" or "My Bucket's Got a Hole in It" greeted me. Even the chickens pecking at the bare ground seemed unusually quiet. I wandered back to the barn where Bobby, one of my dad's hands, told me he was in the tack room searching for a snaffle-bit.

An old plastic radio played Johnny Cash's "Ring of Fire" when I walked in. Daddy was rummaging through a desk drawer.

"Haven't heard that song in years," I said.

He looked up and smiled at me. "Hey, squirt. Found this new station that only plays real country music."

"An oldies country station? That's great. I wondered when someone would come up with the idea."

"What's up?" he asked, pulling a bit out of a drawer, looking at it with a frown, then throwing it back in.

I reached over and ran my hand over the seat of my saddle sitting on a wooden rack. Daddy and Dove gave it to me for my sixteenth birthday. My name was carved across the back of the cantle. I cleaned and polished it so many times that year that Daddy teased I was going to rub my name down to his. I looked at the dust on my hand and laughed. "Needs a good cleaning."

He nodded over at a metal cabinet. "Saddle soap's cheap. Elbow grease a little higher."

"I'll do it soon. Want to meet tomorrow at the cemetery at six?"

"Sure." He dug through the drawer and pulled out another bit, studying it with exaggerated interest.

"Can I ask you something?"

He nodded without looking up.

"Do you know anyone named Gwen Swanson?" I watched his face for any reaction.

He furrowed his silvery brow, then shook his head slowly. "Don't believe I do. Why?"

I hesitated a moment. "It's just . . . well, her name was on that baby quilt Mama's friends back in Little Rock made her, and I was just wondering."

"Didn't really know your mama's old friends from Little Rock that good. We lived on the farm outside of

223

Sugartree, and she'd see them when she went to visit Emory's mama, Ervalean. We went to Sugartree Baptist after we was married until we came out west." His pale blue eyes studied me intently. "There's lots of names on that quilt. What's so particular about this Gwen?"

I shrugged and looked down at the ground. "It just caught my eye. I . . . had a teacher named Mrs. Swanson in college." The lie stuck in my throat a moment before going down.

He nodded, his face unbelieving.

"So even when you were dating you never went to church with her? She never introduced you to any of her friends?"

"I went to church with her a few times. Maybe I met this person you're asking about, but if I did, she didn't stick in my memory."

"What about when you got married? Didn't any of them come to the ceremony?" It occurred to me at that moment that I had no idea where my parents got married or even what day their anniversary was. I felt a deep sadness knowing the date had gone by every year without me even knowing it.

"We got married at the church on a Sunday afternoon with just Ervalean and Boone there. Ervalean played the organ, then stood up for your mama."

"That's it? You didn't even have a reception? What did you do?"

"Your mama didn't want a big fuss. The four of us ate in a nice restaurant in the city, then we called Dove and told her. Your mama's only family was Ervalean, and she already knew. Me and your mama stayed in a hotel in Little Rock for two days, then fetched her things from Ervalean's house and went home to the farm. We lived with Dove until we came out west when you was three."

"What day was your anniversary?" I asked.

His face closed up, and he asked sharply, "Benni, why are you asking all these questions?"

Surprised at his tone, I said, "I just wanted to know what day your anniversary was. What's wrong with that?"

He rubbed a hand over his face. "Nothing, squirt. You know I just . . ."

A twinge of guilt hit me. I knew talking about my mother had never been easy for Daddy, and because of that I'd never asked him why, when she had died so young, he had never remarried. Wasn't he lonely? Did he ever do anything for female companionship? My brain nervously skirted around the idea of sex. Like most people, the idea of a parent enjoying anything of that nature was something I never wanted to dwell on.

He gave me an odd look, then said, "August second."

"Thanks, Daddy," I said softly, hugging him quickly. "I'll see you tomorrow."

He patted me on the back and murmured, "Reckon so."

I went back inside the house, which smelled strangely bland and empty. A scraped-clean casserole dish sat in the sink along with four dirty coffee cups. Without Dove's presence, the house had become just a place for Daddy to eat meals and sleep. What would he do when Dove was no longer here? The thought of our lives without Dove pierced me like a sharp knife.

Before going back to Morro Bay, I called Emory again. "Do you know any friends of your mom's who might have known my mom?"

"Not offhand, but I could call back home and sniff around. Anyone in particular you huntin'?"

"Actually there is. A Gwen Swanson."

225

"Any particular reason?"

"Yes, but I'm not ready to talk about it yet."

There was a moment of silence. "You know I'll do anything for you, Benni, but it would be a lot easier if I knew what I was lookin' for."

"I'd like to talk to her or anyone who knew her or my mother."

He sighed. "I'll do my best. I'll see you at Elvia's tomorrow at one o'clock. I should have something by then."

"Thanks, Emory. You're the best."

"Back at you."

On the drive back to Morro Bay, I thought about my dad's reaction. Maybe it was my already suspicious frame of mind, but it felt like my father was hiding something. But what? What could he possibly have to hide?

Back at Mr. Chandler's house, I wandered around the living room trying to decide what to do next. The trail seemed to have grown cold after the trip to Bakersfield. I took all his wood carving lessons out to the patio and sat in one of the padded redwood chairs. The sun was bright and warm, and Morro Rock glistened. Saturday was a busy day on the Embarcadero, the day tourists flocked from Bakersfield, Fresno, and points north and south, to enjoy the natural ocean breezes and manufactured nautical ambiance.

While sipping a Coke and occasionally scratching Scout's stomach with my foot, I reread the lesson/clues left by Mr. Chandler. I kept coming back to the sentence *The stone is important.* I turned the two flat, white stones over and over. Then it dawned on me what I still hadn't done, talked to anyone in the Wood-carvers' Guild. I drove over to the folk art museum and made my obligatory appearance. While I was there, I looked up the number for the San Celina Wood-carvers' Guild. My contact had been a Mr. Ron Staples, president of the guild. Fortunately he was home. Unfortunately he vaguely remembered meeting a Jacob Chandler, but that was it.

"You say you're looking for him? Have you tried the north county guild? Most of our members are from south county."

I didn't want to go into detail, so I asked, "Do you have the number for the president of the north county guild?"

After thanking him and saying good-bye, I dialed the number he'd given me. A man answered, "Wood-carvers' Museum. Can I help you?"

"Is . . ." I checked my scribbles, "Don Ferron there?"

"He moved to Salt Lake City last month. Can I help you?"

"Who is the guild president now?"

"We're coasting right now. Lucinda Mackey is the vice president, so I guess she's in charge."

I thought for a moment. Should I call this Don Ferron in Salt Lake City? Would Jacob Chandler have made a contingency plan in case one of the people he'd given instructions to moved . . . or died?

"Ma'am, is there something I can help you with?" the man asked.

To get the person's phone number in Salt Lake City, I figured I'd have to at least identify myself and give some explanation. "Well, my name is Benni Harper. . ."

"Oh, Ms. Harper!" he exclaimed. "I have a package for you. Don said you'd probably be calling."

My stomach tightened again. It was getting more than a little eerie how thorough this man had been. "How late are you open?"

"Until five o'clock."

It was three o'clock now, so if I broke a law or two, I could make it. I dropped by the house in Morro Bay briefly to pet Scout and promise him a meaty bone if he'd forgive me for leaving him to guard the place one more time.

"I know you want to go," I said as he whined plaintively behind the gate, "but I really feel better with you protecting the place. Besides, with the speed I'll have to drive, I don't want to risk both our lives. Now remember, Duane and Cole are bad guys. Bite them if they come into the yard."

The Wood-carvers' Museum was about twenty miles up Pacific Coast Highway past the towns of Cambria, Cayucos, and Harmony. I glanced at the turnoff for Harmony as I passed and wondered briefly if Azanna Nybak was mourning Jacob right now.

The museum was located among a strip of highway shops that served passing tourists and the nearby residents of the small town of San Simeon, which crouched below the monolithic Hearst Castle, the only true tourist trap between the artsy shops of Cambria and Big Sur. Tucked among a candy store, a kite shop, and general store selling drinks, beef jerky, and postcards, the museum appeared to be just another gift shop with an emphasis on wood items. But if you looked closer at the wooden items for sale you could tell these weren't some Made in China knickknacks, but one-of-a-kind, hand-carved bowls and animals and even, incredibly, wooden matchsticks carved in the shapes of scissors, forks, and knives.

Since no one seemed to be around, I wandered through the free museum in the back of the store, looking at exhibits by California wood-carvers. They included a mantle, chest, and picture frame carved by Arthur Julius Kofod, who worked on Hearst Castle, and another master carver, the late Rudolph Vargas, who lived in the San Gabriel Valley. Back in the gift shop area, I was studying the detailed sheep and cattle in a rosewood nativity scene when a square, solid-looking young man came out from a door behind the counter.

"Oh, hello," he said, his hand flying up to stroke his dark goatee. "I didn't hear you come in."

I walked over to him. "Hello, Mr. . . ." I glanced at his name tag, then couldn't help smiling. "Burl?"

He gave an ironic laugh. "My father had a very wry sense of humor, and yes, I've heard every wood joke there is. I hated my name when I was a kid, but now I can appreciate its uniqueness. And since I carve now, too, it's a great conversation starter."

"No doubt. My name is Benni Harper, and I just called—"

"Wow, that was fast." He held up a finger. "Just a minute."

In a few seconds, Burl came back carrying two packages. One was a sealed manila envelope, the other was wrapped in white tissue paper. The second package was oval and about eight to ten inches long.

"So, how's old Jake doing?" Burl asked.

I paused a moment before telling him the bad news. His dark eyes blinked rapidly for a moment. "I liked Jake. He never talked down to me when I was a kid. I learned a lot about wood carving watching him." The young man took a deep breath. "He was a pallbearer at my dad's funeral last year."

"I'm so sorry."

He looked down at the tissue-wrapped package with a question in his eyes.

229

Without a word, I unwrapped it, knowing from its weight and feel that it was something Jacob Chandler had carved. A murmur of appreciation came from Burl when I pulled back the last piece of tissue. Wet heat burned at the back of my eyes.

It was a bas-relief portrait in pale oak of my mother. He'd somehow captured in the hard, unforgiving wood her delicate, heart-shaped face; her strong chin; the slight downward slant of her eyes, eyes that stared back at me in the mirror every morning. Her lips turned upward in the shy, half smile she wore in so many of her photographs.

"My dad used to beg Jake to enter his work in competitions," Burl said, touching a finger to my mother's smooth cheek. "But he never would. Said he carved for himself, not to compete with other people."

I quickly wrapped the wood portrait back up and clutched it and the unopened manila envelope to my chest. "Thank you, Burl. I'm sorry I couldn't tell you about his service. He didn't leave me a list of people to call. He's buried in the Paso Robles Cemetery."

Burl nodded, his hand stroking his goatee. "That's okay. I'll let the other people in the guild know."

"Okay, thanks." Then I remembered the stones. I pulled them out of my purse and set them on the counter before him. "Do you know what these are?"

He picked them up. "Sure, they're sharpening stones. Good ones."

"Anything in particular you can tell me about them?"

He set them back down on the counter. "Not much. They're just a couple of good Arkansas natural oilstones. Some carvers think they're the best there is."

"Arkansas? That's the name of the stone?"

He nodded. "Yeah, there's a black Arkansas, too, that's not translucent like these."

The stone is important. Was this what he meant? It was important because it was another link to Arkansas and my mother?

I thanked Burl and started toward the door. Just as I opened it, he called to me. "Hey, I never asked. Were you related to him or something?"

Without turning around and without stopping, I answered over my shoulder. "I honestly don't know."

In the truck I tore open the manila envelope and found another wood carving lesson and five white letter-size envelopes addressed to Jacob Chandler. Every one was addressed to General Delivery and postmarked a different town: Flagstaff, Arizona; Eugene, Oregon; Spokane, Washington; Bakersfield, California; San Bernardino, California.

All of them were in my mother's handwriting.

My hands shook as I arranged them by postmarked dates. The first one was dated June 2, 1961. The last one was a little over two months before my mother died— April 13, 1964.

The cab of the truck suddenly felt stifling. I rolled down the window halfway and pulled the two sheets of thin blue stationery out of the first letter.

Dear Jacob, the letter started.

I refolded the letter and shoved it back in the envelope. I couldn't read my mother's letters in the parking lot of a strip mall. Instead, I read the wood carving lesson.

No matter how carefully you work, sometimes you cut too deeply or break off a piece. Don't lose hope. Stop and think before going on. You may be able to use the mistake to your benefit. Sometimes the mistake can be repaired with wood putty or

231

epoxy resin filler. Cutting too deeply is harder to correct. Often the only solution is to carve around the mistake and attempt to blend it into your design. Sometimes there is no solution, and the wood must be tossed away. Don't be afraid to experiment. Don't copy what others create, but listen to your heart and carve its voice. Details make the carving come alive. One detail may be the secret to the whole piece. Search for that detail.

One detail? What was he talking about? I read it over again slowly, trying to make sense of the directions. There was no doubt that what he was having me search for was somehow hidden in these messages. Was it his true identity? His connection to my mother? Something else?

Maybe the answers were in my mother's letters to him. The miles back to Morro Bay seemed endless. I kept glancing over at the manila envelope, tempted to pull over and read them immediately. Instead I drove as fast as I dared, fighting the evening wind buffeting the truck.

I parked the truck haphazardly in front of the charred garage and rushed through the back gate, expecting an enthusiastic welcome from Scout.

The yard was empty. I called out his name a few times while circling the house. There was no way for him to get inside because I'd locked the dog-door, certain that somehow it would provide a means for Duane or Cole to do something destructive. Just in case, I checked through the house, only panicking when finding the last room empty. I'd owned Scout long enough to know he was not the type of dog to wander off. He was so well trained that not even cats could tempt him to venture off his own property.

"Next door," I said out loud, relieved. "He's probably visiting Rich."

Rich said the last he'd seen of Scout was about two hours ago. "I walked down to the bookstore on the Embarcadero. He was lying on the front porch when I left."

Panic turned my mouth to cotton. I licked my lips, salty with fear. "Rich, he wouldn't run off."

"First, let's not jump to any conclusions. We'll drive around and look for him. Maybe he's just acting out because he's mad you left him alone."

For the next two hours we drove around Morro Bay searching for him, including the narrow, rocky hills across the highway where houses clung to the rocks like barnacles. It was dark when Rich convinced me that we'd be better off going back home and calling the county animal shelter. Maybe somebody had picked him up.

After a call to the animal shelter came up dry, a thought occurred to me. "Duane and Cole are involved with this. I bet they have him."

Before he could stop me, I rushed across the street to their little saltbox house. One light shone through a front window, but no one answered my urgent knocking. I called Scout's name through the window, listening for his frantic bark. The house was silent. I tried the back gate. It was locked.

"Benni, don't you think . . ." Rich started to protest as I climbed the wood stake fence surrounding their backyard. I was over it before he could get the rest of his words out.

He was standing in the front yard, his arms folded across his chest when I climbed back over the fence.

"Nothing back there," I said, ignoring his

disapproving expression. "I know they have something to do with it. I'm going down to Tess's store and find out where they are. Don't try to stop me."

"Benni, I wouldn't even try to, but I am going with you."

"Fine, the more manpower the better."

Tess was sitting behind the counter on a metal stool, reading a *Good Housekeeping* magazine when I burst through the door. Shell wind chimes hanging next to the door clattered from the sharp whoosh of evening air. Her head jerked up from her magazine with a sharp, startled gasp. No one was in the store, though the other Embarcadero shops were crowded with tourists. The room smelled pungently of dust, old mold, and grease from the fish-and-chips restaurant next door.

"Where are Duane and Cole?" I demanded. "They took my dog and I want him back."

Her expression turned into one of practiced denial. "My boys wouldn't do that. They liked Jake's dog."

"Scout is *my* dog, and he's gone. You know he'd never wander anywhere, and your *boys* have been harassing me for a week. I'm warning you, if they've done anything to Scout . . ."

She tossed her magazine on the counter and slipped down from her stool. "I told you my sons liked Jake's dog. Besides, they wouldn't hurt an innocent animal. They—"

"Where are they? I want to ask them myself."

She pressed her painted orange lips together tightly and didn't answer. From behind me, Neely's voice called across the store. "They're over at the Masthead saloon like they always are on Saturday nights. Now leave her alone."

I turned and watched her walk across the store toward

234

us. Her shaggy brown hair was pulled up with a plastic hair clip. In the fluorescent lights of the store, her face was as pale and emotionless as a clamshell.

"Keep cool," I heard Rich murmur behind me.

"You know about this," I snapped at her.

Neely's face stayed calm. "I told you where they are, now get out."

"If I don't find them there, I'll be back."

Her glittery laugh was sharp as glass. "Don't worry, they'll be there."

Out on the street Rich caught my arm to keep me from darting in front of a van full of college students.

"Slow down, kid. We need to think this thing out before we go barreling into a dive like the Masthead."

I jerked my arm out of his grasp and started walking uptown. "If it's too tough for you, then go home," I said over my shoulder. "I'm going to find Duane and Cole and make them tell me where my dog is."

He jogged to catch up with me, his dark face irritated. "You are as stubborn and bullheaded as a donkey, little girl."

"Are you coming or not?" I asked, walking up the steep hill toward downtown.

"I'm with you," he said with an exasperated sigh. "I'd never forgive myself or be able to face your husband if I didn't."

I stopped and faced him. "Look here, Mr. Trujillo, if you think I can't take care of myself, guess again. I'm not afraid to go into that bar and confront them without you."

"I know you're not, Benni. *That's* what really scares me."

The Masthead was the last of the old-time fisherman's bars built back when fish not tourists were the town's

235

biggest economic power. It sat on a corner in an innocuous white building. The gray, peeling sign was shaped like a barracuda. Underneath the sign were black-tinted windows, a small yellow neon light announcing "cocktails," and the ever alluring orange and purple California Lotto sticker.

I burst through the door into a cramped, dark bar that didn't look any different than any cowboy bar I'd ever been in, except for the fact that the music playing was rock and roll instead of country, and the multicolored gimme caps worn by the patrons promoted fishing industries rather than feed stores and tractor dealerships.

I spotted Duane and Cole across the room sitting with a grizzled old man wearing a Greek fisherman's hat and a thin, hard-looking woman with unnaturally bright copper-colored hair. I pushed through the loud, laughing crowd, dodged a moving pool cue, and planted myself in front of their table.

"Where's my dog?" I asked over the deafening voices around me. I felt Rich move up behind me and rest his hand lightly on my shoulder. Deep in my throat a cough from hovering cigarette smoke tickled, threatening to erupt. I swallowed saliva and fought the urge.

"What?" Cole said, his face frozen in genuine surprise. Next to him, the old man picked through a plastic bowl of stale-looking bar mix.

The woman gave a raspy laugh and nudged Duane with her elbow. "Duane, baby, this little girl's lost her doggie. You seen it?"

Duane smiled slyly, then slowly took a sip of his beer.

"Where is he?" I asked, raising my voice an octave. No one in the deafening crowd even noticed.

"We don't know what you're talking about," Cole said, his eyes darting to his brother, then back to me.

236

"I swear, I'll kill you both if you've hurt Scout."

Duane said in a loud voice to no one in particular, "Now, isn't threatening to kill someone, like, some kind of crime or something? Think they'd lock up a police chief's wife for that, or would she just get off with a hand slap? What do you think, Cap?" The man continued picking through the bowl and didn't answer.

I leaned closer, resting both hands flat on the table. "Where's my dog?"

Duane brought his beer up to his lips and drank. Foam dotted the tips of his thin mustache when he smirked at me. "Honey, you're ruining our evening with friends here, accusing us of such a terrible thing as dognapping. Maybe you should use some of those same connections you used to get us harassed by the local pig squad and have them find your mutt."

"I'm only going to ask one more time," I said, anger rising up in me like water boiling. Rich's hand tightened on my shoulder. *"What have you done with my dog?"*

Duane looked over at his brother, who shook his head slightly. He licked his lips and said, "Like I said, if you'd just twitch that fine little ass of yours under your police chief's nose, I'm sure he'd call out the whole force to find your puppy dog."

I grabbed the half-full beer stein sitting in front of him and threw the beer in his face. The woman screamed and jumped up, frantically brushing at her thin silver blouse.

"Shit, you little . . ." Duane yelled, lunging at me over the wet table. Cole grabbed his shoulders, holding him back.

Laughter surrounded us as I felt Rich move between me and Duane and start forcefully pushing me toward the exit.

"Hustle your butt, kid," he commanded in my ear. "Don't look back."

We were outside by the time Duane made it to the doorway of the bar. Yelling out curses at me, he was held back by Cole and another man. "You'll be sorry," were the last words I heard before Rich and I rounded the corner out of earshot.

Rich kept his arm around my trembling shoulders the three blocks back to my house. By the time we reached my gate, I was calmer but still angry.

"I guess I don't have to tell you that wasn't the smartest thing in the world to do," he said.

At this point I was so tired of the whole situation involving Jacob Chandler that I didn't care. "I know."

"I think you should call your husband."

"No."

He gave me a strange look. "He has a right to know."

"He doesn't have a right to anything."

"What happened between you two?"

I frowned at him. "Nothing."

He looked at me for a long moment, his dark face calm. "I realize it's none of my business, but I'm worried about you."

"Don't be. I've got enough problems with one overly protective man, thank you very much."

His hurt expression caused guilt and regret at my hasty words to pull at my heart. This man had not only just ridden around with me for two hours looking for my dog, but also he was willing to try to protect me from a crowd of drunk white men, and here I was treating him like dirt. I was glad Dove wasn't around to see me or I'd be getting a slap upside the head.

"I'm sorry, Rich, that was rude of me. I do appreciate you helping me look for Scout and for everything you've

238

done. The thing with Gabe, it's just so complicated."

"Want to talk about it?" He pointed to my concrete steps. "As Lucy from *Peanuts* would say, the doctor is in."

I didn't think I did, but once I sat down and started telling him the true identities of the photographer and his wife, I found myself pouring out all my feelings about Gabe and how torn I felt about his way of caring for me, the doubts I had about being married to a cop. He listened without comment until like a worn-out battery I eventually stopped talking.

When he saw that I was finished, he spoke. "Now, don't get mad at me, but I'm going to try to let you see things from his side."

"I've already heard it," I said, hating myself for being so ungracious, but not wanting to hear one more lecture, not even from someone as nice as Rich. "His best friend, Aaron; his captain, Jim Cleary; Jim's wife, Oneeda. I've heard all the advice about being married to a cop. I just don't know if it's something I'm cut out for."

"I'm not talking about being married to a cop. I'm talking about being married to a Mexican man."

I looked at him in surprise. "What does that have to do with any of this?"

"More than you probably even realize. Don't you know that he has to be twice as good and work twice as hard as a white man just to get people to treat him the same? On top of that, he's a stranger in town. If he was white and had grown up around here and became police chief, his wife being involved with the things you are would be just something to razz him about at the local bar. In his case, it's a direct reflection on his ability to handle his family as well as be a good police chief."

239

"That's ridiculous! What my family or I do has nothing to do with how well he performs his job."

"That's where you're living in a dreamworld. You're a white woman who belongs to a well-respected ranching family. You gain instant acceptance just for being born who you are. He, on the other hand, has probably had to earn every inch of respect he's ever gotten and probably always will."

Suddenly I felt like the biggest idiot in the world. To be truthful, I didn't think about Gabe's Latino background any more than I did Elvia's, or Señor and Señora Aragon's, or any of her brothers. I'd gone to school with them; stayed with them; been in their weddings; attended their family's baby christenings, *quinceañeras,* engagement parties, and funerals. I'd participated in all aspects of their lives, just as they had mine. Gabe being part Mexican hadn't ever been an issue between us. At least for me. If he'd suffered any prejudice because of his background, he'd never shared it with me, and that made me feel ashamed as well as feel like a failure both as a wife and a friend.

"You're right, we . . . I don't make things easy for him," I said softly, looking up at Rich's kind face.

He put a warm hand on mine. "Just remember, *Quien mas te quiere te hace llorar.*"

"Translation, *por favor.*"

"He who most loves you makes you cry." He smiled. "And that goes for she, too. But in the long run, it's worth it. I promise you."

I squeezed his hand and stood up. "Thanks, Rich."

"*De nada, mija.*"

Inside the house, it was unbearably silent without Scout's presence. I hadn't realized how quickly he'd become a part of my life. My mother's letters were sitting on the counter where I'd thrown them, so I made myself a cup of hot chocolate and took them out to the patio. The lights down on the Embarcadero twinkled on the dark ocean. Morro Rock, barely discernible in the dark, was already shrouded in mist. I pulled Gabe's leather jacket around me, rubbing my cheek a moment against the buttery collar, smelling his scent, then opened the first letter. It was addressed to Jacob Chandler, General Delivery, Flagstaff, Arizona. The postmark was Los Angeles.

June 2, 1961
Dear Jacob,

I've missed you so much. You left so quickly and without much explanation that I was very angry with you for a long time. I understand now and can live with it, though it saddens me that we can never see each other again. There is so much to tell you I don't even know where to start. When I received the letter from you I almost fainted. I was sure you were dead. I have done as you asked and not told Ben about you. You're right, it would just complicate things, and heaven knows none of us needs that right now. You would like Ben. He is a good, solid man and he loves me very much. We met in Little Rock when I was living with Ervalean. We lived with his mother for the first three years and have only been here at the ranch for two months. I am learning to be a good ranch wife. His mother is a wonderful woman who has treated me as if I were her own daughter. I miss Mother, though. It's still hard to believe that she and Daddy have been gone for almost five years now. You never mentioned how you found me, but

241

then I didn't make a secret of where we were going. You always were such a clever man I suppose you found some means to track me down. It is very beautiful here (I am doing as you say and not mentioning the town and will give this to a friend to mail the next time she goes to Los Angeles). It doesn't look at all like where we came from. I miss the thick pine trees, though oaks have their own special beauty. Speaking of beauty, did you know I have a little girl? Her name is Albenia Louise. We call her Benni. I wish you could see her. She seems to grow faster than the weeds that I pull from my flower garden every day. She was three in March, and already Ben has her riding a pony all by herself. And she's not a bit afraid, a trait she certainly doesn't get from me. Ben tries to get me to ride, but you know how frightened I am of animals. Except for cats. Remember the tabby we fed in the alley? I wonder what happened to her.

I stopped reading for a moment when an overwhelming sadness flickered in my chest. Closing my eyes, I tried to picture the face of the woman who'd written this letter thirty-three years ago. My memories were of photos, though, not of a real, flesh-and-blood person. Her touch was something that no matter how hard I tried, I couldn't recall. I brought the thin blue stationery up to my nose, but any lingering scent had dissipated years ago. I stared at the letter for a moment and realized something—she wrote her *B*'s like I did. That small similarity struck me in the heart like a physical blow.

There's so much to say I don't know where to begin. I am happy, don't worry about that, though I miss you and wish things could have turned out differently. I don't yet understand why God has arranged things the way He has, but the minister at our church preached a sermon on faith last Sunday and said that if we knew what would happen every step of the way in our lives, then faith would have no meaning. To be honest, I'm pretty certain I wouldn't want to know what is ahead of me. You always think that if you knew the future you would somehow do things different, but I don't think many of us would. Well, Benni is waking up from her nap now so I'd better go. I'll write again and tell you more about my life. I hope you are safe and well and have friends. The thought of you being alone breaks my heart. I wish I was there to give you a hug. I pray for you every night. Did I tell you she has your smile? All my love, your Ally Lou

Each letter was a little longer but ran along the same vein. She told a little more about me in each one, and I felt like I was watching myself grow up through my mother's eyes. She told this man things that if she ever told my dad, he never passed on to me—like what I brought home in my pockets after playing down at the creek; how I loved fried baloney sandwiches; how the only thing that frightened me was grasshoppers, which she found odd because I'd pick up a spider or a snail without hesitation; and how, when I had just turned five, I'd climbed on the roof of the house with the intention of jumping on my pony's back like I'd seen on television, but instead fell off, gashing my forehead. She didn't tell my father about it when she saw I was okay, because he wouldn't let me watch Westerns with him anymore, and she knew that would kill me.

I touched the scar on the right side of my forehead, the one I'd always had and began covering with bangs when I turned thirteen and became suddenly concerned about my looks. I'd always wondered where it had come from, and no one had ever been able to tell me.

There was something about these letters that bothered me and not just because they were my mother's voice from the grave. It was the intimacy in them. With each one came a slow and terrifying realization that this man wasn't just a friend, that he was more. One line repeated itself over and over in my mind.

Did I tell you she has your smile?

I shivered with an internal chill from the implication in that sentence. The thought of my mother having a lover was shocking. The thought that he might be my biological father was beyond my ability to comprehend. Desperately I tried to reason it away. Surely Daddy would have known if she'd been cheating on him? When in the world could she have seen this man, living out on the farm with Daddy and Dove and the whole Ramsey clan?

Unless she knew him before she met Daddy. I went inside and dialed Dove's number at the museum. She answered on the second ring.

"Dove, it's Benni."

"Honeybun, are you all right? I heard about the fire."

"I'm fine, really. Don't forget, I've got Scout to protect me." I hesitated, then said, "I have a quick question for you. What year did Daddy and Mama get married?"

A long silence answered me.

"Dove?"

"Have you talked to your daddy about this?"

"I'm asking you."

Another silence, then she said, "People made mistakes back in our time too, but they did right by you. Don't you forget that."

"Dove, please."

"It was 1957, but—"

"Thank you," I interrupted, not wanting to go into this until I let it sink in. "I'll see you tomorrow. I'll bring the other things you all requested, that was a large pepperoni pizza, right?"

"Make it two. We're getting tired of canned food in here. And be careful how you talk to your daddy about this. It's a sore spot."

"I love you, Gramma." I said softly and hung up.

August 2, 1957. My birthday was March 23, 1958. According to my birth certificate I weighed 8 lbs. 2 oz. at birth. By no means a premature baby. That meant my mother was probably two months' pregnant when she and my father were married.

I went back outside and sat staring at the ocean, watching the lights sparkle like bits of broken glass on the smooth surface, wrapping myself tighter in my husband's jacket, craving his arms around me. The fact that my mother was pregnant when she and my father were married changed everything. It occurred to me that if Daddy wasn't my biological father, then Dove and all my aunts, uncles, and cousins were no more related to me than the man on the street corner. That I truly had no family left in this world.

I wanted to cry. There was a lot to cry for—my mother and the years I never had her; for this strange man who meant so much to her, a man who could possibly be my father; for Scout, who was lost and maybe hurt somewhere. But tears wouldn't come.

Something was stuck, like a sideways log in a river of floating mill wood, keeping everything trapped in slow moving water.

Sometime during the night, I fell asleep, my dreams troubled with vague, unsettling scenes. In one dream, I was a little girl again, lost in a huge department store, surrounded by stuffed animals that towered over me with grotesque, toothy grins. A wetness on my hand startled me awake. A soft whine broke through my grogginess.

"Scout!" I cried, and he jumped up on the lounge chair, wet and muddy and panting hard, licking my face with his rough tongue. I hugged his thick, warm body, sent a quick thanks up to God, and took him inside.

13

AFTER WASHING AND DRYING AN EXHAUSTED SCOUT, I eventually went to bed at four-thirty. It was past ten o'clock the next morning when we both woke up. I immediately called Rich and told him the good news.

"They must have just dropped him off somewhere," Rich said. "Are you all right?"

"Just a bit groggy. I'm going into town today, so maybe I'll catch you later."

"Be careful, Benni. If you see those Briggstones, run the other way."

"If I see them, they'd better be the ones running."

Taking Scout with me, I walked down to the Embarcadero and ate a quick breakfast at the doughnut shop. Since it was Mother's Day, all the restaurants would be filled with people taking their mothers out for breakfast, and that was something I couldn't bear to experience right now. Two grizzled old fishermen shared the warm, yeasty-smelling room with me. As they argued about the demise of the once prolific fishing industry on the Central Coast, I sat by the window, watching the sky turn dark and cloudy, and reread my mother's letters. I was in a quandary as to where to turn next. If Jacob Chandler was indeed my biological father, that explained why he had left me his estate. What I couldn't understand is why he'd never made an attempt to talk to me all those years he was watching me. Was it out of kindness or fear? Another question that hovered around me like the clouds gathering over the bay was, did Daddy know? Or had he always assumed I was his? Could my mother have been that deceitful? Everything in me cried *no*, my mother would never do that. But in reality I knew nothing about the woman who bore me or about her life before she married my father.

My heart froze when I silently said those words. My father. Just who was my father?

It had grown colder and drizzly by noon when I finally made myself drive into San Celina. I dreaded seeing Dove, fearing she'd pry out of me this information that I wasn't willing to share with anyone yet. I dropped by the pizza parlor and picked up my order. Around the Historical Museum activity had heated up—there seemed to be twice as many newspeople around, probably because this would make one of those amusing, Mother's-Day gone-wrong news bites that television newscasters liked to end their shows with. Miguel, a police officer and one of Elvia's brothers, was guarding the front door of the museum when I walked up, juggling my two steaming pizza boxes and the bag containing their other requests.

"Hi, Miguel," I said.

"Hi, when'd you get a dog?" Miguel asked, bending over to run a large brown hand over Scout's head.

"He came with the house I inherited. You haven't heard?"

His young beardless face sobered. "Yeah, I heard about it. Down at the station we've been bearing the brunt of you being gone. You'd better get home quick, Benni. I swear you're the only thing that keeps him in a decent mood."

"Not always," I said grimly. "There's a week left on my sentence, but I won't guarantee me going back home will soften Gabe's mood."

"Believe me, we can tell the difference when you're not there."

"So, how's the San Celina Seven holding up?"

He shrugged. "I heard some shouting in there a few hours ago, but when I knocked on the door and asked if everything was all right, Dove told me it was nothing."

"Guess I'd better check it out."

Elmo Ritter let me in, and judging by the strained look on his face as well as the frantic stroking of the struggling cat in his arms, I could tell the pressure was getting to him.

"Are you okay, Elmo?" I asked in a low voice, handing him his avocados.

"You gotta break me out of here, Benni. Those women are driving me crazy. They've got me moving furniture so much I'll have to sign all my Social Security checks over to my chiropractor for the next two years. And the fights?" He rolled his watery eyes. "Lord, have mercy, they commence to arguing about situations that happened almost forty years ago. Who really gives a flying fig what color blue the draperies of Mott's Mortuary was in 1959?"

I tried not to crack a smile. "Everyone's getting a little stir-crazy?"

"They've gone nuts," he said, circling his finger around his temple.

"I heard that, Elmo Ritter," June Rae called across the room. "You're not so sane yourself."

After greeting everyone and giving them the pizzas, which they fell to like a pack of starving hyenas, I pulled Dove aside. "Okay, what's going on?"

She gave the group a disgusted look. "I tell you, if these people had been in charge of the American Revolution, we'd all be eatin' fish-and-chips and singing 'God Save the Queen.'"

"What's caused dissention in the ranks?"

"June Rae and Goldie had a big argument last night about whether Rubylee Smythe should have won the blue ribbon for her fudge at the Mid-State fair last August."

"I like Rubylee's fudge. It always wins."

"Well, so do I and so does half the United States. Everyone and his old maid aunt knows the recipe she uses is on back of the marshmallow creme jar."

I groaned. "That's awful. What if the judges found out?"

"The judges *know*. They give her the ribbon every year anyway because she's got those two terrible boys who are in and out of prison so much, and her daughter's married to a podiatrist who was arrested for playing with his patients' feet, and her granddaughter's got diabetes. That blue ribbon is the only thing that keeps her sane, and Goldie Kleinfelder knows that. Goldie's just mad because Oscar took Rubylee to the prom instead of Goldie, and Goldie's never forgotten it."

"Goldie's husband had a fling with Rubylee Smythe?"

"I don't know if they flinged any, but they sure danced close all night, according to Goldie. For heaven's sakes, that was over sixty years ago. These old people need to get a life." Dove glared at them, then looked back at me. "I don't know how much more I can take."

"Well, it looks like things are heating up outside. You're bound to get great coverage, it being Mother's Day and all. Is the mayor or city council weakening at all?"

"Last we heard, the city council was still deadlocked, and only the mayor can break the tie. We're asking for a twenty-year unbreakable lease. Your lawyer friend Amanda is helping us with that. No charge."

"You have the best legal counsel, that's for sure. Anything I can do to help?"

She shook her head. "The pizzas were perfect. You're a good granddaughter."

Her comment must have caused a tiny reaction on my face, because she pulled me in her arms, something unusual for Dove, and hugged me to her. I buried my face in her soft, talcum-scented neck and felt tears for the first time prick at my eyes.

"I know this day is hard for you, honeybun. If there had been any way possible, your mama would be here with you. Don't you ever doubt that. And no matter what, I know for a fact she loved you more than her own life. I seen it myself."

"I have to go," I said, abruptly pulling out of her arms, determined to make it through this day without tears. I gave her the greeting card out of my leather backpack. "As soon as you're free again, I'll take you to dinner."

She took the card, watching me with worried eyes. "I'll hold you to it."

Outside, Gabe lingered at the Incident Command Post, dressed in jeans and a gray cotton sweater. We caught each other's eyes, but I looked away first. Rich's words about how difficult it was for Gabe being a Mexican man echoed through my mind. Guilt and anger congealed inside me, but rather than try to sort the feelings out, I set them aside. I had to figure out this thing with my mother and father first. After a brief noncommittal statement to the *Tribune* and *Freedom Press,* I headed for my truck where I used my cellular phone to call Emory at his house. Scout curled up on the seat next to me.

"You almost missed me," he said. "I'm on my way to Elvia's for the big Mother's Day doin's."

"I'll probably see you later, then, when I drop by before going to the cemetery. I was wondering if you found out anything for me." I reached over and stroked Scout's head as Emory talked.

"Took some huntin', but I didn't fail you. I called the minister at the church my mama attended all her life, and bless those Southern Baptists, they do keep tabs on one another even if a flock member does leave the fold. He's retired now, but he gave me the number of a woman who is apparently the unofficial historian of Little Rock First Baptist. She dug through her extensive records and memories and came up with a woman she remembered had been friends with Mama back in the fifties—one Edith Maxeen Cravens, who left the church to become a Methodist in '62, but still makes it back for the dinner-on-the-grounds anniversary once a year because she says the Methodists never have learned how to make a decent fried chicken. The woman gave me

Edith's last known phone number in Nashville—that's Arkansas, not Tennessee. She wasn't there anymore, given that her husband had died and left her a tidy little sum, but Nashville's not that big, and the woman who now has her phone number knows Edith Maxeen's daughter from PTA and who since last spring lives in— you won't believe this—Nashville, Tennessee. She apparently works for a music publisher. At any rate, I called her and with some finagling and dropping of mutual acquaintances' names managed to get her mama's new phone number in—get this—Arkansas City, Kansas, where she is living with her new husband, a born-again Catholic who talks in tongues and makes windmills—not, I'm assuming, at the same time, which could prove dangerous. You want her number?"

Only Emory could manage to make me laugh on a day like today. "Thanks, Emory. I owe you a double lobster dinner complete with dessert."

"Sweetcakes, if you can keep what all I just told you straight, I'll buy you dinner." He paused for a moment. "You been to see Dove?"

"Things are getting mutinous over there. I'm not sure how long they're all going to last."

"Rumor has it they've got an ace they haven't dealt yet."

"What's that?"

"I don't know, they wouldn't tell me. But it sounds big."

I sighed. "I don't even want to think about what it might be."

"Whereas I, on the other hand, can't wait."

Calling Arkansas City, Kansas, was definitely out of my price range on my cellular, so I walked two blocks down to Blind Harry's to use the phone in Elvia's office. I tied Scout's leash to the wooden bench outside and promised I wouldn't be long. Her office was empty, as I knew it would be, and I settled down in her high-back executive chair, took a long drink of my coffee for caffeine courage, and dialed Edith Maxeen Cravens in Arkansas City, Kansas.

After five rings, a delicate female voice answered in a soft, Arkansas drawl. "Hello?"

"Is there an Edith Maxeen Cravens there?"

"That's me, hon."

My voice froze for a moment. Realizing I hadn't made any plan about what to say, how much to tell her, how I would phrase my questions, I hit my thigh in frustration. Why did I jump so fast into things before thinking them out? Over the phone, her thin voice said, "Hello? Is anyone there?"

"I'm sorry," I said, regaining my voice. "My name is Benni Harper, and I got your name from my cousin, Emory Littleton."

"Ervalean and Boone's little boy? He was such a sweet thing. Always did such a good job raking my leaves and such a talker. I swear, he was a born politician, that one." She hesitated for a moment. "Harper, you said? Now that sounds vaguely familiar. Are you related to JoNelle Harper down around Blevins?"

"I don't think so. My husband's people were from Texas. I hate to bother you, but I have a question about someone you might have known a long time ago."

"Well, hon, my memory isn't as good as it once was, but I'll do my best, seein' as you're kin of Emory's. How is he anyway?"

"He's doing fine. He's living out here near me in California for a while. He's a journalist."

253

"Do tell. Well, he always was a little chatterbox. Now, you hug his neck for me and tell him hello. Who was it you needed to know about?"

"Does the name Gwen Swanson sound familiar?"

"Oh, my, yes. She attended Little Rock Baptist for about five years back in the fifties. She was church secretary for a while until she found herself a better-payin' job down in Pine Bluff. Her and Ervalean were real close. We all stayed in touch for years. Mostly just postcards. Married a man with the last name Felix who raised hogs. It didn't last. He was a Presbyterian."

"Do you know where she's living now?"

"Oh, my, no. I haven't heard from Gwen in over ten years. She retired early because of her arthritis and moved out your way to California there to be close to some relatives. Don't know exactly where. If you can hold on, I can check my old Christmas cards. I think I got one from her about ten years back, and me bein' such a packrat, I'll bet dollars to doughnuts I still have it. Now, you just hold on."

After about ten long minutes, she came back on the line. "Sorry, hon, but I had to climb up into the attic, and it's not as easy as it used to be. Sure enough, I got a Christmas card from her about ten years ago. Oh, my, I guess it's eleven. Here it is, Glendora, California." She read off the address.

"Thanks, Mrs. Cravens. I appreciate your help."

"I hate to be nosy, but do you mind telling me why you're huntin' her?"

"I want to see if she remembers my mother."

"Who was your mother?"

"Alice Louise Banks."

"Oh, my!" she exclaimed. "You're Alice Louise's little baby? Why, you were just a toddler last time I saw you."

"You knew my mother?"

"Oh, my, yes. We weren't in the same Sunday School class because I was a bit older, but I knew her all right. She and Ervalean were just like sisters. They even worked together at the same diner. I remember when she came to live with Ervalean. Such a pitiful thing about her parents being killed in that car wreck. I don't think she ever quite got over it. It was real hard on Ervalean when Alice moved out there to California. That's when Ervalean and Gwen became so close until Gwen up and moved, too. I remember Ervalean sayin' to me, 'People are always leaving me, Maxine. They're just always up and leaving me.' " She rambled on about church picnics and dinners, mutual acquaintances, and gossip about people I'd never heard of. I let her keep talking mostly because she seemed so glad to talk to someone about back home, but also because I hoped somewhere there would be something significant in the abundance of memories.

"There was this one time at the diner when Alice was just datin' Ben Ramsey . . .

"My father."

"That's right. Anyway, I was sittin' there enjoying my hamburger and milk shake—that was back when I could tolerate milk products—and this man kinda sidled in, hat pulled low, and asked for Alice. Why, she took one look at him, turned white as a ghost, and hustled him quick as you please back to the kitchen. About ten minutes later Gwen rushed in, and without so much as a how-dee-do-good-morning, *she* headed back to the kitchen. Then Ben came in, and Ervalean, who was waitin' all the tables at this point and going crazy, went back and got Alice. Alice was as flustered as a sparrow when she took his order.

Then Gwen came out and sat down at the counter and ordered herself a tuna melt, which to this day I thought was odd 'cause I knew for a fact she's always hated tuna."

"Did you see the man again?" I asked.

"Not ever. I tell you, it was a regular Laurel and Hardy skit except no one was laughin'. I don't know if this man was an old boyfriend or what, and I sure don't know what Gwen had to do with it except, like I said, she and your mama were pretty close for a while until your mama moved, but they must've gotten things all straightened out, though, 'cause it wasn't but a month or so later Ben and Alice just upped and got married quick as you please. Next thing I heard, we were bein' invited to a baby shower for you. How is your daddy, by the way? I heard about your mama's passin' a long time ago. I'm sure sorry, hon."

"Thank you. He's doing great. I just have a few more questions. Do you know if Gwen Swanson had a brother?"

"Oh, my, no. She was an only child. I think that's why her and your mama had so much in common. Ervalean kinda mothered them both, though she was not but five years older than either of them herself."

Well, that shot that theory. Jacob Chandler being Gwen's brother would have cleared up a lot. "You wouldn't by any chance have a phone number for Gwen Swanson, would you?"

"I'm sorry, I don't. We didn't keep that good of contact. It was sure nice chatting with you, but I have to go now, my cookies are buzzin'. Good luck to you, and say hello to Ben for me."

I hung up the phone and immediately went downstairs to the bookstore's map section. Glendora was a small

256

town about thirty miles southeast of Los Angeles near the foothills of the San Gabriel Mountains. Back upstairs in Elvia's office, I dialed information and asked for the number of Gwen Felix. I was amazed when the automatic voice came on and gave it. I sat and stared at the numbers I'd penciled on Elvia's personalized memo pad. It was yet another link between my mother and Jacob Chandler, one that I wasn't sure I wanted to delve deeper into. The story Mrs. Cravens had told me sounded an awful lot like there had been a romantic relationship between Mr. Chandler and my mother at the same time she was dating my father, and that this Gwen Swanson Felix knew about it. When I dialed the number, a woman's voice answered. In the background, I could hear rap music playing.

"Hello? Just a minute, excuse me . . ." I heard her yell out, "Would someone please turn down that stereo?" After a few seconds, the music became a soft thump-thump in the background. "I apologize," she said. "My sons are good boys, but very loud." I briefly explained who I was and that I was looking for a Gwen Swanson Felix.

"She doesn't live here anymore," the woman said, her voice instantly suspicious. "Is there something I can help you with?"

There was an awkward silence that made me grit my teeth since I knew how flaky it probably made me sound. "It's a long story, Ms . . ."

"Gloria Carrell."

I stumbled through a lame explanation of looking into my mother's roots, how she'd died when I was six, how I was tracing people who'd known her. "Edith Cravens gave me your name. She knew your . . . Mrs. Felix . . . back in Arkansas. They went to the same church."

She paused for a moment, then said. "Look, Ms. Harper, my aunt Gwen is not really herself anymore. They think it's probably Alzheimer's. I can't let you talk to her alone. I'll have to be there."

That wasn't my preference, but by the unwavering tone in her voice, I knew I didn't have a choice. "That's fine. When can I see her? If it isn't inconvenient, I'd really like to make it as soon as possible."

"How about tomorrow?"

I glanced down at the map I'd brought up to Elvia's office with me. Glendora was about a five-hour drive. If I started early I could make it up and back in one day. "Great. Should I meet you where she's staying?"

"She's at her best in the morning. How about ten o'clock? Meet me here at my house, and we can go together over to where she's living."

Smart woman. She wasn't about to let me sneak in early to question her aunt. I couldn't blame her. I'd have done the same thing if it had been Dove.

After getting her address, I thanked her and then, just in case I forgot to tell her, I wrote a quick note to Elvia explaining the long-distance charges that I'd put on her phone bill so no employee would get in trouble.

On the way to the Aragon house, I picked up my two orders of flowers at the florist. The drizzle had turned into a soft, steady rain by the time I arrived at the Aragons' cheerful yellow-and-white clapboard house. There had to be twenty cars parked out front, so I parked across the street and, sheltering Señora Aragon's roses against my chest, I dashed through the rain, weaving in and out of the Aragon children's vehicles. Emory's shiny new Cadillac Seville was parked among them, so I knew he'd made it for his first Aragon Mother's Day extravaganza. Inside the patchwork

258

house, which had started out a three-bedroom-one-bath and was now a six-bedroom-two bath with a new kitchen and spacious family room, I noticed that some construction was going on in the detached garage. Maybe, now that all the children except Ramon were gone, Señor Aragon was finally getting his dream workshop.

Inside the warm, steamy house, the men had taken over the kitchen, and I found my cousin grating cheese at the round maple table while enthusiastically defending the Arkansas Razorbacks to a bunch of die-hard UCLA Bruins fans. I settled Scout in the corner with a chew stick and perused what the guys had boiling and bubbling in the pots on Señora Aragon's sparkling clean stove.

"C'mon, Emory," Miguel said as he fried homemade taquitos. "Any team where the official battle cry is 'sooiee' cannot be a team that is to be taken seriously."

"I'll have you know, my young and virile gendarme, that it is a well-known fact that pigs are significantly more intelligent than bears."

That comment garnered a lot of hoots and hollers from Elvia's brothers.

"What did he call me?" Miguel asked me when I stole a hot taquito and dipped it into the guacamole his youngest brother Ramon was mixing.

"Check the dictionary," I said, laughing.

"Get out of here," Ramon said, pulling the bowl of guacamole out of my reach. "No chicks allowed until we're finished."

"What's on the menu?" I asked.

"You heard the man, sweetcakes, vamoose," Emory said, winking at me across the room. "The menu's our secret."

The kids had commandeered the big-screen television in the family room, and in the living room the women were sitting around a bowl of fresh, hot tortilla strips and green chile salsa. On the smaller television in the corner played the movie *When a Man Loves a Woman.*

"I would give up M&M's permanently for just one night with Andy Garcia," Ramon's girlfriend, Maria, was saying. The other women nodded and laughed in agreement. Señora Aragon sat in her husband's recliner, knitting. She *tsked* and shook her head in mock disapproval.

"Happy Mother's Day, Mama Aragon," I said, handing her the flowers.

"*Gracias, mija,*" *Señora* Aragon said. "They are *muy bonitas.* You are a good daughter. Have some chips. They are not crispy like mine, but they are *bueno.*"

We all laughed, knowing that letting the men invade her kitchen was not the treat for her that they thought it was. It took great forbearance and patience on her part to allow them this once-a-year access to her exclusive territory.

"I know, but we have to let them think they're as good," I said, taking one and dipping it into the salsa. "Those delicate egos."

"No kidding," Christina, Rafael's wife said. She taught fourth grade over at the school near the golf course development. "I tell Rafael that no one mops floors like he does just so he'll keep doing it."

"I never thought I'd see the day one of my macho brothers mopped a floor," Elvia said, rising up from where she was sitting next to her mother. "Here, I'll put these in water, Mama. You talk to Benni." As she passed me, she reached over and gave me a quick hug, a sign of deep affection from my normally reticent friend.

260

"You doing okay, *amiga?*" Though we didn't discuss it much, she knew how hard this day was for me.

"I'm fine," I said, hugging her back. "It's nice seeing Emory in there feeling so comfortable, don't you think?"

Her black eyes softened slightly, and she answered in a low voice, "I'll deny it if you tell him, but he's starting to grow on me."

"He has a way of doing that," I said, holding her gaze for a moment. This was no small thing for her to admit, and we both knew it.

"So, how's your leg?" I asked Señora Aragon and settled back to listen to her detailed explanation of what the doctor did about the small clot that had formed. By the time dinner was ready, it was ten minutes to six.

"Can't you stay for just one plate?" Señora Aragon asked, her lined brown face fretful.

"I'm really sorry, I can't," I said. "I promised I'd meet Daddy at the cemetery at six. I'm going to be late as it is." I grabbed another taquito and gazed longingly at the *pollo verde* and red chile tamales. "We're going out to eat afterwards, though I know it won't hold a candle to this feast."

"Give Señor Ben my greetings," Señora Aragon said. Her husband nodded his agreement. "This is a hard day for him." She put a plump arm around my shoulders. "And for you, too, *mija.*"

"Let me walk you out," Emory said, peeling off the white apron he was wearing over his pale blue Egyptian cotton dress shirt.

Outside, the rain had stopped, though the clouds were still black as tarnished silver and turbulent with moisture. With his sleeves casually rolled up and his blond hair hanging loose across his forehead, Emory

261

was more happy and relaxed than I'd ever seen him.

"You like the Aragon family, don't you?" I asked.

"Yes, I do," he said, sticking his hands in the pockets of his wool slacks. "They've been remarkably accepting of me. More so than that stubborn daughter of theirs."

"Don't worry, cuz. She really likes you. And she trusts you. That's saying a lot for Elvia."

His emerald eyes darkened. "Benni, what is it with her and men?"

Remembering the married sabbatical replacement professor who so calculatingly seduced then dropped her our senior year at Cal Poly, I shook my head. "That's not for me to tell you. Just keep doing what you're doing and you'll be fine."

"Are you all right?" he asked, pulling his hands out of his pocket and laying them on my shoulders, massaging them gently.

"Don't worry. Daddy and I have done this every year since I can remember. Situation normal." Except that it wasn't this year, and somehow Emory had sensed that.

"I'll call you later," he said, his face creased in worry.

"Get back to your dinner. They're going to eat up all the guacamole."

My father's truck was already parked in the cemetery parking lot. I left Scout in the cab and glanced around. Three other cars were there, and a small family group walked, laughing and talking, toward a grave near the back. Across from them, nearer the highway, my father held his hat in his hands, staring at my mother's headstone. Above me, a squirrel chattered and ran down the gray trunk of an old pine tree. The dense smell of the hothouse roses in my hands overwhelmed the faint scent of pine and fresh cut grass. My boots sank slightly in the soft soil, and though I tried not to think about it, it occurred to me I was treading across a multitude of bodies to reach my dad.

"Hi, Daddy." I kissed his cheek, then immediately sank to my knees, unwrapping the cellophane around the roses. As I arranged them in the sunken vase that my father had already filled with water, I strained to hear the conversation of the other family group, who seemed to be telling some amusing story about the person they were visiting. I envied their easy laugher, their fond memories. But in the brisk wind, tasting of rain and wet dirt and something sharp and pungent, like mustard, I silently picked dead leaves off the roses and trimmed the stems with my pocketknife. When I finished, I stood up next to my father.

"They're real pretty, Benni," he said as he did every year. "She would have liked them."

"Why?"

He turned to me, his wind-reddened face surprised. "What do you mean?"

"I mean why would she like them? Were pink roses her favorite flower?"

He looked away, putting on his hat and pulling it down to shadow his face. His shoulders hunched slightly under his canvas Carhartt jacket. "She liked them."

"Yes, you said that, but why?"

"Benni, I don't know, she just did."

In the long silence, we could hear a rumble of thunder behind us. My father looked up at the dark sky. "Looks like we're in for some more rain."

I shoved my hands deep into the pockets of my Levi's jacket, trying to think of a way to coax him to talk about my mother.

"Daddy, about when you and Mama got married . . ."

263

"Benni, why do you keep bringing that up? It's old business."

"I'm just curious is all. There's so much I don't know about her, about the both of you."

"She loved you more than her own life," he said, his normally laconic voice sharp and defensive. "That's all you need to know."

"You're wrong," I said, feeling like the most horrible person in the world for making him go through this, but I couldn't seem to stop myself. "I need to know more. I want to know about the circumstances surrounding my birth."

"What do you mean, circumstances? We got married, and then you was born. *That's* the circumstances."

I inhaled deeply and said, "I was a normal baby?"

"Of course you were a normal baby. You was as normal as they come."

"How much did I weigh?" I knew, but I wanted to see if he'd lie.

"I don't know. It's written down on your birth certificate. You was born a normal weight. You was normal all the way around. We thanked God for that."

"Except I was born seven months after you and mama were married."

He looked at me, his face flushed with anger and embarrassment. "Your mama was a good woman. We got married. Don't you be thinking bad about her now. Not now or ever. She was a *good* woman."

"I'm not making any judgments about her morality, Daddy, but she was pregnant when you got married, and I wanted to know—"

"I've had about enough of this. I think I'll just skip dinner and go on back to the ranch."

"Daddy," I called after him. "Wait, I'm sorry, I didn't

mean to imply she wasn't a good person. I just . . ."

He turned to look at me, the deep lines of his face dark with anger. "We made our mistakes back then, little girl, but we did right by you. Don't be judging us now."

"I'm not," I said, my eyes hot and burning. "I just wanted to know. I wanted to know about who I was, how I came to be."

"You are the daughter of Ben and Alice Ramsey. *That's* who you are. How you came to be is our business. Let the past stay there."

His back was stiff as he walked away from me. I wanted to run after him, beg forgiveness, take back everything I said. But another part of me was angry— angry that he wouldn't talk to me about this, angry that there were secrets that concerned me and that no one would talk about them, angry that this man who taught me to ride, showed me how to shoe horses, patiently explained over and over how to doctor sick calves, might not even be my biological father. That my father might be a horrible, manipulative man who had changed everything in my life by leaving me his estate. A man who might be a murderer or a drug dealer or both. Daddy's truck pulled slowly up on the highway, belching white smoke in the cold evening air. I watched him, my heart heavy as concrete, until the truck was out of sight.

I turned back to my mother's headstone, wanting to react. I wanted to yell and scream at her for . . . I didn't know what. Loving two men? Desperately marrying the first one who asked? Not leaving me some kind of instructions on how to live? *Leaving me when I was so young and vulnerable.*

As if she had a choice, a voice deep inside me said.

265

But I pushed that sensible voice aside, not wanting to feel anything but the anger that caused my chest to burn like fire. She left me before I could ask her all the things a daughter needs to know—what was it like when she was pregnant with me, who gave her her first kiss, what her relationship with her own mother was like, how she coped with her mother dying.

Another distant roll of thunder sounded, and the rain started slowly, then picked up in speed, as if someone knew that I, who hated to show emotion, needed a substitute. Soon rain was streaming down my cheeks as if it were my own tears. But still I couldn't cry.

I jumped when I felt the hands on my shoulders.

"Just me, sweetcakes," Emory said.

I leaned my head back against his chest and gave a long, shuddering sigh. "Daddy just left. He's real mad at me, Emory. I pushed too hard, like I always do. He . . ."

"He loves you, Benni. He'll be all right."

I turned and looked up at him, his blond hair wet and plastered against his forehead. "Your jacket's going to get ruined."

"It's wool. I imagine the sheep spent a fair amount of time in the rain."

I tried to smile but couldn't. He brought out a linen handkerchief from an inside pocket and handed it to me.

"Thanks." I wiped the rain off my face.

"Are you ready to tell me what's going on?" he asked.

Slowly, as the rain continued to soak both of us, I told him, in broken sentences, all my suspicions about Jacob Chandler, my mother, and my father.

When I was finished, his eyes were shiny with the tears I couldn't seem to shed. "I had no idea."

"Apparently neither did I."

"What are you going to do?"

"What can I do, ask my father for a blood sample to compare our DNA? He won't even talk about what happened when he and my mother got married. He thinks I should let the past stay in the past."

"Maybe he's right."

I scowled at him. "Easy for you to say."

"That's not what I mean."

"Do you realize that if Daddy isn't my biological father that I don't have one person on this earth who's related to me by blood? That Dove isn't . . ." A painful lump formed in my throat.

"That's not true," he said quietly. "You have me."

I looked up at him, realizing what he said was true. We were related on both sides of my family. The lump eased, and I swallowed, tasting salt at the back of my throat. The rain slowed to a soft drizzle, and I shivered in my wet jacket. "Thanks, Emory."

"You need to get in dry clothes," he said.

"I'll run the heater on high driving back."

"No, go by your house and change clothes. I insist. Remember that bronchitis you had in February. You don't need a relapse."

"Yes, Mama Littleton," I said, smiling weakly. "You do the same."

"I will. Elvia and I have a date later on, so I was heading home anyway."

"How did the dinner go?"

"No one grates cheese like I do, though I do believe I'm going to purchase Señora Aragon a food processor for Christmas. All in all, I think I held my own."

I put my arms around his neck and hugged him. "I'm sure you did, Emory."

It was almost eight o'clock when I pulled into our driveway. I could see Gabe in the kitchen window

267

putting away a sack of groceries. Part of me had hoped he wouldn't be home, that I could slip in and change clothes without speaking to him. Another part of me wanted to fling myself into his arms, rest in the comfort of their strength and love.

"Gabe, it's just me," I called, coming in the front door followed by Scout.

He walked out of the kitchen, his face concerned. "Are you all right?" he asked.

"Emory called you, didn't he?"

He nodded, not denying it.

"What did he say?"

"Only that you'd been out to see your mother's grave. That you were having a hard time."

Suddenly, without warning, I felt myself start to shake. Before I could stop them, sobs swelled up from deep inside me, and my legs buckled. Gabe caught me before I hit the floor, holding me close to his dry, solid body. I buried my face in his sweet-smelling T-shirt and let the tears flow freely. Scout whined and nudged his nose between our legs, upset at my burst of emotion.

"Scout, lie down," Gabe said. The dog obeyed him immediately, sensing that this was no time to argue.

Murmuring softly in Spanish, Gabe helped me into our bedroom, closed the door, started peeling off my wet clothes, drying me with a thick white towel. Soon I was under our flannel-covered down comforter, my freezing body pressed up against his warmth. Tears trailed down my cheeks while I tried to explain about my father and my mother, about Jacob Chandler and who I thought he might be. Disjointed apologies tumbled out of my mouth for what I'd done, what my family had done, how hard it must be for him . . .

"Shhh," he said, putting a finger on my lips, stopping

268

me before I could get a coherent story out. "It doesn't matter. Just lie here with me." He held me close, my face wetting his chest as I cried for him and all he'd had to suffer in his life, the ugliness he'd seen, the humiliation he'd experienced, for the mother I would never have, the father I never knew, and for the one I did.

He kissed my lips, my cheeks, licking the salty tears staining my face, his large, familiar hands stroking a slowly rising heat into my arms and legs. I arched toward him, aching to feel his strong heavy body on me, inside me, to forget all the things I'd learned in the last few days, to lose myself in this pure physical moment, to never have to go back and think about who I thought I was, who I might be. At that moment, all I really knew for certain was I would go anywhere on earth with this man.

His broad hand cradled the small of my back, lifting me toward him. When I cried out, his voice murmured words of reassurance, *"Tu puesto es aquì. Ahora y siempre. Todo serà bien.* Everything will be okay. *No te preocupes, estoy aquì. Te amo, te amo.* I love you. *Mientras yo vivo sólo a ti amaré."*

Filled by his warmth, I lay spent and exhausted in his arms, wanting just to sleep for days and, when I woke up, to be living somewhere else, anywhere other than this town where everyone thought they knew everything about me.

His rough knuckles gently caressing my cheek startled me awake. "Sweetheart, it's almost eleven. You have to go."

I bolted up, gripping the sheets to my chest, confused for a moment about my surroundings. Gabe sat on the edge of our bed dressed in jeans and a dark sweatshirt.

He touched his lips to my temple. "You have to go," he repeated.

Still drowsy and disoriented, I lay back against the pillows. *This is where you belong,* I told myself silently. *This is your bedroom, this is your husband.* "No. *I* don't care about the house or anything of Mr. Chandler's. I give up. Let the government have it all."

He studied my face a long time before answering. "I can't let you do that. As much as I'd like to, I can't. You have to be back in Morro Bay before midnight."

"Just like Cinderella," I said, my voice bitter.

"Benni, I don't know what happened between you and your dad at the cemetery, but whatever it is, I know one thing for certain, you'll never forgive yourself if you quit now. I want you to stay here with me, heaven knows, I want that with every fiber of my being. It goes against everything I am to let you go back to that house. But this thing, whatever it is, has to be resolved before you can go on with your life. Until then, we can't go on with ours." He leaned over, kissed my lips, then the hollow of my throat. "I'll be here waiting. My life is braided with yours, *niña,* in a braid so tight nothing will loosen it. Remember that."

I realized that my disjointed rambling when we were making love hadn't made sense to him. He deserved an explanation. He deserved the truth. "I . . . it's . . . my dad . . . and you and what you've . . ."

He weaved his hands into my tangled curls and made me look straight into his deep set eyes. They were gray with fatigue but resolute. "Not now, Benni. Tell me later, when you've had time to think about it. Right now, we just need to get you back safely to Morro Bay."

A rush of love for this man struck me like a blow, and the thought of life without him filled me with an

270

overwhelming despair. In that moment, I knew, if something happened to him, if he died before me, I'd simply want to die, too. "It'll all be over soon," I said. "One way or another. I promise."

He stood up, holding out a hand to me. "You'd better get dressed. I'm going to follow you to Morro Bay."

At Mr. Chandler's house, Gabe walked through it, turning on the heater, checking the place out, his eyes vigilant and searching. Finally satisfied, he locked the door behind him, and through the front window I watched him drive away, the sound of his Corvette growing fainter until only the sound of the wind remained.

I lay in bed, staring at the shadows on the ceiling. The night wind rustled the bushes outside my window, while next to me, in his cedar-chip bed, Scout snuffled and growled in his sleep, his front paws busy and diligent, digging dream holes to China, or maybe dreaming of the strange man whose scent still permeated this room. The man who had invaded my life so completely. The man who might possibly be my father.

14

I LEFT FOR LOS ANGELES AT FOUR A.M. WHILE I dressed, I realized that during last night's turmoil, I'd forgotten to tell Gabe where I was going today. Not wanting to wake him this early, I called his office and left a message on his voice mail, giving him my destination, but not why I was going. His promise that he'd step back and let me do what I needed, explaining it all to him when I was ready, removed a huge weight from my shoulders. Slowly we were

271

working out this balancing act of a relationship, this struggle to be our separate selves while trying to become connected. There was no doubt in my mind that I wanted to spend the rest of my life with this enigmatic, often exasperating man who filled a place in my heart that no one ever had, but I also couldn't lose myself in him, something so tempting at times with his confident, unwavering view of life.

I knocked on Rich's door, feeling awful for waking him, but I didn't want to leave Scout alone again.

Bleary-eyed, he brushed aside my profuse apologies. "I'll watch *el lobo*. *You* just be careful, *comprende*?"

"Yes, sir." After a few minutes of wrangling with a stubborn Scout, who didn't want to leave me, I was on my way south down Interstate 101.

The drive was easy and pleasant through Santa Barbara, Ventura, Oxnard, and Camarillo. Then I hit Thousand Oaks. It had been years since I'd driven down to the L.A. area. Like most Central Coasters, I tried to avoid it as much as possible. As I gripped the truck's steering wheel and inched behind the thousands of cars on their way to jobs in Los Angeles and Orange counties, I remembered why. The only good thing was that the molasses-slow traffic gave me plenty of time to think about what I would say to Gloria Carrell. It was a little past ten-thirty when I found the correct off-ramp and pulled over in a strip mall parking lot to check my Thomas Bros. street map again. Gloria Carrell's house was only six blocks away. I called her on my cell phone, hoping she hadn't given up on me. She answered on the first ring.

"Ms. Carrell? This is Benni Harper. I'm sorry I'm late. I forgot how bad the traffic is down here. I'm only a few blocks away."

"That's fine, Ms. Harper. I work at home, so it's no problem."

I pulled up minutes later in front of a fifties ranch-style house across the street from a busy red-brick hospital. An older Dodge van was parked in the driveway, and evidence of teenagers—basketballs and soccer balls, in-line skates and a fat-tired bicycle—was splashed across the front lawn. Gloria Carrell was obviously watching for me, because she was waiting on the tiny front porch before I could get my truck locked. She appeared about my age and was tall and dark-haired with a face full of rust-colored freckles. Her denim overalls were worn white in spots from age. She wasn't smiling, but her expression was mild and congenial.

I held out a hand. "Ms. Carrell, I'm Benni Harper."

"Nice meeting you. Let's drop the formalities. I'm Gloria." She reached out her own hand, stained dark brown. "Don't worry, it won't rub off. I've been working on some walnut dining chairs this morning." Her handshake was firm and dry. "That's what I do. Refinish furniture."

"I'm sorry to interrupt your work, but I'm sure what I have to ask your aunt won't take long."

She shifted from one bare foot to another, studying me with an open frankness. "We can go see her right now," she said. "But as I told you on the phone, she's in the middle stages of Alzheimer's. I don't know what she can tell you."

"I'll try not to upset her. It's just that she's my only lead at this point."

"Lead?" She tilted her head in curiosity. "You make it sound as if a crime's been committed."

I backpedaled quickly. "Sorry, habit. My husband's a police officer. His slang slips into my vocabulary."

One eyebrow arched slightly, its meaning unclear to me. "Let me get my shoes, and we'll head on over to my aunt's residence." She slipped on some brown leather clogs next to the porch swing and closed the front door without locking it.

"Want me to drive?" I asked.

"No need," she said, giving me a half smile. "We can walk."

I followed her across the street to the back of the hospital parking lot where a large, tree-shaded building stood. A gold-lettered sign in front said, "Hillside Convalescent Hospital."

"I don't know why on the earth they label them convalescent homes," she commented as we walked into the pale lavender lobby. "They make it sound as though old age is a disease for which there is a cure." A teenage Hispanic girl at the front desk smiled and waved at her, then went back to her whispered phone conversation.

"Fidela has a new boyfriend," Gloria said as I followed her down a hall of glass-encased offices toward a set of elevators. Next to the elevators were bulletin boards decorated with colorful Mother's Day construction paper art created by young children. "Unfortunately she hasn't informed her old boyfriend yet, so trouble lurks on the horizon."

"I wouldn't be that age again for all the cattle in Texas," I said.

"I hear you there."

We rode up to the third floor and walked down an aisle crowded with elderly people in wheelchairs. Some called out names when I walked by them, my face causing a stir of memory, remembrances from a past that still burned bright in their cloudy minds. Gloria

274

greeted many of the residents by first name, stopping to shake a hand, kiss a cheek. It was obvious she was a regular and much-welcomed visitor.

She stopped in front of room 317 and turned to me. "She tires easily," she warned me, "and much of what she says is incoherent. Don't expect much."

One of the beds was empty, though a white afghan laid across the thin blue bedspread and some pictures of children tacked on the wall told me that the bed had an occupant somewhere. I followed Gloria to the other side of the curtain, to the window bed, where her aunt sat in a wheelchair, staring out at the emerald-green foothills of the San Gabriel Mountains.

"Aunt Gwen, it's Gloria, your niece," she said in a normal voice. A respectful, noncondescending voice I'd noticed that she'd used with all the people she'd greeted in the hallway. "You have a visitor."

Her aunt didn't react, but continued to stare out the window. Gloria kept talking as if her aunt had responded. "She's related to Alice Banks. You remember Alice? You knew each other back in Arkansas. You went to the same church. Alice was a waitress at that diner you used to tell me about."

Gwen Swanson Felix slowly turned her snowy white head and stared at Gloria with filmy blue eyes the same pale shade as the cloudless sky outside her window. "Alice had a kitty."

"She did?" Gloria said. "Well, now, I didn't know that. What kind?"

Gwen looked beyond Gloria at me. Her blue eyes filmed over with tears. "Oh, my," she said. Her age-spotted hand reached up and covered her mouth. "Alice, the kitty died. I'm sorry." She held out a trembling hand. I looked up at Gloria for permission, and she

275

nodded. I went to her aunt, knelt down next to her, and took her cold hand.

"It's okay," I said.

"He just cried and cried," she said, her voice cracking.

"It's all right," I said, looking up at Gloria, who just smiled and nodded at me.

I held her aunt's hand for a moment, then asked softly. "Mrs. Felix, do you remember anything about a man named Garrett?"

She stroked the top of my hand with her other one. "Alice, you need your Jergen's. Your skin is so rough."

"I will," I said, not knowing how much I should press her for memories. "Do you remember Garrett?"

She pulled her hands abruptly back. "Garrett's dead. We're supposed to say that."

"You're right, I forgot. Tell me why again. Why are we supposed to say Garrett's dead?"

She folded her hands primly in her quilt-covered lap. "He's just like his daddy. The apple doesn't fall far from the tree." Her voice dropped down to a murmuring, words and phrases that made no sense. Then she looked up. "Alice, where's the bow for my hair? You know I always like the red one with that dress."

"Garrett," I prompted her. "Why are we supposed to say Garrett's dead?"

Her eyes filled up with tears again. "We loved him, Weezie, didn't we? He said he would come back." Her gnarled hand hit the handle of the wheelchair. "Oh, Weezie, the kitty died. I tried to save it, but the kitty died, and he never came back for me." In a few seconds, heart-rending sobs came from deep in her chest.

"Wait outside, please," Gloria said, pushing around me. I stood outside the room and listened to her comfort

276

her aunt, finally getting her calmed down. While I waited, it suddenly occurred to me that "Weezie" was a nickname for Louise. My mother's middle name.

Gloria's face was grim when she came back out in the hallway. "I think that's about all she can take today," she said. "She's very confused these days."

"I'm sorry for upsetting her. That wasn't my intention."

"It's not your fault," she said. "She just isn't with us anymore. I wish you could have met her when she was herself. She had a great sense of humor and knew everything there was to know about baseball. She worshiped the Kansas City Royals. You would have liked her. Sure makes you really think about putting that request for a potassium chloride cocktail in your will."

"What?"

She laughed nervously. "I'm sorry, old and very bad habit. I meant for myself, of course. I'd never kill anyone. I was a geriatrics nurse for fifteen years before I found true happiness in furniture. It was a joke among us nurses that we'd rather have a quick potassium chloride cocktail with an IV push than spend years as a living vegetable. I even knew of a couple of nurses who had verbal pacts with each other to administer it to the other if they ever got like Aunt Gwen. After a rough day we used to offer to pour each other a PC with a twist. There were a few doctors we would have liked to serve it to, believe me."

I gave a small laugh. Nurse humor reminded me a lot of cop humor. When you worked every day with the realities of death, grotesque jokes were like letting air out of an overblown balloon. "Is any doctor really worth going to prison for?"

"That's the beauty of the drug. Mimics a heart attack. No one would ever guess. It's the doctor's choice for suicide, you know. Don't you watch television? I thought everyone knew about potassium chloride."

I shook my head. "Guess I missed that little piece of trivia."

We walked back toward the elevators. "Is Mrs. Felix your aunt on your mother's or your father's side?" I asked, not wanting to end our conversation, hoping for any small bit of information.

"Actually, she's my father's cousin. We've just always called her Aunt Gwen. She came out here to live when she retired, since my father was her only living relative."

"And this name Garrett doesn't sound familiar to you?"

"Not a bit."

"What about Jacob Chandler?"

She shook her head no. "Sorry."

"Do you know much about your aunt's life back in Arkansas?"

"Not really. She was in her early fifties when she came to California and didn't talk much about her life back there. She lived in a house down the street until she started getting sick a few years ago. We were lucky to get her into Hillside. But my father knew one of the hospital's owners from some work he'd done on his house—my father was a cabinetmaker—and so Aunt Gwen's name got moved to the top of the list." The elevator came to a stop. "Two months after she went in, my father passed away. My mom died when I was seventeen."

"I'm sorry," I said.

"That's why I allowed you to come talk to Aunt

278

Gwen," she said as we walked out into the late-morning sunshine. "I know what it's like not to know who your mother is." She paused for a moment. "I wish my father was still alive. He probably could have told you more about Aunt Gwen's life, since he grew up back there. All I know is she worked for years as a clerk for some judge back in Pine Bluff and she came out here when her arthritis became so bad she couldn't type anymore. As far as I know, she or my father have no living relatives back in Arkansas. At least none close enough to claim."

We walked across the street to her house. "When she moved to the convalescent home, did she have any correspondence? I was thinking . . ."

Gloria shook her head. "I'm sorry, but there's not much left. That's how we knew she was starting to get sick. I was looking for a photo album I'd made a few years back of all her old photographs, and she told me she'd thrown it out ages ago, that she didn't know who those people were and couldn't imagine why she had pictures of them. When she started accusing the neighbors of sneaking into her house and leaving carrots and tomatoes in the sink, we took her to a doctor. By then, I guess she'd thrown almost all her old letters and stuff out. The doctor said that was pretty common with early Alzheimer's patients. I went through what she had left after you called and didn't find any mention of the names you asked her about."

Not knowing what else to ask, I held out my hand. "Thank you, Gloria. I appreciate you taking the time to help me."

"Good luck, Benni Harper," she said, shaking my hand with her large, calloused one. "I hope you find what you're looking for."

The drive back at noon was faster since most people were already at work. Once out of the extensive Los Angeles county limits, I stopped at a McDonald's near Calabasas and with incredible speed downed a Big Mac, an order of fries, and a Coke. With sugar and grease to fuel my brain, I could seriously contemplate the scanty information Gwen Swanson Felix had given me.

There was obviously some kind of relationship between her, my mother, and this Jacob/Garrett man. But what? From the little bit I gleaned, it appeared that as I guessed, my mother was dating two men at the same time. Was she sleeping with both of them? Or was she sleeping with Jacob/Garrett and when she found herself to be pregnant, married my dad? Did she trick Daddy into marrying her, or did he know she was pregnant with another man's baby and married her anyway? Was that why he was so angry when I asked him about my birth? Or was he just embarrassed that he and my mother had slept together before being married and I was evidence of it? Back then, being pregnant out of wedlock was definitely more shocking than in today's society. The hamburger and fries churned in my stomach, making me consider pulling over to throw up. The pure image I'd maintained of my mother all these years was being trampled by the reality of the person. Would I have liked this person? What if she had tricked my dad into marrying her? Who was this woman who so haunted my thoughts, this woman whose eyes stared at me out of my mirror every morning? If she hadn't died when I was so young, would I have loved her as an adult? Would I have been like her? Could I still be?

My brain was beginning to feel bruised from all the possibilities, so I purposely turned my thoughts to another piece of information that Gloria Carrell had

280

given me. Potassium chloride. PC with a twist. Doctor's choice for suicide. Undetectable. Mimics a heart attack.

Jacob Chandler had supposedly died of a heart attack. No one thought a thing about it because of his heart condition. Maybe he committed suicide. But why? And where was the empty needle? What if . . . ?

No, it was too impossible to believe. Too hard to pull off. Why would he let anyone give him an injection?

A tremble went through my body as the possibility formed in my mind. Maybe the whole reason that Tess and her sons were upset was not just because they'd expected to inherit Jacob Chandler's estate, but also because they'd killed him to get it sooner rather than later. With me living there, maybe they were afraid I'd stumble across something that incriminated them. As frightening as it was, I thought about that instead of my mother. Even death threats seemed less terrifying than my mother's past.

When I hit Santa Barbara, I dialed Gabe. His secretary, Maggie, answered.

"He's down at the Historical Museum, Benni," she said. "Apparently there's something big going down tonight."

"Oh, geeze, that's all he needs. Can you call him and tell him I'm outside of Santa Barbara and I'll be there soon? If I try dialing one more number while I'm driving I'll run off the road, and I don't want to stop." Actually I didn't want to launch into a huge discussion about where I'd been and why until I could see him face-to-face. He was trying hard to be understanding, but this abrupt trip to Los Angeles would be impossible for him not to comment on.

"You got it," she said. "See you in a couple."

It was past six o'clock when I reached San Celina.

The closest parking space was six blocks away and once I reached the historical museum, the reason became clear.

In front of the museum, in all their purple-and yellow-gowned glory, stood the adult, youth, and children's choirs from St. Stephen's Baptist Church. All two hundred of them. They stood on portable risers and had already started their first song. Two huge speakers blasted music on both sides of them as they swayed and clapped, encouraging the crowd to join in.

"We Shall Overcome" never sounded so . . . loud.

From the second floor of the museum, the San Celina Seven hung out of the windows, waving at their adoring public. There were so many flashbulbs you'd have thought it was the Academy Awards. St. Stephen's choirs swayed and sang. People applauded. Vendors hawked candy apples and T-shirts printed with "Save the San Celina Seven."

I walked over to the police command post where Gabe was nowhere to be seen. Jim Cleary, his captain and next in-command, as well as head deacon at St. Stephen's, grinned when he saw me.

"Did you know about this?" I asked, laughing.

"Now, Benni, I'm a police officer."

"This I know, Jim. But it doesn't answer my question."

He just grinned again and didn't answer. Gabe came up when the choir launched into "Onward Christian Soldiers," a rousing but somewhat confusing choice, I thought.

"Did Maggie get a hold of you?" I asked immediately.

He struggled not to look irritated, and I loved him like crazy at that moment. "Yes, how was your trip?"

"Kind of confusing. I'm not really sure yet. I think I

need to contemplate what I learned for a day or so."

He started to say something, then reconsidered and just put his arm around me, kissing the top of my head. "I'm glad you're back safe."

"When did all this commence?" I asked, changing the subject.

He looked over at Jim, his face resigned. "Maybe we should ask Brother Cleary here."

Jim held up his hands. "I swear, boss, I didn't know a thing about it."

Gabe looked at me and gave a tired smile. "But he's enjoying it immensely."

Jim laughed. "The choirs are getting more television exposure than they ever got with their Christmas and Easter cantatas."

"This could start a whole new direction for them," I said. "Protest cantatas. You could hire them out by the hour. Bet it would make a lot more money than car washes."

"We do need a new parking lot," he said, stroking his chin.

"Okay, you two, you can plan the filling of the church coffers and destruction of society later," Gabe said. "Right now Benni needs to talk to Dove and see if we can get a general date as to when this is all going to end."

I looked up into his exhausted face and felt a pang of guilt, remembering what Rich had told me about how much harder it was for Gabe to be in his position because he was Hispanic. He was holding up with remarkable forbearance and good humor.

"I'll see what I can find out," I said, glancing over at the museum and hesitating just a split second. Looking into Dove's face right now, with the realization that she might not be my biological grandmother, would take all the acting skills I had.

Gabe caught my hesitation. "Benni, is something wrong?"

I looked up at him. "No, no, I'm okay."

We stared into each other's eyes. He knew I was lying. He reached over and ran a finger along the edge of my jaw, tapping my chin gently. "Hang tough, *niña*."

"Always do, Friday."

A few reporters shouted questions, which I studiously ignored, as I walked up the museum steps. Inside, the only person downstairs was Elmo Ritter. The dark, heavy bags under his dramatically mournful face looked almost painful.

"Hi, Elmo, how are you doing?" I asked.

"Not good, Benni, not good at all. When is this going to end?"

I patted his arm sympathetically. He'd lost his beret somewhere, and his hair was standing up in stiff little peaks. "Are the women still driving you crazy?"

"I'm ready to throw in the towel, young lady. You'd better inform your gramma of that right quick."

"I'm on my way up to talk to her now. It can't be much longer."

"From your mouth to God's ears," Elmo said. "If the sound can make it past all their cackling."

Upstairs, the women were much less despairing than Elmo. In fact, the mood in the air was one of triumph and jubilation.

"Honeybun!" Dove said, turning away from the window, holding her fist up in a power-to-the-people gesture. "Think we got 'em on the run?"

I laughed, feeling warmed by her familiar face and voice. She was my gramma. Nothing, not DNA or

284

letters from a strange man or anything else on this earth, could change that. "I'd say you got them beat, Dove. Boxstore Billy doesn't stand a flying fig of a chance."

All the women turned back to the windows, but Dove walked over to me. "Gabe sent you, didn't he?"

"Yes, ma'am. I'm supposed to ask you if you have any idea when this is going to end. He needs to make plans."

"Poor boy, I feel so bad doing this to him, but it couldn't be helped. I'll make a nice blackberry cobbler for him when this is over. But as to when this will end, he'd best be asking Mr. Butter-Wouldn't-Melt-in-His-Mouth Mayor."

I drew her farther away from the rest of the ladies, including the mayor's mother. "Seriously, Gabe's getting a little worried. What if the mayor doesn't give in? Elmo's looking a little peaked down there. Do you have a contingency plan?"

"Honeybun, are you asking me to quit? Why, you know better than that. Ramseys aren't quitters. It's not in our blood."

Her words froze my heart for a moment at the word blood. "I know."

Her sharp, knowing eyes caught something in my expression. "What's wrong, child? Is this affecting Gabe's health? I'll quit in a moment to protect my kin."

"No, he's fine."

"Then what is it?"

I turned my head, unable to look in her eyes. "Everything's fine, Dove. Really."

I could feel her eyes scrutinizing me, but she didn't say any more.

"We do have a contingency plan." she finally said. "Tell Gabe that this'll all be over by Wednesday no matter what, but tell him not to tell the mayor or the newspapers. I want his word."

"I'll tell him."

She pulled me to her, and I rested my head for a moment on her soft shoulder, just like when I was a kid. Except that now I had to bend down slightly to do it. Right then I decided that no matter what I found out, I'd never tell Dove or Daddy. Ever. As far as I was concerned, they were my family and always would be.

"Things will be fine," she murmured, patting me on the back. "Now, you know they will."

"I know, Gramma. You're always right."

"And don't you forget it, honeybun."

Outside, I gave a quick statement to the few reporters lingering around, revealing nothing significant, then headed for the command post.

"Well?" Gabe asked.

"Walk me to my truck," I said.

On the way there, I told him about her assurance that it would be over by Wednesday.

"Did she say what they were going to do?"

"No, but I'm sure it won't be illegal."

He laughed, a bit ironically. "I'm glad you're so confident."

Dusk turned the air a lavender-gray, and in the neighborhood where I'd parked, lights were starting to blink on. When we reached my truck, I unlocked it, then abruptly turned, slipped my arms underneath his jacket, and hugged him.

"*Querida*." he said, burying his face in my hair. "Why don't you tell me what's going on?"

"I can't yet." I said into his chest. "I will soon. But not yet. Not until I have it all figured out."

His chest inflated in a sigh, and I almost gave in and

poured out the whole story. But I didn't. He had enough to contend with at this moment with Dove and her band of merry lawbreakers. Though he thought knowing what was going on would be easier on him, I knew it would just be one more problem for him to worry about.

"There is one thing, though," I said, pulling out of his arms. I told him what Gloria had told me about potassium chloride and the suspicion I had about Mr. Chandler's death.

"It's a long shot," he said, shaking his head. "Without something more substantial to go on, we can't exhume the body for an autopsy. I'm not even sure if they can detect that drug anyway."

"But don't you think it might be a possibility?"

" 'Might be' are the key words. At this point, it doesn't matter."

"Are you saying it doesn't matter that a man might have been murdered?"

"No, I'm saying until there is more evidence, it's not an issue." He gave me a stern look. "And it's not up to you to find any evidence. Frankly, I think living alone surrounded by that man's things has turned your brain a little crazy."

"Thank you for showing so much confidence in my ability to assess a situation," I said stiffly, opening the truck's door.

He pushed it closed with his hand, holding it there so I couldn't open it. "Sweetheart, this has nothing to do with me not having confidence in you. It has to do with you seeing crimes where there aren't any."

"You admit that Tess and her sons had a reason to kill Mr. Chandler."

"They might have, but to be honest, this sounds too clever for the likes of those two lowlifes. Besides, do you really believe that this Tess would kill Jacob Chandler?"

Remembering how upset she'd been at the funeral, I had to concede he was probably right. Still, it was a good theory, one I wasn't willing to give up yet.

"I guess we'll just have to wait and see."

He let go of the door and ran his hand down his face. "Man, I'll be glad when this is over and you're back home."

I stood on tiptoe and kissed him hard on the lips. "Nobody wishes that more than me, Sergeant Friday."

Back in Morro Bay, Scout was so overjoyed to see me, he ran around in circles like a puppy, jumping up on me and ignoring my laughing command of "down." Rich asked me how my trip went, and I answered simply, "Fine."

"Okay, never let it be said I can't take a hint," he said, trying not to look hurt.

"I'm sorry, Rich, I just can't talk about it yet. All I can tell you is I'm a little closer to figuring this thing out. When I do, you'll be among the first to know the whole story."

He handed me a large Tupperware container of chicken and rice and a smaller one containing guacamole. "I knew you'd be tired and hungry so just heat this in the oven and get some sleep."

"Thanks, Rich. For dinner and for watching Scout."

"My pleasure, Señora Harper."

After feeding Scout and eating Rich's chicken and rice, I spent some time petting and talking to my canine side-kick to make up for my long day away from him. Then I decided to settle down on the sofa and reread Mr. Chandler's wood carving lessons. There had to be something in them I was missing. But what? After reading them three more times, the stress of the day as well as the weight and warmth of Scout's body on my feet lulled me into a deep sleep. The next thing I knew, it was morning.

I called Elvia and heard the details about her and Emory's date and then updated her on my situation, leaving out the part about Jacob Chandler's possible identity.

"You know how I hate agreeing with Gabe on anything," she said. "But I'll be glad when this is over and you're home safe."

"You and me both," I said.

Then I called Amanda. I didn't really have anything new to tell her except my theory about Mr. Chandler possibly being murdered, but I was stymied at this point and needed a sensible voice to help me sort things out.

"I'll have to agree with the gorgeous chauvinist on this one, cowgirl. Your murder theory is a bit far-fetched."

"I know. It's just that everything seems to have come to a complete halt. I don't know where to go from here."

"You only have five days left. Hang in there."

"I'm trying. But I miss Gabe like crazy. Especially at night."

"I'll just bet you do. Well, not much to report on this end. Your friend Beau Franklin called me and tried to pull his scam on me. I told him exactly what I told you to tell him—no proof, no money."

"And how did he react?"

"He hung up on me. I'm considering suing for damage to my inner ear."

"Maybe I should go talk to him again."

"Maybe you should just hang loose and let the time run out on this thing. That fire spooked me. It could just as well have been your house as the garage. If there is homicide involved in this, let your hubby deal with it."

"My hubby thinks I'm slowly going as crazy as he thinks Jacob Chandler was."

"Just be careful," she said, her voice more serious than I'd ever heard it. "When I was a prosecutor I saw a lot of people do some pretty raunchy things for less money than you're getting. Your life is worth a lot more to all of us who love you than that ole house and bank account."

"Why, Amanda Aurora Lucille Landry, you're getting sentimental on me. I'm deeply touched."

"No comment. Just heed my words, babydoll."

"Duly heeded. And don't worry, there's absolutely nowhere for me to go at this point. I'm just sitting here waiting for something to happen."

"That alone is enough to give me shivers. Toodles."

Two minutes after I hung up the phone, the doorbell rang. Scout bounded over to the door, barking, his tail wagging furiously. I opened it expecting to see Rich and instead found Emory.

"I've come to escort you to breakfast," he said. "Your treat."

"Best offer I've had all morning." I said. "I'll get my jacket."

As we walked past the blackened garage, his face tightened with worry. "I don't like this, sweetcakes. Not one little bit."

"Where do you want to go?" I asked, not feeling like assuring one more person one more time of my safety.

He took my arm and slipped it through his. "Anything new on Mr. Chandler? How did your trip down south go?"

"How did you hear about that?"

He patted my hand. "Sources. Answer my question."

"Not until you answer mine. Where do you want to go for breakfast?"

"How about this Cafe Palais you've been raving about?"

"Okay, but I hope it's Neely's day off. She's none too happy with me right now."

"Oh, boy, then I hope we get seated at her station."

I pulled my arm out of his and punched his shoulder. "What's wrong, cuz, slow news day?" There was a small crowd of people waiting in front of the cafe, so I put our name on the list, and we sat down on one of the blue benches in front.

"No, it's just that—"

"Well, look who's out and about," a voice interrupted him. "Our own local heiress." We turned to look up at Duane and Cole.

"Good morning, gentlemen," Emory said evenly, not getting up.

Duane snorted. "Yeah, right." He turned to me. "Look, we didn't have nothing to do with your runaway dog and we didn't have nothing to do with that fire, so tell that husband of yours to call off his cop buddies and quit harassing us."

"I don't have any control over what my husband does," I said coldly.

He stepped closer to me, and Emory calmly stood up and moved between me and Duane.

"That's enough," he said.

"Move aside, asshole, I've got something to say to—"

Before he could finish, in one swift movement, Emory grabbed Duane's arm, whipped it behind him, and hustled him to the side of the building away from the crowd. By the time Cole and I made it around the building, Emory had Duane's face pushed up against the mottled white stucco.

"Let him go," Cole said, starting toward him.

Emory shoved Duane's arm up higher; his other hand pressed at some spot on Duane's neck that caused him to squeal.

"Call off your brother," Emory said in Duane's ear, grinding his face deeper into the rough wall, "or I might just have to break your cheekbone on this here wall and I reckon that might sting a bit."

"B-b-back off, man. Back off, Cole," Duane managed to get out, his face contorted in pain.

Cole scowled but took a step backwards.

"Now, you listen to me," Emory said, his voice low and pleasant, as if he were talking to the mailman or a friendly stranger, " 'cause I only want to say this once. I don't want you comin' near my cousin again. I don't want you within two hundred feet of her. I don't want you to even look at her if she walks right by you. I don't want you callin' her, harassin' her, sendin' her anything in the mail, or comin' on her property. I don't even want you thinkin' you can think about her. Am I makin' myself clear?"

"She's the one—"

He grounded Duane's face deeper into the stucco. Duane yelped.

"Now I'm startin' not to feel so hospitable toward you, Mr. Briggstone. As the great John Shelton Reed once said, 'Southerners will be polite until they are angry enough to kill you.' But I was raised until I was eleven by a Southern belle of the highest quality, so I'll be givin' you one more chance and I'll repeat my very reasonable request . . ."

"Okay, okay," Duane croaked before Emory could say another word. "We'll leave her alone."

Emory let go of Duane's arm and stepped back,

292

casually pulling down the sleeves of his tailored jacket. Duane, his cheek raw and bleeding from the stucco, gave his brother a furious look.

"Why didn't you do something, jackass?" he asked.

Cole shrugged and with his knuckles rubbed his own cheek as if contemplating how its smoothness would have taken that stucco wall.

Duane turned back to Emory, his wind-cracked lips turned into a sneer. "Better watch it, buddy. Next time I won't let you catch me off guard."

"As delightful as it has all been, I suggest that this little dance is something neither of us would care to repeat."

Duane pointed a shaky finger at Emory, cocky again now that there was some distance between them. "Look, asshole, if her police chief husband and his little cop buddies haven't stopped us, what makes you think you can?"

Emory's face remained genial. "Well, now, I'm surprised, Mr. Briggstone. That's an almost intelligent question, one to which there are no less than three answers. One, unlike the highly esteemed and capable Chief Ortiz, I do not have a career or public opinion to consider. Two, I have a filthy-rich daddy who dotes on me and is quite adept at buying off judges to insure the freedom of his only son and heir, and three . . ." He smiled slowly at them. "As my sweet little cousin could tell you, I'm as crazy as a loon and have absolutely no scruples to boot. Take away my meds, and I might just do any crazy ole thing. Do you really think the cops in this county would investigate very thoroughly if your mama reported your two sorry carcasses missing?" He raised his eyebrows and smiled wider, and if I wasn't sure I knew my cousin like the back of my own hand,

293

I'd swear the light in his green eyes had taken on a rather insane glow.

Duane hesitated, started to say something, then stopped when his brother grabbed his arm. "C'mon, this guy's nuts. Let's split."

Duane glanced over at me, scowled, then followed Cole out to their truck parked on the street.

I nodded my head. "Very impressive, cuz. You almost had me going there for a moment."

He grinned at me. "How do you know what I was sayin' wasn't true?"

"For one thing, I know your college minor was drama. I am impressed by the brute strength, though. Quite an impressive display of machismo."

He shifted his shoulders around, settling them deeper in his cashmere jacket. "Now, what good were all those kung fu and karate lessons my daddy spent so much money on unless one doesn't utilize them occasionally in the name of familial loyalty?"

"Cousin Emory, you are one unique specimen of testosterone, and I do believe they are calling our name."

Unfortunately . . . or fortunately, depending on whether you were asking me or Emory, we were seated at Neely's table. Even though she probably hadn't heard about the latest scuffle between me and the Briggstones, she was not happy to see us. Emory went out of his way to be engaging, but she served us politely and quietly, giving me anxious side glances, not melting one degree at Emory's witty comments and cajoling smile.

Emory's frown at her retreating back held a small pout.

"Sorry, Romeo," I said, digging into my ham and cheese omelette. "Guess there are a few women left in this world capable of withstanding your charm. Eat your French toast."

Over breakfast, I told him all the details of what I'd learned from Gloria Carrell and the confused words of her aunt.

"Sounds like this Jacob fellow was on the run," Emory said.

"That's sure what it sounds like. But from what? My first thought is it was something illegal especially since he stole this Jacob Chandler's identity. And what happened to the real Jacob Chandler? How was he connected to my mother? This Gwen sounds like she had some sort of relationship with him, too, but whatever it was, it's lost somewhere in her mind." I stopped eating for a moment, staring at the melted cheese and ham on my plate. "It was so sad. Our memories are not only our connection to the people we love, but to . . . everything. If you lose them . . ." I didn't know what to say, how to explain what I was feeling. Memories were what this whole situation was about. In a way, Jacob Chandler had stolen my memories of my mother and replaced them with this mystery woman.

Emory reached across the table, took my hand, and squeezed it. "We'll figure this out, Benni. And no matter what happens, we have each other."

I smiled at him through blurry eyes. "You plagiarist, those are the exact words I said to you when you came to stay with us the summer your mother died."

"I know," he said and squeezed my hand again.

We changed the subject and talked about Dove and tried to guess what she and the others had planned for their secret weapon.

"With the mayor's mother in on it, it could be

anything. Dove told you that Wednesday was the big day?"

"If Mayor Davenport doesn't take back his vote. She didn't say when on Wednesday, but knowing them, they'll do it in time for the six o'clock news." I folded my napkin and laid it next to my plate. "I gotta use the bathroom. Meet you out front."

"Nice trick, Harper," he called after me. "Stickin' me with the bill . . . again."

"You can afford it, havin' that filthy-rich ole daddy who can buy judges and all," I called back.

Neely came into the bathroom as I was washing my hands. She stood next to me in front of the mirror, staring at my reflection.

"Say what you have to say," I finally snapped when her silent staring irritated me long enough.

She spoke to my reflection. "Everything was fine until you came into town. Why don't you just leave?"

"I will on Sunday."

"Oh, yes," she said bitterly. "You have to make sure you get your inheritance. You wouldn't want to do anything to screw that up."

I turned to her, forcing her to look directly at me. "Look, Neely, I don't know what your problem is and frankly I don't care. This situation between Mr. Chandler and me is really none of your business, none of Tess Briggstone's business, and most certainly none of Duane and Cole's business. Now, I know you all thought you had a sure thing in Mr. Chandler that was going to eventually pay off, and there is nobody— believe me, *nobody*—sorrier than me that he decided to leave me his estate, but it was *his* choice, for whatever reason, and if you don't like it, I suggest you all go take a flying leap into that bay out there. Otherwise, you leave me alone and you tell your boyfriend and his brother to leave me alone, or I'll find out who set that fire and who killed Mr. Chandler, and that person will spend the rest of his or her life scrubbing toilets in state prison."

Her mouth opened slightly. Fear or some other emotion caused her face to turn ashen. "Killed Jake? What do you mean?"

It was only then that I realized what had popped out of my mouth in anger. I grabbed my purse and walked out of the bathroom without answering her. Silently I screamed to myself, *You idiot!*

"What's wrong?" Emory asked the minute he saw me outside.

"Nothing."

His mouth straightened at my sharp tone.

We walked back up to the house in silence, me lambasting myself the whole way about my reckless words. Once inside, I broke down and told Emory about my heedless revelation to Neely in the bathroom.

"Not a wise move," he said.

"Don't you think I know that?"

He didn't answer, just gave me one of Aunt Garnet's pursed-mouth looks.

I couldn't help laughing. He was such a good mimic. "I'm sorry, Emory. It's just that when I do something stupid . . ."

"Everyone around you has to pay."

"I'm not that bad!"

"Ummm," he said and brushed at imaginary dirt on his jacket sleeve.

"I said I was sorry."

"Apology accepted. Now, the next thing on our agenda is damage control."

"Not much I can do now," I said, flopping down on the sofa. He sat in the recliner across from me. "Uh, you might not want to sit there."

"Why not?"

"It's where Mr. Chandler died."

Emory didn't flinch. "You know I'm not superstitious except when it comes to betting on horses."

"Okay, just wanted to inform you. Anyway, maybe it's a good thing I said something to Neely. If she or the Briggstones had anything to do with Jacob Chandler's death, this might flush them out."

"Or it might get you killed."

"Don't worry about me. I'll be all right."

"Famous last words."

"Look, thanks for breakfast, but I've got things to do, so why don't you go make up some news to report or something."

"You're getting more premenopausal every day, sweetcakes."

"That is a downright nasty remark, Emory. Not to mention chauvinistic. I'm surprised at you."

He leaned forward, resting his elbows on his knees. "Seriously, enough bantering. I'm worried about your safety."

"I know and I do appreciate it, but what can I do? I can't give up now. There are only a few days left. And the thing with my mother, you know I have to find the answer to that or I'll never rest."

He nodded, knowing I was right. "So, what's your next step?"

I shrugged. "Read through the wood carving lessons again until something hits me. That's what Gabe says detectives do to solve cases, study the evidence over and over until something clicks. I know there's something more than what I'm seeing. I just haven't figured it out yet."

"Let me look at them."

While he read through the notes, I washed the few dishes I had in the kitchen and watered the houseplants in the window there. Outside, the blackened frame of the garage reminded me once again how this game he'd started could have devastating consequences. When I went back into the living room, Emory was sitting in the chair, his chin resting on his palm, staring at the burnt logs in the fireplace.

"So, did you come up with any ideas?" I asked.

"He's an odd character, no doubt about it. And a control freak. But he's not stupid. These lessons are actually quite profound. They could pertain to any art form."

"Or to life itself."

"So, the question is, did he intend for you to take them literally or symbolically? There are lots of sentences that suggest to me that he's speaking metaphorically, like *your powers of observation are your most valuable tools,* and *one detail may be the secret—search for that detail.*"

"Like I said, they seem to be telling me something, I just can't figure out what. That's why I've decided that my next step will be the library. I'm going to look up every reference I can find in quotation books and reference books pertaining to stones and wood. Maybe I can find the source to that quote on the wall. That might tell me something."

Emory stood up and went over to the carved plaque. He read it out loud in his slow, Southern accent." 'Raise the stone and thou shalt find me; cleave the wood and there I am.' " He turned back to me. "Sure does sound as if he was tryin' to tell you something, doesn't it?"

299

"Yeah, well, I wish he'd just sent a fax."

"How's things between you and your daddy?"

I looked at the ground. "I need to go out and see him. Knowing Daddy, he'll just act like nothing happened, and I'll go along. That's how it's always been with us."

"This has to be hard for him, too," Emory said gently. "If he did know about your mama and this man, it can't be a good memory."

"I know. Whatever I find out, though, I've decided not to tell Dove and him. As far as they are concerned . . . and for that matter, as far as I'm concerned, they are my family."

"But you will tell Gabe."

"Yes. I tried to explain it all to him Sunday night but I was so upset, and he told me just to tell him everything when it's over."

"He's a good man."

"I know. All I want is for this to be over so I can go home. I miss our life. I miss him."

A quick shower of pain flashed over his face. "I envy what ya'll have."

"It'll happen for you, too."

"I'm not so sure."

"Oh, Emory, don't get discouraged now. Take it from someone who knows Elvia better than anyone. She's starting to thaw."

"I want to be married, Benni. I want to have kids. I want to marry Elvia. I love her. I always have." For the first time since he'd come west, doubt clouded my cousin's eyes.

"Emory, you don't realize what a coup it was for you to be invited to the Mother's Day celebration at her house. She's *never* invited a man to that. Why, that's practically as good as an engagement announcement in the Aragon family."

He smiled slightly.

"Don't worry, we'll figure this out," I said, smiling back. "And remember, no matter what happens, we have each other."

I held out my hand, and he took it, shaking it solemnly, just like an eleven-year-old boy did twenty-four years ago next to a gurgling creek bottom while blackbirds flitted from tree to tree and a twelve-year-old girl cried for the first time in six years.

15

AFTER HE LEFT I CLOSED UP THE HOUSE AND HEADED for the San Celina Library. Set on a low bluff overlooking Laguna Lake, its large parking lot was almost empty on this Tuesday morning. I tied Scout to an empty bicycle rack where I could see him from a reference room window. For the next two hours, I searched every quotation and reference book I could find, looking up the words "stone," "rock," and "wood." I discovered there were a vast amount of quotations with the words stone and wood in them, and not one of them cleared up anything for me. I did discover the origin and history of the quotation on the wall plaque, however. First attributed to the claimed sayings of Jesus recounted in the third century, it was also later quoted by Henry Van Dyke and Rudyard Kipling. That also didn't illuminate much. So I turned to the dictionary and looked up the word "cleave" to make sure I was getting the meaning right.

"To adhere closely; cling. To remain faithful. To split

or divide by, or as if by, a cutting blow, especially along a natural line of division, as the grain of wood. To cut off; sever. To penetrate or advance by or as if by cutting."

To split or divide as if by a cutting blow. To sever. Exactly. It felt like he'd severed me from my history, from the family I thought I knew, from the perfect mother I'd formed in my mind.

The small black print in the dictionary blurred in front of me. Above me, a florescent light flickered. The buzz sounded like a large insect let loose in the quiet room. An old man two tables away coughed into a white cotton handkerchief.

A line in his last set of instructions kept coming back to me.

One detail may be the secret to the whole piece. Search for that detail.

My instincts told me that detail was in this ancient phrase. But I still couldn't figure out what. I put away the reference books and went back outside. After giving Scout some water, I dropped by the Historical Museum, which was surprisingly calm this afternoon. Only one reporter sat outside, and one police officer manned the command post, a young blond female officer I knew slightly—Bliss Girard.

"How are they doing?" I asked her, nodding at the museum.

"Everything's quiet, ma'am," she said.

I smiled at her. "You can call me Benni. Ma'am makes me feel a little old."

"Yes, ma'—uh, Benni. Your grandmother talked to me this morning through the door and said they were all feeling fine. I guess that's all to report." She shifted from one foot to the other, her belt, loaded down with

302

all the paraphernalia a street cop carries, squeaking in the quiet afternoon. She struggled to keep her smooth, girlish face stern and authoritative. I could tell she was taking this assignment with great seriousness. Gabe had talked about her before, told me she was a good cop, one of his best rookies. But to me she just seemed like a vulnerable young girl, someone who should be gabbing on the phone with her friends or riding her horse in the hills. Certainly not toting that loaded gun and solid nightstick. Inwardly I sighed. Looking at her made me feel as old as the bricks of the Historical Museum.

"I'm going to go in and see if they need anything," I said. "Could I leave Scout with you?"

"Sure," she said, her face softening slightly at Scout's wagging tail.

"Be good," I told him. "She has the power to lock you up."

As I walked toward the museum, she started talking softly to Scout, then a spontaneous giggle erupted from her. I smiled to myself and didn't turn around.

Inside the mood appeared lighter than my last visit. Elmo sat in a corner watching a soap opera on a thirteen-inch television. When I asked him where the ladies were, he pointed a finger straight up and didn't say a word.

"Are you okay?" I asked.

"I will be on Wednesday night when I'm home in my own bed."

"So, Wednesday's the day, huh? For sure?"

"Better ask the general. All I know is I'm going home Wednesday night even if I have to crawl out of here under gunfire."

I tried not to smile. "Elmo, I'm sure it's not going to come to that. In fact, I can almost guarantee it."

"Hmmph," he answered and turned his eyes back to the screen.

Upstairs, the women were working on a quilt, laughing and talking as if this were just another afternoon get-together.

"Benni, pull up a needle and sit down!" June Rae exclaimed, moving over. Next thing I knew, I was gamely pushing a needle through a burgundy and tan pinwheel quilt.

"This one's going to be auctioned off at the benefit next month for Corrie's House," Dove said. Corrie's House was a local shelter for abused and neglected children. Dove's quilt guild, the Churn Dash Quilters, made quilts regularly for the kids at the shelter and often for fund-raisers the shelter was always hosting.

"It's gorgeous," I said, working my needle through the three layers. "Are you sure you want me working on it, though? I'm kinda rusty." I didn't have much time to quilt these days, and my stitches didn't come close to the quality of theirs.

"That's okay, honeybun," Dove said. "We'll rip out and do over what doesn't look good."

"What else do we have to do?" Melva, the mayor's mother, asked cheerfully.

I looked at her curiously. "Isn't this upsetting you at all?"

"Not a bit," she said. "That boy always was too big for his britches. It was his daddy and his grandmother who spoiled him, not me. I always thought he needed to be brought down a peg or two."

"And she's the woman to do it," Dove said, beaming at her. The rest of the women echoed Dove's look. It appeared they had a new and very welcomed member to their guild and historical society.

"So, what's the secret weapon you're going to unleash tomorrow?" I asked.

The women looked at each other, their faces smug.

"Sorry," Dove said. "Classified information."

"Well, considering who I'm married to, I had to at least try to find out."

"We wouldn't have respected you if you hadn't," Goldie said.

"So, what's going on in your life?" Edna asked. "We need a little distraction from each other. Spare no details."

As we worked, I told them about my inheritance, the wood carving instructions Jacob Chandler had left me, the convoluted trail he'd led me on, the people who felt they should have inherited his money and possessions, and my frustration that the trail seemed to have come to a dead end. Once they got me talking, I even told them about my suspicions that he might have been murdered. Everything except the connection to my mother.

"Why, you do seem to land yourself in some interesting situations," Goldie said. "Pass me the thread, sweetie."

"Those people mad about being shut out of his inheritance worry me," Dove said. "I agree with Gabe. This man's a kook and didn't seem to care one hoot about your safety. Why in the world did he pick you, anyway? That's got me all stirred up. Seems kinda perverted, if you ask me." The other women murmured in agreement.

I shrugged, looked back down at the quilt and concentrated on my stitches, avoiding Dove's penetrating eyes. She knew I hadn't told her the whole story and also knew if I looked at her too long, I'd spill my guts. This time, for her sake, I was determined not to give in.

"So, what're you going to do now?" Edna asked.

"Frankly, I have no idea," I said.

"What about secret compartments?" Goldie asked.

"What?"

"You know, like on TV. There's always a secret compartment somewhere and there's always a clue in it. Have you discovered any secret compartments yet? Seems like a man so interested in wood might have a secret compartment somewhere."

"Sounds a little Nancy Drew to me. Gabe knocked around on some of the walls but didn't find anything."

"No, I mean in his carvings. Did you look for a secret compartment in any of them?" she persisted.

"It never occurred to me." I didn't want to say it sounded downright silly, too obvious and predictable, like . . . something Nancy would have discovered before George and Ned.

"Well, Jessica Fletcher would've looked for a secret compartment the first fifteen minutes. She's a sharp one, but then, she grew up during the Depression." The other women nodded.

I stuck my needle in the large, tomato-shaped pincushion on the table next to me and stood up. "When I get back to the house I'll check out your theory," I said, humoring them. "Right now, though, I'd better get going. I want to talk to that Beau Franklin again and see if I can get him to reveal what he invested in with Mr. Chandler. Maybe he knows more than he's telling."

"Be careful," Edna said, the others echoing her. "Good luck."

"Back at you," I replied, and they laughed.

"Oh, don't you worry any about us," Melva said. "We're on the side of right, no matter what my loony son says."

Dove walked me to the front door.

"Do you need anything?" I asked.

She reached up and took my face in her soft, warm hands. "I need you to tell me you're safe. That this thing with this strange man is not hurting you."

I swallowed hard. "I'm okay, Gramma. I'll be back home with Gabe soon."

"See that you are," she said, pulling me into a hug. I rested my head against her shoulder for a moment, wishing I was a little girl again. Wishing I had never heard of Jacob Chandler. Wishing my memories of my mother had never been tampered with.

"I love you," I whispered.

"Oh, honeybun, you're my sweet little baby girl and you always will be."

Back in Morro Bay, I dropped the truck off and then walked over to Beau Franklin's house. His wife informed me he was down on the Embarcadero playing chess at the giant chessboard.

"Please don't upset him," she said, her voice trembling. "He has high blood pressure." Her pale face pleaded with me. "Things are . . . hard, Miss Harper."

"Thank you," I said and made no promises, picturing her husband's angry face when he confronted me in my yard last week. High blood pressure, hard times or not, he was acting like a jerk and had possibly invested in something illegal. I was determined to find out just exactly what he knew about Mr. Chandler.

Down at the chessboard, about a dozen people watched Beau and a somewhat younger man move around three-foot-high chess pieces. Beau glanced up when he saw me join the crowd, but turned his attention back to the game, his face neutral.

The game took another twenty minutes to finish. Beau

lost and took quite a bit of ribbing for it. Apparently he was a regular player, and losing was something out of the ordinary.

"Mr. Franklin," I said when the crowd around him had broken up, "can we talk?"

"Unless you plan on writing me out a check, there's nothing to talk about."

"I might consider it if you'd tell me what you'd invested in with Mr. Chandler. If you have some written—"

"Young woman," he snapped, "what I invest in is none of your business."

His tone caused Scout to rumble low in his throat. I grabbed Scout's leash close to the collar and pulled him next to me, saying coolly, "It is if you want your ten thousand dollars back."

"Oh, I'll get my money. One way or another."

"Is that a threat, Mr. Franklin? Because if it is—"

"Miss Harper, you don't know who you're dealing with."

"Is it something illegal, Mr. Franklin? Is that why you can't show me any proof? Does it have something to do with the trips Mr. Chandler made to Mexico? Are drugs involved?"

His face drained of color, and instantly I knew I'd hit on the truth. I felt sick to my stomach having it verified that this man who could possibly be my father was a drug dealer.

He pointed a thick finger at me. "You'd better watch your mouth." He moved toward me, and Scout bared his teeth, pulling against the leash. Abruptly Mr. Franklin stepped back, then turned and walked away without another word. A few people looked at me curiously, then went back to their conversations.

My legs were shaky the whole walk back to the house. For at least the hundredth time in the last week and a half, I gave thanks to God for Scout. There would be no way I could sleep in this house without his protective and alert presence.

"Looks like we've got yet another person royally pissed at us," I said when we reached the house. When I opened the gate and went through, Scout started growling again, and I stopped dead.

Beau Franklin stood by the front door waiting for me. I started to turn away, to head over to Rich's to call the police, when Beau's choked voice stopped me.

"Wait, please, Miss Harper. I'm not going to hurt you."

I turned slowly around to face him, Scout rumbling low in his throat.

"What do you want?" I asked.

"I need to talk to you. I need to explain."

"As far as I can tell, there's nothing to talk about." I'd found out what I needed to know, though he hadn't actually said it. One of my fears had been verified. This man who might be my father was something that, especially since I'd known Gabe, I'd come to despise—a drug dealer. Until Gabe had told me some of what he'd seen as an undercover narcotics officer, I hadn't completely realized the havoc and pain those cruel people perpetuated on our society, how far their devastation reached.

"It's not what you think," he said, his florid face sad. "I'm not a bad person, Miss Harper. I just needed money and I needed it fast. Jake was a good man, a good friend, and he was trying to help me. He knew how to make money fast."

"He dealt drugs," I said, "and you were going to join him. There's *nothing* good about that."

309

"It was just that one time! I needed the money really bad. My wife . . ." His voice caught. "She's got colon cancer. Our insurance cut us off. The insurance my company promised after twenty-seven years of working. We got caught up in red tape and can't qualify for Medicare for months. She needs those shots, and they cost a thousand bucks apiece." Tears started rolling down his cheeks. "Miss Harper, she'll die without them. She'll die in a lot of pain. I can't let that happen."

Shocked at this sudden reversal, my mouth went dry, and I couldn't answer. Was his story true? Even if it was, did it excuse his actions?

"Ten thousand dollars was the rest of our savings," he said. "All her medicine and doctors took the rest. Jake knew that. If he hadn't had a heart attack, this never would have happened. I'd have had the money he promised."

And more addicts would have had drugs to sniff, smoke, or shoot in their arms, I wanted to say. More children would be born on crack and be neglected, more robberies and rapes and killings would happen, more lives would be wasted. But even with those truths on the tip of my tongue, I couldn't lecture him right now. All he could see was that his wife was dying, and he would do anything to stop it. Would I do that for someone I loved? Hurt someone else so their suffering would lessen? I'd like to think I wouldn't, but I didn't know the desperation born of watching someone I love suffer and die before my eyes.

"I'll see what I can do, Mr. Franklin," I said softly. "Please, just go home to your wife now. She needs you."

He looked at me for a long moment, then nodded

slowly. As he brushed past me and Scout, I could smell the sharp, tangy scent of fear.

A few minutes later, after I'd gone into the house and drank a glass of water to calm myself, there was a knock on the door. Rich's voice bellowed out, "It's me!"

I opened the door. "Come on in. A friendly face is more than welcome."

"What's wrong?" he asked.

His face grew sober as I explained what had just happened between Mr. Franklin and me.

"Poor guy. I know how he feels. Watching someone you love suffer is a living hell." He looked down at his hands. "My wife struggled with lupus for seven years. When it got bad, when she was in the most pain, I think I would have done anything, cut off my own arm, kill myself, to give her some relief."

"Oh, Rich, I'm so sorry."

"I think it was pretty good of Jake to help Mr. Franklin."

I thought about what he said for a moment before answering. "No, loaning him or giving him the money would have been good. Helping him earn more money by dealing drugs that will hurt other people is . . ." I hunted for the right words. "Selfish and evil. A truly good and kind person would not have put a desperate person in that position. Jacob Chandler had this house. He could have taken a loan out on it and given the money to Beau Franklin. *That* would have been kind."

Rich nodded. "You're right, but all I'm saying is don't be too hard on Mr. Franklin. Sometimes when you're desperate, your morality gets skewed."

"It's not Mr. Franklin I'm blaming." Then I told him about my unfruitful day at the library. "I seem to be at an impasse."

"I wish I could help, kid, but the whole thing's got me stymied. But I did make chilies rellenos for dinner. Want to join me?"

"You have to ask?"

I spent the rest of the evening looking through his photo albums and hearing stories about his three daughters and their dating disasters. We purposely stayed away from any topic concerning my inheritance or Mr. Chandler. It was a much-needed break for me. At nine P.M., while I was trying to hide my third yawn, he ordered me to go home and go to bed.

At home I called Gabe, and like two teenagers, we talked for an hour about everything and nothing. I didn't mention what had happened between me and Beau Franklin. There would be time enough to discuss it later. When my time in this house was up, I'd asked Gabe's opinion about what I should do about Beau's ten thousand dollars.

Not wanting to say good-bye, I said, "This reminds me of when we were dating. Remember, you used to call me every night at eleven P.M. to tell me to dream sweet."

"What I remember is going to bed horny."

I made a sympathetic noise. "Only four more nights, then relief is yours, Sergeant Friday."

"Better get rested up because you're going to need it."

"I like the sound of that."

After we hung up, I went out on the balcony and stared out at the ocean. It was a moonless night, and a thick halo of clouds shrouded Morro Rock. A damp wind whipped my hair around my face, causing my cheeks to tingle. I stood looking at the water for a long time, wondering for the first time where my mother actually was, what I really believed about an afterlife, feeling sadder and more alone than I'd ever remembered feeling.

When the feelings became overwhelming, I went back inside and decided to test Goldie's theory and look for a secret compartment in Mr. Chandler's wood carvings. With the radio playing a blues and jazz station to remind me of Gabe, I started with the wooden plaque hanging on the wall. It did, after all, say, "Cleave the wood." Maybe he meant there was a thin, secret compartment. I pushed and prodded and shook the plaque. It was a good theory, just not the right one. Then I started with the duck decoys and methodically inspected each carved piece carefully, pulling and pushing, trying to find a secret compartment. Two hours later, with a bored Scout stretched out in front of the fireplace, I gave up. There was not a secret compartment to be found in any of his carvings. I flopped down on the sofa, headachy and cranky, deciding that I was going to just lay there for the next four days, wait out my time, then go home. I was so tired of this game I no longer cared who he was, what he'd done, or how he'd been connected to my mother.

I fell asleep and woke hours later to a dark, cold house. After turning on the lights and furnace; I changed into sweats and fixed myself some hot chocolate. Back in the living room, I curled up on the sofa and picked up the carved picture of my mother. Holding it, I stared at the plaque hanging on the wall, mentally rereading the saying once more, trying to discern whether the feeling I had about it being a message was true or just the fanciful thinking all humans resort to when they don't have control over something. If I get through the next three traffic lights and they turn green, he'll call. If two more birds land on that wire before any more fly away, she won't die. If I pretend like none of this happened, it hasn't.

"Raise the stone," I said out loud. Scout's head came up at the sound of my voice. "Cleave the wood," I said to him.

He dropped his head back down when he realized I was just making noise.

"Raise the stone, raise the stone," I said.

Then it hit me.

"Raise the *stone*."

What if he meant literally? What if there was something hidden under a stone somewhere? That's silly, I told myself. The plaque also said cleave the wood, and that didn't mean anything.

What stones were there around the place? I walked through the house, looking for something that could be considered a stone. Nothing seemed to fit. The next step was naturally the yard. I looked out the kitchen window at the fog that had rolled in thick and damp and spooky-looking. Even with a jacket and a flashlight, it wasn't going to be pleasant poking around outside at two in the morning. I could wait until the sun came up, but my curiosity wouldn't let me sleep, and besides, then it would also be easier to observe me. Taking the pocket-size flashlight from my purse, I went outside.

In the backyard there were plenty of rocks and stones placed around. Many of his flower beds were trimmed with stones ranging from the size of baseballs to bowling balls. I lifted each one and poked around with a small hand trowel I found in the wreckage of the burnt garage, coming up empty-handed. Scout faithfully followed me, sticking close to my side, his pungent dog smell becoming stronger as his brown coat grew wet and dark from the fog. The heavy, salty air settled on my skin like a coat of oil.

After checking under all the real stones, I looked down at the stepping stones that led to the lava-stone birdbath where I'd scraped my head the first day I was here. In the cold, the tulips wilted slightly, bending toward me on their long, slender stems. Using my trowel, I pried up each of the flat stepping stones only to reveal damp, undisturbed earth and an abundance of worms and pill bugs.

After dropping the last stepping stone in its place, I looked at the lava-stone birdbath. It was made of stone. I shook my head. He couldn't have buried something under it.

On the other hand, the tulips were freshly planted, unlike most of the other flowers in the garden.

Leaning against it, putting all my weight behind it, I pushed the birdbath over, regretting my actions the moment I did. It was heavier than I'd anticipated, and there was no way I'd be able to put it back in place alone. I'd have to explain my crazy theory to Rich or Gabe after all.

Since I'd already done it, I decided to stick my trowel into the soft, black dirt and feel around. I hated disturbing the tulips, but I'd already come this far so, with the weak light of my pocket-size flashlight, I started digging. Scout enthusiastically joined me, throwing dirt behind him with abandon.

"Thanks, Scooby-doo," I said, laughing softly. "But I think you're more of a hindrance than a help."

Five minutes later my trowel hit something hard.

I froze for a moment, then stuck it in again.

It definitely hit something hard. Something hard and metal. I dug frantically to reveal the top of a one-foot-square hinged metal box. It took me another five minutes to remove enough dirt to pull it out. By now my knees were wet and dirty, and my heart was beating in my throat.

I lifted the box out of the hole and set it on flat ground. It was about six inches deep and weighed at least five pounds. I stared at it for a moment, afraid to open it. This was the end of the quest, this was what he wanted me to find, and whatever was inside would change my life forever.

I opened the box and looked inside.

It was filled with money.

Wrapped in plastic were stacks and stacks of bills. One-hundred-dollar bills. And there was a small wooden box with my name carved on top. *Albenia Louise.* No last name. Why? Was it because he felt it shouldn't be Ramsey? That it should be . . . what? I never found out Garrett's last name.

I opened the wooden box and found a folded piece of paper and two envelopes. One envelope had no address but had my name written across the front. The other was from my mother to Jacob Chandler. The postmark was dated one week before she died.

I sat on the ground for a moment, barely feeling the dampness rise up through the seat of my sweatpants. Avoiding the envelopes, I opened the folded piece of paper, knowing what I'd find—the final lesson.

There are many ways to finishing wood carvings. Most take plenty of elbow grease. Finishing brings out the grains of the wood and grants the piece life. There are two common finishes—tooled and sanded. One is rough, the other smooth. Sanding shows off the wood and

316

makes the piece more abstract. Tooling shows off the subject and makes the piece more lifelike. Finishing is an individual decision. There is no right or wrong way to finish a piece. Only the carver can decide. Some carvers like to leave tool marks to show the work is handmade rather than machine produced. Listen to your carving. It will tell you which finish is the right one and, even more importantly, when the piece is really done.

I set the lesson aside and looked at the envelope written in my mother's handwriting. I couldn't face that yet so I opened the other envelope, the one with my name written across the front in the same printing that Chandler had written every one of the wood carving lessons.

Dear Benni, it said.

Jacob Chandler was finally going to speak directly to me.

In the damp backyard, with piles of dirt and a metal box of plastic-wrapped money next to me, I read Jacob Chandler's words to me. It was dated six months ago.

> *Good job. I knew you'd finally figure it out. I realize it was quite a silly little clue, but sometimes it's the "small details" that make the piece. So, have you had fun? I hope you're not angry at me for forcing you to play this elaborate game, but it was the only way I felt we could spend some time together. Just you and me. For two weeks I wanted your undivided attention, and this was the only way I could figure out to do it.*

317

I stopped reading. A sudden chill caused me to start shivering. This man was perverted, just like Gabe said. I looked back down at the letter.

I know there are a lot of unanswered questions, like why didn't I just call you, or walk up to you on the street, but there's a good reason why. I didn't want to bring any unnecessary danger into your life. I promised your mother I wouldn't, though if she could see what you get tangled up in on a regular basis, I imagine she would definitely say you and I share the same blood. The only difference is the side we play on.

Tears came to my eyes when he verified the fact we were related.

So, do you like your uncle Garrett? Or do you just think I'm a big pain in the ass?

My uncle? But that wasn't possible. My mother was an only child. *That* was something I was absolutely positive about. I'd asked Dove and Daddy many times growing up and always I'd been told she had no brothers and sisters.

I know your mother never told you about me. She never even told Ben or Dove. The reason why was she and I didn't discover each other until I was twenty-seven and she was sixteen. We had the same mother but different fathers. My father was a very rich businessman from Chicago who made his money in not very legal ways. The story goes that he met my mother, your grandmother, while traveling

318

through Arkansas. Apparently I was the product of that single weekend they spent together, but coldhearted man that I always knew him to be, he had no intentions of bringing a naive small-town girl to be his wife in Chicago. The family wouldn't have stood for it. She was foolish enough to think that telling him about me would soften his heart when all it did was get me taken from her. I heard all of this from my father's deathbed when I was twenty-seven. He was trying to confess all his sins in preparation for meeting his Maker, I suppose. Until then, I'd been told my mother had died giving birth to me. After his death, I drove down to Sugartree to find my mother. It was the best three weeks of my life. I even fell in love. Her name was Gwen, and she was a friend of your mother's. But my family in Chicago, my father's brothers, had other plans for me, and I wasn't strong enough at that point to walk away. Your mother and I continued to write to each other, and when our mother was killed, I wanted her to come live with me. But she knew what kind of family I was from, and by that time I was so embroiled in the family business that I understood when she said she could never live that way. This is when things get a little murky. I won't go into detail since at this point it is irrelevant, but I'll just say I was involved in a situation that forced me to make a choice between my father's family and the law. After meeting your mother, falling in love with Gwen, and seeing how real, honest people lived, I wanted to do the right thing. I didn't want to end up like my father and his brothers. When I agreed to testify for the prosecution of my two uncles, it was obvious I needed to disappear. Back in the fifties, they didn't

319

have the elaborate witness protection program they have now. I went on the run with five thousand dollars I'd acquired by hocking my father's jewelry. My encounter with Jacob Chandler was pure chance, though I've always regretted not being able to tell his family what happened to him. I hated sending that postcard from Arizona to his sister, but I didn't feel I had a choice. He picked me up one late afternoon outside Baton Rouge and offered to let me share a motel room with him. He was a good man who took pity on my bedraggled appearance, and before I knew it, I'd poured out my whole story to him. He died that night, a heart attack or something. I promise you, it was entirely natural. The next morning I panicked, until I realized this was the opportunity I'd been waiting for. I stole his identification, dressed him in my clothes, and waited until night when I dumped his body along the side of a bayou. I feel a horrible shame about it to this day. Using his license and Social Security number, I started a new life. It was easier than you would think. Then I started thinking about your mother, how she was the only family I truly wanted to see, but how I didn't want to put her in any danger. I had to see her one more time, explain why she'd never hear from me again. I went to the cafe she worked at in Little Rock and told her and Gwen, and then I disappeared again, this time for a long time. But I couldn't stay away. I missed your mother and wanted to hear about Gwen even though I knew she'd probably find someone else. The simple, good life they led was something I dreamed about all those nights on the road. When I made some discreet inquiries, I found out that your mother had married the man she told me about that day in the cafe and was living in San Celina. I sent her a letter with instructions to burn it for her own safety and mine. I did save hers, though, which you now have. In this box I carved for you I've enclosed the last letter she wrote me. When she told me she was dying, she asked me to watch over you. But that's all in the letter. It'll sound better coming from her.

Now, here's the deal. The reason I set up the will the way I did was entirely selfish. I wanted you to think about me and only me for two whole weeks. I knew if I just left you what I owned in a conventional manner, after a day or two of speculation, your life would go on, and I'd just be a small, peculiar incident. But for two weeks, I wanted to be special. And I wanted you never to forget me. Thank you for indulging my last request. The money is yours to do whatever you want with. Some of it I saved from my salesman job, but when your mother asked me to watch over you from a distance, I had to find another way to make money so I could live near you. Unfortunately some of the lessons I learned growing up kicked back in, and I used them to make a living for myself. I did what I had to do to survive and to carry out your mother's wishes. That's really all I can say. I guess, in the long run, we are more like our parents than we realize. I wish we could have met, Benni. So many times I was tempted to strike up a conversation with you. We stood next to each other in lines as often as I could manage it. You are a wonderful woman. I fell in love with your smile. It was just like your mother's. I don't know exactly when you'll be reading this, but I sense it will be soon. My heart

has not felt right lately, and I'm very tired. Remember me with some kindness, if you can. If this game I set up for you has caused you any pain, please forgive me. Use the money as you see fit. I trust your judgment.
With love, your uncle Garrett

The last few sentences I read through a sheen of tears. I didn't know what to think. My uncle. My mother's only brother. Well, half brother. A person even my father hadn't known about. The feelings were too complex and confusing for me to sort out right now. I folded the letter and slipped it back in the envelope. What I needed to do was go see Gabe. Show him this money. Show him Jacob's . . . my uncle Garrett's letter. I wanted his arms around me as I cried for the man who was so desperate and so lonely. I needed to talk until I had no energy to talk anymore.

I picked up my mother's letter and stared at it a moment—the last words of hers I'd ever read. I stuck it back in the box with my uncle's letter and the money and stood up. Inside the house where it was warm and quiet would be a better place to read it. Next to me, Scout growled low in his throat, then before I could stop him, he barked.

"Scout, no," I whispered loudly, but it was too late. Someone walked through the back gate. I held the flashlight toward the direction he was looking and saw Duane.

"What's goin' on back here?" he asked, his voice slurring. Obviously he was on his way home from another night of closing down the Masthead.

"Get lost," I said, clutching the box to my chest. "This is private property."

322

"Now, you're holding on to that box like it was your long-lost baby or something. That makes me real curious. Lemme see it."

Scout growled again. I grabbed his collar, struggling to hold the box with one arm. "I mean it. Get off my property, or I'll call the police."

"Get off my property, or I'll call the police," he mimicked in a falsetto voice. Then he pulled a small hand pistol out of his jacket pocket. "Let me see the box."

The trembling pistol in his hand captured my attention like a swaying cobra. His glassy-eyed expression froze my blood. If he was sober, I was certain he'd never be this foolish. But alcohol-induced bravado is not something to mess with. I slowly set the box on the ground in front of me, bending down to open it. "Let me just get my letters . . ."

"Get back," he said, walking toward it. Scout growled, and I gripped his collar tighter, whispering no. Duane opened the box and pulled out a wrapped stack of bills. "Shit, I was right about ol' Jake. My brother said I was nuts, that Jake didn't have no treasure hidden, but looky here. It's like winning the lottery."

"Get real, Duane," I said. "Do you really think you can walk out of this yard with that money and have me not tell anyone?" The minute the words were out of my mouth, I wanted to grab them back. *Smart move, Harper. If he needed a reason to shoot you, you just gave him one.*

He stared at me a moment, the gun still in his hand. It was taking a while for his booze-soaked brain to formulate a plan. Murdering me would not be a logical, sensible solution. Then again, I wasn't dealing with the crown prince of Mensa. I started to tell him to just take the money, that I wouldn't tell, praying he'd be stupid enough to buy my story, when someone spoke behind me.

"Put the gun down," Rich's voice said from behind me. I turned around and watched him come through the hidden gate in the ivy-covered fence. He trained a huge automatic handgun on Duane's skinny chest.

Duane gaped at him, slack-mouthed.

"Lay the gun on the ground in front of you. *Now*," Rich said, his voice harder and more authoritative than I'd ever heard it. He sounded almost like a . . . well, Gabe.

"Do it, asshole!" he commanded.

Hearing language he could finally understand, Duane did as he was told and placed his hands on his head without instructions. He obviously knew the steps to this dance by heart.

"Step back two paces," Rich said.

Duane slowly took two long, shaky steps backward, almost tripping over his own feet because he was so drunk.

"Get on your knees."

Duane complied, his mouth still open.

"Now lay facedown."

After Duane was flat on the ground, Rich came around me and in seconds had Duane's hands cuffed behind him.

"Get the gun, Benni," Rich said, pulling Duane to a sitting position.

Letting go of Scout's collar, I scrambled forward and picked up Duane's small pistol.

"Call the police, *mija*," Rich said.

I stared at him a moment, my own mouth open. "Where did you get those cuffs? Why do you have a gun?"

"Call the police. We'll talk later."

After the Morro Bay police arrived and they took my statement and took Duane down to the station to book him for assault with a deadly weapon, I called Gabe. The sun had just started to peek up above the horizon, and I'd made a pot of coffee for me and Rich. While we waited for Gabe to arrive, Rich explained the gun and cuffs.

"I was an arson investigator," he said, sipping his coffee. "We have to go to the police academy just like cops. And we carry a gun and cuffs. No big mystery. And in case you're wondering, it's Scout's bark that woke me. I knew it wasn't normal for him to be outside that time of morning, much less barking, so . . ." He grinned at me. "Like a good cop, I assumed the worse and came prepared."

We both looked at the box of money sitting on the table between us. "Are you going to tell me what that's all about?" he asked.

"Yes, but I want to tell Gabe first. I . . ."

"It's okay," he said, putting a warm hand on mine. "I understand. I'll just sit here with you until your husband arrives."

Rich left when Gabe arrived wearing rumpled jeans and a worried expression.

"I'll come over and explain everything later," I promised Rich.

"What happened?" Gabe asked.

I opened the metal box. The sight of all that money caused his eyes to widen. "Before I let you read his letter, I have to explain some things." Then I started to talk.

16

AFTER I'D TOLD GABE EVERYTHING AND HE'D READ MY uncle's last letter to me, he took my hand and pulled me onto his lap, holding me close. Exactly what I needed.

"I'm so sorry you had to go through this," he said finally.

I looked down into his tired face. "I'm . . ." I paused, trying to put into words how I felt. "I'm fine . . . I'm glad it's over. There're still questions, but the biggest one was answered. And I'll be home soon. That's the most important thing."

"What was in your mother's letter?"

"I don't know. I haven't read it yet."

He answered by kissing me softly on the lips. "Let's see how much money there is." The final count was 80,300 dollars.

"Is it legally mine?" I asked.

Gabe nodded. "I believe so. There's no proof except the vague references in his letter that this money was gained illegally. It's not as if you found it wrapped in a bank's money bag. And some of it he stated he'd saved from working. There's no way to tell how much is what. I'd check with Amanda to be certain, but I'm willing to go out on a limb and say it was found on your property, so that makes it yours."

It only took me ten seconds to make the decision. "I don't want any of it. Since we don't know what he made by illegal means, I'll give it all away. I don't want our life tainted with it."

At a little past nine A.M. Gabe got ready to leave, taking the money with him to lock up in the police station's evidence locker until I could deposit it in a bank account somewhere. "I need to shower and get dressed for work," he said. "Don't forget, today's the big decision day at the Historical Museum."

"I'll come down as soon as I get cleaned up."

"Try to get some sleep," he said, cupping my chin in his hand. "You look beat."

"You, too, Friday."

After he left, I lay down on the sofa, Scout at my feet, and studied the envelope containing my mother's letter, probably the last one she'd ever written. For the first time I wondered why she never thought to write a letter directly to me. Not believing she was really going to die? Not knowing what to say? Perhaps the second one. What would you say to your child when you knew she had her whole life ahead of her and you wouldn't be there while she lived it? How to choose the words, how to put down all the things you wanted her to know? Maybe it was just too overwhelming a task when all you were doing was trying to take another breath.

Part of me didn't want to read it, ever, needing instead to keep the possibility of its words always there, like a kind of hope. I'd learned one sad fact about life a long time ago: that often the truth isn't nearly as beautiful or easy as your dreams. But truth was real. And in the long run, real was better than any illusion. The letter was sent to Jacob Chandler, General Delivery, Sacramento, California. I slowly opened the letter.

> *Dear Garrett,*
>
> *I'm using your real name this one last time, because it is the last time. I want to write to my brother, not some man I've never heard of. I'm dying. I didn't tell you this in the other letters because I didn't want you to worry or feel bad.*

Your life has been tragic enough. But I can't wait any longer. I'm so weak these days that my writing looks like that of an old woman. I can't even go to the bathroom by myself. The indignities are something you can't even imagine. I just wanted to tell you how much I love and have missed you all these years. How often I wished our lives could have turned out differently. And I have a request. Please look out for Benni. I know she will be taken care of and loved by Ben and Dove and their wonderful family, but you are her family, too. Except for Ervalean, you are the only family I have left. I know you can't actually tell her who you are, but if you can, once in a while drop by this area and see that she is doing okay. I cannot bear the thought of not being with her. I am trying so desperately to understand why God has chosen to take me away from her, but it is beyond me. I am grateful she has Dove, but I am so afraid she won't remember me. That, perhaps, is the cruelest blow of all. I have tried writing her a letter, but the task overwhelms me. There is just too much to say. I don't know where to start. I will trust Ben and Dove to tell her what she needs to know, to give her the love I won't be there to give. I love you, dear brother, and hold in my heart the hope we will be reunited in eternity.
Always, your Ally Lou

I was right about why she hadn't written me, but that didn't ease the ache of sadness. Why couldn't she have at least tried? A few sentences. Something. Anything. One thing to take with me through my life. Except for my hazy, little-girl memories, she would remain someone whose personality I knew only through her relationship with others. As she said in her letter, that was maybe the cruelest blow of all. I sat for a long time before the tears came. Slowly at first, like the trickle of a summer creek, then wet and loud and violent as a spring flood. Scout stuck his nose in my face, whining, licking at the tears, and I sobbed into his thick, furry neck until I felt there wasn't any drop of moisture left inside me. Then I fell into a deep dreamless sleep.

When I woke, the clock said four o'clock. I jumped up hoping I hadn't missed the San Celina Seven's triumphant moment. I fed Scout, took a quick shower, and threw on a thick blue sweater and jeans.

I arrived at the museum just in time. Uncaring, I parked next to a fire hydrant and ran with Scout to the police command post. Mayor Davenport was being escorted by Gabe up the museum's steps. Two uniformed police officers flanked them. Reporters and media people snapped pictures and yelled out questions.

"What's going on?" I gasped.

"The San Celina Seven and the mayor are having a meeting," Bliss said. "They are presenting their ultimatum."

"Their 'Hail Mary pass,' so to speak," Jim Cleary said, his black eyes twinkling.

We stood anxiously drinking bad coffee from a dispenser in the back of the police van, waiting for the mayor and Gabe. Twenty minutes later they emerged. I could tell by Gabe's relaxed face that it was over. Behind him marched the San Celina Seven with Dove in the forefront. Reporters flocked around the mayor and the senior citizens. As the mayor began his statement to the media, Gabe slipped away and walked toward us.

I ran to meet him halfway. "What happened?"

"Over here," he said, trying unsuccessfully to hold back his grin.

When we were safely away from curious ears, he said, "The mayor changed his vote. The historical society will get its twenty-year lease."

"They actually did it! What in the world changed his mind?"

"A small picture his mother has of him. One she threatened to give to the newspapers and television stations."

"A picture? He changed his vote 'cause he didn't like his picture? I mean, I know he's vain, but . . ."

Gabe laughed out loud, a hearty, masculine sound I'd really missed living apart from him. "The bong pipe in his mouth might have something to do with it."

"Oh, no! You mean he . . ."

"Yes, he inhaled, and his mother was willing not only to give the picture up, but reveal that little fact as well. Seeing as he ran on a ticket that was very heavily antidrug, antimarijuana legalization, it could look bad."

"Blackmailed by his own mother. Man, some psychiatrist is going to build a new vacation home with the business from that one."

"I wouldn't be surprised."

We turned back to watch the San Celina Seven pose for pictures and give their statements to the reporters with Emory out in front. Then they all joined hands and gave a deep bow, like actors in a play. Gabe and I looked at each other and burst out laughing.

"Just you watch," I said. "That one's going to be on the front page of the *Tribune* with Emory's story."

When I got back that night, I went over to Rich's house and told him the end of Jacob Chandler's story, including the part about me thinking he was my father. He shook his head after reading my uncle's letter.

"You have to feel sorry for the guy," he said. "What a sad life."

I didn't answer. I still wasn't sure how I felt about my uncle and what he did. He got his dying wish, to be foremost on my mind for two weeks, and there was no doubt I'd never forget this time, but I still wasn't ready to grant him any sympathy. Not yet. I couldn't forget how he'd earned his living all those years he was stalking me. Maybe later, when I was back home and had time to think about what had happened, who he really was, I could feel differently.

Then I called Elvia and told her everything.

"Oh, *chiquita*," she said, her voice sad. "It's time for you to go home."

"Sunday," I said. "And I can't wait."

I spent the next few days getting things straightened up around the house, packing up my uncle's clothes and possessions, deciding what to do with everything. I purposely stayed away from Cafe Palais and Tess's store. I wrote letters to everyone I'd encountered on my search for Chandler's identity, sending each of them one of his wood carvings. The rest of the carvings I would donate to the Wood-carvers' Museum so people could enjoy his work for a long time or sell it, donating the money to the carvers' guild. The only things I would take with me were the head he'd carved of my horse, Harley, the wooden portrait of my mother, the plaque from the wall, and Azanna's pot.

Friday morning, I went to the cemetery alone and took flowers to his grave, standing there for a moment, still trying to grasp that this man was a member of my family. On the way back. I stopped at the mortuary and asked for one thing to be changed on his headstone. It would read—Garrett Jacob Chandler—so he'd at least have part of his real identity back in death. I realized after looking through everything, including his last letter, that he'd left no clue to his last name. I would never know who he really was, and perhaps that was as it should be. Then I drove out to my mother's grave and just sat with her awhile. The roses Daddy and I had left were already wilted, but I'd brought some tulips from her brother's garden to replace them. On the way out, I stopped by Jack's grave and brushed the grass off his flat stone. Leaving the cemetery, my heart felt lighter than it had in years. I felt like I'd hiked a treacherous mountain and was now taking long strides downward on a clear, smooth trail.

Gabe and I talked every morning and every night. The break, I think, had done us good. We were ready to start on this next leg of the journey together that would, I hoped, carry on for many more years to come. I went out to the ranch and told the story to Daddy and Dove. I asked for my father's forgiveness, which he gave without hesitation. Seeing how quickly he gave me grace, I rethought my feelings about my uncle, and my heart softened just a little. I never told them my suspicions about who I thought my uncle was and I never would.

On Saturday, my last day in Morro Bay, Emory came by to see if I was all right. He'd had breakfast with Gabe.

"He's really itching for you to come home tomorrow," Emory said, sitting on the sofa, watching me carefully wrap my mother's wooden portrait in tissue paper.

"The feeling's mutual," I said, touching a finger to my mother's smooth brow before covering it with tissue.

"He said he'd leave a light on."

"He doesn't have to. I could find him in the pitch black dark."

He came over and put his arm around my shoulders. "So, how are you, really?"

"I don't know. All of this happened so fast. It's hard to believe the two weeks are up tomorrow and I'll be back home as if nothing happened."

"Only plenty did."

I nodded. "My journey has certainly felt rather like Odysseus's."

"With a dog named Scout, not Argos."

Hearing his name, Scout got up from where he lay in front of the fireplace and nosed Emory's leg. Emory reached down and scratched his chest. Scout stretched his neck in pleasure and smiled in that way that I knew would always make me laugh.

"Scout's the best thing to come out of this," I said.

"Well, I came to know my mother better, too. That's something."

"That's definitely something, sweetcakes. So, when can I write my story?"

I looked into his kind green eyes. "I don't know. Maybe never."

He took my hands in both of his and squeezed them gently. "I'll ask again in a month or so."

After he left I watered the plants and pulled weeds in my uncle's garden. I went down to the nursery near the highway and bought some more red tulips to replace the ones I'd uprooted around the lava-stone birdbath, which Rich and Gabe had set back in place. Maybe, when I sold the house, I'd keep the birdbath. Eventually Gabe and I would buy a house together, and this birdbath in my future flower garden would be a reminder of the sad, troubled man who meant so much to my mother and whose blood did indeed run through my veins.

By eight o'clock that evening, I had everything done that needed to be. My duffel bag and Scout's dog dish were already loaded in the truck. I'd put his fancy dog bed in first thing in the morning. Feeling as restless as a couple of barn cats, Scout and I walked out to Morro Rock and sat out there, watching the pier lights snap and blink across the dark ocean. I thought about my mother and the brother she lost, then found again—right before he lost her to death—about how our losses form a big part of who we are, soften us or harden us, depending on how we take them, how glad I was that I'd never told Dove or Daddy about my suspicions about Jacob Chandler—my uncle Garrett—being my father. That would have been a wound that would have taken a long time, if ever, to heal.

It was almost 11:30 P.M. when I got back to the Embarcadero. It was a busy evening since the weather was balmy and spring was definitely here. I stood on the dock next to a bar called Harpoon Hank's that was well known for being a place where singles liked to meet and connect. The band was good with a lead singer who had a decent, whiskey-soaked voice. He was singing "Stardust" in a gravelly, Willie Nelson way when I felt a tap on my shoulder.

"Thought I'd find you somewhere down here," Rich said. "I was afraid you'd leave without saying goodbye."

"You know I'd never do that."

"I'm going to miss you," he said, bending over and giving the back of Scout's ears an affectionate scrub. "Not to mention *el lobo* here."

"We're only twelve miles away. We'll visit you. We

334

have to. I've become addicted to Rich Trujillo's famous Mexican cuisine."

"I'll expect regular visits. You haven't tasted my *ropa vieja*."

"I promise Scout and I will come back often."

"What are you going to do with the house and all that money?"

"Sell it and split the money between the Historical Museum, the Wood-carvers' Museum, the Humane Society, and the new drug rehabilitation center that's part of the homeless shelter. That seems right to me, considering how he earned some of it. And I want to send some money to the real Jacob Chandler's sister in Texas. Money can't replace all those years she didn't know what happened to her brother, but I feel like I should do something. And I'm going to give Beau Franklin twenty thousand dollars."

"Even though you suspect he was investing it in drugs?"

"Yes. I don't think what he did was right, but I can't think of a better place for it to go than for medicine for his wife. I've talked to Amanda, my attorney, and I'm going to pay the rent and utilities for Tess Briggstone's store for the next year. That should help her out without me worrying about her taking the money and handing it over to her flaky sons or bailing them out of jail. Maybe that will give her enough time to get on her feet. Also, I'll ask her if she wants the quilts she made for Garrett and let her pick some of his wood carvings. She deserves that much. I've already sent a wood carving to all the people I met who knew him and I'll donate the rest to the Wood-carvers' Museum. I'll probably have a yard sale for the rest of his furniture and stuff. That money I'll give to the folk art museum. Heaven knows, our budget needs it."

"You certainly have this all thought out."

"I've had a lot of time to think these last three days. It's important to me that I don't profit from my uncle's death."

"So, what do you think happened there? Do you think it was natural?"

I shrugged. "I don't know. Maybe someone helped him along, maybe not. Gabe says there's not enough evidence to exhume the body, so I guess we'll never know. I'll just tell myself he died peacefully in his sleep. The way we'd all like to go."

He nodded. "I'll light a candle for him the next time I go to church."

I looked over at him. "So, what's next for you?"

"Maybe I'll light a candle for myself, too, and pray that my new neighbors are as fun as you've been."

I laughed. "Maybe God will answer your prayer and send a feisty widow lady who can't cook, loves to fish, and has always secretly lusted after firemen."

He grinned at me. "Now there's a dream a man can hold on to."

We stood staring at the bay, listening to the music in a companionable silence. I would miss Rich, too, and realized it hadn't taken me long to start a life here in this little town. I suppose that was the way most people are, more adaptable than we realize when forced into it. As Dove had always said, it doesn't matter whether God gifted you with a persimmon patch or a rock farm, because one made good jelly and the other good fences. There was no doubt He gifted me with a woman who could show me the beauty in both.

"I'd better get on back," I said to Rich. "The quicker I go to bed, the quicker it'll be tomorrow."

He glanced at his watch. "Benni, it's already tomorrow."

I looked at his bulky black diver's watch. It was three minutes after midnight.

"You're right. Technically it is Sunday, isn't it?"

"Go home. Surprise your husband."

I gave him a quick hug. "Thanks, Rich, for being my friend these last two weeks. I wouldn't have made it without you."

"Yes, you would. But you wouldn't have eaten as well."

The drive back to San Celina seemed endless. Why does going home always seem longer than going *to* a place? I drove down Lopez Street passing Blind Harry's where the Mother's Day window display was gone, replaced by one that celebrated graduation and new beginnings. The clock above San Celina Savings and Loan flashed 12:41 A.M. Students bunched around the open bars down near Gum Alley, but the rest of the street was quiet and empty, waiting for tomorrow. On my street, the houses were dark, and the truck's headlights formed a single beacon in the blackness. Next to me, I could feel the anticipation in Scout, obviously caught from my own.

When I pulled into our driveway, Gabe sat on the porch, waiting. Next to him, a votive candle burned. It was the decorative religious candle I'd bought him at the grocery store once on a whim. It showed a determined, strong-chested angel holding a sword in one hand and scales in the other. The angel was beating down a weak, bat-winged devil. On the side was written *Oración a San Miguel Arcángel*—Prayer to St. Michael. The prayer talked about defending us in battle and God thrusting into hell Satan and all the other evil spirits who wander through the world seeking the ruin of souls.

337

"For some reason," I'd told Gabe, "it reminded me of you."

"That's probably because St. Michael is the patron saint of police officers," he'd answered.

The candle flickered, and Gabe stood up. He thrust his hands deep into the pockets of his hooded sweatshirt. Later I would tease him about what he would have done if I hadn't come home until later that morning, and he would tease me by saying he knew me better than that.

I turned off the ignition and opened the passenger door to let Scout jump out. He bounded toward the porch, and Gabe stooped down to scratch his chest, laughing when Scout licked his face. I stepped out of the truck, pulling my duffle bag with me, slamming the door shut. Gabe looked up and smiled, a smile I knew I'd never grow tired of, a smile I wanted to see on the last day of my life on earth. Without hesitation, I dropped my bag and ran across the dew-soaked grass toward home.

Dear Reader:

I hope you enjoyed reading this Large Print mystery. If you are interested in reading other Beeler Large Print Mystery titles or any other Beeler Large Print titles, ask your librarian or write to me at

Thomas T. Beeler, *Publisher*
Post Office Box 659
Hampton Falls, New Hampshire 03844

You can also call me at 1-800-818-7574 and I will send you my latest catalogue.

Audrey Lesko chooses the titles I publish in Large Print. Our aim is to provide good books by outstanding authors—books we both enjoyed reading and liked well enough to want to share. We warmly welcome any suggestions for new titles and authors.

Sincerely,